Northpointe
Chalet

THE Jane Austen SERIES

Northpointe Chalet

A CONTEMPORARY RETELLING OF
NORTHANGER ABBEY

DEBRA WHITE SMITH

BETHANYHOUSE
a division of Baker Publishing Group
Minneapolis, Minnesota

© 2005 by Debra White Smith

Published by Bethany House Publishers
11400 Hampshire Avenue South
Bloomington, Minnesota 55438
www.bethanyhouse.com

Bethany House Publishers is a division of
Baker Publishing Group, Grand Rapids, Michigan

Bethany House edition published 2018

Previously published by Harvest House Publishers

Printed in the United States of America

ISBN 978-0-7642-3070-7

Library of Congress Cataloging in Publication Control Number: 2017963589

Unless otherwise indicated, Scripture quotations are from the Holy Bible, New
International Version®. NIV®. Copyright © 1973, 1978, 1984, 2011 by Biblica,
Inc.™ Used by permission of Zondervan. All rights reserved worldwide. www.
zondervan.com

Cover design by Connie Gabbert

Author is represented by Alive Literary Agency

Cast

Alaina Tilman: Based on Eleanor Tilney from *Northanger Abbey*. The sister of Ben Tilman, Alaina meekly lives from day to day under the thumb of her overbearing father.

Ben Tilman: Based on Henry Tilney from *Northanger Abbey*. Ben is as gifted a pastor as he is charming. A true gentleman, he enjoys a strong relationship with his sister, Alaina, and a strong attraction with Kathy Moore.

Caleb Manley: Based on Eleanor Tilney's boyfriend from *Northanger Abbey*. Caleb is Alaina Tilman's secret love and the son of Thurston Manley.

Dory Thaine: Based on Mrs. Thorpe from *Northanger Abbey*. Dory is the high school friend of Gloria Avery and Ron and Liza Thaine's mother.

Gloria Avery: Based on Mrs. Allen from *Northanger Abbey*. Mrs. Avery is a longtime friend of the Moore family. She is Kathy Moore's godmother.

Jay Moore: Based on James Morland from *Northanger Abbey*. A high school coach, Jay is Kathy Moore's beloved elder brother.

Kathy Moore: Based on Catherine Morland from *Northanger Abbey*. Kathy, a delightfully charming scatterbrain, spends her days working in her new bookstore and her nights reading thrillers.

Liza Thaine: Based on Isabelle Thorpe from *Northanger Abbey*. The sister of Ron Thaine, Liz has a charming personality as captivating as her beauty.

Michelle Moore: Based on Mrs. Morland from *Northanger Abbey*. Kathy Moore's mother, Michelle has everything she's ever dreamed of in life: happy children and a doting husband.

Raymond Moore: Based on Richard Morland from *Northanger Abbey*. Kathy Moore's father, Raymond, enjoys his life as a successful pastor in west Texas.

Ron Thaine: Based on John Thorpe from *Northanger Abbey*. The brother of Liza Thaine, Ron is enchanted with Kathy Moore.

Sigmund Avery: Based on Mr. Allen from *Northanger Abbey*. Mr. Avery is a longtime friend of the Moore family. Like his wife, Gloria, he serves as a parent figure to Kathy Moore.

Thurston Manley: The father of Caleb Manley (Alaina Tilman's boyfriend), and Zachariah Tilman's enemy.

Zachariah Tilman: Based on General Tilney from *Northanger Abbey*. Zachariah, a retired army captain, rules his family with as much zeal as he once did the military men assigned to him.

One

It might have been midnight, or perhaps earlier, or later, for I had taken no note of time, when a sob, low, gentle, but very distinct, startled me from my revery. I felt that it came from the bed of ebony—the bed of death. I listened in an agony of superstitious terror—but there was no repetition of the sound. I strained my vision to detect any motion in the corpse, but there was not the slightest perceptible. Yet I could not have been deceived. I had heard the noise, however faint, and my whole soul was awakened within me. I resolutely and perseveringly kept my attention riveted upon the body. . . . I felt my brain reel, my heart cease to beat, my limbs grow rigid where I sat . . .

Kathy Moore relished the tremors penetrating her soul. She'd read everything Edgar Allen Poe had written so many times she'd lost track of the number. But each time she read this passage from *Ligeia*, delightfully creepy goose bumps spanned her body. The flickering candle on her nightstand provided the only light in the shadowed bedroom. She'd promised herself years ago she'd never read Poe unless the lights were off and a candle was on. The effect was beyond exhilarating.

To make matters even more gratifying, an unexpected boom of thunder rattled the dilapidated apartment's windows. Kathy jumped and yelped as a flash of lightning extinguished the room's thick darkness. She blinked and, in the aftermath of momentary blindness, was almost certain her drapes billowed with the imprint of a person, hidden and waiting . . . an invader, fumbling to free himself from the curtain's bondage.

Just like Ligeia, she thought. Kathy scooted deeper under the sheets and bit the fresh-smelling linens to stop the scream. Her eyes wide, she clutched her book and commanded herself to scramble to the other side of the bed, away from the intruder. But her body refused to cooperate. She was stranded in the clutches of living rigor mortis.

A gust of wind whistled around the aging building. The apartment, nestled atop Kathy's bookstore, groaned like a soul tormented from ancient days. The drapes fiercely surged.

I must have left the window open. The practical thought both disappointed and comforted. Then Kathy remembered shutting and locking the window before donning her satin pajamas and crawling into bed. Both comfort and disappointment plummeted.

Kathy glanced toward her cell phone sitting on the nightstand on the other side of her bed. The shadowed distance between her and the phone stretched into an insurmountable chasm, too difficult to span for a terrified soul trapped by rigid terror.

For but a second the drapes halted their activity, only to shiver through the final throes of the captive's determination to reveal himself. Kathy released her copy of *Edgar Allen Poe's Complete Works*, gripped her throat, and lunged for the phone. Nothing could stop her calling for help now . . . nothing . . . except the phone was dead.

Panting, Kathy glanced around the room in desperate search for any sign of the charger. Her frenzied mind conjured no memory of what she'd done with it. She glanced toward the curtains again, fully expecting a menacing hand to extend from the folds.

A scream erupted through her terror. In response, a faint, questioning "Meow!" floated from the curtains.

Kathy whipped around and gazed into the inquisitive, golden stare of her furry roommate, Lucy. After flopping her hand against her chest and collapsing onto the bed, she stared up at the watermarked ceiling. A shaky giggle accompanied another of Lucy's feline queries.

"That was a good one, Lucy!" Kathy cheered in her heavy Southern accent. "You got me good, girlfriend! I haven't been scared like that in absolutely ages. Ha! I love it! What a riot!"

Kathy crawled back to her side of the bed. She blew out the candle and flipped on the brass-plated lamp. "Come on, sugar," she crooned and patted the side of the bed. Lucy stretched her golden striped torso, jumped onto the bed, and trotted toward her owner. Purring, she nudged her head against Kathy's waiting hand and shamelessly drank up the fond affection.

"You need some kind of an award for that one," Kathy claimed. She slid her feet out of the bed and wiggled her bare toes against the worn taupe carpet. When she stood, the floor planks creaked. A new boom of thunder sent a shock through her body. Kathy jumped again and released a yelping giggle.

She stooped to pick up the cat and said, "Too much more and I'll have five years off my life by ten o'clock." Kathy glanced at the clock and noted that was only five minutes away. She'd been on her own here in Northpointe, Colorado, for a whole month, and her mother had called her exactly thirty times. Every night between nine and ten, Kathy's phone rang. And every night Kathy stopped herself from reminding her mother that she was twenty-two and could take care of herself. Now she realized that, with her phone dead, she was missing her mom's call tonight, and her mom was probably worried sick.

"Where is that charger?" she mumbled and plopped Lucy on the end of her bed's rumpled eyelet comforter. Picking up a framed black-and-white poster of Lucille Ball on the kitchen table, and pawing through a pile of bills mixed with three of last week's blouses, Kathy found the charger, plugged in her phone, and saw six missed calls.

"Phooey!" Kathy fretted just as the phone started ringing. When she placed the receiver to her ear, her mother's concerned voice came through the line.

"Hi, honey! Are you okay?" Michelle Moore nearly shrieked.

"Hi, Mom. I'm sorry, I guess my phone died. How was your day?"

Her mother sighed relief, then immediately began chatting about the new chicken casserole she'd cooked for the church board members' luncheon, as Kathy stepped toward the haunted drapes. She pulled the drape cord and double-checked the window lock. As she remembered, it was tightly secure.

"And how was your day?" Michelle questioned.

"It was great!" Kathy imagined her mother's ginger-eyed stare, penetrating and analytical. She squirmed. Kathy didn't bother to add that she had only sold twenty-five dollars' worth of merchandise in the last two days.

At the age of fifty-four, Michelle Moore looked like she was in her early forties, but at times Kathy thought her mom had an eighteenth-century mindset. Michelle had been certain that if her twenty-two-year-old daughter moved all the way from Amarillo, Texas, to Northpointe, Colorado, all manners of disaster would unfold. So far, the worst that had happened besides her car trouble and a minor flood downstairs was the doorknob falling off her bathroom door. She glanced toward the knob lying in a sea of folded clean clothing stacked atop her dresser.

"Did you get a mechanic to see about your car's overheating?" Michelle queried.

"No, not yet," Kathy admitted. "I called the mechanic and . . ." Kathy peered through the rain-splattered window and hoped the storm didn't get much worse. Two weeks ago it rained so

hard water leaked through her store's front door and ruined a
lower shelf of used books.

"And?"

"Oh . . . he said to bring it in Monday." A movement near the
street's edge snared her attention. A person wearing a flapping
dark poncho ran the short distance from the curb toward her
window. At first Kathy assumed he was going to continue his
journey past her store and cut down the narrow alley behind
it. She'd noticed the first week of her arrival that many teens
used that trail. But that was normally during the day and when
it wasn't raining.

"What about your plumbing?" Michelle continued. "Is your
toilet still making that noise?"

"Well . . . yes."

Soon the man halted outside Kathy's window. Frantically he
waved toward Kathy. A flash of lightning highlighted a drenched
masculine face beneath a hood.

Her mother's voice fading into the distance, Kathy glanced
to the left, then the right. "Me?" she mouthed and rested her
index finger against her chest. She looked down at her black
satin pajamas and recalled the lecture her mother had given her
about standing in front of open windows at night.

The man waved more wildly.

A hint of a warning suggested she should close the curtains
and let the guy find someone else to help him if he was really
in need. But a tide of anxiety insisted the poor guy might catch
pneumonia and die before he could find any help on this deserted
street. Kathy's was the only store that featured an apartment
above it. The rest of the small town's merchants had long ago
gone home for the evening.

"Just a minute, Mom," Kathy said. "I think I've got an emergency here."

"What? What's going on?" Michelle interrogated.

"Just a minute," Kathy repeated. "I don't know. Don't hang up, okay?" Not waiting on her mother's response, Kathy dropped the phone onto the pile of clothes on her dresser. It slammed into the bathroom's doorknob.

Kathy unlatched the window and flung it outward. A blast of wind whipped a sheet of rain into her face and she squealed.

"Hello, up there!" The harsh weather broke up the man's distressed voice, but Kathy managed to understand his message. "Sorry . . . phone . . . car broke down . . . left cell . . . home."

"Okay, meet me at the front of the store," Kathy screamed over a receding roll of thunder.

The man waved and moved down the sidewalk.

As Kathy snapped the window closed and relocked it, she recalled her father's admonition from the day she got her driver's license:

"Remember, Kath, don't be stopping on the side of the road to help out any men. Sometimes guys set up traps for ladies. If a man is really in trouble, he can deal with it himself or wait for another man. I know you well, and there's no need for you to risk getting attacked because your heart is bigger than your head."

Kathy grabbed her house robe from the end of the bed and slipped into it. She tied the waist tight and wrinkled her brow. *What if this guy is up to no good?* she worried. *But what if he really needs help?* Kathy countered and couldn't imagine being out in this weather with a broken-down vehicle. She made her decision and headed toward the room's doorway. A faint, high-pitched voice stopped her. Kathy pivoted toward the sound. The phone was still nestled in her dresser's clutter.

"Oh my word, I forgot Mom!" Kathy trotted back to the

phone, snatched it up, and put it up to her ear. "I'm so sorry, Mom," she rushed. "A man just saw me standing at the window. He needs a phone and—"

"A man?" Michelle exclaimed. "At this hour? It's ten o'clock there."

"I know!" Kathy responded and hurried from her bedroom. She wove through the musty-smelling living room—an obstacle course of used furniture and piles of unopened boxes. "But he says his car's broken down and—"

"*Oh no!*" Michelle exclaimed. "Don't you dare go down there, Kathy! It's probably a setup! Don't tell me you were standing at your bedroom window with the light on inside?"

"W-well yes," Kathy admitted. She stopped at the locked door that opened onto the stairway leading down to her book and coffee shop.

"Kathy, you can't!" her mom urged. "Call the police and tell them there's a guy down there. If he needs help, they'll help him."

"But I told him I'd come down," she reasoned. "Besides, it's raining and there's not much protection on the sidewalk in front of my shop. He'll die of pneumonia before the police come. Those guys are slow!" She unlocked the door.

"Kathy, don't!" This time Michelle sounded like she was disciplining a six-year-old.

Gritting her teeth, Kathy whipped open the door and trotted down the stairs. "Mom," she said, "in the first place, I'm a twenty-two-year-old woman who can make my own decisions. And in the second place, the crime rate in Northpointe, Colorado, is zero. That's why the police are so slow. The worst thing they ever have to worry about is an elk wandering down the street or a fender bender in the grocery store parking lot. This town's so tiny it barely ranks a spot on the map!"

"There's no rule that says mass murderers only strike in large towns!" Michelle stated.

The stairs creaked as Kathy turned the corner and descended the second section that led into her store. She paused by the stair doorway and flipped on a series of lights that illuminated the store inside and out. Dubiously Kathy eyed the front door and took comfort in the familiar smells of books and gourmet coffee. A shrouded man stood in front of the glassed doorway, gazing into the store. Even though his rain hood incited images of the grim reaper, the pathetic look in his wide-set eyes confirmed that Kathy was making the right move. When he spotted Kathy, he meekly waved and offered an apologetic smile.

"Mom," Kathy said, "I know a mass murderer when I see one, and this guy isn't one, okay?" She didn't bother to acknowledge that she'd never encountered a mass murderer in her life. "He even looks a little familiar," Kathy added and rattled through her file of memories in search of a name for the face. *He might even be someone from church*, she thought, and the notion increased her determination to help.

"Are you looking at him now?" Michelle's voice rose a decibel with every word.

"Actually, yes," Kathy admitted. While weaving past a row of bookshelves, she returned the man's wave and threw in a friendly smile. "He's standing outside the store's door. It's glass, remember?"

"Listen to me, Kathy—"

"I'm going to have to go now," Kathy claimed. "I need to let him use this phone." She stopped inches from her door.

"Uuuuhhhhh!" Michelle huffed. "Okay, but I'm giving you three minutes to call me back. If you don't, I'm calling you. And if you don't answer, I'm calling the police!"

"Okay . . . okay . . ." Kathy agreed only because she knew she couldn't stand here for an hour being lectured when a fellow citizen was in need. After a harried farewell, she ended the call, laid the phone on the polished coffee bar, and wrestled the door's ancient lock.

Finally she turned the knob. The door creaked open. The merry bell attached to the knob by a red ribbon emitted a faint jingle. And the smell of cool June rain ushered in a new acquaintance.

Two

"I'm so sorry to bother you." The man's cultured voice, soft and trustworthy, heightened Kathy's assurance.

She flung open the door and said, "It's no problem. I'm just glad I could help. You're having car trouble?"

"Yes." He nodded and eyed the empty store behind her.

"Why don't you come on in?" she urged. "You can use the phone, and I'll make you a cup of hot chocolate while you wait for help."

"Oh no," the man replied. "I'm all wet." He glanced down at her robe and bare feet. "If you'll just let me use the phone, I can place the call here and wait until my dad or sister arrives."

Kathy wiggled her toes. For the first time, she considered her appearance. She never wasted time worrying about makeup anyway, much to her mother's exasperation. So her lack of it mattered little. She slid her hand down the back of her cropped hair and was certain by the feel that it must look like a dark rat's nest. A gust of wind hurled raindrops against Kathy's feet and face like icy needles. A shiver erupted in its wake. Summer in northern Colorado was definitely different from summer in west Texas.

"You can't stand out there in this! We're both going to catch the flu and die on the spot." Kathy grabbed the slender man's arm, tugged hard enough to affect his balance, and used the moment of weakness to drag him inside.

"Whoa!" the guy barked. "Hang on, will you?"

The bell's angry ring accompanied the door's closing thud.

The phone's peal began with the bell's final clink. "Oh brother," Kathy mumbled. "That's my mother. She thinks you're a mass murderer."

The guy laughed out loud and gingerly observed the puddle his wet poncho was creating on the wooden floor.

"My thoughts exactly," Kathy replied. "She lives in Amarillo and thinks their crime rates apply here. Has Northpointe ever even *had* a murder?" The persistent phone didn't stop.

"No, not that I know of, anyway." The man shook his head. "But I will agree that it's probably not safe for a young woman alone to ask a strange man into her store . . . even in Northpointe."

"Then why did you come in?" Kathy asked.

"Did I have a choice?" He nudged his hood back to reveal a headful of damp brown curls and a soggy Band-Aid clinging to his forehead.

"Well, it was either that or get soaked myself," Kathy defended and once again tried to place the man. Maybe he was a customer. "Here, you talk to Mom." Kathy shoved the noisy phone into his hands. "I'm in charge of hot cocoa. When you get through, make your call, okay?"

"But . . . but . . ."

"Just deal with her, will ya?" Kathy said. "She's driving me crazy!"

With a chuckle, the man shook his head and swiped the phone to answer.

Kathy giggled and would have given fifty bucks to see her mother's face when he said hello.

She walked behind the old-fashioned counter at the same time the phone beeped. Kathy's questioning look prompted his reply.

"She just said, 'Sorry, wrong number,' and hung up before I could tell her differently."

"Oh well." Kathy waved her hand and tried not to focus on the Band-Aid. "Don't worry about it. Trust me. She'll call back. Go ahead and make your call."

Tuning out his conversation, Kathy busied herself with filling a carafe with water. According to the real-estate agent, this ancient strip of buildings was a hundred years old, and her store used to be an old bar. A druggist bought it in 1958 and turned the bar area into a soda and snack section. When the druggist died a year ago, so did his retail business. Kathy bought the store from his widow with the nest egg her grandmother left her in her will.

The whole setup was perfect for Kathy's use. Once her parents realized she couldn't be persuaded from her dream of being a store owner, they and Kathy's brother, Jay, helped her clean the shop from top to bottom. Plus they'd assisted her in putting the coffee bar into top working order with the latest in equipment. Every time Kathy entered the store, she thought of the old western series *Gunsmoke*. Before her parents left, they'd fondly dubbed her "Miss Kitty," after the classic series' leading lady.

In the midst of all the teasing, her father had dropped hints the size of atomic bombs about how managing business revenue was totally different from managing a personal account. All Raymond Moore seemed to remember was the fact that Kathy had bounced a few personal checks back home. Now he was as obsessed over Kathy's finances as her mother was over her car, the plumbing, and who she let into her store.

I only bounced eleven checks, and that was two years ago, she grumbled and poured the carafe full of water into the Bunn coffee maker so she could quickly reap hot water. Next, Kathy grabbed a thick mug from the rack that housed a dozen just like it. *I haven't had a check problem since,* she argued and wished her father were present to hear just how convincing she sounded. *And okay, my car might be a '67 Chevy, but it does run.* An attack of brutal honesty insisted she amend her claim. *Well, most of the time, anyway.*

By the time her parents finished helping her set up the new business, her father was insisting she let him manage her store's money online. Her mother was wanting to buy her a new car. Kathy refused both. She was her own woman, and she was going to live like it. That involved completely managing her own business, driving the car she bought for herself, and . . . She darted a glance to the guy on the phone. *And using my own judgment when it comes to helping people.*

Kathy grabbed a package of peppermint hot chocolate mix. After filling the mug with hot water, she whipped up her best offer of the warm beverage, topped in whipped cream. The treat looked so appealing, she fixed one for herself. By the time she served the cocoa, the man was finishing his conversation.

"Thanks, Alaina," he said. "I'll be waiting for you here. Tomorrow I'll call Drake to tow the car to his shop."

He hung up the phone and eyed the cup of hot chocolate. "Wow! That looks great!" he said and rubbed his hands together.

"Glad you think so," Kathy answered and didn't even try to stop herself from thinking that this man looked like he'd stepped out of the pages of one of her favored novels. *Not that he was what her college friends might dub a "yummy guy" by any means. But his candid blue eyes, straight nose, and high cheekbones created an effect that wasn't half bad, either.* The oversized Band-Aid hinted at a dramatic past.

Maybe it's more the way he showed up than anything else, she thought and eyed his dripping rain gear. What could be more adventurous than breaking down on a dark and stormy night and asking a woman for help at her window?

"Why don't you take off your rain jacket and have a seat?" Kathy asked.

"Well . . ." the guy hedged. "My sister is going to be here in about ten minutes. I hate to drape this thing somewhere and get the store even more wet." He looked down at his rain gear. New droplets plopped onto the freshly scrubbed floor.

"Oh, for Pete's sake," Kathy fussed and rounded the bar. "Two weeks ago this whole front section was flooded. A little more water isn't gonna hurt a thing."

The man's indulgent smile merged into a chortle. The fine crow's feet around his eyes hinted that he was around thirty. "And you say you're from Texas?"

"Yes, Texas."

"I'd have never guessed," he teased and allowed her to help him slip out of the poncho. Underneath he wore a simple pair of slacks and an oxford shirt. "And I guess you like books, too?" He took in the shelves crammed with everything from used cookbooks to new classics.

"Why would you assume that?" Kathy quipped.

"I have no idea," the man responded and shook his head. "Just a whim, I guess."

With a broad grin, Kathy gingerly placed his rain jacket on a row of empty bar stools. She picked up his mug and extended it to him. "Have a seat," she said and patted a stool. After he sat down and took his first swallow, she perched on a stool and indulged in the warm sweet brew.

"Mmmm, this is great!" he exclaimed again before gingerly touching his wounded forehead.

"Thanks," she replied and was certain she could have glowed in the dark. "It's my best seller." Kathy glanced at the bandage and decided she could stifle her curiosity no more. She was on the verge of posing the question when the telephone bleated anew. Kathy squeaked and jumped. Her cocoa sloshed onto the bar. "Oh man," she confessed, "I'm just so high-strung, everything sends me straight up."

"That's probably your mom."

"You're right, I'm sure. I guess I'll have to talk with her." With
a crooked smile, she said, "I wonder what she'd do if I screamed
bloody murder instead of saying hello?"

"Please, lady, don't do that." The man's eyes rounded in earnest appeal. "She might call the cops on me or something."

"Good point." Kathy held up her hand, and then she answered
the phone. "Hi, Mom," she said in a singsong voice before Michelle had a chance to emit one syllable. "I'm still alive. We're
having hot chocolate."

"Kathy," Michelle said in a tone that transcended Kathy's
worst discipline memories. "I'm worried sick, here! I've been
trying to call you back *forever*, and the phone's been going to
voicemail!"

"He's been calling his sister to come pick him up. We're fine.
I'm fine," Kathy asserted. "Here, you talk to him. He's harmless.
I got him to answer the phone earlier."

"You mean that was him?"

She winced and pulled the phone from her ear. "Yes. Here he
is again." Kathy extended the telephone to her visitor.

"Say hi, will ya?" she asked and enjoyed another generous
swallow of sweet liquid.

The man took the receiver and voiced an awkward greeting. "Yes, I know," he said after a few seconds. "Yes, ma'am. I
agree. No, ma'am. I don't blame you. Of course, I'd feel the
same way if it were my daughter. Uh-huh. I told her nearly
the same thing a few minutes ago." He observed his mug of
hot chocolate resting on the bar and toyed with the handle.
"Yes, it concerns me, as well. I understand. . . . Yes, of course,
I'll be glad to tell her."

Kathy frowned. *Whose side is he on, anyway?*

Once he disconnected the call, the man laid the phone on the
bar and didn't bother to look at Kathy.

She placed her hand on her hip and turned down the corners

of her mouth. It was bad enough to feel like a bug under her parents' microscope without having them rope the town citizenry into the act.

"I think she's just concerned about you, that's all," he finally said. "And I can't say I blame her. You really don't need to be letting stray men into your store at night."

"Well, you started it!"

"I know," he meekly agreed and finally possessed the decency to look at her. "But really, all I wanted was just to use the phone. I was going to stand outside, remember?"

Kathy drummed her two-toned fingernails against the bar. "For whatever it's worth," she said, "I've never done this before, and I'm not sure I ever will again." Her fingernails' rhythm increased. "And I probably wouldn't have tonight if Mom hadn't treated me like I was ten. But there comes a point . . ."

Her fingers halted, and Kathy examined her freshly painted nails. She'd never understood why so many women painted every fingernail the same color. Today, during the height of boredom, she'd painted hers green and blue. Now every other nail bore the contrasting color. Kathy hadn't bothered to paint her nails in months and decided if she was going to give herself a manicure, it should be memorable. When she noticed one of her nails was already chipped, she forgot all about her momentary irritation.

"Ah man," Kathy blurted. "Would you look at that?" She extended her fingernails under the man's nose. "There's a chip!"

"Heaven forbid," he said and pressed the heel of his hand against his forehead. "What's the world coming to?"

The doorbell's jingle preceded a soft feminine voice. "Hello in here!"

Kathy glanced up to encounter a young woman with eyes as blue as the drenched stranger's. Her pale blond hair hung in stylish ringlets around her face. She held a closed umbrella and offered a familiar smile to Kathy's visitor. "Are you ready?" she asked.

"Oh sure," the guy replied and stood. He reached for his rain jacket but stopped and turned back toward the bar. With a sassy grin, he scooped up the mug and guzzled down the hot cocoa. When he finished, a smudge of whipped topping clung to the corner of his mouth. He licked it away.

"How much do I owe you?" he asked.

Smiling, Kathy replied, "This one's on the house."

He tugged his wallet from his back pocket and shook his head. "Not on your life," he said and flopped a five-dollar bill onto the counter.

"No!" Kathy protested. She retrieved the money and attempted to foist it back on him.

He grabbed his rain jacket and shook his head in a firm manner that ended her protests. "I've taken your time, used your phone, and given your mother a stroke. All that is worth something, don't you think?"

"Well . . . I guess I could put it toward my mom's medical bills," Kathy agreed and slipped the money into her robe pocket.

"I'm sure she'll appreciate it." His steady lips belied his jaunty eyes.

The blond woman was striding back to the vehicle parked at the curb by the time the man shrugged back into his rain gear. He flipped up the flimsy hood and prepared to step outside when he shot a glance back at Kathy.

"Thanks again," he said. "You were a lifesaver."

"You're welcome," Kathy replied and fidgeted with the money. When he opened the door, she realized they hadn't even introduced themselves. "I never did catch your name."

With a mischievous smirk he straightened his hood. "I'm the Ghost of Christmas Past," he said and slyly winked.

"Nice to meet you," Kathy replied. After a mammoth exertion

of self-control, she managed to refrain from even the hint of humor. "I'm Miss Kitty."

His raucous laugh simultaneously erupted with a boom of thunder. "Oh man," he exclaimed, "I almost forgot. Your mom said to tell you that the main reason she called tonight was to let you know someone's coming to visit you named Mr. and Mrs. Av—Av—" He looked up.

"Avery?" Kathy asked.

"Yes. That's it. Avery. They'll be here tomorrow."

"Tomorrow?"

"Yes."

"Did she say how long they'll be staying?"

"Maybe all summer."

"All summer?" Kathy asked and wondered if they expected her to fit them into her tiny apartment.

"I believe that's what your mom said." He shrugged. "You might want to call her back. . . . Bye now!"

"Later, gator!" Kathy called, and her attempt at a wave stopped at half gesture. The door bumped to a close, and the pleasant stranger was gone.

Kathy smiled. The first week she was open for business, the owner of the next-door barbershop came over for a cup of coffee. After a lazy thirty minutes, he commented that he hoped she wasn't looking for any excitement around this town. He said the Christmas parade was about as exciting as it got.

But I already know differently, she thought. During the last few weeks, her trusty Impala had overheated three times, her bathroom doorknob fell off, the front section of her store flooded, she'd been scared out of her mind tonight, and now she had met "the Ghost of Christmas Past."

"How much more excitement can I stand?" she asked.

Sobering, Kathy contemplated the stranger's message about the Averys' imminent arrival and lengthy visit. Undoubtedly, her retired godparents would be their usual helpful and supportive selves, but they'd also keep Kathy's parents well-informed about her life. She imagined Paul Revere riding the streets of Northpointe shouting, "The Averys are coming! The Averys are coming!" Kathy laughed under her breath and examined her chipped nail. Maybe they'd be okay with staying at the colonial-styled bed-and-breakfast across the street. The accommodations would certainly be more comfortable.

Oh well, she thought, *I'll be thrilled to see them. Even if they are Mom and Dad's spies, I love 'em to death.*

"And I love Mom and Dad to death, too," she whispered and shook her head.

Kathy walked toward the front door and manhandled the ancient lock until it slipped back into place. Then she eyed the sidewalk to the left and right. The street, lined with gift shops and antique stores, was deserted. Only the dwindling rain and distant thunder offered a reprieve from the silence.

Stepping back toward the service bar, she silently prayed for more business . . . and maybe a few new friends. Kathy contemplated her recent guest and wondered why he hadn't told her his real name. "Maybe he's married," she mumbled but didn't recall a gold band on his left hand, even though she couldn't be certain.

Kathy pulled the five-dollar bill from her pocket and stared at it. The longer she observed the bill, the more she began to realize that the stranger looked somewhat familiar, and she strained to remember where she'd seen him before. Soon an image materialized in her mind.

"Yesterday's newspaper!" she exclaimed. Kathy shoved the money back into her pocket and hustled behind the service bar. She knelt beneath the cash register and snatched up a stack of disorganized newspapers from the open shelves.

Hugging the papers to her chest, Kathy stood, then unceremoniously dropped them on the bar. She tackled the newspapers, carelessly scattering them in the wake of her urgency.

"Come on . . . come on . . ." Kathy mumbled as the smell of stale ink on newsprint urged her on. When she was on the brink of despair, Kathy flopped open a fold and spotted her "Ghost of Christmas Past."

"Yes!" she whispered and devoured the caption she'd only skimmed yesterday. *Local citizen saves boy's life. See page 12.* Before searching for page 12, Kathy raised the newspaper and scrutinized the image. Even without reading the article, she easily could decipher the story. A burning compact car was turned upside down on a street in the outskirts of Northpointe. An ambulance sat nearby. "The Ghost of Christmas Past" stood beside a worried-looking woman hovering near a child-laden gurney. Kathy's new acquaintance held a bundle of gauze against his forehead. His attention was riveted on the flaming vehicle perched near a gulley.

"Oh my word," Kathy mumbled as the implication sank in. *He must have pulled the boy from the car before it caught fire.* She nodded in affirmation of her own assumption and focused on the gauze pressed against his forehead. "The Band-Aid," she whispered and wondered what her mother would think now. *He's not a mass murderer. He's a hero!*

Kathy flipped through the section of newspaper she held, only to discover it stopped on page eight. By the time she'd scrounged through the rest of the stack, her toes were chilled and disheveled newspaper cluttered the bar and floor. She also possessed a vague memory of discarding part of the stack yesterday.

"But it should have been only the old ones," she fussed. Another perusal of the newspapers confirmed that the rest of the article was missing.

Oh well. Kathy examined the photo again. *It doesn't take a brain surgeon to figure out what happened.* The longer Kathy concentrated on the man, the more she became convinced that he was exceptional.

"I think I could really like this guy," she muttered, glancing at his hands in the picture. Unfortunately, the camera's angle prevented even a peek at his left ring finger.

Three

"Now, tell me about your car," Sigmund Avery said. "Your mom says you're having problems with it." He set his mug of coffee on the service bar with a decisive thud that insisted Kathy tell the truth, the whole truth, and nothing but the truth.

Kathy glanced from Gloria Avery to her husband. Last night after the kind stranger left, Kathy called her mother to confirm that the Averys were indeed planning to spend the summer in Northpointe. Even though Michelle Moore had known of the pending visit for a week, she'd not told Kathy.

She was probably afraid I'd figure out they're her spies, Kathy thought.

The Averys had arrived only thirty minutes ago, just as Kathy was opening her store. After a round of hugs and greetings, they settled at the coffee bar for some of Kathy's coffee and cinnamon rolls. They announced that they had indeed checked in at the bed-and-breakfast across the street late last night. Kathy couldn't have been happier if she'd planned their lodging herself. The pastries, hot from the toaster, filled the store with the smells of cinnamon and Kathy's own secret cream-cheese filling.

Now, both the gray-haired seniors awaited her answer. "I really wish you'd just let us buy you a car while we're here, dear," Gloria cooed. The diamonds crusting her pleasingly plump fingers glistened as she indulged in a sip of cappuccino. "It would be so easy, then Sigmund wouldn't have to work on yours."

"Nonsense!" Sigmund exclaimed with a defiant gaze at his wife. "Kathy's got a classic. What would she want with some ol' plastic replica of a vehicle?"

Kathy straightened her shoulders. Sigmund Avery was the only person who understood her love for her antique automobile.

Gloria shook her head, looked from Kathy to her husband, and mumbled under her breath, "Beats me."

Turning from the service bar, Kathy glanced toward the picture-laden wall above her beverage equipment. She had scoured the countryside for old photos and memorabilia from days gone by. As a result, the wall was filled with everything from an ancient Coca-Cola sign to a black-and-white photo of Elvis. In the center of the collection hung an 8 x 10 framed picture of Kathy next to her '67 Impala. Her brother, Jay, had taken the picture with his digital camera. He used Photoshop to transform the image into a replica of the past.

Gazing up at the black-and-white photo, Kathy was astounded anew at how it appeared to have been taken in the late sixties. Her snug capri pants hugged her slender frame and resembled the pedal pushers that were once all the rage. Her short hair, tossed by the wind, favored one of the popular cuts of that era. And, just for the fun of it, Kathy had plastered on a thick layer of red lipstick that looked garish in color but perfectly sixties in black and white.

The first time she stumbled on the low-mileage car in an Amarillo neighbor's garage, Kathy nearly drooled over the thing. According to the ninety-two-year-old owner, she had driven it around town for twenty years and then parked it in her garage once she was unable to drive. When her son came home once a month, he'd drive it to the store. The vehicle had just over 30,000 miles on it, and the inside showed only gentle wear.

The owner, Mrs. Everette, sold it to Kathy for $3,500—as long as she promised to take good care of it and not sell it to "some old mean-spirited, used-car salesman." Kathy had gladly agreed. Even though Mrs. Everette passed away six months later, Kathy refused to break her promise. She'd drive the vehicle until it fell apart, then either give it back to Mrs. Everette's son or find a place to store it.

Kathy reached for an empty mug and filled it with fragrant decaf. When she was stirring in her second packet of sugar, Sigmund said, "So are you going to tell me what's the matter with your car?"

"Oh, the problem." Kathy turned and smiled at her godfather. "I guess I didn't get around to that, did I?"

His deeply lined face softening, he shook his head. "As absentminded as you are now, child, I dread seeing what you'll be like when you get to be my age."

"You don't have any room to talk, Sigmund," Mrs. Avery teased. "You're on the verge of calling the police every time you look in the mirror because you mistake your own reflection for an intruder." She looped her hand under his arm and threw in a kiss on the cheek to round off her loving jibe.

"Don't listen to her, Kathy," Sigmund said and patted his wife's hand. "She's just mad because I can remember my own name."

"Oh you." Gloria pursed her carefully made-up lips.

Kathy chuckled, sipped her sweet coffee, and smoothed the front of her vintage-looking T-shirt that read, "Kathy's Book Nook." So far she was the only one in town who'd purchased one of the shirts. Twenty more shirts just like it hung on a rack across the store beside a display of Christian fiction.

"Come on, Kath," Mr. Avery said and stood. "Take me to your car, and we'll talk about what needs to be done. At least I know *you* appreciate my brain."

"Hey, I appreciate your brain," Gloria claimed. "That's why I married you—for your brain. And I'm staying with you until I see some evidence of it." She winked.

"Such support," Sigmund groaned and clutched his chest.

Kathy giggled. A full year had lapsed since she spent any quality time with the Averys, and she'd almost forgotten just how entertaining they could be. "Well, come on, Uncle Ziggy," she said and rounded the coffee bar. Kathy had used the familial endearment since she was a child, even though the Averys weren't literal relatives. At age three, her parents coaxed Kathy to call him Uncle Sigmund, but all that came out was Ziggy . . . Uncle Ziggy. The endearment stuck.

"My car's overheated—as in three times in the last two weeks," Kathy continued. Sigmund fell in beside her as they neared the door. "I thought Mom would have told you."

"Nope," he said. "She just mentioned you were having trouble."

"I'll stay here and try to hold this chair down," Gloria said.

Glancing over her shoulder, Kathy noticed her godmother walking toward one of the overstuffed chairs strategically positioned around the store. She gave Mrs. Avery the thumbs-up. "That chair tries to float around a lot, so I really appreciate your holding it down."

"I've got it covered," Gloria claimed. Her face never even twitching, she yanked on the front of her denim vest like a soldier preparing for battle. "You can count on me. Oh, and don't worry about customers; I'll manage everything, just like I said, okay?"

"Sure," Kathy agreed. One of the first topics of conversation had involved the Averys' offer to volunteer their mornings to her store. "If you have any questions, just stick your head out the door and yodel. The parking lot is only a hundred yards that way." She pointed north.

"I know this might come as a grave shock," Sigmund inserted, "but your Aunt Gloria doesn't know how to yodel."

"Listen, buckaroo," Gloria parried, "if Kathy wants yodeling, I'll yodel. Got it?" She pointed her index finger at Sigmund's nose.

"Oooweee!" he teased. "I like 'em feisty!" The two broke into adoring smiles.

Kathy's sixty-year-old godmother claimed the cozy chair. Next to the chair sat a narrow mahogany table, perfect for holding a mug. Mrs. Avery deposited her cappuccino atop a coaster and picked up one of the novels lying near her mug. She examined the cover.

Sigmund opened the door and warm Colorado air wafted into the store.

Grinning, Kathy followed Sigmund out the door. Even on the hottest days, northern Colorado couldn't compete with the west Texas heat. After last night's rain, the whole town smelled clean. Even the aspen-laden mountains surrounding the village looked like they'd endured a heavenly scrub.

Several cars purred down the street, and Kathy peered toward one end of the road, then the other. According to the Chamber of Commerce, the town usually teemed with tourists this time of year. The only thing teeming today were the elk. The barber next door said those critters roamed the streets during the summer and took to the mountains when hunting season set in. Presently, Kathy counted four hanging out near the feed store across the street. Occasionally, the owner took pity on them and gave them some of his leftovers. A cow lifted her head and stared at Kathy and Sigmund as if their traipsing down the sidewalk was royally interfering with her day.

"That elk's kinda got an attitude, doesn't she?" Sigmund said.

"Yep," Kathy responded. "I just wish they'd take up reading and coffee sipping. I could make a killing. Business hasn't exactly been booming yet. Most of my customers have been heavy on browsing and light on the spending."

"Well, maybe that will all change now that we're here. Where there's honey, there are always bees, ya know."

"Right," Kathy drawled.

But nobody's gonna top that man from last night, she thought and scrutinized the street anew. There was no sign of "the Ghost of Christmas Past," and Kathy awoke this morning wondering how long it would be before she encountered him again. This town was so small, she didn't doubt that another meeting was inevitable. So far, he was the only person of the male persuasion who had posed any potential distraction. The church she chose to attend was friendly yet small; the singles group limited. But even if the group had been flourishing with social gatherings twice a week, Kathy had been too busy establishing her store to participate . . . or even to attend services every Sunday. Now that she was officially away from home and out of her parents' sight, Kathy was free to go to church or not. Since she'd regularly attended her whole life due to her parents' expectations, Kathy had begun to question her place in the church. Now, thoughts of meeting "the Ghost of Christmas Past" in some local congregation encouraged her to increase her floundering attendance.

She rubbed her index finger along the top of her thumbnail, slick with polish. Her parents were always so worried about her. Nothing would make them happier than for Kathy to find a respectable, responsible churchman to settle down with. While Kathy wasn't losing any sleep over the prospect, the idea wasn't exactly displeasing to her, either . . . especially if he was anything like last night's visitor.

Her sandals crunching against the sidewalk, Kathy kept up with Sigmund's long-legged gait and observed his attire from the corner of her eye. He had never chosen clothing that hinted at his family's massive oil fortune. Today was no different. His baggy golf shorts, the color of olives, were held in place by green suspenders. He wore black lace-up shoes with striped socks that sagged around his ankles. When they arrived in the parking lot beside the store, Kathy got a good look at what his T-shirt read. The words, "Kiss Me!" were scrawled beneath a neon-green bullfrog. Of course, Kathy had noticed the bullfrog the minute the Averys stepped into the store, but she'd been so caught up in conversation and in listening to their entertaining banter that she hadn't bothered to read the caption. As skinny as Sigmund was, he looked like a stick with a frog in the middle. Kathy giggled.

Sigmund, pausing beside the blue Impala, glanced at Kathy, then examined his shirt. "Glad you like it," he said with a stubborn lift of his chin. "Gloria told me when I bought this guy that if I ever wore him in public she'd vow she didn't know me. So I named him Jeremiah—no other name would do—and told her where I go, he goes. Now that's telling her, isn't it?"

"Jeremiah?" Kathy questioned.

"Oh," he waved his hand, "I guess you're too young to remember that song 'Jeremiah Was a Bullfrog.'"

"Uh, yeah," Kathy agreed and quirked her eyebrows. "Somehow that one escaped me."

"Well, it was a doozy," he admitted with a broad grin that Kathy was sure had instigated plenty of female attention in the past and present. "Okay, let's look at your girl here and see what's up."

"Well," Kathy began as Sigmund pulled the hood latch, "she just keeps overheating, that's all."

He raised the hood.

"The first two times the temperature gauge went up, I stopped long enough for it to cool down. Then three days ago she blew the top off the radiator."

"Hmmm." Sigmund rested his hands on the frame. Like a doctor examining a patient, he gazed at the spotless engine. "Did you put some more water in it?"

"Yes, but I haven't driven it since. I was scared to."

"Probably just needs new hoses," he determined. "Have you ever had them replaced?"

"No," Kathy admitted. "Other than having the oil changed, I really haven't had to do much to it."

"Man, this is a beaut of a car," he mumbled, and Kathy was certain he was on the verge of drooling like she did the first time she saw it.

"Yodelady-hooo!" Gloria's squawking yodel floated from the store.

Kathy, breathless with the potential of a live customer, whipped around and gazed toward her godmother, wildly waving from the doorway. "Aunt Gloria needs me," she exclaimed. "Maybe it's a customer!"

"What a concept!" Sigmund said.

"Who'd have ever dreamed this!" Kathy replied and trotted back toward the store. "Oh!" she hollered and stopped. She twisted toward Sigmund, pulled the car keys from her pocket, and tossed them toward him without warning him about the nearing missile. "Look out! Keys!" she bellowed one second before they crashed into his thigh and clanked to the concrete.

"Ugh!" he exclaimed. "Thanks for the warning." Sigmund bent to retrieve the keys.

"Just do whatever you have to do to fix it, okay? I'll reimburse you."

He shook his head. "No deal! I'll fix it, but it's on me."

"But—"

Sigmund held up his hand. "If I were your father, I'd do the same. You're the closest thing to a daughter we'll ever have, so indulge an old guy, okay?"

Kathy's shoulder's sagged. Any time Sigmund brought up this daughter business, Kathy could never resist him. She had to admit that she was more in tune with him than with her own mom and dad. While she dearly loved her parents, neither of them understood her free-spirited need for adventure or her independent streak. They were forever trying to make her live up to her brother's example. Jay finished his bachelor's degree in three years and was now a successful football coach. Kathy took four years to complete two years toward a bachelor's degree and finally decided she couldn't be stifled another minute in a dull college class. There was a world to explore! While Uncle Sigmund told her he thought she needed to finish her degree, he hadn't judged her because of her choice. Her parents, on the other hand, overheated as badly as her Impala.

"I know you!" Sigmund's claim interrupted her thoughts. "You're planning your argument. It won't work!" He placed his hands on his hips. "If I don't cover costs, I don't fix it. Understand?"

"Okay," she acquiesced, "I won't argue."

"Good," Sigmund said and bent back over the engine.

At least he's not trying to make me trade it in on a new one, she thought and hurried toward her store.

Before she went inside, Kathy perused the sidewalk across the street and cast one last glance toward the passing traffic. Not even the potential of a customer could diminish her desire to spot "the Ghost of Christmas Past." Fleetingly, she debated whether or not he was married and decided he couldn't be . . . not even a little bit. All those heroes in the novels she loved were never married. The only thing that could make the mysterious guy more exciting was for her to learn he had a dark past he was desperately trying to hide.

Maybe that's why he didn't want to tell me his name, she mused and narrowed her eyes. *What if he was sent to prison for a murder he never committed and he escaped? Now he's hiding from the FBI in this little bitty town.* Her imagination hungered for more information as Kathy scoured the street anew.

"Or maybe he witnessed a murder," she mumbled and decided that was a more probable scenario. His guileless blue eyes just couldn't belong to even a falsely accused killer. "If he witnessed a murder, he must be in the Witness Protection Program." *That overturned vehicle in the newspaper might have been wrecked because of a wild car chase.* Kathy imagined her ghost zooming in and out of traffic with a bad guy on his tail and an innocent driver getting in the way. She rubbed the corner of her mouth and recalled the full-blown plot from the novel she just finished last week—a suspense that kept her up until two in the morning. The hero had thought when he entered the Witness Protection Program he was safe. But the very people he trusted turned out to be his worst enemies. They pursued him until the last five pages of the book. Kathy imagined hiding the guy in her apartment, slinking around town to buy him food, looking over her shoulder for the mafia . . . because no adventure was worth a hoot unless the mafia was involved. A shiver danced across Kathy's shoulders. She smiled.

Her attention trailed to the lone chalet nestled on the mountain that towered over Northpointe Village. Her smile diminished. And Kathy began a new series of what-ifs regarding that chalet, which was surrounded by aspens and pines. Bits and pieces of town gossip had been her only source of information for the Swiss-style home that possessed an ominous aura. So far she had gleaned that the townfolk referred to it as Northpointe Chalet, and the home belonged to a man—a Mr. Tilman—who seldom came into town. For the hundredth time, Kathy wondered what that man was doing up there all day by himself.

Her palms grew damp, and she curled her fingers. *What if "the Ghost of Christmas Past" is hiding up there?* she wondered. A shaft of sunlight burst on the cedar-crested dwelling like a beacon from heaven confirming her curiosity. Kathy determined to discover the secrets that lay within the chalet walls.

But what if there are no secrets? she thought and immediately dismissed such nonsense. Every mountain chalet had secrets.

"Kathy!" Gloria's insistent voice pierced her fantasies.

Kathy jumped and spun to face her shop.

Her godmother stood with the door ajar and shook her head. "I promise," she fretted, "I think you're as big a daydreamer now as when you were a child." She leaned closer and wrinkled her nose. "There's somebody here who wants to meet you. Some new friends."

"Oh!" Kathy exclaimed and recalled the reason she'd walked back to the store. *Customers!* She gazed past Gloria. Three people browsed her bookshelves. Two of them, a man and woman, appeared to be in their late twenties. The third one, a lady, looked sixtyish and stylish.

She stepped into her shop, and the delightful smell of cream-cheese cinnamon rolls obliterated all traces of Colorado clean.

Gloria closed the door behind Kathy. The young man, a tall blonde, observed her. His candid smile, warm and inviting, hinted that he needed new friends as much as Kathy.

Four

"Kathy," Gloria began as the newcomers neared, "believe it or not, Dory Thaine is my friend from high school." Gloria stepped to the matron's side and looped her arm with Dory's. "We were almost inseparable then. We called ourselves—"

"Dory and Glory," Dory interrupted.

"Wait, I thought it was Glory and Dory," Gloria countered.

"No, I specifically remember," Dory argued. "Dory and Glory. It was in the school yearbook that way." The two fell into a three-second stare down.

"Oh well," Gloria said. "I haven't seen her since our tenth-year high school reunion. Can you believe this? It's such a small world, isn't it?"

"Hi!" Kathy extended her hand toward Dory. "It's nice to meet you."

"You must be Gloria's daughter?" Dory raised her finely penciled brows.

"No, she's my godchild," Gloria explained. "Sigmund and I never had any kids."

"Oh!" Dory's green eyes widened in dismay. Her turquoise eye shadow sparkled nearly as much as the rhinestones on her decorated T-shirt. "How perfectly dreadful," she breathed. "I've got three kids." Dory motioned toward the two young adults standing nearby.

Kathy glanced at them. Dory's daughter, a strawberry-blonde

with narrow wire-rimmed glasses, offered a friendly smile. The glasses, coupled with her precise application of makeup and high-fashion shorts set, reminded Kathy of a gorgeous intellectual she'd attended college with. The combination of beauty and brains had gone straight to that woman's head. This young lady's soft brown eyes lacked the intense genius spark but reflected a desire for honest friendship.

"My eldest son is a lawyer," Dory continued. "Anyway, I can't imagine life without my kids."

"Well," Gloria held her head high, "Sigmund and I don't feel like we've missed out on much." She stepped away from Dory and placed her hand on Kathy's back. "Kathy and her brother, Jay, have been as good for us as any of our own kids could have ever been." The sharp glint in her eyes dared Dory to defy the claim, and Kathy wondered if the two ladies might have had a negative history in high school.

"Hi, I'm Ron." The young man's introduction distracted Kathy from the undercurrents between Gloria and Dory.

"Hello," she responded and extended her hand for a brief shake. "I'm Kathy Moore." Ron's brown eyes were as dark as his sister's were soft. His fair hair, fashionably spiked, offered a nice contrast to his light tan.

"And I'm Liza, Ron's sister."

While Gloria asked Dory if she'd like some coffee, Kathy shook Liza's hand and said, "I'm thrilled to meet both of you." Always glad to make new friends, she had never been more delighted than now. Kathy hoped the Thaines were planning to stay in town for a while. "How long will you be in North-pointe?"

"About two months," Ron explained and rested his thumb in the belt loop of his surfer-style shorts. "Mom wanted us to do some traveling with her while Dad's out of the country. He's a Dell executive and travels all over the place."

"Mom loves this part of Colorado," Liza explained, "and has booked us at the B and B across the street."

"Really?" Kathy exclaimed. "That's where my godparents are staying! They'll be there 'til the end of August."

"Mom and Liza are booked until the end of August," Ron countered and lifted his chin with an assured air. "But I'm staying until the first of August. Then I've got to get back to work. I'm a high school football coach."

"No way!" Kathy blurted. "My brother is, too!"

"Wait!" Ron held up his hand, palm outward. "Didn't you say your last name is Moore?"

Kathy nodded.

"So your brother would be Jay Moore?"

"Yes."

"He doesn't happen to live in northern New Mexico, does he?"

"Yep!" Kathy pumped her head up and down. "Do you know him or something?"

"Know him?" Ron whipped his sunglasses off the top of his head and waved them as if they were a director's baton. "His team has beaten mine the last three years. If he and I weren't golfing buds, he'd be my archenemy!"

"This is just amazing!" Liza exclaimed.

Ron leaned his head back and said, "Ha! I can't believe this!"

Kathy laughed. "How totally crazy!" she exclaimed. "I wish he were here! We could probably find plenty to do around here together." She cast a glance toward her burgeoning inventory.

"Of course, we'd have to plan most everything for after hours," she added. "I've got a store to run."

"So this place is yours?" Ron questioned with a doubtful lift of his brows.

"Yep." Kathy pivoted toward the bookshelves and inserted her hands into the pockets of her slacks. "It's all mine. Jay and I got an inheritance when my grandmother died. I used mine to put myself into business. I love to read, so . . ." She motioned toward her inventory.

"I'm impressed," Ron said and inserted his sunglasses into his indigo shirt pocket. "You don't look old enough to own your own store."

"Ron!" Liza slapped his arm.

"Oh, it's okay," Kathy said. "I get that all the time. I look younger than I really am. One customer the other day thought I was only sixteen." Kathy didn't bother to explain that that customer had been the only one for the whole day. "But actually I'm twenty-two."

"I guess I'm the old guy here," Ron admitted and slid his fingers along his square jawline. "I'm right in there with your brother—twenty-eight."

"And I'm twenty-five, and I teach tumbling and ballet." Liza curtsied like a ballet dancer.

Kathy laughed and hoped the humor hid her thoughts about Ron. In her opinion, he thought a little too highly of his good looks.

"Hey! I've got an idea!" Ron exclaimed. "Why don't I call Jay and see if he'll consider driving up for a few weeks? The last I talked to him he didn't have any big plans."

"I don't think he does," Kathy said. "Does he even know you guys came here for the summer?"

"No." Ron shook his head. "This was a last-minute thing on Mom's part. I haven't seen Jay or talked to him in a couple weeks."

"Well, why not call him?" Kathy asked and lifted both hands.

A crease formed between Ron's brows, and he examined Kathy's fingernails. "Great nails, there," he said with an engaging smile.

Liza laughed. "I love it! Green and blue," she said and tugged on one of Kathy's hands. She turned Kathy's fingers over, nail side up. "Do you have time to do mine like this?" she asked as if the two had been friends for years. "I'm seriously chipping here." Liza wiggled her fingers.

Kathy examined Liza's fingers and detected several imperfections in her rose-colored enamel. "Sure!" she said. "We can go up to my apartment and bring my manicure set down here. We'll drag a couple of chairs together in the back and get busy."

"Oh good," Liza purred. "I've wanted to do something daring here lately. I'm so bored with all these pinks and peaches!" she huffed and looked at her nails.

"To tell you the truth," Kathy explained and began the short trek to the stairway, "I almost never do my nails." She glanced at her new friend walking nearby. "But when I do, I always make sure it's somehow different. I figure if I'm going to do them, I want them to be . . ." she shrugged, "I don't know, memorable, I guess."

"Well, green and blue are memorable," Liza said.

"Hey, what about poor ol' me?" Ron's words held a pathetic note. "Are you two going to just go off and leave me? I guess I should ask to have my nails painted, too."

With a broad grin, Kathy stopped and faced Ron, who feigned a pout. Even though the guy came across as a little arrogant, she was so glad to meet potential friends, she decided to overlook his fault.

"Sorry," she said, "I wasn't thinking. You can come up, too. That is, as long as you don't mind dodging boxes and clutter. I've put almost all my effort into getting the store in shape. Except for my bedroom, my apartment is still not set up."

"Maybe you could use a hand, then," Ron offered and rushed to Kathy's side. He placed his arm along her shoulders and moved in for a close smile that said "I hope you think I'm as good-looking as I do."

"Oh sure!" Kathy agreed and backed away. "I'm not going to turn down any help."

"Great!" he said.

"No way!" Dory's ecstatic exclamation bounced from the coffee bar.

Kathy halted and looked toward Dory, who was gazing at her in gaping wonder. "You mean you've got a whole section dedicated to Sherlock Holmes?"

Kathy eagerly nodded.

Dory slid from her stool, and her heavy chest jolted with the effort. "Show me where!"

"Follow me!" Kathy motioned for Dory to follow. "I just love him, don't you?"

"Absolutely! At least the ones I've read. I'd like to read all of them."

"Well, I've got everything—including collector's editions of the complete works. I've also got all sorts of other classic mysteries."

"Perfect!" Dory said. "That's exactly the kind of books I love!"

"Great!" Kathy said and wove through the shelves placed in the store's center. The smells of new and used books fueled her enthusiasm. She stopped at the last shelf and opened her arms wide. "Here they are! The Sherlock stuff is on this half." She motioned to the left. "The other half has the other classics."

"Let's see," Dory mused. She neared the shelf and began grabbing a variety of titles. One by one, she moved them to the shelf's open slot.

Kathy's heart soared as she mentally tabulated the cost of nine books. When Dory turned to her and straightened, she said, "I have the ones I've set aside. I want to buy what's left."

"Wonderful!" Kathy sputtered and hoped dollar signs weren't glowing in her eyes. "I'll—I'll go get a shopping basket and get you fixed right up." She rushed a few steps toward the front door and stopped. This meant Dory would be buying twenty-eight books! *I'd better get two baskets,* she added to herself.

When Kathy rounded the bookcase nearest the cash register, she spotted Ron and Liza sitting at the coffee bar. Gloria was handing them both drinks. Liza accepted a tall glass of lemonade while Ron, holding his cell phone to his ear, nodded his thanks for a bottle of root beer.

"Hello, Jay?" he asked. "Ron Thaine here. You're never going to believe where I am!"

On an impulse, Kathy hurried behind Ron and bellowed, "Hi, Jay!"

Ron and Liza both looked over their shoulders and smiled.

"Maybe that's because it *was* your sister!" Ron replied into the phone. "Why didn't you ever tell me you had such a cute sister?" he chided and winked at Kathy. His brown eyes sparkled with masculine speculation. "We're here in her store right now."

After weeks of no company her own age, Kathy beamed and soaked in the compliment. Nevertheless, she reminded herself not to take his encouragement too seriously. Next to Liza's polished appearance and ballerina grace, Kathy didn't even deserve a *cute* rating.

"Listen," Ron continued, "Kathy and I were just talking. Why don't you drive up for a few weeks? My sister, Liza, is here. You remember . . . I told you about her last time we golfed. We were all thinking maybe we could make a foursome and see some sights this summer."

A light tap on her shoulder sent a jolt through Kathy. She jumped and bumped into someone.

"Whoops!" Dory's yelp mingled with the sound of toppling books.

"Oh no!" Kathy whipped around. Dory Thaine, her eyes wide, grappled with a wobbling tower of Sherlock Holmes books. "Oh no!" Kathy repeated. She reached to help the lady but wound up whacking the stack of books instead. The remaining titles collapsed to the floor.

"Kathy?" Gloria said like a surprised mother.

"Oh phooey!" Kathy blurted. "I'm acting like Laurel *and* Hardy." She dropped to her knees and began gathering the books. Soon Gloria was also retrieving the strewn titles.

"It's okay, dear," Dory sweetly soothed. "I guess I didn't realize I was going to scare you. I'd get down there with you, but my knees are just awful."

"Don't worry one li'l bit about it," Kathy chattered and glanced up the length of Dory. "I should be the one to pick all these up. I was the one who—"

"Here, let me help, too," Liza offered.

Kathy smiled her thanks and noticed Ron had neared the door. The cell phone still to his ear, he pressed his finger against his other ear. "I guess we interrupted Ron's call," Kathy observed.

"He'll be fine." Liza waved gracefully toward her brother.

The three women stood, each holding several books.

"Let me have yours," Gloria said. "I'll put them down here by the cash register." She pointed to the end of the bar and gingerly accepted the stacks from Liza and Kathy.

"That sounds fine," Dory said. "And if I could just get a couple of those shopping baskets . . ." She gazed toward a stack of the plastic baskets strategically placed at the end of the bar.

"Good grief!" Kathy covered her eyes. "I got distracted over Ron's phone call and forgot everything."

"Isn't she the cutest thing you've ever seen?" Dory exclaimed.

Lowering her hand, Kathy appraised Dory, who shot a meaningful glance toward Ron. He slid his phone in his pocket and hurried toward his mom. The hardwood floors creaked with his approach.

"That's what I was just telling her brother," Ron agreed. He strolled within inches of Kathy and invaded her comfort zone again. This time she even caught a whiff of spicy cologne. She edged back.

Liza cleared her throat. "Ron's subtlety is his best trait. Don't you think?"

"What normal guy could be subtle at a time like this?" he responded.

Kathy giggled and took Ron's every word exactly for what it was . . . the request for a summer flirtation. While she wasn't interested in a meaningless flirtation, Kathy determined not to spurn his friendship. She hated to come across as rude.

"Look," Dory said, "why don't I just get Gloria to help me? You kids get back to whatever it was you were doing. We old women will take care of business. I've seen several things I think I need." Dory ambled toward the cash register.

"I guess we were going to paint my nails," Liza said while tucking a wayward wave of hair behind her ear.

"Right," Kathy agreed. "But I went off with your mom and left you high and dry, didn't I? Then I left her holding the bag . . . or I guess, that would be the books," she corrected.

Ron and Liza chuckled.

"If we're going to be seeing each other this summer, you might as well know right now, I am soooo ADHD," Kathy explained.

"Really?" Ron quipped and winked. "I would have never guessed."

Liza wrinkled her brow.

"That means I'm hyper, and I can't pay attention for long," Kathy explained. "I also have trouble staying on task, until it comes to reading and setting up my business. That's why my apartment is still a wreck. I spend all my time here." She glanced toward the meticulous store.

"Ah!" Liza nodded her head slowly. "One of my ballet students has that. She's on medication, I think."

"Yes," Kathy affirmed. "I've gone the whole medication route, too, but it makes me feel bad. I don't really like it. So you get the real me!" Kathy ran in place for a couple of paces. "I hope you can take it!"

Liza laughed. "We need somebody to keep us from getting bored." She grinned at Kathy. "Looks like you're the perfect prescription."

"And guess what else?" Ron asked and eagerly stroked his hand across the front of his cotton shirt.

"What?" Liza and Kathy said together.

"Jay says he'll be here Saturday night and can hang out 'til the first of August."

"No way!" Kathy said.

"Yes," Ron said. "He asked me to tell you to call him. I told him they have a small room available at the bed-and-breakfast across the street."

"Great!" Kathy said. "I doubt he'd want to sleep on my couch's pull-out bed. The thing's so lumpy it feels like it has grapefruits in it. Hey," she continued chattering, "maybe he'll come over and clean my apartment. His place is always spotless!"

"I'm not sure he'll have time," Ron said. "He says he really wants to meet Liza." He waggled his eyebrows at his sister. "I've been telling him all about you."

"Oh, really?" Liza questioned and adjusted her narrow gold-rimmed glasses. "That's a first for you. Trying to marry me off or something?"

"No," Ron admitted, "I just can't get over this gut feeling the two of you would like each other."

"My brother is really handsome," Kathy admitted. "He's got high morals, too," she added. "Goes to church, even." She examined Liza for her reaction. Many women had tried to snare Jay Moore, but he'd yet to find the right one. One of his requirements was a woman of strong morality who lived her convictions.

"That's exactly the kind of man I'm looking for," Liza admitted.

Kathy smiled—more for her mother than anything else. Michelle Moore was beginning to despair that her son would ever find the right woman. While their father encouraged Jay not to rush into anything, their mom was ready to be a grandmother and didn't try to hide it.

Well, Mom, Kathy thought, *who knows? You just might get your wish this time.* As they headed toward the stairway, Kathy examined Liza's profile. She dismissed the prospect of Liza's being an intellectual but sensed that her new friend probably had a good heart. Kathy didn't believe in making snap judgments about character, for good or bad, but she was willing to hope that her brother and Liza just might make a good match.

Five

Saturday morning, Kathy opened her store as usual. And as usual, Ron and Liza Thaine arrived ten minutes later for coffee and a cinnamon roll.

Kathy looked up from the first round of cinnamon rolls she was pulling out of the oversized toaster oven. The smell of cream cheese and cinnamon nearly made her swoon. "No matter how many times I make these babies, I never get tired of eating them . . . or smelling them." She glanced toward her godmother. A butcher's apron covered Gloria's clothes, and she wore a pair of thick plastic gloves that reached halfway to her elbows.

"I know how you feel," Gloria admitted. "And I'm afraid it's going to show up on my hips if I'm not careful." Gloria Avery had worked in the store every morning as promised. After Sigmund finished fixing Kathy's car, he'd proclaimed a golfing holiday and had already met some new buddies around town. This morning, Gloria arrived at the store before Kathy came down. She let herself in with her key and began scrubbing down Kathy's sink and counters. Equipped with a bottle of cleaning spray in one hand and a brush in the other, Gloria never looked up from her task. The smell of liquid cleanser mingled with the aroma of freshly brewed coffee and bespoke industry and success.

Mrs. Thaine's large purchase seemed to open a floodgate of business for Kathy. So far, this week had been her most successful. The whole town suddenly realized there was a new gal in town who made dynamite cinnamon rolls and carried hard-to-find books to top it off. Kathy glanced at the corner where a pair of elderly gentlemen sat with a checkerboard between them. That was the exact fate Kathy had planned for the cushioned chairs and antique tables scattered across the store. This was the third morning that pair had arrived to play checkers. They each ate two cinnamon rolls and drank nearly a pot of coffee. Before they left by noon, both usually found a Louis L'Amour book they couldn't live without.

"I think Ron and Liza are as addicted to these cinnamon rolls as those guys over there." Kathy set the pan on the counter and removed her oven mitt.

"Liza maybe," Gloria mumbled. "But I don't think Ron's here for the cinnamon rolls." She threw in a wink.

"We're just friends," Kathy whispered and rubbed at a smudge of cream cheese streaked across her linen blouse, "and I plan to keep it that way." She waved at Ron.

With a self-assured smile, he claimed his usual stool at the end of the service bar.

Liza hopped onto the seat next to her brother's and chirped, "Hi!" with added emphasis on the long *I*.

"Hi," Kathy returned, and the two girlfriends shared a laugh. All week Liza had occasionally teased Kathy about her Southern accent. Ron often joined in the fun. "You guys want the usual?" Kathy asked.

"Yes," Ron replied. "At least I do, anyway." He looked at his sister.

Liza nodded, and her reddish-blond hair shimmered in the morning sunlight pouring through the numerous windows. "One cinnamon roll and a mug of coffee," she said.

"Got it!" Kathy turned back to the industrial-sized coffee-maker. She grabbed a pair of mugs and began filling one with dark, rich brew.

The whole time, she pondered what Gloria said about Ron. While Kathy wasn't naïve enough to miss his wanting more than friendship, she also wasn't gullible enough to imagine the man was playing for keeps. Since Kathy wasn't interested in a relationship that might result in a painful breakup at summer's end, she returned Ron's overtures with kindness and nothing more.

Besides, he's really not my type, she thought and reminded herself to convince Gloria of that truth. Ron was a tad too confident for her taste. A few times, he'd even bordered on cocky. He was also too convinced that he was good-looking and somewhat over-certain of the effects of his looks on her. She stole a glimpse of him. His spiked blond hair offered an engaging contrast with the dark hues of his black T-shirt. The last few days Kathy noticed young ladies taking a second look at Ron, but he did precious little to stir her own heart.

When Kathy set aside one mug and began filling the next, images of "the Ghost of Christmas Past" floated across her mind. Even though she'd only met the mystery man once, a sixth sense insisted he was her type. At least he looked like her type: clean-cut, honest eyes, masculine, but not overtly handsome like Ron. And he acted like her type. His rescuing the child proved he was a man of bravery and character—exactly what Kathy wanted in a future mate.

If I could only run into him again! she thought and wished he would return to the store. *Maybe he'll be at the cookout this afternoon*, she mused.

On Saturdays Kathy closed her store at noon. Today, she and Gloria were scheduled to be at the community barbecue. She learned at church the annual fundraiser had been a tradition for a hundred years, and it brought out most of the town. All proceeds went toward beautifying Northpointe.

Kathy stifled a yawn and released the coffeemaker's fill spout. After the picnic, she planned to come home for a nap. Once Jay arrived tonight, he, Ron, Liza, and Kathy were scheduled to go to dinner and a movie in Denver. While Kathy couldn't wait to go out with her friends and see if Jay and Liza hit it off, she also determined to keep all interaction with Ron light.

Both coffee mugs in hand, she approached Ron and Liza and served them their brew along with a generous grin. "Howdy strangers," she said. "How's thangs around Dodge?"

"Thangs is fine," Ron returned. He flashed her a smile that would be labeled captivating by many women. "What was that you said about the cocker spaniel puppy that woman brought in yesterday morning?"

Kathy tilted her head and tried to remember. Yesterday she'd decided her store must be turning into the center of culture for Northpointe. The doorbell's present jingle punctuated her assumption. Kathy waved to a klatch of aging women, all wearing red hats and purple shirts. According to the local rag's society pages, the "Circle of Red Hats" was one of the town's strongest and most vivacious social clubs. No woman was allowed to be a member unless she was over fifty, feisty, and a little wild and crazy. So far the club bragged of forty members. Several times Kathy noticed a small group of them out on the town.

One of the men playing checkers released a low wolf whistle and stood. He approached a gray-haired matron, took her hand, and bestowed a kiss on her cheek. She returned the endearment, and one of her red-hatted buddies giggled.

"I wonder if those two ever met before?" Kathy quipped.

"Either that, or that guy's a fast worker," Ron mumbled. "I wonder if he gives lessons?" He cocked his head and leveled an inviting ogle at Kathy. She turned to retrieve a crockery dish full of sugar and creamer packets and pretended she didn't see him.

"I remember what she said!" Liza said.

"Who?" Ron and Kathy said together.

"You!" Liza exclaimed and pointed at Kathy. "Ron was trying

to remember what you said about that cocker spaniel puppy in the store yesterday morning." She fidgeted with the top button of her sleeveless blouse.

"Oh yes, the puppy!" Kathy replied. "I said he was as cute as a—"

"Bug's ear," Liza finished for her.

"Cute as a bug's ear," Ron repeated and winked at Kathy. "That's what I was wanting to say about you when you said, 'How's thangs around Dodge?' You're as cute as a bug's ear."

"Oh, so you're comparing her to a cocker spaniel now?" Liza quipped and laughed out loud.

"I didn't mean it that way." Ron held up his hands, palms outward.

Kathy, glad for the diversion from a serious compliment, placed her hands on her hips and said, "Exactly what *did* you mean, then?"

Before he could answer, she scratched the top of her head. "Oh man! These fleas are driving me nuts! My owner changed my brand of flea collar, and it was a huge mistake." She lowered her hand and panted like a canine. "Have either of you seen my doggie bone around here?"

Both Ron and Liza laughed so hard the red-hatters stopped shopping and focused solely on them.

Smelling the potential for some serious sales, Kathy headed down the length of the coffee bar. "Is there something I can help you ladies with?" she asked. By the time she stepped from behind the bar, one of the ladies adjusted her feathered hat and said, "I'll have an extra-large cup of what *they're* having!" She pointed at the red-faced Ron and Liza.

The rest of the crew exclaimed, "Us too!"

"It's called my laughter brew," Kathy claimed. "Do you want it served at the coffee bar or would you rather pull some chairs together and get comfy?"

"I say we live dangerously and sit at the coffee bar!" A pretty, dark-skinned lady dressed in a neon-purple dress hustled forward and perched atop one of the stools. "Maybe we'll even get rowdy and slide our mugs up and down the length of it!"

"Now, now, ladies!" Kathy admonished, recognizing the woman from her church. "If you get too wild, I'll have to get my bouncer after you." She pointed toward Gloria.

Gloria held up her scrub brush and growled. "I'll take you down with this," she warned.

The red-hatters couldn't have been more enchanted. While Liza and Ron regained their composure, Kathy committed to charming her new customers. By the time she served their coffee, they were ordering cinnamon rolls and begging for Kathy's recipe.

The group didn't leave for two hours and so monopolized Kathy with requests and purchases she completely forgot about Liza and Ron. At last the fun-hearted group exited, each having purchased one of Kathy's T-shirts, along with a bag full of books, and promising they would be back.

Kathy waved them off with a cheerful grin even though a yawn would have been more appropriate. She'd stayed up past midnight reading Edgar Allen Poe. Once Kathy finished the last page of "The Tell-Tale Heart," she turned out her lamp, snuggled under her covers, and nearly drowned in her own adrenaline. All she could think about was how perfectly horrible it would be for someone to do what Poe wrote—murder a person and then hide his body parts under the floor.

Edgar Allen Poe had a wild imagination, she thought. *I wonder what causes someone to have a wild imagination?* Baffled, Kathy shook her head and noticed a message lying where Liza and Ron had been sitting. She hustled forward, picked up the note, and read: "Glad to see you're so busy. We have to go. Mom wants to do some sightseeing. See you tonight at seven. Meet Jay and us at the B and B as planned. Ron and Liza."

Six

Just past noon, Kathy eased her Impala into a parking place at the city park, a green meadow that stretched to the base of Northpointe Mountain. The smell of carpet shampoo testified to Sigmund's arranging to have her automobile cleaned after he fixed her overheating problem. Kathy admired the gleaming dashboard and clear windshield. The very thought of trading in her classic was as heinous as betraying a steadfast friend. She stroked the leather seat as if the vehicle were her pet.

While Aunt Gloria chatted about the profitable morning, Kathy put the Impala in park and gazed toward the chalet, perched on the side of the mountain like a royal entity ready to deliver judgment. At closer vantage, the chalet's floor-to-ceiling windows took on the appearance of great glassy eyes glaring at anyone who dared approach. A flashback to last night's Poe story sent a shiver through her soul. She imagined all sorts of similar scenarios . . . vengeance, murder, a conscience so tormented the chalet's owner had become a hermit. Kathy held her breath and wrapped her fingers around the gear shift. The longer she stared at the chalet, the more an invisible force beckoned her into its dark passages.

It's like the house has a personality all its own, she thought. *And it's not a good one.* Her throat tightened. The only thing that could make the house more ominous was a thunderstorm with life-threatening lightning crashing into the mountain. *It was a dark and stormy night,* she thought.

Trying to calm her racing mind, she focused on the park and resisted the home's silent summons. Sunshine christened the gathering of nearly a hundred people who meandered around numerous picnic tables. A huge barbecue pit, emitting trace puffs of smoke, claimed the center of attention. Kathy's mouth watered. The portable sign posted at the park's opening read, "All you can eat for $8." The chalet's presence faded into the distance.

"This looks like it's going to be fun!" Gloria enthused.

"I think I'll eat my eight dollars' worth," Kathy said and glanced at her godmother. "What about you?"

"At least! I'm starved. I didn't get a chance to eat breakfast this morning. Did you?" Gloria pushed at her cropped gray hair. Never did Kathy remember her looking so disheveled.

"Not a bite," Kathy admitted. "And I'm feeling a little trembly, too."

"Are you going to be okay?" Gloria worried. "You look hollow-eyed. You aren't going to faint, are you?"

"No, I haven't fainted in over a year," Kathy said. "My hypoglycemia has really leveled off in the last year or so. I just need to get some protein down me and I'll be fine." Kathy's stomach growled. Her head began a slow thud. She didn't tell Gloria that the last time she fainted had been because she skipped breakfast. Part of the reason she'd been able to control her low blood sugar was her own conscientious commitment to eating right.

She glanced down at her wide-leg linen pants and yellow sleeveless top, and grimaced. All week she and Gloria had enjoyed a quick breakfast of yogurt or cheese and a cinnamon roll at nine thirty. But not today. Instead, Kathy was wearing the cinnamon rolls. Aside from the cream cheese's dark streak on her blouse, her clothing was rumpled and showed signs of wear along the seams. A smudge of dust even marred one leg of her pants.

Gloria looked at Kathy's clothing. "We're going to have to go shopping for you," she said.

Turning off the ignition, Kathy said, "Me? Why?"

Her godmother sputtered over a laugh. "Your wardrobe is as worn out as this old car! I gave you that outfit three years ago. Haven't you shopped for anything since?"

"Well . . ." Kathy hedged, "I bought two of my store T-shirts from myself and a new pair of jeans three months ago."

"That's it!" Gloria proclaimed. Her pink lips firm, she popped open her door. "Monday afternoon we're going to get Sigmund to run the store, and you and I are going into Denver to shop. We're also going to get you a makeover." Gloria shook her finger at Kathy's nose.

"Have you been talking to my mother?" Kathy sighed. She removed the keys from the ignition and dropped them into her duffel purse. They clinked toward the bottom.

"Of course." Gloria never blinked.

Kathy laughed and picked up her purse.

"What?" Gloria prompted.

"Oh, nothing," Kathy said and recalled the yearly "people are going to think you don't care about your appearance" lecture Michelle Moore usually delivered. A former Miss Texas, Michelle had never understood Kathy's lack of interest in most glamor products.

"You and Mom are just two peas in a pod, that's all," Kathy finally said and shook her head. As much as she hated to admit it, the two were about to wear her down.

"And you're a pea in a pod of your own," Gloria teased, her gray eyes alight with a fondness that nearly convinced Kathy to go through with the makeover. "Seriously, I think a little makeup might at least make you look older."

"The Lord knows I need that," Kathy replied. "Did you hear that lady today ask me when I'd graduate from high school?"

"That's what I mean." Gloria nodded. "You're a business-woman now. You need to look the part."

Kathy clicked open her door. "You might be right," she admitted. The smell of smoky beef sashayed through the open doors. Kathy's stomach roared.

Gloria laughed, and the fine lines around her eyes only added to her beauty. "Enough about all this shopping, let's get you fed," she quipped and climbed out of the vehicle.

When the two met in front of the car, Kathy said, "I guess if it will make you and Mom happy, I'll go for a makeover. But the clerk better understand she's going to have to do some teaching. I can barely tell a mascara wand from a lipstick."

Gloria patted her back. "We'll get you all fixed up," she promised as they meandered toward the park entrance.

More cars flowed into the overcrowded parking area, and Kathy was thankful Gloria had spotted the space between a large truck and a tree. They paused at the entrance table. After Gloria insisted on paying for both their lunches, she dug into her purse in search of her wallet.

Kathy smiled politely at the neatly dressed woman sitting near the sign and then scanned the crowd. *I wonder if he's here*, she thought and caught the eye of a sundress-clad blonde setting her full plate on a picnic table. The woman's cascade of pale ringlets reminded Kathy of someone, but she couldn't remember who. When she smiled at Kathy and offered a shy wave, Kathy remembered.

"That's his sister!" she exclaimed.

"Whose sister?" Gloria asked and wrestled her wallet back into her purse.

"The Ghost of Christmas Past," Kathy explained. She beamed toward the blonde and waved back.

"What?" Gloria handed Kathy a blue meal ticket.

Kathy turned toward her godmother and gushed, "I'm sure Mom told you about the man who used my phone Monday night."

"Of course," Gloria said. "Your mother tells me almost everything. She was really worried about all that."

"I know . . . I know." Kathy swept away the issue with the flick of her wrist. "But this guy was okay. I promise. Anyway, when he left, I asked him his name. He said he was 'the Ghost of Christmas Past.'"

"Oh, really?" Gloria puzzled. She zipped her purse and slipped the strap onto her arm. "I guess it takes all types. Doesn't it?"

"No, he's not a type," Kathy claimed. "He was just kidding . . . just having some fun. So I told him I was Miss Kitty—you know, from *Gunsmoke*."

Gloria chortled and shook her head. "I've heard it all now."

"Mom and Dad started calling me that when they saw my store."

Kathy glanced back toward the willowy blonde who smiled again. She figured that was invitation enough. Without bothering to inform Gloria, she hurried toward the picnic table and descended on the young woman.

"Hi!" she said and extended her hand. "I'm Kathy Moore. I own Kathy's Book Nook. Didn't I see you Monday night during the storm?"

The blonde stood and nodded. "Yes," she said and shook Kathy's hand. "I'm Alaina Tilman, Ben's sister," she murmured. After brief eye contact, she lowered her head.

If Kathy hadn't been so weak for need of food, she would have been hard-pressed not to run in place and scream for joy. Determined to keep her voice even, she said, "So your brother's name is Ben Tilman?"

When Alaina's smile turned curious, Kathy figured she must

have sounded as eager to Ben's sister as she did to herself. "I thought you two knew each other." Alaina tilted her head and eyed Kathy.

"No." Kathy shook her head. "I just let him into the store so he could use my phone that night. When he left, I asked his name and he said he was 'the Ghost of Christmas Past.'"

Alaina squinted and strained her mouth. "That's strange," she said. "Why would he say something like that?"

"I have no idea." Kathy shrugged.

"Why would who say something like what?" a masculine voice queried.

Kathy looked to the left and encountered her ghost. Except for the fact that his brown hair was dry, he looked exactly as he had five days ago—except the Band-Aid's absence revealed a nasty cut lined in stitches.

"You're Ben Tilman," Kathy accused and placed her hands on her hips. "You lied to me," she teased. "You told me you were 'the Ghost of Christmas Past.'"

"And you believed that line?" Ben replied.

"Well, of course." Kathy's sandal-clad feet reminded her she'd been on them all morning. She shifted her weight. "I'm a gullible newcomer. What was I supposed to believe?"

"You can be sure he doesn't even believe in ghosts," Alaina fondly replied and laid her hand on her brother's arm. "He actually pastors a church just outside Northpointe."

A pastor! Kathy thought and immediately assigned to Ben all the character her father had exhibited in his ministry and home. Even though spiritual issues weren't presently at the top of her priority list, Kathy decided she could reevaluate that list—and fast—if it involved interesting Ben. But Kathy's elation and schemes were short-lived.

His wife might appreciate his character qualities even more than I do, she suddenly thought.

Never adept at the art of subtlety, Kathy wasted no time examining his left hand. No gold band claimed his ring finger. "You're not married!" she exclaimed like a kid who just learned she was going to the circus.

Ben's brows quirked. Alaina softly snickered.

Kathy smacked her hand over her mouth. Eyes wide, she stared at Ben for several seconds before he broke into a relaxed grin. Never one to blush, Kathy couldn't deny the rush of heat to her cheeks. In three rash words she clued in Ben to her thoughts over the last five days.

"No, not married yet," he replied and slipped his hands into the pockets of his shorts. "And I'd hazard to guess you're not Miss Kitty, either." His indulgent grin resembled that of a doting elder brother.

"Miss Kitty?" Alaina echoed.

Somehow Kathy gained the fortitude to lower her hand.

"You know, you're a fine one to accuse me of lying," Ben teased and rocked back on his heels.

"I guess you got me on that one," she parried. "I'm actually Kathy Moore," she explained, glad for the diversion from her embarrassment.

"I can't remember now," Ben said and narrowed his eyes. "Did you tell me you're the owner of the bookstore? Or is it someone else who owns—"

"I'm the owner," Kathy affirmed.

"I'm guessing you're not eighteen, then?" he said, and Kathy detected a glimmer of interest in his eyes.

Her heart soared as one word marched through her mind: *Chemistry!* Her friends back home had talked about it, but Kathy had never experienced that unexplained spark that screamed, *I need to get to know this guy!*

"No, not eighteen," she said and decided that makeover was a must. "Actually, I'm twenty-two."

Ben's eyes dulled, and he gazed past her as if she weren't there. "Well, not much over eighteen, huh?" he said with a tolerant smile.

"You're young to own your own business," Alaina thoughtfully asserted. "That's quite an accomplishment." Her tone held the trace of admiration Kathy longed to hear in Ben's voice.

"Thanks." Kathy tried to hide the wilt in her voice. Obviously even twenty-two was too young for Ben Tilman. She noted the laugh lines around his eyes and decided he was somewhere between thirty and thirty-five. While thirty didn't seem too old for her, thirty-five was probably pushing it.

But Dad's thirteen years older than Mom, she reminded herself.

"Kathy, aren't you going to get something to eat?" Gloria's voice invaded her thoughts.

She turned toward the end of the picnic table where Gloria stood holding a plate laden with a barbecue sandwich, coleslaw, and potato salad. Her blue knit top blurred as an unexpected dizzy spell demanded Kathy find something to eat—and soon. She gripped the edge of the picnic table and steadied herself.

Ben looked over his shoulder.

"Oh!" Gloria exclaimed. "Are you Kathy's ghost?"

He chuckled. "I guess I am."

"Aunt Gloria," Kathy said, "this is Ben Tilman. He actually isn't a ghost at all. He pastors a church. . . ." She turned to Alaina as Gloria deposited her plate on the table. "Where did you say he pastors?"

"Just east of Northpointe—actually between Northpointe and Denver," Ben supplied. "It's called Aspen Community Church."

Gloria scurried forward and extended her jeweled hand for a brief shake. "Let me guess," she said. "It's surrounded by aspens."

"What makes you think that?" Ben queried.

"I don't know. I was just guessing." The group laughed.

"We'd love for you and Kathy to visit sometime."

"Oh, sure!" Gloria replied. "That sounds good, doesn't it, Kathy?"

While Ben's invitation sounded promising, his voice's professional polish was all about being polite . . . and nothing more.

"Sure!" Kathy agreed and averted her gaze.

So much for spending five days daydreaming, she thought. *On top of all that, it doesn't take a genius to figure out he doesn't even have a dark past.*

While all her grandiose adventures crashed into a heap of rubble, Ben said, "I still haven't gotten anything to eat. Want to join me?" He looked at Kathy and pointed toward the service line.

"Yes, she needs to eat," Gloria insisted.

"I'm a moderate hypoglycemic," Kathy asserted, her words as limp as her legs.

"By all means, let's get in line," Ben insisted. "We could probably even arrange for you to cut to the front of the line."

"No, that's okay. I'll be okay," Kathy insisted and walked beside Ben toward the swiftly moving line. With Ben only a couple feet away, he seemed taller than he had Monday night or even when he was standing near the picnic table.

"This is going quicker than last year," he explained. "They got smart this time and made everybody pay as they walked into the park. Last year, we had to pay in the same line where we got our plates. I thought I'd never get my food. I almost died of hunger right there on the spot. I started hallucinating my own tombstone under those oaks over there." He pointed toward a clump of regal trees.

Kathy chuckled. "I feeeeeel yo' pain!"

Ben gazed downward. "Texas," he mumbled and shook his head.

"What?"

"Oh, I was just thinking I could hear the Texas in your voice," he replied.

"Yep," Kathy admitted. "And I'm unrepentant about it."

"I would have never guessed."

They stopped at the end of the line, and an awkward silence descended on them. During the lull, a dread depression swooped into Kathy's spirit and mingled with the beginnings of "low blood sugar grouchies." *This has to be some sort of a cruel joke,* she groused. *I'm standing in a gorgeous Colorado park with a guy I'd give my life's savings to get to know better, and he's not interested.* The cool breeze tumbling from the snow-crested mountains sounded like the whispers of a thousand mockers.

Well, if he's not interested, she thought, *why did he ask me to stand in line with him?* She chewed on the tip of her index finger and reminded herself not to nip off the polish. Kathy withdrew her finger and examined her nails. Last night Liza and Ron had come to her place for sandwiches. After they ate, they worked on getting her apartment more organized. When they grew tired, she and Liza repainted their nails. Today, Kathy's fingers were tipped in red, white, and blue stripes.

"So . . . uh . . . why did you move to Northpointe, of all places?" Ben queried.

Kathy looked up. His gaze trailed from her wild fingernails to her eyes. The kind interest in his baby blues answered her question about his asking her to stand in line with him. Ben Tilman was a gentleman. And as a gentleman, he would have asked her to stand in line with him if she were eighty and married.

"My family and I visited here a few months ago," she explained, her voice as lively as a ghost town. "And I just knew this was the place." She shrugged. "After living in Amarillo, it's a nice change of pace. I love Colorado. Plus it gives me some space from my parents."

"Oh," Ben acknowledged and didn't pose the silent question that hung between them.

"It's not that I have a bad relationship with them or anything," she hurried. "It's just that . . ." She hesitated and decided to come out with the truth. "They don't seem to realize I can take care of myself and make my own decisions. It can get stifling at times. At least this way I've got some space on it all."

"And the lady you're with is your aunt, you said?"

"No. That's my godmother. She and her husband are the people my mom told you to tell me were coming. Remember? The Averys."

"Oh, yes." Ben nodded his head.

"I just call them Aunt Gloria and Uncle Ziggy because . . ." She shrugged. "I just always have." *Why I'm telling him all this stuff is anybody's guess*, she thought. *I'll probably never even see him again.* "Really," she continued, "I think they're here partly to help baby-sit me." Kathy rubbed her aching forehead and braced herself against the tantalizing smells wafting across the park.

"Yes, I gathered that the other night," Ben mused.

"Sometimes I feel like my mom thinks I'm still fifteen."

The line moved forward, and Kathy stepped in sequence with Ben.

"I think my sister feels the same way at times. She's only three years younger than I am," he said. "She's twenty-seven."

"Really?" Kathy questioned but was more interested in knowing that Ben was only thirty—only eight years her senior. *How can he think I'm too young for him?*

"Yes. My father seems to have forgotten she grew past seventeen."

"What about your mom?"

"She passed away a couple of years ago. She and my sister were really close." He fingered the stitches near his hairline, and Kathy debated how best to introduce the subject of his heroic rescue.

"So your dad's more like my parents than your mom was?"

"Definitely," Ben affirmed. "There are times he even gets on *my* trail."

"And where does he live?" she asked.

"Funny you should ask," Ben said and pointed to the chalet. "He lives right there. That's the house I was raised in."

Kathy imagined gothic organ music as chills swept her torso. Earlier in the week, she'd wondered if Ben might somehow be linked to the spooky chalet. The reality that he was only heightened her disappointment that he wasn't interested in getting to know her better. Not only would she not experience a budding romance, she would also miss out on a summer of potential intrigue.

She looked down and nudged a clump of grass with the toe of her sandal. *Even though Ben probably doesn't have a dark past,* she reasoned, *the chalet must. It's just too weird looking.*

The chalet tugged at her attention, and Kathy's gaze trailed up the mountain once more. She made herself look away for fear of Ben suspecting her thoughts. Her sight focused on a strange-looking man only twenty feet away. He was staring at her. The guy reminded Kathy of a shriveled-up cowboy who'd spent one too many decades in the sun. The man's piercing eye centered on her while the other one, clouded and bloodshot, sagged at an odd angle.

Kathy's thoughts flew to "The Tell-Tale Heart," to the murder victim's evil eye—the eye that drove the narrator to commit his heinous crime. She stiffened against a shiver. As the cowboy continued his scrutiny, she was overcome with a deep realization that this was more than a passing observation. The man had a motive. Kathy's flesh erupted in goose bumps.

"Kathy, have I somehow offended you?" Ben's question shattered the moment.

"Who, me?" Kathy looked up at him and tried to expunge the old man's evil eye from her mind.

"No. There are three Kathys standing behind you. I was talking to them."

Without thinking, Kathy looked behind her and glimpsed

where the cowboy had been standing. Thankfully he was gone. She laughed. "You got me," she admitted.

"So I did," Ben replied.

Their momentary banter diminished into another stiff silence. They moved closer to the food. If not for her dire need to eat, Kathy would have slipped away and headed home.

"You didn't answer me," Ben prompted.

"About what?" she queried.

"I asked if I've somehow offended you."

"Oh, that!" Kathy looked away as a rush of fatigue weighted her spine. Her nap was beckoning. This week had been quite fulfilling but highly exhausting.

"Are you pleading the fifth on me?" he pressed.

"I'm just tired," she explained and wondered if she should mention the stranger. She decided not to say anything. Ben might think she was paranoid. "And, well," Kathy added, "when my blood sugar drops I get grouchy."

Thankfully, Kathy was next in line. She went through the buffet and chose a barbecue sandwich, baked beans, and coleslaw. In her haste she passed the beverage table. "I guess I'll see you 'round town," she called over her shoulder and purposefully strode toward Gloria. She hoped Ben took the hint and kept his distance. Kathy wasn't in the mood to chat with someone who might be her dream man but who wasn't interested—especially after she'd blatantly clued him in to her interest. Presently, even his story about the rescue was losing appeal.

"Kathy!" Ben's voice floating across the crowd ended her hopes of his taking the hint.

She hurried toward their table, and her cheeks warmed anew as she recalled blurting, *"You aren't married!"* Kathy pressed her fingertips against her forehead and groaned.

"Are you okay?" Gloria looked up from a session of chitchat with Alaina.

"Uh . . ." Kathy eyed her food. As much as she wanted to sit down and inhale the whole meal, she decided eating on the way was the most sane option. "I really need to go," she explained and glanced over her shoulder. Ben was steadily moving toward them. "I think it would be best for me to just eat on the way. Do you mind driving?"

Seven

Clutching his plate full of food, Ben strode toward Kathy. He'd never considered himself adept in the ways of women, but he knew he'd somehow offended the young store owner. How was anybody's guess.

"Kathy!" he called again and hurried across the park.

She was standing at the picnic table by her godmother and never bothered to look at him this time.

Ben attempted to step around a klatch of elderly ladies when one of them exclaimed, "Ben Tilman, is that you?"

He forced himself to concentrate on the gray-haired woman demanding his attention. Her brown eyes and plump cheeks brought back memories from his junior high days. Mrs. Dodd was the study hall monitor who retrieved his paper footballs on a regular basis. Ben never would forget the time he'd misaimed and smacked the teacher right between her eyes. She had not been a happy camper that day.

"Mrs. Dodd!" Ben said. While he welcomed her brief hug, Ben stole another quick glance at Kathy. Still standing, she nibbled on her sandwich as her godmother threw away her plate. "It's been so long since I've seen you. How are you?"

"Fine. Just fine," the matron claimed. "And I'm so proud of you," she crooned and patted his arm. The smell of her heavy powdery scent brought back memories of musty books and old desks and a corner reserved for boys with flying paper footballs.

"I saw your dad in the store just last week, and he said you'd just received your Master of Divinity and were a senior pastor. I would have never imagined . . ."

Mrs. Dodd's chattering faded as Ben cut another glimpse toward Kathy. She was waving at his sister while Gloria patted Alaina's back. Still munching from her plate, Kathy turned and walked toward the parking lot.

She's leaving! Ben thought and considered breaking away from his former teacher.

"Ben! Ben Tilman!" Mrs. Dodd's sharp words whipped him back to attention.

He gazed down at Mrs. Dodd and said "Sorry" like a thirteen-year-old caught daydreaming. "What were you saying?"

"I was saying I hope you've learned to listen better than you did when you were in school," she said with a rap on his arm.

He smiled. "I try." Ben gazed toward Kathy, who was on the edge of the parking lot.

When he looked back at Mrs. Dodd, she was following his gaze. "Well . . ." she mused. "I guess it's the same as always. You boys always were more interested in girls than your schoolwork. Your dad told me you still aren't married, so—"

"It's not that," Ben defended. "I just . . . I'm afraid I offended her. She's a newcomer."

"By all means," Mrs. Dodd winked, "we don't want to offend newcomers."

"No, it's not like that," Ben insisted and peered toward Kathy again. Gloria at her side, she walked into the parking lot and disappeared behind a truck. Ben sighed.

"Well, whatever you say." Mrs. Dodd nodded. "It was good to see you nonetheless."

"And you, too, Mrs. Dodd," Ben replied with an assuring grin.

Soon he wove through the crowd toward his sister. One of

Ben's goals in life was to fulfill the New Testament command "As much as lies within you, live at peace with all men." So he always made extra effort not to offend people, and if he did, he exerted just as much effort to clear the offense. But this time it didn't happen. After a significant exertion of willpower, he chose to release the whole Kathy Moore incident. He probably wouldn't see her more than a few times a year anyway.

Oh well, he reasoned as he placed his plate near Alaina's. *Maybe she really didn't feel well and that was all.* In the middle of his musings, Ben realized he failed to thank Kathy again for allowing him to use her phone Monday night. *Maybe I should just drop her a note,* he thought and examined the parking lot. A light-blue Chevrolet, about forty years old, was rolling toward the exit. Ben caught a glimpse of a woman with short dark hair in the passenger side.

He recalled the spark and interest in Kathy's eyes. Her concern over his marital status was beyond blatant. While a personal note would be the gentlemanly thing to do, it might also give Kathy the impression he was interested in more than friendship. Kathy Moore was far too young for him to leave that impression—despite the fact that he'd thought about her off and on since they first met.

"You really scored big, didn't you?" Alaina asked, never taking her attention from the brownie she was tasting.

"Huh?" Ben questioned while settling next to her.

"With Kathy," she continued and cast him a sly sideways glance.

Ben silently stared back. "Did I say something that could have offended her?" he questioned. "I got the idea she wasn't exactly happy with me."

Alaina rolled her eyes. "Men!" she huffed.

"What?" Ben picked up the cellophane package containing his plastic knife, fork, and spoon.

"Kathy Moore is a business professional, and you treated her like she was a child."

"I did not!" Ben defended.

"Oh, please." Alaina laid down her brownie. "When she told you she was twenty-two, you said that wasn't much older than eighteen and acted like she was of no consequence at all."

"I did not!" he denied again, this time with the bossy, elder-brother voice that usually ended their arguments.

"Suit yourself," Alaina returned with a shrug. "But you asked, so I told you."

"Well, what was I supposed to do?" Ben demanded and gazed at his sandwich. "She didn't make any bones about being, well . . . you know . . . interested in me." He freed his plastic fork from its wrapper and jabbed at the mound of potato salad.

"You mean you aren't interested in her at all?"

"Of course not!" Ben denied and hoped his wayward mind caught on. "She's way too immature."

"I don't know if I would call her immature," Alaina debated. "Free-spirited, maybe, but being a store owner at the age of twenty-two isn't exactly the stuff that immaturity is made of. Who knows? We both just met her. I hate to see you snub an opportunity before you give it a chance. You aren't getting any younger, and your options aren't exactly that broad these days."

"Whatever," Ben grumbled and frowned at his sister's profile. "But I'm not interested in a flirtation with anyone or to date just to be dating. And I seriously doubt Kathy is ready to settle down at her age. Besides, I have to be careful. I'm a pastor now. Do you know how many women have . . ."

Ben trailed off. He hated to sound egotistical, even to his own sister. But the truth was, he probably could have gotten married about ten times last year. He didn't know what had overcome the female population in northern Colorado these days. Ben had never considered himself overly handsome or even a remarkable catch, but it would appear that a few women didn't agree—including the mother of the boy he'd pulled from that car seconds before it exploded. Ben touched his forehead and ran his finger across the stitches. That lady had wasted no time telling him she was a widow when Ben visited the boy in the hospital.

One of the new church attendees had even dropped hints the size of boulders. When Ben continued to ignore the hints, she finally asked him out. He had respectfully declined and hadn't seen her since. Once Kathy Moore blurted her glee over his being single, Ben decided to end a new pursuit before it even began.

"I can't take up with every woman who's new in town," he finally said. "People would start talking."

Alaina picked up her iced tea. "You asked me why Kathy Moore was irritated," she softly asserted. "I told you what I thought. No sense getting in a huff over it." She took a generous swallow of her tea.

Ben looked straight ahead. His sister was being unusually pushy over this. She normally let Ben be his own person and make his own choices without remarking. He made it a habit of returning the favor.

He hadn't even mentioned that he knew Alaina was secretly seeing Caleb Manley, the son of Thurston Manley. Zachariah Tilman and Thurston had despised each other for as long as Ben could remember. At Ben's mother's funeral, he even overheard Thurston tell someone he wouldn't be surprised to learn that Zachariah killed his wife.

If Dad found out Thurston said that . . . Ben tensed and wondered if his father would ever allow God to heal him over the Thurston issue. *Unless he does, Alaina is in for trouble if Dad discovers her romance with Caleb.* Ben didn't know what was getting into Alaina these days! She had never crossed their father. Few people did, especially not his timid daughter.

"I guess I really liked Kathy," Alaina mused. "I know I just met her, but there seems to be something," she shrugged, "I don't know . . . something special about her."

"Maybe," Ben said and filled his mouth with a generous bite of tart potato salad. After a swift chew and swallow, he said, "But I still don't think she'd be a good fit for me. Whoever heard of a pastor's wife with striped fingernails, anyway? Monday night she had them painted blue and green. I can just see the Women's Auxiliary now." Ben rolled his eyes as he imagined a whole room full of ladies—half of them much like Mrs. Dodd.

Alaina chortled. "Maybe you're right. But I just think she's cute, and she seems really sweet. Besides, somebody like her would stop you from getting boring. You know you have that tendency." She placed her hand on his upper arm and didn't blink.

Ben, in the process of picking up his sandwich, gaped at his sister. After grappling with a dozen responses, he quipped, "I don't think Mrs. Dodd would agree."

"Who's Mrs. Dodd?"

"You remember. The study hall monitor from junior high." Ben turned and scanned the park. He pointed toward the teacher, still locked in conversation with her cronies.

"Yes, I remember her," Alaina agreed.

"I used to pop paper footballs all over that study hall. Once, I hit her between the eyes."

Alaina giggled. "I think you're making that up," she said. "You were so dull in high school, you were listening to elevator music."

"I'm not *dull*!" Ben defended. "I nearly got killed pulling a kid from a car! Last year I raised over a hundred thousand dollars for that orphanage in China! And I—" He scrambled for something—anything—to add to the list. "I'm—I'm a killer chess player!"

"Ooooh," Alaina mocked. "Chess! The most exciting game known to man." She eyed his stitches while Ben grimaced.

"Okay," she acquiesced, "I'll admit you have had an exciting week. That was pretty brave of you, even if I do say so myself."

"Thanks a lot," Ben drawled. "It's funny you should say *I'm dull*. . . ."

"I'm not dull," Alaina claimed, and Ben recognized a confident gleam in his sister's eyes he had never seen before. "I've never listened to elevator music."

"Well, you're not exactly a live-wire, either," he retorted and wondered how much of Alaina's increasing poise could be attributed to Caleb's influence. "Your idea of an exciting evening is reading the phone book."

"You don't know everything," Alaina said with a mystical grin.

"If you're talking about the thing with you and Caleb . . ." Ben trailed off and wondered at his own wisdom in introducing the subject.

Alaina gasped. Her face blanched. She frantically glanced around them. Ben followed suit. No one in the crowd even registered their presence.

"I don't know what you're talking about," she whispered. Alaina lowered her head and toyed with the napkin in her lap.

"I saw you guys last week at the lake," Ben admitted. "I saw him kiss you," he mumbled under his breath. "Alaina, what has gotten into you? Two years ago you would have never crossed Dad."

Alaina didn't look up. "Two years ago, I had Mother." Her ringlets hid what her shaking voice revealed.

Ben placed his elbow on the table and rested his forehead against his palm. "I'm sorry," he breathed. "I didn't mean to make you cry."

"I—I know." She sniffled and dabbed at her eyes with her napkin. "It's just that you—you've got your ministry. Dad's in his own world. And there I am . . . up there in that chalet with no life."

"What about your job?"

"What about it?" Alaina challenged. She raised her head and tossed her rumpled napkin in the center of her empty plate. "I'm cooped up in a hospital lab all day, and then I come home. Caleb is the only thing . . . the only person . . . everyone deserves to have someone."

"But Caleb Manley?" Ben questioned. "Alaina, if Dad finds out—"

"Why should he find out?"

"Well, are you two . . . are you planning to get married?"

"Caleb hasn't asked, but . . ." She stared into the distance.

"Then Dad will find out for sure."

"By then it will be too late." Alaina squared her shoulders. "I am twenty-seven, you know. It's time, Ben. Dad can't keep me cooped up there on that mountain my whole life. At least he gave you the freedom to leave. He won't even let me move out on my own! The last time I hinted at getting an apartment, he hit the ceiling."

"I know it's hard," Ben said and examined his sister's empty plate. At least she had started eating right again. After their mother died, Ben was worried sick she had fallen into some sort of eating disorder. Alaina had gotten bone thin, and her eyes lacked sparkle. But during the last year she'd put on some weight and regained some fortitude. Now Ben began to wonder how much of her improvement involved overcoming grief and how much could be attributed to Caleb.

"How long have you and Caleb been together?" Ben gently asked.

She touched the rim of her cup full of iced tea. "Nearly a year."

"That long?" Ben exclaimed and wondered how he'd missed the beverage table.

"Shhh!" Alaina snapped up her head, leveled a glare at Ben, and peered toward the crowd. "I saw his dad earlier. Keep it down!"

Ben glanced across the park but didn't see anyone who even resembled the prune-faced, one-eyed man.

"Caleb and I liked each other in high school, okay?" Alaina whispered.

"You did?"

"Yes. One day last year I was in the cemetery leaving flowers for Mom's grave. He was there. His grandfather had just passed away. They were close."

"So the two of you started talking, and . . ."

Alaina nodded. "One thing led to another, and here we are." She lifted her hand like a helpless child.

"Are you in love with him?"

She gazed toward the chalet perched on the mountain. "What do you think?"

Ben sighed and focused on his father's home.

When he was a kid, Ben had often lamented being the middle child. His elder brother, Phil-the-overachiever, was usually up to his neck in awards and accolades. Alaina had been everyone's sweetheart. Their father had especially doted on her. And Ben, a fairly good student who enjoyed basketball, never felt he measured up to either of them.

Now that he was an adult, Ben thanked God he was the middle child. His father had stayed as busy pressuring Phil to follow his footsteps in the army as he had making certain Alaina remained under his control. That left Ben to pursue his own interests, to develop into his own person, to answer God's call. Zachariah Tilman, never a deeply spiritual man, hadn't been wild about Ben becoming a minister. But given his obsession over his elder son's successful military career and overprotecting his daughter, he'd finally learned to tolerate Ben's profession. Nevertheless, pursuing his call had taken every ounce of courage Ben possessed—even with his mother's support. In the eyes of all three of his children, Zachariah

Tilman's disapproval was nearly as dreaded as the disapproval of God himself.

If only I was brave enough to find a wife, Ben derided himself. Part of the reason he was still single involved the determination to marry a woman of whom his father would approve. Aside from the fact that he dearly loved his father, his whole childhood his mother had been the victim of in-law war. Some of the wounds had yet to heal, and the last thing Ben wanted was to repeat the battles from his childhood.

Grandma Tilman, still spry at age eighty-five, was as strong-willed as her son. Laura Tilman, as gentle-spirited as her daughter, had endured pure grief from her mother-in-law. Ben couldn't recall a Christmas in his childhood when his mother wasn't crying. The tears usually started when Grandma Tilman came and didn't end until she left. Ben vowed as a teenager never to marry a woman unless they could live in peace with his family and hers. So far, he hadn't met a lady he thought could get along with his father. Therefore, except for the usual high school and college flirtations, he'd kept his distance on the whole lot of them.

"I'm through," Alaina said, and her words took on a determined edge Ben found difficult to absorb. She stood, picked up her plate, and walked toward a trash can.

Sighing, Ben enjoyed a mammoth bite of his barbecue sandwich and thoughtfully chewed the smoky beef. He didn't know exactly what he was looking for in a woman. Whoever she was, she needed to be as close to perfect as possible.

She won't have striped fingernails, that's for sure, he thought and imagined his father's eyes at the sight of such.

But despite her wild fingernails, Ben couldn't deny that Kathy Moore would have interested him had she been a few years older. Her animated personality was both refreshing and endearing . . . as endearing as her upturned nose and ready smile. All that was part of the reason he'd dubbed himself "the Ghost of Christmas

Past" Monday night. Her carefree spirit had induced him to respond in like manner. Ben shook his head and decided he was best served to stop thinking about Kathy Moore and just eat.

She's too young anyway! he reminded himself and promptly recalled all the couples he knew with five to ten years' difference in their ages.

Eight

Something cold and wet and spongy dabbed Kathy's cheek. Half asleep, she rolled onto her side and rubbed at her face. The tiny cold sponge assaulted her ear. This time it was accompanied by a low hum Kathy recognized. Her eyes slid open, and she encountered feline whiskers only centimeters away. Lucy's purring grew more insistent. The cat released a pitiful meow.

Kathy drowsily smiled, rolled onto her back, and pulled her furry friend onto her stomach. "Lucy, you sound like you haven't eaten in weeks," she admonished.

The golden-eyed feline complained anew. Kathy checked her wristwatch. "Five after five," she said over a yawn. "No wonder you're hungry. It's five whole minutes past your mealtime. How perfectly horrible!"

The striped cat rubbed her face against Kathy's arm and flopped onto her side. Chuckling, Kathy sat up and swung her feet to the floor. She'd eaten her lunch on the way home from the park and dropped into bed the second she entered her bedroom. Now she felt like she'd been hit over the head with a two-by-four.

"Oh man," she groaned and stretched. "My mouth feels like it's got glue in it." She grimaced and planned for a cold glass of water after she fed Lucy.

The cat on her heels, Kathy made a necessary trip to the restroom. Once through, she gritted her teeth, closed her eyes, flushed the toilet, and awaited the otherworldly moan.

The plumbing didn't disappoint. Lucy arched her back, inched toward the wall, and hissed at the toilet. The hair on her tail stood straight out.

Kathy chuckled. "I love it," she mumbled, turned on the water, and began washing her hands. The smell of country apple hand soap did nothing to stimulate her senses. She was as sleepy as ever.

After a lazy yawn, Kathy turned off the water, grabbed a towel, and examined her appearance in the mirror. Dark circles marred her eyes. Her cheeks were unusually pale, which made her sparse freckles stand out like blotches of cinnamon on a sugar cookie. Her bobbed hair was crushed on one side and protruded straight out along the bangs. Kathy laughed again.

I couldn't look worse, she thought and planned for a quick shower.

Her brother had texted last night, saying he was supposed to arrive by six, an hour before their outing with Ron and Liza. He also said he couldn't wait to meet Liza. Kathy was beginning to think something good might come of this new friendship with the Thaines. Kathy's mother, forever fretting over her children's welfare, would be thrilled if Jay found the right woman.

Thoughts of her mother motivated Kathy to examine the jagged crack marring the mirror's upper right corner. During the move, Michelle Moore insisted that Kathy buy a new mirror to replace the old one, but Kathy refused. She looped the towel over the tarnished brass rack and commended herself for her fortitude. Old apartments with haunted plumbing, creaking floors, and cracks here and there were the stuff adventures were made of.

"The Lord knows I need an adventure," she mumbled under her breath. Ben Tilman turned out to be one huge disappointment. Kathy had purposed to extinguish thoughts of Ben but failed. Now that she'd formally met him, his memory was more vivid than ever.

If only I was going out with him tonight instead of Ron, she pined.

Lucy's insistent meow blended into a feline squawk. As Kathy hurried from the bathroom, the cat scurried toward the kitchen, her tail straight in the air. Kathy stepped from her bedroom into the neat living room, brought to order with Liza and Ron's help.

A twist of guilt burned her chest and left Kathy feeling like an ungrateful wretch. Ron had worked hard all week to help Kathy with her apartment. The bookshelf was neatly filled. Kathy's collection of black-and-white posters from classic TV shows were arranged along the far wall. Dick Van Dyke hung between Andy Griffith and a picture of the whole *Leave It to Beaver* cast. Of course, Lucille Ball reigned from the grouping's center. On her way through, Kathy stroked the arm of the used love seat Ron found for two hundred dollars at the nearly new shop. The earth-toned upholstery clashed with the dormitory green sofa Kathy had in college. The love seat was the only piece Kathy owned that Gloria approved of.

The least I can do is try to enjoy an evening out with Ron. Maybe he'll grow on me, she mused. *He's not that bad.*

"But he's not Ben, either," she whispered and hustled into the kitchen.

By six o'clock Kathy had showered, changed into a skirt and cotton shirt, and meandered down to her store. With Jay arriving any second, Kathy opened her shop's door, stepped onto the sidewalk, and looked up one length of the street, then the other. The smell of hamburgers and fries attested to the presence of The Diner on the Corner. The collection of cars around the street corner assured that tonight was the all-you-can-eat buffet. Still there was no sign of her brother's silver Thunderbird. Sighing, Kathy made a tent of her hand above her eyes and looked the other way again. The evening sun nearly defeated her determination but didn't overcome it. Finally, Kathy lowered her hand and decided to wait inside. As she was turning for her door, she glimpsed Northpointe Chalet and was riveted by its appearance. The westward sun hurled bucketfuls of sunshine on the home, highlighting the cedar woodwork and expansive windows. Despite the balmy evening's warmth, a chill shook Kathy.

Something strange is going on in that chalet. I just know it! she thought. *Or maybe something strange has gone on there.*

"So what do you think of it?" a gruff voice questioned.

Kathy jumped and whipped around to face a man with weathered skin. One of his gray eyes focused on her while the other clouded eye angled away.

It's him! she thought. She blurted, "You were at the cookout!" A rush of dread immobilized her. Her heart pounded.

"I see yore lookin' at Tilman's house," he said as if she'd never spoken. "Whatcha think?"

"Uh . . ." Kathy hedged and tried to recall seeing the guy before today. While his straw cowboy hat and leathery skin might belong to any of the older men who drank coffee at her shop, Kathy couldn't remember this man.

He leaned closer, and his bloodshot "evil eye" paralyzed her. "I think it's spooky," he hissed. The tinge of alcohol on his breath heightened Kathy's terror. "And the man who owns it ain't worth the nails holding the place together."

"Really?" Kathy asked. Torn between her thirst for knowledge and concern for her safety, she debated whether to stay or dash into her store.

"I saw you talkin' to Ben Tilman today at the cookout," the man continued.

"I know." A rush of sweat assaulted Kathy's forehead.

"Yes. I've been waiting on you to come out ever since ya came home."

"You have?" Kathy gripped her throat.

His curt nod was answer enough. "I tried to catcha earlier but I was too late. You'd already locked yore store."

"Really?" Kathy repeated, her voice shrill.

What if he's a stalker? she thought. Her legs began to shake, and she regretted not mentioning the man to Ben.

"If you have any sense at all, you'll stay away from that Tilman bunch," the man continued.

"I will?"

"You will." He didn't blink. "Zachariah Tilman killed his wife."

Kathy's eyes bugged. She relived the conversation with Ben. He said his father was overprotective of Alaina. But what if there was more—much, much more—to the whole ordeal? What if Alaina knew her father killed her mother, and Zachariah was trying to prohibit her from telling the truth?

"Are you sure?" Kathy pressed, and every dark thought she'd entertained about the chalet took on factual undertones. The mingled plots of all the murder mysteries she'd read cavorted through her mind. Each scenario grew in a credence Kathy could not ignore.

"Sure?" The cowboy ground his bootheel against the sidewalk and pulled a silver flask from his jeans pocket. "As sure as I'm Thurston Manley," he growled. "And one day the whole truth is gonna come out." He unscrewed the lid and tilted the liquid into his mouth.

The nauseating smell of whiskey left Kathy struggling to breathe.

Thurston lowered the flask and stared at Kathy awhile longer. Mutely she stared back and debated the wisdom of taking the word of a drunken stranger.

Tears brimmed his eyes. "I loved her," he wobbled out. "She looked a lot like you."

"She did?" Kathy croaked and tried not to stare at his bad eye.

"Yes."

He touched the edge of Kathy's hair, and she was too astounded to even flinch away.

Thurston's gaze grew hard. He glared at Kathy with a mute fury that flushed his lined cheeks and sent cold horror through her soul.

"Then she hauled off and married that sorry, no 'count—"

A car horn's repeated toots jolted Kathy. She jumped from the man's mesmerizing stare and pivoted toward the noise. Jay's silver Thunderbird cruised toward her store and rolled into the nearest parking place.

The sight of her brother broke the dreadful spell. "*Jay!*" Kathy hollered and raced forward.

Jay hopped out of the vehicle and opened his arms to his younger sister. Kathy flung herself against him and wrapped her arms around his torso. Jay stumbled backward and slammed into the vehicle with a surprised "Uumph," as he clutched his sister.

"There was a man . . ." Kathy rushed, her arms and legs trembling with a violence she hadn't perceived until now. She cautiously looked over her shoulder, but the cowboy had vanished.

"Hey, sis, you're shaking like a leaf," Jay said. "What's going on?"

"Uh . . ." Furtively, Kathy glanced in all directions but detected no sign of Thurston Manley. Ready to tell all, she moved away from her brother and crossed her arms. "There was this man," she repeated and encountered Jay's brown eyes, every bit as intense as her mother's. A warning blasted through Kathy. If she told Jay everything, he might leak the information to her parents. They'd make sure the Averys knew. The Averys probably wouldn't let Kathy out of their sight for a month!

"Oh, um, there was just this cowboy guy who . . . he just gave me the creeps." She hid a shiver and perused the street once more. Her attention settled on the chalet. She stiffened and twined her fingers behind her back.

"Are you sure that's all?" Jay pushed. He suspiciously eyed her and then the front of her store.

Kathy, honest to a fault, searched for some way to minimize the incident without lying. Finally she decided the best tactic was a change in subject. Jay had been so interested in meeting Liza, she took a gamble that mentioning the new aquaintance would sidetrack his suspicion.

"So, are you ready to meet Liza?" she asked with more fortitude than she felt. "She's certainly looking forward to tonight." Kathy leaned closer and repeatedly winked.

Jay laughed. "Good," he said. "Now, what do you think about her? I mean, really." He slammed his car door, and Kathy nearly cheered with the success of her subject change.

"Well," she began and walked toward her store, "she's really pretty and very nice." She eyed her brother's auburn hair and light tan. While Kathy didn't strongly favor either of her parents, Jay looked like their mother except for his prominent nose, which resembled their father's. "I think you guys will make an attractive couple. She has light brown eyes, and her hair is lighter than yours but has a lot of red in it." Kathy placed her fingers against her temples and closed her eyes. "I can see the two of you with six kids—all with red hair and brown eyes."

"Whoa!" Jay jumped back. "Has she said she wants six kids or something?" He observed Kathy in round-eyed horror.

Kathy giggled. "You know I'm just teasing." She tugged his arm. "Come on in. I'll whip up some of my famous lemonade while we wait. We're not supposed to meet for about forty-five minutes."

She opened the store door and nudged her brother ahead of her. Before Kathy stepped into the store, she stole a last glance up the street. No sign of the cowboy. While Kathy relished the potential for any intrigue, a stalker wasn't on her list of desirable adventures. *Maybe he is just a crazy drunk who is trying to scare me*, she reasoned.

Kathy scurried inside and closed the store door. The bell

swung on the red ribbon and jingled like a prophet of cheer but did nothing to extinguish Kathy's anxiety. She engaged the door's ancient lock and prayed she never saw that whiskey-loving cowboy again. But no matter how hard she prayed, she couldn't stop his tale of murder from bombarding her mind.

Nine

One week later, Alaina Tilman eased her Volkswagen into the parking lot of the Walmart Supercenter, the biggest grocery-and-department store for miles around. How Northpointe, Colorado, population 9,322, had ranked a Walmart two years ago still left the citizenry thunderstruck. But the store, nestled at the base of the Rockies, drew customers from numerous small towns and stayed busy twenty-four hours a day. Alaina attributed the store's huge success to its manager, Caleb Manley, who was the youngest Walmart manager in the nation . . . and also the love of her life.

As she'd told her brother Ben, Alaina stumbled on Caleb a year ago in the cemetery, and the two of them had gotten acquainted . . . or rather, reacquainted. The next Saturday, Alaina had purposefully wandered into Walmart, hoping to see him. He spotted her in the pet department, right before his supper break at six, and asked her to join him. Caleb bought some chicken and potato salad in the deli, and they ate in his office. What began as an awkward restart on an old friendship soon blossomed into the beginning of love.

After the first three months, her weekly meetings with Caleb had grown into twice a week. A year later, they were up to three secretive meetings a week, and they exchanged daily text messages. Now Alaina went to Walmart every Saturday to "shop for groceries." When she came home with the car loaded down, her father never suspected his daughter had enjoyed more than a pleasant shopping trip.

Alaina turned off the VW Beetle's engine and pulled down the vanity mirror. Every blond ringlet was still in place, just like Caleb liked them. The sight of her ecstatic blue eyes made her smile, and she reveled in the flutters that tickled her tummy.

She hadn't fancied herself in love since high school—and that had been with Caleb, too. What Ben and nobody else knew was that she and Caleb Manley had experienced more than a high-school crush all those years ago. They were a hot couple before he went off to college and married Sonya. He'd been the first and only boy she ever kissed. And he'd promised her the week before he left for Colorado State University that she'd always be his one-and-only love. That Christmas he brought Sonya home with him and broke Alaina's heart. As a shattered sophomore, she'd buried herself in her schoolwork and convinced herself the breakup was for the best. After all, their fathers hated each other. The match was destined for failure from the start.

Alaina touched the corner of her glossy lips and removed a rosy smudge. She wrinkled her nose and puckered up for a midair kiss. *If only I were so brave with Caleb*, she thought and couldn't imagine herself even reaching for his hand. That would take a level of courage she had never learned to embrace—not with Zachariah Tilman as her father. Her eyes stopped dancing. Alaina's lips wilted. She flipped up the mirror. The Volkswagen's new smell drove her from the vehicle. She'd wanted a snazzy red Honda. Her father insisted on the black Beetle. Alaina didn't have the strength of will to thwart him, even though she was the one making the payments.

With her purse and jacket in hand, she double-checked the car door's lock and strode across the parking lot toward the store entrance. A chilly breeze sashayed around the parked cars and swirled up the smell of recent rain on warm concrete. Shifting her purse, Alaina slipped her arms into her denim jacket and eyed the sky. A bank of gray clouds hung low over the mountains, blotting out their snow-crested peaks and the blast of six o'clock sunshine. The closer she got to the store, the less she worried about the weather and her father. Whatever the dire circumstances in the real world, nothing could darken this precious hour she spent with Caleb Manley. *Nothing.*

Her spirits soaring, Alaina stepped through the doorway and appeared to aimlessly wander toward the back of the store, near the shoe department. When no one was looking, she ducked through the doorway that read "Employees Only." Alaina turned right and trotted up the short flight of stairs to the tune of her high heels clicking against tile. Glancing over her shoulder, she rushed down a short hallway. Fortunately, Caleb was the only management employee who worked Saturday evenings. After passing a trio of office cubicles, she paused outside a door marked "Manager." The faint smell of rotisserie chicken confirmed Caleb's purchasing of their deli meal.

Alaina's heart gently thudded, and she urged herself to turn the knob. Instead, she softly knocked and awaited Caleb's usual answer.

"Come in," he called.

Alaina eased into the cluttered office, shut the door, and offered Caleb a tentative smile. "Hi."

Caleb looked up from the spread of food on his desk and whistled. "Wow!" he exclaimed. He dropped the lid to a tub of broccoli salad and rounded the desk. "That outfit looks great on you!" Towering inches above Alaina, he was as tall as Ben. But her brother was a lean runner; Caleb, a muscular weight lifter.

"Thanks," Alaina breathed and looked down at the leopard-print skirt and black high heels she'd purchased last week in Denver. Her denim jacket had a leopard-print collar that perfectly matched the skirt and complemented her chocolate-colored blouse. She set her purse near the door and was nearly overtaken with the same concerns that accosted her when purchasing the outfit.

"I was worried it was too, uh, not quite me," she explained and ached for his embrace.

Caleb's dark widened eyes ended her anxiety before he ever uttered a word. "Baby, you've never looked better," he said and wrapped his arms around her in the hug she'd hungered for all day.

Alaina wilted against him, enjoyed the whiff of aftershave, and regretted the brevity of their closeness the second Caleb backed away. But that was the way it always was with Caleb, even in high school. Alaina drank in the fire in his eyes but never doubted the gentleman's heart. Forever respectful, he'd never once pressured her. He hadn't even kissed her last year until they'd been secretively dating for six months. Even though Alaina wasn't experienced in the ways of the world, she'd listened to her friends at work enough to realize that his behavior wasn't typical of current morals. Not at all. But then his dedication to God wouldn't be considered typical, either.

"I've missed you." Her words trembled out of a heart vulnerable and burning with love. She gazed into his soul and received the force of his answer without any words passing between them. His attention trailed to her lips and lingered there. Alaina sensed the power of their attraction as strongly as if he'd already kissed her.

"Uh . . ." Caleb backed into his desk, stopped, then pointed toward the deli meal. "Are you hungry? I bought us some marriage, as usual."

Marriage? Alaina thought. Her face went cold and her legs began a slow tremble. The smell of lemon herb chicken and broccoli salad couldn't begin to tantalize her now.

He pressed his fingertips against the top of his head. "I mean chicken," he rushed. "I bought some chicken." Caleb closed his eyes and took a slow breath.

"Okay," Alaina said over a nervous giggle laced with panic. During these clandestine dates, Alaina purposed to push her father's disapproval from her mind and focus solely on Caleb. It was only after their dates, when she was lying in bed at night, that Alaina stressed over the depth of their relationship. They'd been seeing each other for a year, and while she longed to be Caleb's wife, she also dreaded the very thought. Hinting to Ben that she'd go against her father's wishes and marry the son of his enemy was one thing. Following through with the deed required a level of valor Alaina wasn't certain she would ever grasp.

I've never crossed Dad, she fretted. *How could I now? And if I did, wouldn't that anger God?* Thoughts of God ushered in fresh guilt. *What am I thinking? Every time I meet with Caleb I'm crossing Dad,* she thought and resisted the urge to look over her shoulder.

Caleb yanked at the knot in his red tie. He whipped off the tie, dropped it onto his desk, and clawed at the top button of his starched shirt. A prominent vein pulsed at the base of his neck. He turned his back to Alaina, placed both hands flat on the desk, and hung his head.

Alaina laced her fingers together and squeezed hard. Neither of them had mentioned marriage during their whole courtship— not that Alaina would have ever hinted at such. She sensed Caleb fully understood the subject was taboo and why. This silent discernment between them had brought peace early in their relationship. In the past few weeks, it had increased the ever-heightening frustration.

Caleb straightened, walked across the room, and stopped by the window. He tugged on the blind's cord. Watery sunlight filtered into the room while lazy raindrops plopped against the pane. After several tense seconds, Caleb pivoted to face her. He rubbed the side of his face, inserted his hands into his casual slacks, withdrew them, and toyed with the edge of the blinds.

"You know, I really wasn't thinking about the chicken," he finally said.

"I know," Alaina breathed and leaned against the wall.

"So . . ." His eyebrows, as black as his mother's Cherokee ancestors', barely twitched.

Alaina had never hyperventilated in her life, but a stressed voice suggested she might be on the verge.

"We've been seeing each other for a year."

She swallowed hard and nodded.

"I spent the first few months wondering how anything could come of it. I wondered that in high school, too," he added and hung his head. "Our dads are like oil and vinegar."

Curling her fists against the wall behind her, Alaina pressed hard and prayed she didn't slump to the floor.

"Then about six months ago I stopped analyzing all of it. I was just happy we were back together." Caleb walked forward and stopped at a proper distance. His eye twitched. "I can't keep going on like this," he whispered. "I love you, Alaina." He closed his eyes and took in a slow breath. "You know I love you."

"I—I love you, too," she murmured, and the room tilted. Alaina staggered to the nearby chair, dropped into it, placed her elbows on her knees, and rested her face in her hands. Too overwhelmed to release any emotion, she sat in rigid uncertainty. The last thing she needed was for Caleb to propose, but that was also what she wanted more than life.

Caleb's footsteps neared and stopped behind her. He placed his hands on her shoulders and said, "When Sonya died, I never thought I'd ever—" His fingers flexed against her shoulders. "Then I moved back home and there you were just like always— like, like you'd been waiting for me all these years."

I had been, she wailed to herself.

"I can't keep this up much longer," he groaned.

Alaina's stomach rolled in a nauseous twist. She hugged her midsection and gently rocked. "I can't . . . I can't . . . What about my dad?" she wobbled out.

"What about him?" Caleb released her shoulders and knelt in front of her. "Alaina, you're twenty-seven years old!" he exclaimed. "You can't stay under his thumb forever."

"But he'll never speak to me again!"

"And that's bad?" Caleb snorted, his dark eyes sparking.

"But—but—you don't understand," she stammered. Alaina shook her head and grappled for a way to explain what she didn't fully comprehend herself.

"No, you don't understand." Caleb tugged her hands into his. "Alaina, I thought when we broke up the first time it was for the best. I thought you'd find somebody your father approved of and you could be happy. But here we are again. It's almost like . . . like God is determined to put us together no matter what!" He raised their twined hands.

Tears blurring her vision, Alaina nodded and didn't doubt that Caleb's love was any less fierce than hers. What she did doubt was God's approval of their relationship. *The Bible says children are to obey their parents!* The echo of her father's recurring words laced her in an invisible shroud of condemnation. Alaina had spent the last year accumulating disobedience on top of disobedience.

"So, I guess what I'm saying is," Caleb finally continued, "it's time for you to make the choice." Ribbons of agony and doubt marred Caleb's features. A sheen of perspiration dotted his dark skin. His fingers flexed against hers. "It's either me or your father."

Ten

Kathy inserted her key into the store's lock. "Okay," she glanced over her shoulder at her companions, "this could take thirty minutes," she exaggerated. "This lock is older than dirt and has a mind of its own. This last week it's gotten more and more cantankerous."

"Here, let me see it," Ron said and moved to Kathy's side. "It probably just needs a man's touch." Without permission, he brushed away her hands.

"Oh brother," Liza complained as Kathy hid a frown.

"Hey," Jay teased, "he's probably right."

Backing away from the door, Kathy glanced toward her brother, who held Liza's hand. She playfully punched him in the arm, and he pretended to stagger sideways. The two laughed, and Jay smiled into Liza's eyes with a *Where have you been all my life* awe. Liza's adoring expression matched Jay's. During the last week, the two had been almost inseparable as they enjoyed sightseeing or shopping with Ron and his mom. At night, Kathy joined Jay, Liza, and Ron for dinner in or takeout burgers. Several evenings they'd all hung out in her apartment and watched TV. Kathy couldn't ever recall her brother being so taken with a woman. He usually moved at a turtle's pace with the opposite sex, but Kathy caught them kissing in her kitchen last night.

While Ron wrestled her lock, Kathy yawned, closed her eyes, and tilted back her head. She was too tired to be alarmed. She hadn't told the other three, but when they'd arrived this afternoon for their trip into the mountains, she would have been thrilled to just stay home by herself. The store's increasing traffic coupled with the late evenings had left her exhausted.

Worry over that weird Thurston Manley hadn't helped her sleep, either. Kathy glanced up the street one way, then the other. She hadn't seen the man in a week and hoped she never did again. She purposefully avoided gazing toward Northpointe Mountain and the creepy chalet, but she felt the home's presence like a dark vapor of doom looming on the horizon.

Kathy shivered, checked her watch, and noted it was only seven o'clock. The cloudy sky made the summer evening seem closer to eight thirty. The cool breeze lowered the temperature to that of early fall rather than late June. She tugged the sleeves of her sweater over her hands, crossed her arms, and watched Ron bend over the lock with renewed fervor. He muttered a string of oaths under his breath. During the last week Ron tossed around a few choice words Kathy had never allowed to be a part of her vocabulary. Neither had Jay. But it didn't seem to bother Jay in the least—nor did the fact that Liza released a curse stout enough for a sailor when her pump's heel broke last night.

"Hey man," Jay chided and moved toward Ron. "You're going to lose your religion at this rate. Let me see what I can do."

Clearing her throat, Kathy stepped beside her brother. "Why don't you guys just let me manage this lock business? This is my store," she added with an edge to her voice.

"Why don't we just get snappy?" Jay said and pressed his lips together.

"Okay, okay!" Ron gave her the key and backed away. "Forgive me for trying to help."

Kathy placed the key into the lock and jiggled it into what she hoped was the right position. The lock turned with her first effort. Masking her surprise, Kathy opened the door.

"Oh, what a low blow!" Jay exclaimed. "Man, she just made you look bad."

"You go, girl!" Liza said from close behind.

Kathy turned toward her friend and winked like she had everything under control. Little did they know she had worked with the lock for ages last night before getting it secured.

"I guess that'll teach me to offer help," Ron said over a good-natured laugh.

You didn't offer help, Kathy thought. *You just took over.* Adjusting her purse strap on her shoulder, Kathy allowed the other three to step inside. Nobody had mentioned crashing in her apartment, and Kathy hoped she could keep them downstairs at the coffee bar. After their meal at The Diner on the Corner, they all decided to walk to Kathy's store for root beer floats. Kathy had just added the floats to her limited menu three days ago, and she was as glad to indulge as the other three.

Besides, she thought, *the root beer has a little caffeine, and I can use it.* She recalled the last time she drank caffeine this late in the evening. As usual, the stuff had sent her into orbit. She'd started talking and couldn't stop. Then, when she'd gone to bed, she lay with her eyes wide open and stared at the ceiling while her mind raced. So Kathy read *Frankenstein* until two o'clock. She'd gone to sleep with the book in hand and dreamed all sorts of wild stuff, including Frankenstein growing mushrooms in the bottom of her dishwasher.

"Maybe I'll only have half a root beer," she said to herself as she hurried behind the service bar.

"What, Kathy?" Ron called from the corner, where he and Jay were pulling four chairs around a table.

"Oh, nothing," she said. "I was just thinking about limiting my caffeine intake."

"Please do!" Jay said with a nod. "You guys don't want her on too much caffeine. She goes nuts."

"Speak for yourself," Kathy shot back.

"You'll be speaking for yourself—nonstop—if you overdose on that stuff." Jay shook his finger at her in a way that tempted Kathy to drink two "fully leaded" Coca-Colas. Why everyone in her family was determined to boss her around continued to remain a mystery to her. She loved her brother and enjoyed being with him, but at times he acted too much like their mother. He rolled up the sleeve of his bronze-colored Western shirt and turned back toward the table as if he fully expected her to heed his warning.

Kathy clamped her teeth, opened the refrigerator at the end of the counter, and reached for a bottle of root beer. Then she noticed the can of Coca-Cola—by far more caffeinated than the root beer. Twisting her lips into a defiant line, she grabbed the Coke. After popping the top, Kathy guzzled one-fourth of the can. She retrieved the root-beer bottles and removed the lids with the bottle opener bolted beneath the service bar. Soon the first signs of the caffeine's effects kicked in. Kathy's eyes no longer felt heavy; her mind no longer groggy. She recklessly grabbed the can and downed some more.

While Kathy retrieved the tub of vanilla ice cream from the freezer, she awaited the caffeine's rocket effect on her mind. She grabbed four clear glasses from the shelf over the mug rack and pulled her ice cream scoop from the wall hook over the sink. A euphoric rush chased away the last traces of exhaustion, and Kathy downed the rest of the can. After releasing a burp, she tackled the tub of ice cream with an enthusiasm she could have never conjured on her own.

"You aren't yourself this evening," Liza said from nearby. "Are you tired or something?"

"Aahh!" Kathy hollered and jumped at the same time she was digging a scoop of ice cream from the side of the gallon container. A glob of vanilla popped up and crashed onto the top of her sandal.

"Cold, cold, oh, cold!" Kathy wailed and started laughing.

Liza giggled. "I'm so sorry! I didn't mean to scare you."

Kathy cackled. "Oh, it's soooo cold!" she cried and kicked the frozen wad off her foot. The ball flew up, smacked into the front of Liza's denim skirt, and slid to the floor with a soft plop.

"It's alive!" Liza squealed.

And the two women backed toward the service bar as if the ice cream were a snake. With every breath, their hilarity went up a decibel.

"What is it?"

"What's gotten into you two?" The masculine voices mingled with the ladies' laughter.

Still holding the ice cream scoop, Kathy wilted onto the service bar and looked at her brother and Ron, who joined them behind the counter. "Possessed ice cream!" she wheezed.

Liza covered her face and heaved with fresh mirth.

Jay shared a dubious glance with Ron. The two jeans-clad men stood with hands on hips and stared at the clump of ice cream melting on the wooden floor. Neither of them appeared the least bit threatened by humor.

"This is one of those 'you had to have been here' deals," Kathy explained and reached for the napkin canister. She pulled out a chunk of napkins, extended them to Liza, and helped herself to a thick layer.

"Thanks," Liza said. She removed her glasses and mopped at her eyes, then her skirt.

Kathy dropped her scooper into the barrel of ice cream, slipped her foot out of her sandal, and sponged at her cool toes. Then she sponged up the ice cream on the floor and dropped it into the garbage. All the while, intermittent giggles tottered out of the women.

"Looks like we need to take over this operation," Jay said, "before you two have ice cream hanging from the ceiling. Ron, you dip the ice cream. I'll pour the root beer."

"Oh brother," Kathy crowed with feigned irritation. "Here we go again. Don't think you can come into my kitchen and take over, bucko!" She raised her fists, bounced toward Jay like a boxer, and took some fake shots at his nose.

"Hey, stop that!" he hollered and lifted his arm to thwart her advances.

"Here's the problem!" Ron held up the empty Coke can.

"Oh no!" Jay bellowed. "You didn't!"

"I did! I did!" Kathy said. "And so did the ice cream!"

Liza's face crumpled, and she sputtered forth with a new gurgle. "You two are nuts!"

Kathy bounced in closer to her brother. "Move it or lose it," she demanded and gently body slammed him.

"I'm not nuts, she is!" Jay said and playfully shoved at Kathy. "Somebody get her off of me. She's like a giant mosquito."

"I'll get her!" Ron exclaimed.

Before Kathy understood his intent, Ron hauled her into his arms and cradled her like a groom carrying his bride over the threshold. "Got her!" he huffed and smiled down at Kathy. "She doesn't weigh much more than a mosquito."

"Put me down!" Kathy said and kicked.

"Good! Get her outta here!" Jay raised his hands like he'd just scored a touchdown. "Come on, Liza," he motioned her to his side, "you and I will do the floats."

"Oh goody!" Liza crooned and sidled up to Jay.

"Put me down!" Kathy hollered. "Help! Somebody help! My brother stole my kitchen!"

Ron turned and hustled toward the end of the service bar. "He's on the 50, the 40, the 30 . . ." he chanted like a football stadium announcer.

Kathy clutched at Ron's arm, raised her head, and said, "I'm going to get you good for this, Jay Moore!"

He waved her off and focused on Liza and the ice cream, in that order.

Kathy squirmed and huffed, "Really, Ron, you can put me down now. I won't bother them."

He slowed but didn't offer to release her. Furthermore, Ron's cocky smile was a tad too eager for her comfort. Her feminine alarm system clanged through the surge of her caffeine-induced stamina.

"I like you on caffeine," Ron drawled before stopping near a towering case of cookbooks. "You go crazy!" He slowly released Kathy's legs but kept his arm around her waist. His focus trailed to her lips.

Gulping, Kathy glanced toward the service bar and could only see the back of her brother's shoulder and arm. If Jay and Liza turned around, chances were high the bookcase would block their view of Kathy and Ron.

How convenient! Kathy stumbled back toward the corner and bumped into a padded chair. Her fingers, now jittery from the caffeine, shook harder. The last thing she needed was Ron trying to kiss her.

Kathy had done everything in her power during the last week to send Ron a silent message about their relationship: *We're friends and nothing more.* When he'd tried to hold her hand in the buffet line, she stepped away from him. When he'd settled his arm around her at the movie, Kathy excused herself for a trip to the snack bar. When Ron inched too close at a scenic overlook in the mountains, she casually walked to her brother's side. Until now, she thought he was taking the hints rather well. Given his present heavy-eyed intensity, Kathy wondered if Ron had even registered the hints. His chin's assured angle guaranteed he hadn't.

Her overstimulated, tired mind whirled in a frenzied fit. "R-Ron," she stammered and held up her hand. "I think—"

The doorbell jingled, and both she and Ron looked toward the entrance. An attractive young woman wearing a denim jacket with a leopard-print collar hesitantly leaned into the store.

Kathy immediately recognized the blonde's stylish ringlets and peaches-and-cream complexion. "Alaina Tilman," she whispered and stepped forward. "What's she doing here?"

Eleven

Alaina looked toward a movement behind the service bar and noticed a tall, lean guy with auburn hair.

"Sorry, the store's closed," he said. The petite woman near him looked at Alaina with a silent, *Get lost!*

"Oh, sorry!" Alaina said. "I saw the lights on and thought . . ." She lowered her head and stepped out of the doorway. As she snapped the door closed, a familiar voice called, "No, wait!"

The glass door swung inward, and Alaina was staring into Kathy Moore's welcoming face. Even though dark circles marred Kathy's eyes, her vivacious smile belied any exhaustion.

"Alaina!" Kathy chirped. "I'm not open, but you're always welcome. Want to come in? We're making root beer floats."

"Well . . ." Alaina toyed with her leather purse zipper and ducked her head. She figured it wouldn't be long before Kathy noticed her red puffy eyes and streaked makeup. She dubiously glanced through the door's opening. A tall guy with spiked blond hair stood a few feet behind Kathy. Then there were those two people behind the counter. Even though the smell of gourmet coffee and used books invited her to accept Kathy's invitation, Alaina shrank at the thought of those three strangers detecting even a hint of her problems.

"Um . . ." Alaina hedged for more time and deliberated how to graciously bow out without seeming rude. She'd held no plans of stopping by the store, but when she saw the lights on, she hoped to find Kathy alone. After the upheaval with Caleb, Alaina desperately needed a friend. From the minute she shook Kathy Moore's hand at the cookout, Alaina sensed that the newcomer was a special someone in whom she could confide. She seldom felt free to confide in even her best friends. So far no one but Ben even knew about her and Caleb.

The damp breeze nipped at Alaina's skirt and brought with it a spray of fine mist. A distant rumble of thunder announced that more rain was on its way.

"Look," Kathy admonished, "you're getting wet out there. Come on in." She tugged on Alaina's arm; Alaina didn't resist.

Once she stepped into the store's cozy warmth and the door was closed, Alaina felt like a germ under a microscope. Four people focused on her, and only one of them appeared to be happy about her arrival. Alaina held her breath to stop a new surge of tears.

She'd wept from the second she pulled out of the Walmart parking lot. Part of the reason for stopping off at Kathy's involved finding a place to repair her makeup before entering the chalet. Applying mascara in front of an audience held no appeal. Alaina grappled for some excuse that would provide a swift exit.

"Alaina Tilman, these are my new friends, Liza and Ron Thaine. The guy with the root beer bottle is my brother, Jay." Kathy leaned forward and hissed. "But don't tell anyone, okay?"

"Hey!" Jay protested.

Kathy shifted her weight and tapped her toe against the wooden floor. "We were just making some root beer floats," she chattered and gestured toward the service bar. "But if you'd like, I could fix you a soda or coffee or something upstairs in my apartment." She worked her fingers, crossed her arms, and drummed her fingertips against her sweater sleeve. "I'm sure the gang won't miss me for a while." The knowing glimmer in Kathy's sharp hazel eyes assured Alaina her splotchy complexion and red eyes hadn't gone unnoticed.

"I could use some coffee," Alaina said with a nod. "Strong and black." She focused on Ron's square-toed boots.

"I can do that!" Kathy exclaimed. "Come on."

Alaina didn't wait for a second invitation. She followed her new friend through the bookstore and paused as Kathy unlocked a narrow door. When she swung open the door, Alaina glimpsed a cramped staircase.

"What about your float?" Jay asked.

Alaina glanced toward him. Ron now leaned on the service bar and gazed at them like a kid who'd missed Christmas. Liza held an ice-cream scoop and didn't look any happier. Alaina cringed. The last thing she ever wanted was to come between friends.

"We don't have to go upstairs," she offered.

"It's okay. Really!" Kathy's stiff smile and determined eyes hinted at all sorts of things. She gripped Alaina's arm and pulled her toward the stairway. Before closing the door, Kathy looked into the store and said, "Don't worry about my float." She snapped the door shut before anyone replied.

"Come on," Kathy said and charged up the stairs.

Alaina, struggling to match Kathy's pace, fell several steps behind. The narrow stairway's musty smell brought to mind women in long full skirts, gun-toting men, and a hundred years of usage thereafter. Idly, Alaina wondered how many people had traipsed up and down the shadowed steps over the years. Kathy stopped outside another door. She inserted her key again and turned another lock.

"Welcome to my humble abode." She swept inside. "It's not much, but it's all I've got."

Her feet protesting her new spiked shoes, Alaina stepped into the apartment. In one swift glance she absorbed the mismatched furniture, the collection of black-and-white classic TV posters, the ancient television with aluminum foil hanging from rabbit ears, and the new-looking stereo system that claimed the corner.

Just as quickly, Alaina was overwhelmed with an unexpected onslaught of envy.

What I wouldn't give to be on my own! she pined and couldn't hold the tears at bay another second. Two hot testimonies of her overwrought emotions trickled beside her nose. The smell of Freesia candles obliterated all but a trace of "old building musty" and only increased the pain in Alaina's soul. Her father hated Freesia. Alaina associated the odor with the aroma of freedom.

"I've only got one bedroom," Kathy babbled. "The whole place is only about eight hundred square feet, but it works for me." As she closed the door, the floor creaked. "It also makes all sorts of noises. I just love it!" Kathy stepped beside Alaina, shrugged, and inserted her hands into the back pockets of her pants.

Alaina dashed aside her tears and hoped Kathy hadn't noticed.

"Want to join me in the kitchen?" Kathy asked and pointed to the left.

"Sure," Alaina said and followed close behind.

"Look. I even have a breakfast bar." She pulled out a short wooden stool and patted the unpadded seat. Glad to relieve her aching feet, Alaina took the seat.

Kathy bounced into the tiny white kitchen and began banging through cabinets. A box of macaroni and cheese fell out of the first cabinet. She picked it up and shoved it into a second cabinet. The box flopped back onto the counter with the clatter of uncooked pasta.

"I'm a closet slob," Kathy claimed. "And I'm unrepentant. My motto is, you grab whatever you need in the closet," she picked up the box, "open the door," Kathy opened a third door, "close your eyes, throw it in, and slam the door before it can fall back out." She tossed in the macaroni and whacked the cabinet closed.

Despite Alaina's gloomy spirits, she smiled.

"I can't remember what in the world I did with the coffee,"

Kathy continued. The door she'd just slammed creaked open and a bag of gourmet coffee flopped onto the counter. "Oh! There you are!" she exclaimed. "Why don't you just jump right out and bite me next time?"

Alaina giggled.

"I wouldn't be surprised if Jay hid it from me!" Kathy picked up the bag and examined it. "This is the fully leaded stuff. Do you do caffeine in the evening?" Kathy peered toward Alaina and rapidly blinked.

"Yes, that's fine," she agreed. "Caffeine has never had that big of an effect on me."

"Oooh," Kathy said and shook her head. "Caffeine sends me straight up. I start talking, and I don't stop. As a matter of fact, I'm on caffeine right now. I just drank a Coke. Am I talking too much? It's hard for me to tell." She didn't pause long enough for Alaina to answer.

"Now, if I can just figure out what Jay did with my coffeepot! He keeps saying he needs to organize me. Can you imagine why he'd say that?" Kathy glowered toward the lower cabinets and opened one. A trio of stainless steel pans clattered to the floor. "I was doing just fine without his obsessive-compulsive self. Now he acts like he's got to save me from me or something. But then everybody in my family seems to act that way. Do you know what it's like being the youngest?"

Yes, I do! Alaina thought and frowned.

"Oh, gag!" Kathy continued. "They just won't let me grow up. In their eyes, I might as well be twelve." She rammed the three pans back into the cabinet, slammed the door, and whipped open another cabinet.

"Here it is!" she exclaimed. "Right where I didn't put it. I told Jay this morning, I said, 'Jay, I've got a business to run. I don't have time to alphabetize my canned goods.' Then he asked me if I'd mind if he would." She stood, set the coffeepot onto the counter, and gaped toward Alaina. "Can you imagine someone doing something so crazy?"

"Uh . . ." Alaina didn't answer, nor did she think it wise to mention her color-coordinated closet.

"Oh well!" Kathy plugged in the coffeepot. "I guess I'm kinda that way when it comes to the store. But up here, I just slob out." She relaxed her spine and expanded her arms.

Alaina laughed out loud.

"What?" Kathy asked. She tilted her head and blinked.

"You're a hoot!" she explained. "I wish—" Alaina stopped herself from mentioning her desire for Ben to at least give Kathy a chance.

"You wish . . . ?" Kathy prompted and wasted no time scrounging through another cabinet.

While Alaina gripped the breakfast bar's edge and panicked over what to say, Kathy pulled out a package of coffee filters.

"Ah, man!" she exclaimed. "I'm down to one filter up here. I'll have to remember to bring some up from the store." She crammed the last coffee filter into the filter basket and looked at Alaina. "Have you seen those new stainless steel coffee filters? I saw one at Walmart the day 'fore yesterday. It looked really neat. I think I'll just buy one of those for up here. Then I don't have to worry about running out."

The very mention of Walmart made Alaina's face go cold. The next few days were going to require more courage than she ever imagined she possessed. "Uh, I was going to ask if you minded my using your bathroom," she said and picked up her purse. "I need to repair my makeup."

"Oh!"

Kathy reminded Alaina of a big-eyed kitten, all eager curiosity. She could only imagine what her new acquaintance must be thinking about her unexpected teary-eyed appearance.

"Sure. It's right through that door." Kathy pointed across the petite living room. "Through my bedroom. You can't miss it. Also, Lucy likes to drink out of the toilet, so if you need it, you might want to wipe off the seat first."

"Lucy?" Alaina glanced toward the poster of the famous actress hanging on the living room's far wall.

"My cat." Kathy pointed toward an overweight feline curled on a polished-cotton love seat.

Alaina sputtered over another giggle. "You're a riot!"

"Not always," Kathy admitted. "I can get grouchy when I'm tired. Really, I'm tired now but I'm over-caffeinated, that's all."

"Right," Alaina said and was glad she'd followed her instincts to stop by Kathy's store. Just a few minutes in her vivacious presence was proving enough to lift her spirits, at least beyond the realm of tears and fears of the future.

Kathy watched Alaina sashay toward the bathroom. *What I wouldn't give for legs that long*, she thought and looked down at her short legs. She examined her sandals and the red-and-white polka-dotted toenails peeking out.

For the first time that evening, Kathy began to feel warm. She shed the sweater she'd grabbed on the way out the door "just in case." Jay and Ron both laughed at her when she'd put it on because she was wearing her thick-soled sandals along with a sweater. Kathy hadn't cared. Her feet seldom got cold. Her arms were another matter. She walked toward the tiny coat closet near the front door. When she opened it, a trio of tennis balls and their tube casing cascaded from the top shelf. One ball whacked her on the forehead and bounced to the middle of the living room.

"Great," Kathy mumbled and recalled tossing the canister of balls into the top of the closet when they'd fallen at her feet two days ago.

The whole time she was retrieving the balls and hanging up her sweater, one thought commanded the center of Kathy's mind:

What's Alaina Tilman doing here, and why has she been crying? When she closed the closet, Kathy crossed her arms, tapped her toe, and scrutinized her bedroom's entry. Alaina was shy. Kathy knew that from the minute they shook hands at the cookout. Most shy people didn't just drop in on a new acquaintance.

Unless she's in desperate need of a friend because of some horrible something that's happened to her, Kathy reasoned. She marched to the window near the stereo system her parents got her for Christmas. After yanking the blinds open, she glared at the chalet, barely visible in the dreary evening. A layer of dense clouds clung to the top of Northpointe Mountain and made the chalet look more sinister.

Thurston Manley's "evil eye" and murderous claims sent a chill through Kathy's overcharged psyche. Her hands shook. *There's no telling what horror Alaina suffers in that awful place,* she stewed and imagined Zachariah Tilman, a bent, mean old murderer with a whip in one hand and a gun in the other.

The image brought to mind the murder mystery Kathy started writing a year ago. While watching a *Matlock* rerun, she'd thought, *I could write a mystery!* and began the tedious task. But after tapping out the second chapter on her laptop, she'd found herself staring and yawning more than writing. Soon she cast aside the idea and resigned herself to being a mere mystery-reading lover.

She gripped the back of her bobbed hair as her mind reeled with new plot twists and ideas. The chalet loomed larger than life against the domineering mountain, while the characters swayed through her thoughts like vapors in a graveyard.

The old, gnarled murderer, Kathy thought. "He'd be meaner than a junkyard dog," she whispered.

His beautiful daughter. "She's the helpless victim of too much knowledge." Kathy narrowed her eyes and tugged on her hair. "She knows her father murdered her mother, and she's scared to death of what he's going to do to her."

The handsome elder brother. Kathy smiled and released her hair. *He just needs to have a romance.* She wrinkled her nose and stopped her mind from further travel in that direction. Ben Tilman made his stance clear. He wasn't interested in Kathy, and she wasn't about to force herself on him.

She turned from the window and decided to check out her laptop files later that evening. Chances were high she still had that novel saved on her hard drive. She stopped by Lucy, languidly stretching on the love seat, and bent to scratch her ears.

"Want to help me write later, girlfriend?" she asked. "You could hide in the curtains when I'm in the middle of a really scary part and terrify me again."

The cat rolled onto her back and purred. Her pleased meow mingled with the doorbell's off-key dong. Kathy jumped. "My goodness, Lucy, you're starting to chime now," she teased and shook her head at her own joke. "I wouldn't bother to laugh at that one," she crooned and stepped toward the door. But then she stopped in mid-stride as she considered who might be waiting on the other side. She certainly didn't want to face Ron "the octopus" again. When the bell released another dong and the person knocked shortly thereafter, Kathy accepted that she didn't have a choice but to open the door. Ron knew she was up here anyway. There was no pretending otherwise.

With a resigned slump of her shoulders, she marched across the living room, twisted the deadbolt, and opened the door. But the tall man on the other side was not Ron. He was the very man Kathy had just decided needed a romance.

Twelve

"Hi!" Ben said with a brief wave. He gazed past Kathy to note a diminutive apartment void of other occupants. "Uh, your brother said my sister was supposed to be up here?"

"Yes, she is!" Kathy bobbed her head. "She just went into the restroom. Want to come in?"

"Sure."

Kathy opened the door wider, and Ben stepped past her into the smell of yesteryear mixed with something flowery. Kathy's decor was every bit as eclectic as he figured it would be. Not that he'd spent much time considering the lively newcomer or her apartment.

Now I've started lying to myself, he thought and smiled awkwardly as she closed the door.

When she beamed back, Ben noticed a pair of "moon crater" dimples that reminded him of a Christian singer his older brother, Phil, once had a huge crush on. "Has anybody ever told you that you look like that eighties singer Evie?" He tilted his head sideways. "Maybe Evie mixed with Dorothy Hamill."

Kathy's smile intensified. Her dimples deepened. Her cheeks grew rosy. "Dorothy Hamill, yes. Evie, no." Her gaze slid to the scar near his hairline.

"I thought of Evie because of the dimples, I think," Ben explained and couldn't deny the pint-sized gal's body language. Either he was losing it or she was developing a gargantuan crush on him. She drank up his comment like he'd just told her she looked like the princess of England. He broke her gaze and mentally fumbled for something to say. He sensed her question about his wound. If she was enamored with him now, the story of rescuing the boy might send her into full-fledged hero worship. That was the last thing Ben needed or wanted.

He hated doing anything to hurt her feelings, especially after exasperating her at the cookout. Thoughts of the cookout sent him into a mental debate over whether he should apologize for insulting her age. *But what can I say?* he thought. *I'm sorry I think you're too young for anything romantic between us?* He tugged on the neck of his dress shirt. Ben's tie had never felt tighter.

"I guess you're wondering what I'm doing here," he said and coughed.

"I assumed you're after Alaina since you asked for her," Kathy responded.

"Oh, yeah," he mumbled and felt like a blockhead.

"Come on in here." Kathy walked toward a small kitchen. Ben followed. "I was in the middle of making coffee for Alaina. Sit there." She pointed to the lone wooden stool near the breakfast bar. Ben settled on it.

"Actually, I was out making a call at the hospital when Dad called my cell. He said he was worried about Alaina, since the roads were wet and slick." Ben rested his elbows on the counter and watched Kathy begin filling the coffeemaker with water. Her dark bobbed hair shone in the overhead lighting, and an unexpected wish flitted across his mind—a wish that involved Kathy being five years older.

"Dad tried her cell," Ben said, "but she must not have had it on. She does that sometimes—forgets to turn the thing on. Anyway, I told him I'd cruise around and see if I could spot her car. When I saw a black Beetle parked outside your store, I stopped here."

"Good job, Watson!" Kathy said. As she measured a final tablespoon of coffee into the filter basket, she winked at him.

Ben looked down. *Okay, now what?* he thought. *She's cute, she's friendly, and she's winking at me.*

But she's only twenty-two! he hollered at himself. *The whole town would call me a cradle robber!*

He noticed a trio of hardbound books stacked on the bar near a crumb-laden toaster. A library's past-due postcard protruded from beneath the books. Ben nudged at the stack until he could read the spines. The top one was titled *Setting Boundaries.* The bottom two appeared to be part of a *True Crime* series.

"Are you reading this stuff?" he asked and noted the subtitle on one was *Psychotic Criminals, Their Drives and Motives.*

Kathy now knelt on the countertop while scrounging through a tall shelf. She turned around and gazed at him as if he'd just asked her to recite the Pledge of Allegiance in Portuguese.

"What? Oh, that!" she exclaimed. "Yes. I'm trying to find anything that will help me get my parents to let me grow up."

"No, I mean the *True Crime* books. You like this sort of stuff?"

"Sure! Who doesn't?" she quipped. "I like anything, you know, that has to do with mysteries. Right now I'm looking for some cookies that have mysteriously disappeared. You don't see them hanging out of a cabinet or from the ceiling fan or anything do you?"

"Hmmm, no." Ben shook his head and couldn't stop the indulgent smile. Why any woman who read about psychotic criminals would have allowed him to come into her store on a stormy night was anybody's guess. But then Kathy Moore had so far defied all standards of norm.

"Like I just told Alaina," she babbled and went back to her search, "I'm a closet slob. Aha! Case closed. Here they are. Are you okay with Chips Ahoy?" She extracted an unopened bag from the shelf and flashed her dimples.

"And all this can be yours if the price is right!" she exclaimed.

After hopping to the floor, Kathy ran her index finger beneath the bag of cookies and tilted her head like a TV model.

Pretending to silently debate the price, he took in every inch of her appearance, right down to her red-and-white polka-dot toenails. *I could live with polka dots,* he decided and nearly groaned out loud. *She's really getting to me.*

"I bid two thirty-nine!" Ben finally responded and couldn't remember ever sounding so charmed.

"Beeeeep, beeeeep, beeeeep!" she hollered. "You *don't* win the air-conditioned doghouse or the trip to Antartica!" The coffee pot gurgled, hissed, and emitted a heavenly aroma.

"Awwwwww," Ben said, mimicking a studio audience.

"But you can have a cookie!" Kathy placed the bag on the bar, and Ben's stomach roared. He'd had good intentions of stopping at a drive-thru when he left his house but hadn't.

A horrible groaning noise erupted from behind, and Ben pivoted to look over his shoulder. A yellow striped cat with its ears back and its tail puffed darted across the living room and hit the kitchen tile. When the feline rounded the refrigerator, it slid most of the way.

"What was that?" Ben asked.

"My toilet!" Kathy explained. "Isn't it just too hilarious!" She laughed. "Lucy hates the noise. Most of the time she hisses at it. One time she even swatted at the thing. But I guess this time it caught her off guard."

Ben's gaze trailed to the black-and-white poster of Lucille Ball hanging in the middle of a collection of classic TV personalities. He figured Kathy's cat was named after the redhead, but in the face of the possessed toilet, he didn't comment on the subject. Instead, he frowned and said, "Really, you could be having some serious plumbing problems. You should have it seen about. No kidding. I worked with a plumber about eight years ago while I was in college."

"That's what Dad said," she commented, "but I just figured he was worrying too much. When it comes to me, he and Mom can't seem to worry enough."

"I'd be glad to take a look at it while I'm here, if you like," Ben offered.

"Would you? You wouldn't mind?"

"Not at all. It's the least I can do after you let me borrow your phone the other night."

"But you paid me for that."

"It was worth more, believe me," Ben said with a firm nod.

"Ben!" Alaina's exclamation ended the plumbing discussion. "What are you doing here?"

He twisted to face his sister and smiled. "No matter where you go, I'll always be on your trail," he teased. "I guess I could ask you the same question."

Alaina's gaze shifted from Ben to Kathy. "I just . . ." She looked down and toyed with the strap of her leather purse. Ben immediately understood more than she probably wanted him to know. Something negative had happened, and Alaina didn't want to tell him. Ben's first assumption involved Caleb Manley.

"Your sister stopped by for a chat," Kathy said. "We're friends now. Didn't you know?" The crinkling cookie wrapper snared Ben's attention and instigated another stomach rumble.

Kathy's eyes widened, and she looked toward his midsection. "Was that you?"

Ben grimaced. "Sorry. I still haven't eaten supper. I was going to drive through Taco Bell and never got around to it."

"I've got some sandwich stuff." Kathy stepped toward the small refrigerator in the corner.

"No, that's okay," Ben said. "I couldn't—"

"Nonsense. Of course you could. Look, why don't you go check out the plumbing, and I'll have a big ol' fat sandwich a mile high waiting on you when you get through." Her attention shifted to his forehead.

"Don't argue with her," Alaina said and placed her hand on Ben's shoulder. "She's over-caffeinated." She shook her head. "Not good."

Ben glanced at Kathy and laughed. "So that explains why you're bouncing off the walls."

"I'm not bouncing off the walls."

"All right, maybe I should say off the cabinets!" he teased.

Kathy shook her finger at his nose. "I'm like the Tasmanian devil on speed when I'm on caffeine. I drank a whole Coke tonight. Don't mess with me, bucko!"

"Okay, okay!" Ben raised both hands and stood. "I give. I'll go look at the plumbing and come back and eat my sandwich like a good boy. No argument." He reached for a couple of cookies and crammed one into his mouth. "Oh!" Ben looked at his sister and mumbled over the crumbs. "You need to call Dad. That's why I'm here. He's worried about you." Ben swallowed the chocolate-laden treat. "Sent me on a chase after you. I saw your car here."

Alaina's only reply was a silent nod.

Kathy pretended to peer into the refrigerator but sneaked a long look at Ben's retreating back. Earlier, when she saw him standing at the door, Kathy nearly fell into a dead faint. Either he grew more appealing every time she saw him, or her interest was growing tenfold with each encounter. Dressed in a crisp white shirt, navy-and-gray tie, and blue pleated slacks, he looked more handsome tonight than he ever had. The blue in his tie made his eyes appear as brilliant as sapphires, and Kathy wondered if he might be wearing colored contacts. But that didn't fit Ben's nonassuming personality.

As he disappeared into her bedroom, Kathy nipped at her

thumbnail and brainstormed ways to heighten his interest in her. She'd never been one to chase men or even invite interest. But then, she'd never met a male she considered worth the effort. Presently, she was wondering what would happen if she knocked Ben flat and kissed him. With the cold refrigerator air spilling onto her feet, she snickered and covered her mouth.

I could never do that! she scolded herself.

"My brother's really nice, isn't he?" Alaina's soft voice pierced Kathy's reverie.

She shifted her attention to Alaina, whose timid smile suggested Kathy's every thought must be splayed across her features. Not certain what to say, she began grabbing sandwich material.

Alaina approached and said, "Here, I'll take the lettuce and cheese."

Keeping her gaze down, Kathy released the items into Alaina's hands.

"If it's any consolation, I'm on your side," Alaina softly assured. "I've wished since the cookout that Ben would—" She broke off and tugged her top lip between her teeth.

"He thinks I'm too young, doesn't he?" Kathy asked. "At the cookout—"

"I knew you were insulted. After all, you're a business professional, and he pretty much dismissed you because of your age."

"Yes, but I think it was obvious he dismissed more than just my professional accomplishments."

"Maybe he'll reconsider," Alaina encouraged.

Kathy's spirits soared. "Do you think so?"

"I can't exactly promise anything. He might be my brother, but he's still a man. And you know how unpredictable they can be."

"And they say *we* are," Kathy complained. "I promise, I think my brother sometimes has PMS."

Alaina snickered, but the laughter barely touched her red-rimmed eyes. While her fresh makeup hid the after-effects of emotion, a closer perusal revealed plenty of hints about her recent tears. Once again Kathy wondered what could have so disturbed the attractive blonde.

Abruptly, Alaina looked away and turned toward the kitchen counter. "I guess I need to call Dad. He always worries about me if he can't get me on my cell."

"Sometimes I forget to turn mine on, too," Kathy admitted. After filling her arms with a large package of turkey breast, tomatoes, mayo, and a jar of pickles, she shut the refrigerator with her foot and followed Alaina to the counter.

"To tell you the truth, there are times when I forget on purpose," Alaina admitted.

"If I didn't know any better, I'd say you were the youngest in your family, too," Kathy said with an impish grin.

"Bingo," Alaina replied. "But I have a feeling your parents aren't quite as suffocating as my dad." She looked toward the living room with a wistful longing that spoke volumes and left Kathy conjuring all sorts of scenarios about Alaina's murderous father.

Silently, Alaina reached for her purse, which was lying on the counter, and pulled a cell phone from a side pocket. "He was bad before my mom died, but since then it's been awful. I look just like her. It's like he's worried sick I'm going to suddenly die, too."

Kathy retrieved a table knife from her dish drainer. "Ben mentioned her death at the cookout. I was so sorry to hear . . ." She deliberated what to say next.

"It was a heart attack." Alaina's admission echoed with haunting sorrow. "She got up that morning. Everything was fine. Then I found her dead in their room after lunch."

"I'm so sorry," Kathy breathed and recalled the book on forensic medicine she'd read a few months ago. She knew for a fact that some substances mimicked heart attack symptoms and had fooled more than one autopsy team. *That would be the perfect way for a man to kill his wife*, she thought.

"Are both your parents still living?" Alaina questioned.

The pain in her eyes made Kathy repent of ever being exasperated with her mother for any reason. She nodded.

"Count your blessings," Alaina said, and Kathy decided to call her mom before bedtime just to tell her she loved her. She also considered telling her father how glad she was she never had to worry about his killing her mother.

They'll think you're crazy, she told herself, and decided that probably wouldn't be the first time.

While Alaina placed her call, Kathy retrieved a loaf of bread from the bread box and busied herself preparing Ben's sandwich.

"Hello, Dad," Alaina said. "Ben found me." She paused.

Kathy did her best to act like she wasn't interested in the conversation while straining for every word.

"Yes, everything's fine. I stopped in to see a new friend—Kathy Moore. You know, she owns the new bookstore in town, Kathy's Book Nook."

Kathy slapped a thick layer of mayonnaise onto a piece of whole wheat and didn't bother to diminish her curiosity.

"Yes, that's right. It's beside Blake's Barber Shop. Anyway, I'm upstairs in her apartment now. Ben's here. She's fixing him a sandwich."

After picking up three slices of turkey breast, Kathy piled them atop the bread.

"Sure! That sounds great. I'll ask her!" Alaina exclaimed. "Just a minute."

Kathy glanced toward her new friend, who placed her fingers over the cell phone's mouthpiece. "Dad said I should ask you over for dinner," she reported with a welcoming smile. "Are you free sometime in the next few weeks?"

"Who, me?" Kathy pictured herself entering the dreaded chalet and being swallowed alive.

"Yes, you," Alaina replied. "You're the only person in the kitchen, aren't you?"

She grinned. "Yes, I guess you're right." A rush of chills assaulted her arms. Horror mingled with anticipation. *The only way to decide if Alaina's father murdered her mother is to go meet him,* she told herself. *Maybe I can act like Matlock and even look for clues.*

"I'm free any Friday," she admitted. "I'd love to have dinner with you."

Alaina lifted the phone to her ear. "It's a go, Dad. Any Friday is good for her. What's good for you?" she asked and waited.

Imagining herself stalking the chalet's corridors, Kathy wondered if the scenario would be less like Matlock and more like her favorite Don Knotts movie, *The Ghost and Mr. Chicken.* Kathy imagined herself, like Don Knotts, nearly having a nervous breakdown while trapped inside some secret passage in the mysterious home.

"Sure, I'll see." Alaina angled the cell phone away from her mouth. "Dad's leaving for a mission trip with a church group tomorrow morning. He won't be back for two and a half weeks. What about three weeks from yesterday at seven o'clock?"

A church mission trip? Kathy thought. *What a perfect cover!*

"Works," Kathy affirmed and tried to sound like Matlock even though she felt like Mr. Chicken. "That'll give me time to close the shop and get ready."

Alaina moved the cell closer to her mouth. "Kathy says that's fine," she said and waited. "Sure, I'll ask Ben, too. I think that's a great idea!" she added and demurely grinned at Kathy.

Thirteen

After Ben admonished Kathy that she was definitely in need of a plumber, he devoured two sandwiches. Then the three amiably chatted about everything from Northpointe's worst winter to Kathy's love of old movies. During that hour, Kathy's caffeine rush diminished and left her simply perky. She even found herself relaxing with her new friends more than she had with any of Northpointe's citizens.

Soon, unrelenting music invaded Kathy's apartment and so distracted the three that they decided to investigate. While Kathy said she thought the music was coming from the barbershop next door, Ben and Alaina suspected a kid with a boom box in the alley.

Halfway down the steps, Kathy decided the familiar musical beat sounded too close to be next door. The mixture of clapping, foot stomping, and cat calls mingling with the music sounded suspiciously close, as well. She looked back at Ben and Alaina and raised her brows.

"Sounds like it's coming from your store," Ben said.

"Is that the theme music for the Charleston?" Alaina asked.

Kathy snapped her fingers. "Yes. I knew it sounded familiar. But why would my brother and Ron and Liza be listening to that music?" Kathy's curiosity drove her down the rest of the stairway. She didn't even bother waiting on her friends before flinging open the door.

A circle of clapping people stood near her store's front entrance. Jay, Ron, Liza, Dory, and three red-hatted women dressed in purple surrounded Gloria and Sigmund, who were doing the Charleston. Gloria, dressed in a floppy magenta dress, grabbed the long strand of tacky orange beads around her neck and started twirling them. Sigmund bent forward and wobbled his knees back and forth while passing his hands from knee to knee.

"You go, Uncle Zig!" Jay whooped.

Kathy burst into uncontrolled laughter. "These people are crazy!"

"Are all your friends caffeine sensitive?" Ben drawled. "Maybe they've all OD'd." He pointed toward the service bar lined in coffee mugs. The smell of cappuccino and gourmet coffee attested to the group's indulgence.

After darting Ben a sassy glance, Kathy hustled forward and squeezed into the circle between Jay and a red-hatter. As the song ended, Kathy applauded the pair as loudly as the others. Uncle Ziggy held his wife's hand. She curtsied; he bowed.

"And that is how the Charleston is done!" Gloria chimed, her cheeks flushed.

"Now call an ambulance," Sigmund teased and clutched at his chest in feigned exhaustion. Tonight, he wore the usual neon-green suspenders with a pair of baggy slacks. His T-shirt featured a bull with enormous horns. The caption above the bull read, "Eat Mor Chikin!" A national chicken chain's advertisement claimed the space beneath the bull.

"More! More!" Ron cheered. The rest of the group joined him, including Kathy.

"Hey!" Sigmund looked at Kathy. "When did you get here?"

"Just now," Kathy explained. "We came down to check out the music."

"Well, in that case . . ." Sigmund bellowed and grabbed Kathy's hand, "you need to learn the Charleston."

Gloria grabbed the unsuspecting Ben and paired him with Kathy. The whole group went into a cheering fit. Ben lifted his hands and backed away. He bumped into one of the red-hatters, who jovially shoved him toward Kathy. Rolling his eyes, Ben shrugged and accepted his fate. Caught in the moment, Kathy laughed and decided to be a good sport.

After taking off her beads, Gloria slipped them over Kathy's head while Sigmund hurried to the CD player behind the cash register and started the music again. Neither Kathy nor Ben had a clue what they were doing. Twenty seconds later the whole rowdy group knew they were Charleston-challenged. Kathy mimicked gestures she recalled from old movies but wound up whacking Ben in the face with the beads three times. He bumped into her twice. The first time she bounced off Liza; the second time Ben slammed Kathy against Ron, who grabbed Kathy's waist and yelled, "She's falling for me!"

When Ben bent forward and tried to pass his hands from knee to knee, Kathy was concentrating on trying to complete a circle and rammed into his backside. Ben crashed forward and landed on his hands and knees. His back to her, he rolled to his side and clutched his midsection. Her heart leaping, Kathy covered her mouth. A gurgle of horror erupted from her throat. The raucous bunch stilled. Only the loud music remained . . . and outlandish laughter exploding from the floor. Ben rolled to his back, and Kathy realized the laughter was coming from him. The whole group burst into a new round of shrieks.

"You knocked him off his feet, Kathy!" Sigmund roared.

Out of the corner of her eye, Kathy noticed Ron's frown and hoped he recognized defeat.

Still laughing, Ben sat up, and the circle began to break up. Kathy reached for his hand. He hopped to his feet and didn't distance himself from her. Instead, Ben held her hand, looked into her eyes, and said, "I haven't had this much fun in . . . I don't even know when—*ever*!" Open admiration pranced across his features.

Kathy held her breath and prayed this might be the beginning of something special. She didn't doubt that Ben enjoyed the evening in her presence. The only thing that could have made the hour happier would have been his lack of constant restraint. Now, in the aftermath of their flailing arms and Kathy's bead-slinging, Ben seemed to have forgotten he should remain guarded.

"I've had a great time, too," Kathy purred and was tempted to rise to her tiptoes and kiss his cheek and then his scar.

Ben's face stiffened. He dropped her hand and backed away. The Charleston music came to a thumping halt, and Kathy averted her gaze. Her mother always said Kathy's expressions were transparent. She prayed Ben didn't know she'd thought about kissing him. His comments about her age stung anew. Her head began to thud.

"I'll start the music again, and everybody who wants to can try this time!" Sigmund announced.

"I've got the beads and the chart that shows all the moves!" Dory claimed and ran to the service bar, where a shopping bag sagged open. A profusion of multicolored beads spilled from the bag. The oversized blonde grabbed the beads, hurried forward, and began handing them out to the ladies. "We'll spread the chart out on one of the tables and all look at it," Dory continued.

Kathy gazed after Ben, who stopped near his sister. She was standing by the door, talking on her cell phone again. Kathy immediately wondered if the call was from Alaina's father. She frowned and added some warts to her gnarled image of Zachariah Tilman.

Doing her best to act normal, Kathy stepped near Gloria. "Where did you guys get all this stuff, anyway?" Kathy lifted the strand of beads around her neck and let it drop.

"At the new party shop in town out in that shopping strip by Walmart," Gloria said and shoved at the sides of her disheveled gray locks. "We bought the CD and the beads. They even had some hats and outfits from the twenties, but we didn't get them. Dory and I decided we were too fat!" She laughed and patted her plump hips.

"How fun!" Kathy exclaimed and absorbed Ben's every move. Alaina had just pocketed her cell phone and said something to him.

"We ran into those wild red-hats at the ice-cream parlor next to the party shop," Gloria explained and pointed to the trio who were gladly accepting their beads from Dory. "When we told them what we found, we all decided to try it out tonight. We were going to see if the bed-and-breakfast owner minded if we used the parlor, but then we saw your lights on. So . . ." She shrugged.

"I love it!" Kathy enthused and noticed Ben out of the corner of her eye. One of the red-hatters had moved to his side. He was laughing at something she said and shaking his head no.

The sixty-something woman's expression said, *If only I were thirty years younger!*

If only I was a little older! Kathy pined.

"I've got your next dance . . . or maybe we should just call it an aerobic workout." Ron's voice penetrated Kathy's reverie. She jerked her attention to him. He'd moved to her side without her even realizing it. His ardent brown eyes begged for more than a round of the Charleston and suggested he hadn't forgotten the near miss on their kiss.

Kathy swallowed hard and decided she might have to get a little blunt. "I'm really sorry," she begged, "but my head has started killing me." *Now, that's really being blunt,* she mocked herself. Kathy stroked her temple. "I probably need to go upstairs for some aspirin." While her mind was still energized, her body was beginning to start complaining about the exhausting week all over again.

"I'm sorry," Ron crooned and slipped his arm around her

waist. "Want me to go up with you?" He shot a triumphant glance toward Ben.

Growing nauseous, Kathy shook her head and tried to not look at Ben. The urge would not be denied. Her fear was confirmed. Ben had noticed. But even worse than that, he acted like Ron's clinging didn't bother him in the least. He calmly ended the conversation with the red-hatter and spoke to his sister again.

Alaina nodded at something he said and walked toward Kathy.

Kathy pulled the beads off her neck and handed them to Ron. "Would you please hold these?" she asked and stepped away from his clutch as he accepted the beads.

Approaching Alaina, Kathy never looked back. "Sorry! I didn't mean to ignore you," she said. "I just got roped into that Charleston."

"No, it's quite all right," Alaina said. "I enjoyed the entertainment. I've never seen Ben in that position before." She laughed over the final words. "You really bring some life to him." Her lips twitching, she leaned forward and whispered, "Sometimes he can be boring."

"Never!" Kathy gasped and didn't add that she found his understated charm captivating. Long ago Kathy's father told her she needed to marry someone low-key because if she got a man with her energy level, she'd probably blow a fuse. Ben fit the description—if you could call dragging a kid out of a burning vehicle low-key. Kathy was dying to pry for details but had yet to find an appropriate opening.

"I'm afraid we're going to have to leave," Alaina continued. "Ben's got to get home to prepare his sermon for tomorrow, and I need to get back to Dad. He called again. He's waiting on his ice cream."

Kathy picked at the top of her scoop-necked blouse. "You've had ice cream in your car all this time?" she asked and wondered what flavor a murderer would eat. *Probably Double Death Delight,* she thought.

"Yes, but it's okay." Alaina began slipping on her denim jacket. "I have a cooler I always put the cold stuff in."

"Who said they wanted root beer floats?" Jay's call rang over the first notes of the music.

Dory and Gloria began to swing their beads and hop to the tune like a couple of teenagers. Over the last week, Kathy had noticed a decided lack of the rivalry that had characterized Dory's first day in town.

Kathy glanced toward her brother. He and Liza were behind the service bar. She held a bucket of ice cream, and he grasped a scoop. Those two were starting to act more and more like a team, and Kathy hoped her brother didn't throw all common sense to the wind. But even concerns over her brother didn't stop Kathy from eyeing the empty mugs lining the service bar. She began to calculate how much all these festivities were costing her and wasn't pleased with the outcome.

Uncle Sigmund lowered the music's volume and asked, "How much do you get for your floats, Kathy?"

"Two-fifty," she answered, "but let's say two even for tonight!"

"And the cappuccino and coffee?"

"A dollar fifty a mug on the cappuccino," Kathy supplied. "Seventy-five cents on the coffee."

"Let's keep it simple and make it a dollar a mug for both. Okay?" Kathy nodded.

"Did everybody hear that?" Sigmund bellowed. "If you've gotten anything, make sure you pay for it before you leave."

"Not a problem!" Liza interjected.

The group agreed.

Sigmund nodded toward Kathy, and she mouthed a thank-you.

"Anyway," Alaina continued while straightening her jacket collar, "thanks again for everything." She gripped Kathy's hand.

Her eyes reddened, and she rapidly blinked until they cleared. "You've helped me more than you'll ever know."

"You're welcome," Kathy responded and suppressed the questions that stormed her mind: *What's going on? Why have you been crying? Does it have anything to do with your father? Look, did he kill your mother or not?*

Alaina's attention trailed to a point beyond Kathy, and Kathy followed her gaze. It rested on Ron, who was watching her. He lifted his chin in an assured manner that implied every female in the room should be looking at him. Ron waved and winked.

Kathy snapped her focus back to Alaina. A silent query hung between Kathy and her new friend.

"He's driving me crazy," Kathy mumbled. "He wants us to get together." She shook her head.

Alaina nodded. "I see. I think Ben was wondering."

"You do?"

Slipping her purse strap on her shoulder, she nodded. "I also think he'd never admit it."

"Oh." Kathy's shoulders slumped, and she relived the seconds after she assisted Ben to his feet. Her hopes had been dashed aside then as swiftly as now.

"Well, I guess we're still on for dinner in three weeks. Right?" Alaina asked.

"Right," Kathy affirmed.

Alaina glanced down and fidgeted with the button on her jacket. "Would you mind if I maybe called you between now and then?" Her faint request was hardly detectable over the crowd's noise, and Kathy strained to make sense of the words. Finally Alaina's meaning struck her.

"I'd be thrilled!" Kathy enthused. "Maybe we could get together and go shopping or something!"

"I was thinking the same thing," Alaina admitted and lifted her gaze back to Kathy. Her eyes, every bit as blue as Ben's, communicated a deep, silent desire for a close friendship. Kathy didn't know what all was going on with Alaina, but she sensed that her new acquaintance was carrying a burden that was better borne by two.

"Call me tomorrow, okay?" Kathy said. "And maybe we can set up a time."

"Tomorrow's Sunday," Alaina mused and thoughtfully looked at Kathy. "Hey, would you like to go to church with me?"

"Sure!" Kathy answered. "I'd love to. I've been going, um, sometimes to a little church just up the street—Northpointe Lighthouse."

"Well, Dad and I drive to Ben's church."

Kathy was simultaneously enthused and dismayed, but she masked her feelings. While she'd be thrilled to see Ben again and even hear him speak, she didn't want him to think she was chasing him, either. Even though her attraction for him was growing to mammoth proportions, his subtle rejections weren't easy to take.

"His church is about twenty minutes away," Alaina explained, "but we think it's the best."

"Naturally," Kathy teased.

"Of course," Alaina added with a smile. "Anyway, since Dad's leaving on his trip tomorrow morning he won't be going." She nudged a stray ringlet from the corner of her eye. "Want me to stop and pick you up?"

"Um . . ." Kathy hesitated and decided to just be honest about her misgivings. "Do you think Ben will think . . ." She wrinkled her brow and hoped Alaina understood her implied meaning.

"Not in the least!" Alaina gestured and rolled her eyes. "His church has gotten so big, he probably won't even notice you're there."

"Oh," Kathy answered and didn't know whether she was relieved or disappointed.

"Look," Alaina said, "why don't I pick you up here at nine? That way we'll be able to make Sunday school, as well."

"Sure," Kathy said. As the two new friends exchanged their final farewell, Kathy refused to even look Ben's way. She decided she'd rather him think she was rude than think she was pushing herself on him. If he saw her at church tomorrow, he might draw the worst conclusion anyway. So Kathy walked toward the service bar and pretended interest in Jay and Liza's endeavors. She was so intent on blocking out Ben that she didn't realize someone was beside her until he tapped her shoulder. Kathy jumped and turned toward the person.

"Sorry," Ben said, the laugh lines around his eyes deepening.

"It's okay," Kathy said and tried to act as natural as possible. "You just surprised me. I was a million miles away, and I'm, well, I've been told I'm jumpy." She didn't dare maintain eye contact for more than a few seconds. Kathy's imagination spun with a dozen different motives for Ben's approach.

Maybe he's going to ask me out! she enthused and tried to look as receptive as possible without stooping to silent begging.

"Before I leave, I just wanted to make sure you remember what I said about your plumbing," Ben said.

"My plumbing?" Kathy squinted and searched Ben's eyes for some clue to his comment.

Undaunted concern flowed from him as he nodded. "Yes, remember, it's groaning and I told you—"

"Oh, yes!" Kathy grabbed the top of her head. "My plumbing! You said I need to have it seen about."

"Right. Don't forget, okay? I've heard of whole houses flooding in old buildings like this. If you flood upstairs it could leak down here." He looked up, and then gazed around her store. "You could lose inventory."

Kathy nodded and crossed her arms. "I understand. Really,

thanks for your concern." *Plumbing!* she thought. *How can you worry about plumbing at a time like this?*

"Sure." Ben hesitated, looked down, and peered past her. "Well, I guess Alaina's told you we need to go."

"Yes."

"Thanks for the sandwiches and everything."

"My kitchen's open any time!" she quipped and hid a grimace. *No telling what he thinks now!*

His smile couldn't have been more halfhearted; neither could his good-bye. The second he pivoted from her, Kathy turned back toward the service bar and slid onto a stool. She stifled a groan and kept her expression pleasant. All the while she wanted to creep behind the bar and hide until Ben was gone.

Feigning interest in Jay and Liza, Kathy was highly aware of Ben and Alaina's exit. Only when Kathy was certain Ben wouldn't notice, she strained for a final glimpse of him out the store's front window. Through the twilight mist, Kathy detected his silhouette as he got into a sporty pale vehicle parked at the curb.

Funny, she thought, *I wouldn't have guessed Ben would drive anything sporty.* The racy image didn't quite fit an understated gentleman pastor. Then Kathy eyed the photo of her and the Impala hanging above the store's kitchen area. *Nobody but Uncle Ziggy seems to think I need to be driving the Impala, either,* she reasoned and decided the sports coupe only added to Ben's appeal and hinted there was much more for Kathy to learn about him.

If only he felt the same about me, she lamented.

Kathy stared at the service bar, spotted with drops of cappuccino, and tapped her finger. The shopping and makeover trip with Aunt Gloria had never happened. They'd both been so exhausted by the store's demands, neither had wanted to drive to Denver after work. So they'd tabled the whole idea for later.

Kathy considered her meager wardrobe at the same time she checked her watch. It was just after eight. The last time she was in Walmart, she noticed they had some inexpensive business suits that looked high-end. *They also have all sorts of cosmetics and hair products*, she mused and wondered if she might be able to pull together an older look by morning. Even though Alaina said Ben might not notice her, Kathy wanted to be prepared in case he did.

She had never considered herself a fashion-savvy chick, but Kathy did have a good eye for color and balance. She glanced toward the shelves and shelves of books, their neat arrangement, and the way the scattering of tables and chairs created an inviting appeal. Maybe she could pull off the same effect with her appearance . . . and maybe Ben would not only notice, but would take a second look.

But by tomorrow morning? she worried and nipped her thumbnail. *Well, where there's a will, there's a way*, she told herself and made her final decision. As soon as she could politely leave, Kathy would slip out to the store. When she got home and the crowd cleared out, she'd spend the rest of the evening trying to make herself look less like an adolescent and more like the business professional she was.

"First float up!" Jay bellowed before setting the foamy treat on the service bar.

The faint whiff of vanilla ice cream and root beer tempted Kathy, but she asserted her willpower to decline more caffeine. *I'll get some ice cream later*, she decided.

Jay glanced at Liza, who was busy dipping ice cream into another glass, then he leaned toward Kathy.

"I think she's the one," he hissed.

Kathy, feeling like she'd dropped three stories in an elevator, stared into her brother's earnest hazel eyes. He didn't blink. The determined set of his features didn't waver.

"But you've only known her a week!" Kathy insisted. "You can't be thinking of asking her to—"

"I'm not ready to propose now, silly," he whispered. "I just mean that I think she's . . ." he shrugged, "the one. I'll propose when we've known each other awhile."

"Good." Kathy laid her hand over her heart. While Kathy's mother had long ago labeled her "spontaneity personified," Kathy knew the limits. Capriciously jumping into a marriage was not an option. Ironically, Kathy's parents usually referred to Jay as the levelheaded one.

He turned down the corners of his mouth and wagged his head back and forth. "I figure the proposal can wait three, maybe four weeks."

Kathy's elevator went into a free fall to the basement. "But— but—" Kathy stammered. "That's still not enough time. Don't you think you need to at least pray about this?" she questioned and wondered why she, of all people, would come up with something that sounded so spiritual.

"I am!" His insinuation of spiritual seeking didn't match the fervent, masculine glee in his eyes.

Speechless, Kathy helplessly observed her brother and doubted he'd prayed at all.

"Look, Ron's been trying to get Liza and me to meet for a while. He knew we'd hit it off. Now that I've found her, I don't want her getting away from me," he argued, his voice low and urgent. "I've got to go back to my job in five weeks. She's not scheduled to leave 'til the end of August. I don't want to leave town unless my ring is on her finger."

"But, Jay!"

"Another float's up!" Liza said, and Jay turned his back on Kathy to accept the treat.

Fourteen

Two and a half weeks lapsed before Ben acknowledged his sister had a serious problem. Ben didn't know whether it broke his heart more to admit the issue existed or that he was stooping to actually spying on Alaina. He had never doubted his sister's integrity and would have never questioned her morals if she hadn't sneaked out of town after his father went on the mission trip. The fact that Caleb Manley was conveniently out of town, too, hadn't escaped Ben's notice. Today, Ben just happened to see Alaina and Caleb entering a Denver hotel at three in the afternoon. Shortly after spotting them, Ben attributed the unexpected sighting to an act of God.

He now sat outside the Holiday Inn Express in his church's new passenger van and leafed through the latest copy of *Pastor's Life* magazine. A church member had driven him into Denver for the sole purpose of picking up the van. Little did Ben know he would stop at a red light and spot his younger sister walking across the hotel parking lot with Caleb on her heels. By the time Alaina and Caleb entered the hotel, Ben was claiming a parking spot one row away and ten cars down from their vehicles.

Now, two hours had crept by and Ben was not only tired of waiting, he was sick of the new-van odor. He clicked the ignition key and lowered the passenger and driver windows. A cool breeze whipped through the van. Even though the five o'clock air sent a chill along Ben's arms, he was thankful for the reprieve.

This Colorado summer had been the coolest one on record for several decades.

He gazed at the snow-crested Rockies to the west of Denver. Ben had come to expect his sister to be like the mountains, always present, always the same. Alaina lowering her level of morality was as unthinkable as the Rocky Mountains disappearing.

But now, Ben was far past the long list of rational excuses for his sister's trip inside. The truth settled into his soul like a heavy chunk of lead.

"Somehow, Caleb managed to get to her," Ben mumbled. His clammy fingers tightened on the magazine, and Ben felt like he was ten years old again and needed to defend Alaina from a first-grade ponytail-pulling brat. Then he reminded himself that Caleb Manley had a reputation as solid as Alaina's, and he hadn't been dragging her into the hotel. She'd willingly hurried in.

"She was smiling, even," Ben mumbled and tried to focus on the magazine article. As usual, this piece featured a pleasant young man with an attractive wife. The title read, "Co-Pastoring with Your Mate."

"Oh, great. Like we all have a mate!" he grumbled and was tempted to submit an article on being a single pastor.

Despite his disenchantment, Ben examined the woman standing outside a white frame church with her husband. She wore a fashionable black suit and had short dark hair and a cheery smile. Mentally, Ben added some dimples to the gal and reduced her size by fifteen pounds. What he got was Kathy Moore—despite the fact that the model was part Asian. The longer he looked at the woman, the more she resembled the perky brunette who made him laugh when he least expected it and propelled him to odd behavior—like telling her he was the Ghost of Christmas Past and doing the Charleston. "Whoever heard of such?" Ben grumbled and wondered what the Ladies Auxiliary would have thought of him—or of Kathy's polka-dotted toenails. After minutes of internal vacillation, Ben came to a definitive verdict. *Who cares!*

Closing the magazine, Ben laughed out loud and relished the relief. In an act of new independence, he decided to stop making his life choices based on what others might or might not approve. Kathy seemed to be a good, moral, sweet lady. What she did to her toenails was her business. *If the Ladies Auxiliary doesn't approve, then that's their problem.* He closed the thought with a nod and recalled how nice Kathy had looked in his congregation.

Two weeks ago, when Kathy attended church with Alaina, he hadn't seen her until he stood at the pulpit to deliver his sermon. Somehow, in a crowd of four hundred, his attention rested on the attractive newcomer beside his sister. He'd been so overwhelmed by the difference in her appearance he'd nearly forgotten his message's text. Overnight, she'd gone from a lively sixteen-year-old to a classy twenty-two-year-old.

Ben flopped the magazine into the passenger seat, closed his eyes, and propped his head on the back of the seat. He'd acted like a coward that Sunday and vanished after the service.

Part of the reason Ben's church was growing so rapidly involved his ability to empower the members to be the arms and hands of Jesus. Ben had successfully delegated a whole host of duties traditionally viewed as the "pastor's job" to committed laypeople. Along with numerous other teams, Ben established a Meeters-and-Greeters unit that shook hands with everyone who arrived and left. However, Ben always made a point of being in the foyer after services. Not the Sunday Kathy was present.

"Nope. I hid in my office," he mumbled. "I ran from her." Ben shook his head, unbuttoned the top button of his Polo shirt, and fanned himself with his shirt. The cool breeze did nothing to assuage his increasing body temperature.

I ran from her the night before at her store, too, he thought. Once she helped him to his feet after the Charleston fiasco, Kathy's expression confirmed Ben's every assumption about her interest in him—except Ben realized Kathy's feelings weren't a crush. Kathy Moore was stricken with a case of undaunted, adult-stuff admiration.

"If I didn't know any better, I'd say she wanted to kiss me," Ben mumbled and relived the magnetism that sprang between them. *Yeah, well, maybe I wanted to kiss her, too!* He briskly rubbed his face.

"I'm going off the deep end," he groaned as he reflected over the last couple of weeks.

Like a lovesick adolescent, Ben had purposefully driven by Kathy's store numerous times in hopes of seeing her. Once he even stopped by, ordered a coffee, and bought a fishing magazine. Unfortunately, Gloria and Sigmund were the only ones there. Ben, feeling an illogical need to explain his visit, had mumbled something about a camping and trout-fishing expedition he and his friend Heath were planning this fall. He finished his excuse by saying he'd been looking for the magazine all over town. Of course, every word was true, but he would have stopped at Kathy's store that day regardless of the fishing magazine. Ben didn't know whether or not Gloria had even told Kathy he'd been by.

"I shouldn't even care," Ben rasped. "She's too young for me." But the argument that started as a verbal iron wall now crumbled like straw. All he could do was relive the time he'd spent with Kathy. In the short season he'd known her, she made him laugh . . . made him feel more alive than any other woman he'd ever met.

He'd nearly dropped through the floor the night that spike-haired model-looking guy put his arm around her. In the aftermath, all Ben could come up with when he told her good-bye was some inane comment about her plumbing.

Wow! he thought and rolled his eyes. *I am soooo good with the lines.*

When they left Kathy's store that night, Ben hadn't bothered to worry what Alaina thought when he asked about the blond man. Alaina reported that Kathy said the affection was all on the guy's side. Ben had never been so relieved!

Okay, he finally admitted. *I'm interested in her—a lot. Now what?* He lifted his head, opened his eyes, focused on the hotel's entrance, and beseeched God for His perfect will. Ben meditated before his Creator, awaiting any indication that he should not pursue Kathy. All Ben sensed was an ever-deepening longing for a mate—a longing God had placed within him. The dinner party at his dad's was only two days away.

The memory of Ben's grandmother slapping his mother blew through his mind. Ben flinched. He'd been six. It was Easter Sunday morning. He was so proud of his new black suit with white shirt. It matched his dad's. Ben's mom had dressed Alaina, then three, and herself in pink. Zachariah's mother had entered the room with a lacy white dress she fully expected Laura to change Alaina into. When Laura refused, Ben's grandmother had slapped her. Ben didn't remember much after that—except that his father had arrived in the room and witnessed the abuse. The eruption that followed assured that Easter had been as miserable as the last Christmas.

"If Dad likes Kathy . . ." Ben mused and drummed his fingers on the steering wheel.

The hotel door opened and a familiar woman wearing a red blazer and navy slacks exited. A tall, muscular guy with dark hair and a deep tan followed close behind. Thoughts of Kathy vanished. Ben grabbed his magazine and buried his face behind it. Feeling like a second-class detective in a B movie, he scrunched lower in the seat and peeked around the magazine's edge. With the windows down, he registered the approach of footsteps. By the time Alaina and Caleb stopped at Alaina's Beetle, Ben concentrated on picking up snatches of their conversation through his open window.

" . . . love you," Caleb said.

"You know I . . ."

Ben strained to hear the rest of his sister's remarks but failed.

" . . . father finds out?" Caleb replied.

"He won't—not until . . ."

His eyes narrowed, Ben observed Caleb opening the door for his sister, who was glowing like Ben had never seen her glow. After stroking Caleb's face and intimately resting her hand against the front of his tailored shirt, she settled into the vehicle and lowered the window. Caleb bent down and placed his forearm on the window's ledge. Even though Caleb wasn't what Ben would dub handsome, his highly toned form brought to mind a few of the models he'd seen sprawled across the front of mushy romance novels.

Ben tightened his gut. *I never imagined Alaina could be so carnal!* He reached for the large Taco Bell cup in the beverage holder and sucked down the remains of the Pepsi. The icy liquid seeped into his stomach and created a chill that wracked his body.

Hearing the rest of the conversation was no longer an option. All Ben detected was low mumbling. Finally Caleb straightened. Alaina cranked her Volkswagen engine while Caleb walked toward a Ford pickup closer to Ben's parking place. As Alaina whizzed out of the parking lot, Caleb waved at her like a man who had the world by the tail.

Bile rose in Ben's throat, and he wondered if Alaina had been sneaking around longer than he thought. At the cookout she'd hinted about marriage but still acted like she had some huge secret she couldn't reveal. Ben narrowed his eyes and considered the remote possibility that his sister and Caleb were already married.

"No," he whispered and shook his head. "She would have told me." Alaina had never kept secrets from Ben. *Yes, but she didn't tell me she was seeing Caleb in the first place, either,* Ben reminded himself.

"But marriage?" he mumbled. *Why lurk around like this if they're already married?*

In search of a telltale gold band, he prayed for a glimpse of Caleb's left hand and lambasted himself for not noticing whether or not Alaina wore a wedding ring. Still watching Alaina's departure, Caleb inserted his hands into the pockets of his twill slacks.

What I wouldn't give for some binoculars, Ben griped. He dared lower the magazine a few more centimeters and squinted. With a sexy smile, Caleb removed his left hand from his pocket and stroked his chest. His fingers were ringless!

Ben winced and lifted the magazine. The only thing that stopped him from chasing Caleb down and defending Alaina's honor was the awful fact that she was every bit as willing as Caleb. When Caleb strode toward his truck, all Ben's hope, all excuses plummeted to a sickening death. The sister he'd blindly trusted to never lower her morals had done exactly that.

If Dad ever finds out, it will not be pretty! Ben thought and brooded until Caleb's blue truck rolled from view.

Tomorrow, Zachariah Tilman would arrive home from his Mexico mission trip. Ben had overheard Alaina telling him she planned to spend the time he was gone with Kathy. A couple of times his sister even told Ben she and Kathy were getting better acquainted. They'd gone shopping together last week.

Maybe she just wanted to keep me and Dad off her trail, Ben thought. As he cranked the van, Ben's heart went cold. *I wonder how many months this . . .* thing *has been going on?* He refused to use the word *affair* in relation to his sister. While he knew she couldn't remain innocent forever, Ben had pictured Alaina only one notch below the Virgin Mary. The very thought of her violating one of the Ten Commandments was nearly too much for him. His sweet-looking sister had managed to betray and dupe him, and Ben began to wonder if he knew Alaina at all.

Fifteen

Alaina steered her vehicle through the streets of Northpointe and cruised down Main. She parked outside Kathy's Book Nook and shut off the engine. Alaina checked her appearance in the visor's mirror and noted that her lipstick was smudged, her blusher was gone, and her mascara was flaking. Despite the damage to her makeup, her eyes shimmered with the same light she saw in Caleb's. She did her best to repair her lipstick and dashed aside as many mascara flakes as possible. She had never so thoroughly not cared about looking drab.

After flipping up the visor, Alaina examined the wide gold band on her left hand. She and Caleb both loved wearing the symbols of their matrimony and put them on the minute they were together. Today, Caleb removed his band before they left the hotel, but Alaina decided to wait until she absolutely *had* to take hers off. Sighing, she stroked the ring and wondered how long she'd be able to hide her marriage from her father. The day after Zachariah left for Mexico, Alaina arranged for some vacation time. She and Caleb flew to Las Vegas and said their "I do's." The last two weeks had been nothing short of heavenly.

Several times she'd been so tempted to tell Ben and Kathy that she almost broke the promise she'd begged Caleb to keep— that neither of them would tell a soul. The last thing Alaina needed was for Caleb to tell his mother, who might tell his sister, who might tell another someone, who might tell her dad's housekeeper, who might tell her dad. Northpointe was a small town, and Alaina never ceased to marvel at the grapevine's swift accuracy.

But Kathy doesn't know enough people to put it on the grapevine, Alaina reasoned and dubiously eyed the bookstore. *Besides, she'd keep her promise and not tell. I just know it! Dad wouldn't find out if I just told Kathy.*

Even though Caleb wanted to immediately tell Zachariah about the marriage and have Alaina move to his apartment, Alaina implored him to allow her to handle those details. Therefore, Caleb had agreed to conceal their marriage for six months. Somehow, Alaina would find a way to use the time to soften the blow and make the ordeal less explosive. Even though her heart irrefutably belonged to Caleb, and he understood that, she also convinced him of her desperate need to tell her father in her own way in her own time.

She further hoped to find relief from the guilt that wouldn't release her. Alaina had irrefutably gone against God's command that she should obey her father. The day she said "I do," Alaina stopped praying. In her heart, God's eyes took on her father's cold disapproval. She wondered if she would ever feel His smile again.

Frowning, Alaina stepped out of the Volkswagen, snapped the door shut, and locked it with the button on her key ring. She strode across the sidewalk toward Kathy's shop and wondered if her new friend was busy. Kathy would be closing her store in fifteen minutes. Tonight Caleb had to work the evening shift, and Alaina planned to invite Kathy out for dinner. When she shifted her purse to her left shoulder, she noticed the gold band still on her finger.

"Oh no," she whispered and darted a furtive glance toward Kathy's shop, up one side of the street, and then down the other. Since no one was watching, Alaina subtly slipped the ring from her finger, unzipped her blazer's pocket, and dropped the ring inside. The gold clinked against the loose change left from today's lunch, and Alaina rezipped her pocket. Releasing her captured breath, Alaina strode the rest of the distance to Kathy's shop. The door was barely open before Kathy offered her greeting.

"Hey, Alaina!" she exclaimed with an eager smile and kind eyes that said "I accept you just the way you are." Kathy's unconditional friendship was such a rare find; Alaina marveled that she could be so at ease with anyone but Caleb and Ben.

"Hi," Alaina replied and moved toward the row of stools lining the service bar. Her wedge heels tapped the hardwood floor and reverberated with the echo of a century of customers. "Am I too late to order one of your famous lemonades?" she asked. Alaina laid her leather purse atop the service bar and claimed a stool. The faint smell of freshly squeezed lemons twisted her taste buds and made her glands ache. Alaina glanced behind Kathy to a scattering of spent lemon halves near a juicer.

"Believe it or not, I was just making myself one," Kathy said. She wiped her fingers on a checked dishtowel and smoothed the cloth along the front of her T-shirt, which read "Kathy's Book Nook."

"I just sprayed myself with a lemon that was full of juice." She blinked, closed one eye, and dabbed it with the towel.

"Sounds like my kind of lemons!" Alaina said.

"You're on, then," Kathy said and pointed at her friend. She turned back to her task, sliced more lemons, and inserted them into the juicer. Over the appliance's hum, Kathy began chatting about her busy day.

Alaina idly listened and contemplated the long evening ahead. Every night since her marriage, she and Caleb had somehow managed to be together. A few times, she sneaked to his place. Three times, he'd waited until sunset and left his truck at a park near their chalet. Then he'd walked the rest of the way. They'd met at a hotel, as well. But not tonight. Caleb had to work late, which was fine since Alaina's father was due home tomorrow morning, anyway. So they'd met earlier in the day in Denver. All that meant Alaina would be alone . . . unless Kathy was free.

"Do you have plans for tonight?" Alaina asked.

Kathy shot her a smile over her shoulder. "I was just about to ask you if you wanted to come up to my apartment for a movie and some taco salad. I've got all the stuff ready to go; I just have to warm up some leftover taco meat. We could check out what movies are streaming to see what we're in the mood for. I think there may be some old Alfred Hitchcock movies."

Glad for anything to take her mind off the time she wasn't with Caleb, Alaina beamed. "That sounds great! I was going to see if you wanted to go out and eat or something, but this is even better."

"Good! I'll sip my lemonade while I close out my cash register and run the 'lectric sweeper. Why don't you just sit here and enjoy yours. I'll be done in a jiffy."

"Or I could run the sweeper while you do the cash box."

"No." Kathy held up her hand. "You look tired. I can take care of it."

Even though Alaina hadn't ever felt so euphoric, she didn't argue. The fact that her makeup was smeared away made her look less than fresh. Alaina didn't want to have to explain why she appeared drab and felt so wonderful, so she remained on her stool and accepted the straw-laden, mile-high glass full of shaved ice drenched in lemonade.

Kathy wasted no time dealing with the cash register. Alaina had barely sipped the tart beverage when the doorbell jingled. She swiveled toward the newcomers and stiffened. Ron Thaine shifted his sunglasses to the top of his head and swaggered in with Kathy's brother and Liza close behind.

Last Saturday afternoon, the three hadn't been happy when

Kathy chose to go shopping with Alaina rather than to a movie
with them. Even though Kathy assured Alaina she and Ron
weren't a couple, he still acted like he owned Kathy. The man's
mere presence rankled, and Alaina was so thankful Caleb had
never adopted such an attitude.

"Hello, Mizz Store Owner!" Ron exclaimed. Dressed in fashionably loose-fitting jeans and a knit shirt, he strode over near
the cash register.

Kathy smiled toward the newcomers. "What are you guys
up to?" she asked.

Jay draped his arm on Liza's shoulders and said, "Liza and
I are driving into Denver for dinner." Alaina noted Liza's chic
blouse and skirt and Jay's sport jacket. Apparently, this wasn't a
trip to McDonald's. "Ron wanted to see if you two could make
a foursome out of it." Jay's voice sounded less than enthused,
but Ron's assured expression never wavered.

Instead, he edged closer to Kathy and looped his arm around
her waist. "They're going to the new fancy place—Impressions.
They even have a jazzy swing band. We could have a night on
the town!"

Kathy inched away from Ron. Her lips fleetingly turned down
before she offered an apologetic-yet-relieved grin. "Sorry." She
pointed toward Alaina. "Alaina and I just decided to have a taco-
salad-and-movie night."

As one, the three peered toward Alaina as if she were an alien
entity they'd never before encountered. She weakly smiled. Jay
and Liza both responded with grins as enthused as Alaina's. Ron
didn't bother to offer any silent greeting.

Jay's insincere smile soon turned to a silent *Aha!* He shifted
his attention to Ron and said, "That sounds like fun. Don't you
think, Ron? You could hang out with *two* ladies if you stay here."

Alaina feigned nonchalance while sipping her lemonade and
watching the exchange from the corners of her eyes. Jay's forced

tones were accompanied by a silent, wide-eyed plea to his sister. Kathy responded with tight lips and a hard stare.

"Sure! That sounds even better," Ron said and darted a direct glance toward Alaina. "Especially if we were alone." He did nothing to soften the barb.

Kathy's eyes rounded. Alaina's spirit sank, and she backed away from the lemonade straw. She didn't want to be with Ron any more than Kathy did. Kathy darted a nervous glance toward Alaina and beseeched her not to bow to Ron's hint.

"Well," Kathy hedged, "I already invited Alaina over, and she and I—uh, we—"

"I really have something I need to talk to Kathy about." Alaina's soft voice punctured the room's heightening tension; and she was amazed at her own assertiveness as much as she was by the admission. But the statement spoke her heart. Even though she had made Caleb vow not to tell a soul about her marriage, Alaina had to share her joy with someone or she was going to explode.

Ron narrowed his eyes and glared at Alaina. Her bravery melted in the face of his heated appraisal, and she looked down. Alaina had learned early in life that existing in peace often meant being invisible. Eliciting rancor was impossible when no one noticed you existed. This was the first time in her life she'd ever reaped such animosity, and the experience left her baffled.

Forever a pleaser, Alaina was ready to relinquish her rights to the evening when her friend's decisive voice ended all debate. "Ron, didn't your mom want someone to go to a concert with her tonight?"

Alaina sucked hard on her straw, gulped the lemonade, and nearly sank in the heavy silence. She didn't dare look up from her fixed focus on the hump of ice floating in pale gold liquid. Finally Ron stomped away and slammed out the door.

"Did you have to be so cold?" Jay demanded.

"Well, I already had plans," Kathy defended, "and he was being . . ." She hesitated, and Alaina dared a glimpse in their direction. Kathy offered a silent apology to Liza and looked at her brother.

"I just had plans," Kathy repeated and went back to her money counting.

Liza observed Alaina. While her eyes lacked Ron's unmasked animosity, she did little to hide her disenchantment. Jay rubbed his face and said, "Okay, fine," and ignored Alaina. "Come on, Liza," he continued and didn't lower his voice. "We can't let this ruin our evening."

Without a farewell, the couple walked out of the store. The door's clap punctuated their disapproval.

Alaina lifted her straw, stirred the lemonade, and decided that Kathy Moore had more backbone than her carefree personality implied. *I could probably learn a thing or two from her,* she thought and decided she was right in sharing her secret. In a few months, she was going to have to face her father. *Maybe Kathy will help me figure out how to tell him.*

She smiled at Kathy, who rolled her eyes as her shoulders drooped. "I was glad when they came to town because I needed friends, but now I'm looking forward to the first of August."

"They're leaving then?" Alaina asked.

"Well, Ron is, anyway. Jay, too, for that matter. They've got to get back to work. Liza's staying with her mom until the end of August. Normally, Jay and I get along like two pigs in a deep mud hole, but this time has been different."

While Alaina stifled a snicker, Kathy stared at the front door. "I just hope Jay's not actually going to—" She jiggled the change in her hand and looked straight at Alaina. "What do you think about quick engagements and marriages?" she probed. "Think they're smart?"

Alaina blinked and nearly choked. Even though she and Caleb

had known each other forever, their marriage had definitely been a quick development.

"I've been accused of being free-spirited a time or two," Kathy continued without recognizing Alaina's lack of response, "but hauling off and deciding to get married after you've only known someone a few weeks is asking for trouble. And to think my parents are always fretting about *me!*" Kathy fumed. "They need to be worried about Jay—the levelheaded one." She dropped the rest of the change into the register drawer and banged it shut. "He's the one losing it here, not me!"

Choosing not to comment, Alaina detoured the straw, picked up the frosty glass, and gulped the lemonade. *Maybe Kathy won't be as understanding as I thought.* The last thing Alaina needed was a friend's negative judgment on top of her father and God's disapproval.

"Why don't we just go on up to my apartment?" Kathy said as she trudged toward the front door.

"Okay," Alaina agreed and hoped Kathy didn't remember her mentioning something important to talk about.

"I'll count the money and run the sweeper in the morning." Kathy flipped the sign in the window to "Closed" and clicked the deadbolt above the doorknob. "I never can get the money drawer to come out right anyway. Half the time I just don't bother."

Sixteen

Friday was the longest work day of Kathy's life. She checked her watch every five minutes and was certain each minute was dragging into an hour. After days of frenzied business, this Friday reaped one disinterested customer. By noon, Kathy had earned a whole $8.53. Her boredom was driven to new heights by the absence of her godparents, who left at ten this morning for a leisurely trip to Mesa Verde National Park. Jay departed an hour ago with Liza. Neither commented on where they were going or when they'd be back. Thankfully, Ron hadn't been with Liza when she arrived and still hadn't appeared today. As desperate as Kathy was for company, she was ready to dodge the octopus.

After polishing her front windows twice, Kathy slumped onto a stool and set her glass cleaner and cloth on the service bar. She rested her elbow on the gleaming walnut bar, placed her chin in her hand, and huffed. Her chalet dinner engagement at seven loomed into the future like an elusive event that would never materialize.

The dull sunlight filtering through heavy gray clouds did nothing to appease Kathy's impatience. She scowled toward the cool mist that had begun at eight. The near-invisible droplets hung in the air like eternal minutes forever suspended in time. A lone Chevy pickup cruised the deserted street and braked in front of the feed store. The elk weren't even around today!

Groaning, Kathy checked her digital watch: 12:16. She laid

her arm on the service bar and rested her forehead against her forearm. "This day is never gonna end!" She stared at the dark wood grain, only centimeters from her eyes. The scent of her citrus body spray entwined with the pungent odor from the damp dust cloth lying nearby.

Her labored mind searched for another project to tackle. Nothing came to her. The store was in tiptop shape. Her apartment, as usual, was a wreck, but Kathy found no desire to do a thing about it. The only thing she could conjure that interested her was preparing her outfit for tonight.

During Alaina's visit Wednesday evening, they agreed that Kathy should wear the new pants she'd purchased at Walmart, and they settled on a nice top—casual, but not too casual.

Kathy raised her head and eyed the door. The Chevy pickup was still the only vehicle in sight. After brief deliberation, Kathy made her choice.

"This is my store," she mumbled. "I can close for lunch if I want to." She hopped from the stool and found a piece of paper and a magic marker near the cash register. Kathy scrawled, "Gone to lunch. Be back at 1:30" on the paper and taped it to the door. After turning the deadbolt, she switched her sign to "Closed" and trotted up the stairs.

She breezed into her apartment, stepped over a laundry basket burgeoning with towels, and headed straight for her bedroom. Lucy reigned from her usual spot on Kathy's pillow surrounded by a chaos of covers. The cat lifted her head, yawned, stretched, and blinked at Kathy.

"Hey there, Lucy," Kathy crooned. "Surprised to see me home at this time?" She neared the bed and plopped beside her furry friend. Kathy rubbed Lucy's ears, and the cat purred her enjoyment. With a final pat on Lucy's back, Kathy rose and pivoted toward her closet door where her pants were hanging on a hook.

Before she took one step, her attention shifted to the laptop nestled on her dresser in a mound of clothes that had started as a neat pile but was now a mound of T-shirts mingled with jeans and shorts and underwear, plus the *Setting Boundaries* book that had found its way there after she finished her second read-through. But putting away her clothes or studying the liberating book could never propel Kathy like the laptop.

"I should have taken this to work with me this morning," she mumbled and couldn't believe she hadn't thought of it before now. Kathy had fallen asleep last night at midnight while revising the mystery novel she'd abandoned months ago. When she awoke at one o'clock, Kathy shut the laptop without turning it off.

Now she picked up the computer and settled onto the side of the bed. After sliding the latch, she lifted the screen and the laptop came to life. Kathy drank in the most recent lines she'd penned on the book once titled *The Castle*. As of eleven last night, the title was *The Chalet*.

Kathy kicked off her loafers, scooted to the head of the bed, propped two pillows behind her, and reveled in the rush of expectation. Revisiting the book had been far more stimulating than starting it had ever been. Kathy now had a real-life mystery on which to base the plot, and a real-life Colorado town where the story could unfold. She'd changed the name Northpointe Village to Northington Village; the name Ben to Barry. Kathy became Kay, and Alaina was Alissa. Last night the only thing that halted her word flow was her own exhaustion.

She considered the basis for her latest scene—none other than the encounter with that weird Thurston Manley. Even though Kathy looked over her shoulder every time she entered and exited her business, she hadn't seen Thurston since the day he'd told her Zachariah Tilman murdered his wife. Now Thurston Manley's creepy words took on new life as Kathy wove them into her manuscript. She devoured the latest scene while her mind raced with new plot possibilities:

> "If you have any sense at all, you'd stay away from that Taylor bunch," the man threatened.
>
> "I would?" Kay asks.
>
> "You will." He doesn't blink. "Zebediah Taylor's wife was *killed* by him."
>
> Kay's eyes got really big. She relived the talk she had with Barry. He said Alissa was overprotected by his father. But what if Alissa knew her mother was killed by her father, and Zebediah didn't want her telling the truth?
>
> "You're sure?" Kay questions. The chalet seemed darker and darker.
>
> "Sure?" The guy rubs the heel of his boot on the sidewalk. He pulls a flask from his pocket. . . .

The scene continued. Kathy's writing flowed anew, unchecked, unedited, much loved. When the opportunity came for Kathy to introduce her hero, Barry, she alloted two pages to his description alone. His eyes were as blue as Ben's, his smile as captivating. Her Barry was a pastor, of course. And he hadn't the first clue about how to do the Charleston.

Kathy giggled and relished the character she'd created. Her gaze shifted from the computer screen to the rumpled bedclothes as she daydreamed about the first kiss between the hero and heroine. As far as she was concerned, that scene couldn't happen soon enough. Deciding to skip ahead in the novel to the first kiss scene, Kathy scrolled down a page and held her breath.

She closed her eyes and twitched her sock-clad toes against the sheet. Her heart pounded as she imagined Ben's lips on hers. Nothing could be more thrilling . . . unless they were being stalked by a killer in a dark, twisted jungle. With a convinced nod, Kathy decided her hero and heroine's first kiss would definitely be in a jungle infested by boa constrictors and huge apes and crocodiles.

Nothing else will do, she thought and didn't bother to figure out how she was going to justify a boa-infested jungle in the Rockies.

She opened her eyes and positioned her fingers on the keyboard. Kathy had barely typed her first letter when the phone rang. She jumped and squealed. Lucy lifted her head and released a startled "Meow."

"Oh my word!" Kathy laid her hand across her chest. "Lucy, what are you going to do with me?" she asked and reached across her bed for her phone. After fumbling to swipe it on, she managed to answer with a breathless, "Hello."

"Kathy?" a male voice questioned. He sounded so much like Ben Tilman, Kathy debated whether he really was Ben or her imagination was on a tangent.

"Y-yes, this is Kathy Moore," she stuttered and shifted the laptop to the bed.

"This is Ben."

"Ben?" she squeaked.

"Yes. I'm down here outside your store. Your sign says you're closed until one thirty. It's two o'clock. Is everything okay?"

"It's two?" Kathy checked her watch, which validated Ben's claim.

"Yes," he drawled.

"You're downstairs *now*?" Kathy moved to her knees and began finger-combing her hair.

"Yes. I was just going to my dad's for tonight's dinner party. I'm early on purpose—wanted to visit with him and my brother awhile. Phil—that's my brother—came in yesterday. He's on leave from the army. Anyway, Dad asked me to stop and get some

coffee on my way. He's out and wants some for dinner tonight.
I thought I'd buy a bag of your gourmet stuff."

"Oh, yes! Right! Sure!" Kathy exclaimed and scrambled to
the bed's edge. "I just came up here to, uh . . ." She glanced
to the rumpled slacks still hanging on the closet door's hook.
"I've had almost no business today, so I came up to my apartment for a lunch break." Her legs unsteady, Kathy rounded the
bed. Her stomach rumbled. Her head suddenly felt light. The
phone trembled in her hand. "Except I didn't eat," she rushed.
"Now I'm hungry." *Great! What a time for my blood sugar to be
dropping*, she thought and decided to grab a slice of cheese on
the way out the door.

"If you like, I can go to The Diner on the Corner and get us
some burgers. I haven't had lunch, either."

"You'd do that?" she blurted and dared hope this might be
their first date.

"Well . . . yes," Ben said. "It's not that big of a deal. I'd do it
for anyone."

"Right," Kathy agreed and swallowed her disappointment.
"Okay, well, you go on and get the burgers. By the time you get
back, I'll have the door open."

"Great!"

"Don't worry about drinks. I've got those in the store."

"Okay. Do you want fries?"

Kathy's stomach growled like a rabid mountain lion. "Yes—
lots of 'em."

"Got it covered!" Ben said.

The second Kathy hung up, she looked at Lucy. "Oh my
word, he's here!" she squawked. "Now what?"

The cat answered with a golden-eyed blink.

"A lot of help you are!" Kathy complained. She moved to her
dresser mirror and examined her appearance. Her hair, fluffed
from the finger-combing, wasn't half bad. But as usual Kathy

hadn't bothered with makeup this morning, and she wore a white T-shirt with a pair of jeans.

Kathy grimaced. "I look sixteen again!" she complained and raced into her bathroom. Within fifteen minutes, she'd slapped on a light layer of makeup and volumized her wedged hair with some mousse and a hair dryer. She finished the look with a light application of spritzer and prayed the whole thing didn't flop. She managed to change into a short-sleeved sweater without rumpling her hair, and decided the jeans would have to do. Kathy finished with a generous mist of the citrus body spray along her arms and neck. Not bothering to put up the hair dryer, makeup, or hair-care products, Kathy tossed the body spray into the mix on the counter and headed for the bathroom door.

When she passed the toilet, her bare toes encountered something wet. Kathy looked down. A small puddle of water oozed from behind the toilet. "Oh, great!" she griped. Closer inspection revealed that the intermittent drip she'd noticed near the wall water valve last night had grown to a steady drip. Kathy reached for the towel she'd dried off with that morning. It lay crumpled near the overflowing trash basket. She mopped up the puddle and left the towel beneath the drip.

The memory of Ben's admonishment about a plumber nibbled the back of her mind. Fleetingly, she considered phoning a plumber but decided it could wait until tomorrow. *I can't think about plumbing at a time like this!* she fumed and dismissed the whole problem.

After slipping on her loafers, Kathy zipped from her bedroom. On the way out the door she grabbed a thick slice of deli cheddar. Her hands trembling, she crammed a fourth of it into her mouth and hoped the protein at least partially steadied her blood sugar before Ben arrived with the burgers. Once, she'd read something about men not liking women who inhaled their food. Presently, Kathy's shaking metabolism was so desperate for sustenance she didn't trust herself not to beat Ben up for his burger after eating her own.

By the time she descended the stairs and unlocked the store door, the cheese was history. She considered the bag of pretzels by her store fridge, but a glimpse of Ben exiting The Diner on the Corner ended all chances of a pretzel encounter.

After a dull, wet morning, the mist had cleared. The sun christened the town with liquid gold. Like a flying flower, a yellow butterfly flitted toward Kathy's store and darted up the street. The snow-tipped mountains towering in the distance had never seemed more picturesque. It was as if Ben's very presence had metamorphosed nature itself.

"What'll I do? What'll I do?" She fidgeted with nothing and brushed her dampening palms along the front of her jeans. While the cheese was already taking the edge off her desperate hunger, her hands still quaked, her body continued to demand more protein.

Look calm! Look natural! she told herself and raced toward the service bar.

Kathy dropped onto the customer stool nearest the front window and tried to appear casual while straining for another glimpse of Ben. Her efforts weren't in vain. He was halfway down the block. Dressed in a pair of pleated shorts and a polo shirt, he held a white burger bag and steadily strode forward.

She touched her hair, smoothed her sweater, and rubbed her hands together. *Whoever heard of a store owner sitting around like this?* she worried and decided she couldn't be more conspicuous. Kathy raced toward the cash register, grabbed the feather duster, and trotted to a nearby bookshelf. With her back to the door, she fluffed the feathers along the dust-free shelf.

Then she thought of the sodas she'd said she would supply for lunch. With the feather duster posed in midair, she thought, *Ben's going to think it's weird if I'm dusting and the sodas aren't ready!*

Kathy hurried back toward the cash register, flung the duster next to it, and slipped behind the bar.

When she opened the refrigerator, the doorbell clanged. Feigning leagues of composure, Kathy turned to face Ben. "Hi!" she said.

Seventeen

"Hey," Ben replied with a smile powerful enough to stop an avalanche. "Ready to eat?" He closed the door and neared the service bar. "I'm starved. I nearly stopped on the way and ate both burgers."

Kathy's heart thudded. The last time she talked with Ben was the night they'd attempted the Charleston. From the start of that whole evening, he'd been kind, considerate, yet constrained. Only when she helped Ben to his feet had his constraint slipped to reveal a dash of admiration that took Kathy's breath and made her want to kiss him.

Now the doting light in his eyes was identical to what Kathy had glimpsed after the Charleston. And it had the same effect. The boa-infested jungle kiss scene pranced through her mind. Kathy prayed her imagination wasn't playing tricks on her. The refrigerator air oozing against her torso was real enough. The closer Ben grew, the more she was convinced his jaunty appraisal lacked constraint and revealed that the guy was every bit as attracted to her as she was to him.

He set the white bag on the counter and said, "What do you have to drink in there?"

"To drink?" Kathy rasped.

"Didn't you say you'd supply the drinks?"

"The drinks! Oh yes, the sodas!" she exclaimed and pivoted toward the open refrigerator. "Let's see, there's root beer—"

"Sounds fine!" Ben stated. "Anything—as long as it's wet."

160

She grabbed a brown, long-necked bottle and a can of Caffeine-free Diet Coke for herself. The last thing she needed was caffeine and sugar. *No telling what I might say if I get revved on caffeine. I might propose or something,* she thought and swallowed a giddy giggle.

Kathy closed the fridge and braced herself before facing Ben again. Chances were high he wasn't half as thrilled to see her as he'd first appeared. Her palpitating heart insisted she was wrong.

"One root beer," she said. With the smells of beef and fries sending her stomach into flips, Kathy pressed the bottle cap into the opener fastened beneath the bar. She tilted the root beer. The cap clinked into the box beneath the opener, and Kathy placed the soda near his hand.

Without making eye contact, she set her Coke across from Ben and reached for the only stool she kept behind the bar. After dragging the stool close, she plopped onto it.

"Here's your burger," Ben said and extended the sandwich wrapped in plain brown paper.

Keeping her gaze down, she reached for the burger and gripped it, only to have Ben cover her other hand with his. Kathy's fingers flexed. While she managed to swallow her gasp, she couldn't stop herself from looking him full in the face.

Even though concern clouded his eyes, Kathy could no longer hope his constraint had vanished. The hour of hoping was past. She was flung into accepting her assumption as fact. Ben had somehow changed his mind about her being a possible girlfriend. A thrill surged through Kathy and nearly knocked her flat.

"You're really shaking," he said. "Are you okay?"

"I'm starved," Kathy admitted with a dizzy grin that felt as goofy as her cavorting emotions. "I have low blood sugar," she rushed. "I usually keep it under control, but I've blown it today. I didn't eat much breakfast, and here I am eating a late lunch."

"By all means, let's eat, then!" Ben insisted. "I got both our burgers fully loaded. Hope that's fine."

"Whatever you did is *fine*," Kathy affirmed, crinkling wrappers punctuating her words.

"Oh, I *did* have them cut the onions. I can't stand them, and I decided to play it safe with you."

"That's fine, but I *love* onions. I'd eat 'em with my pancakes if I could."

Ben laughed, bit his burger, and chewed. Kathy forgot whatever she read about men not liking women who inhaled their food and gobbled her burger. The taste of tomatoes and lettuce and mustard had never been so appealing. Neither spoke again until after their last bite.

Her trembling subsiding, Kathy guzzled her cold soda and observed the bag. "Are the fries in the bag?" she said.

"Yes. Two extra-large orders." Ben winked and went for the sack. "I like to see a woman with an appetite," he said.

"Then you must be beyond thrilled now," Kathy teased and dabbed the corner of her mouth with a napkin.

Ben chuckled. "I guess you could say that." He pulled out an order of fries and passed them to Kathy.

"When my blood sugar drops like that, I feel like I could eat cow patties and love 'em." She set the fries on the counter.

He laughed again and looked into her eyes. "You mentioned at the cookout that you have low blood sugar. Is that a big problem with you?"

"No, not usually. I've learned to control it by eating right. But sometimes I don't."

A companionable silence settled between them, and Kathy popped a salty fry into her mouth.

"You know what I like about you, Kathy Moore?" Ben asked.

"What?" Kathy drank in his doting blue eyes, pinched a fry, and decided this was indeed a date.

"You always make me laugh."

Kathy's loafer slipped off and she realized she'd been rubbing her foot against the stool's rung. She didn't bother to retrieve the shoe.

"By the way, you look great!" Ben's gaze slid to her hair and roved her face.

"Thanks," Kathy said and hoped she didn't have pink lip gloss smeared across her cheek or a chunk of lettuce dangling from her mouth.

Ben looked away and rotated his root beer bottle in his fingers. His lips hardened with a hint of the old constraint, and Kathy prepared herself for the inevitable rejection. A flash of unexpected irritation heated Kathy's gut, and she lost interest in the fries. Nearly every time she encountered Ben Tilman, he somehow managed to make her hope they could be together, and then he destroyed all expectation.

"I'm looking forward to tonight," he said, his tone less animated. "Dad's really interested in meeting you."

"Really?" Kathy asked, her voice flat.

Ben looked up and briefly narrowed his eyes. "Yes," he answered. His lips twisted a bit. "Don't sound so excited," he taunted. Despite his light tone, his open admiration was now replaced by restraint.

Kathy turned away, but not before Ben detected the red splotches marring her cheeks. Her back stiff, she crumpled her burger wrapper, stalked toward the waste can, and tossed the wad inside. While Ben never claimed to be an expert regarding women, he wasn't a dunce, either. Something had angered Kathy—something he'd done. Maybe he'd presumed too much when he assumed Kathy was keeping the dinner date tonight.

"You are coming tonight, aren't you?" he asked.

"Sure," she said. Her back to him, Kathy walked toward a

coffee display at the end of the service bar near the front window. She reached across the bar and retrieved a gold foil bag from the display's top section.

"I'm sending the coffee, compliments of yours truly." Her rigid smile matched the blank stare she aimed just past him. While the splotches were fading from her cheeks, Kathy's face had never been more rigid. She plopped the gold bag near his arm, reached beneath the counter, and pulled out a small wooden box full of soda bottle caps.

Ben gripped his cold root beer, and Kathy dumped the bottle caps into the waste can. As the caps clinked into the receptacle, he relived the last half hour. From the minute Ben offered to buy Kathy's lunch, he argued himself into believing the impromptu date was "something he'd do for anyone." When he opened the store door, he'd expected to encounter the "energetic adolescent" Kathy; instead, he had been captivated by the "pretty woman" Kathy. Ben had been as taken aback by Kathy's appearance as he had the Sunday she visited his church. His argument that the burgers were "something he'd do for anyone" dissolved.

Before Ben realized it, his glib tongue had overtaken his commitment to constrain all flirtation until he determined tonight if his father liked Kathy. That had been the original plan, but he was trapped in the throes of unguarded admiration before he knew what hit him. The unchecked hero worship oozing from Kathy had sealed his doom. But the mere thought of Kathy meeting his dad jolted Ben back to harsh reality. The last thing he wanted was verbal violence and in-law friction for the next twenty to thirty years. If Zachariah Tilman didn't like Kathy, there was no sense in his even thinking of her as a potential wife.

Potential wife! he croaked to himself and stiffened. *I've only known her six weeks! It's crazy to even think in those terms!* Ben

downed a mouthful of root beer and wished the sting would cata-
pult him into saying something clever—something that would
pave his way to a swift and painless exit.

Kathy turned from the trash can. Head lowered, she scraped
the box into place under the bar.

"Did I—Did I make you mad or something, Kathy?" Ben
stammered. *Well, obviously, you idiot!* he taunted himself.

Eyes narrowed, she peered at him and never flinched.

Ben winced and shrugged. "Sorry . . . whatever it is."

Kathy balled her fist near the fries. "I just don't get you," she
finally said.

"What do you mean?" he asked and couldn't have felt more
ridiculous. And yet he couldn't stop his feet from walking to
her.

Her face pinched, Kathy leaned toward him and scrutinized
him. The intensity of her appraisal scared the stuffing out of Ben.
If she looked too closely, Kathy might see just how enamored
he was with her. She might detect traces of those crazy dreams
he'd endured . . . enjoyed . . . the last few nights—dreams that
always ended with Kathy in his arms, his lips on hers.

A hot rush of anticipation insisted Ben should make those
dreams a reality. Right here. Right now. The traces of adoration
still lingering behind Kathy's irritation increased the magnetism.
Suddenly the Reverend Ben Tilman sympathized with Samson as
never before. The power of this growing attraction was enough
to make him let Kathy Moore shave him bald and paint nail-
polish polka dots all over his fingernails *and* toenails.

The Ladies Auxiliary would not be happy with me! Ben thought
and just as quickly dismissed the notion. He had decided two
days ago to quit worrying about what those ladies—and, for that
matter, everyone else—thought.

Everyone except my father, he reminded himself.

As Kathy's gaze melded with his, as the ire drained from her, as her features softened with wonder, even that reality faded from Ben. All that mattered was Kathy—his Kathy—begging to be kissed. Ben didn't realize his hand was trembling until he touched her cheek. She closed her eyes. Ben inched nearer and admonished himself to keep the kiss short and sweet.

Sweet it was. But short? Never!

Tugged into the river of Kathy's soul, Ben lingered, relishing every nuance of the encounter . . . the feel of her lips against his . . . the smell of her summery fragrance . . . the impact of her sigh. He relived every encounter he'd enjoyed with Kathy. She'd tickled his fancy that rainy night she let him use her phone. At the community cookout, he'd entertained thoughts of how cute she was—despite the fact that he'd convinced himself she was too young. And Ben had never laughed so hard as he did the evening she bounced around her kitchen and later knocked him flat during the Charleston.

Now Kathy was once again delivering the unexpected with a kiss that insisted she was all woman and in no way the adolescent she could appear to be. Ben longed to tarry in the web of ardor, but as with all good things, the kiss gradually came to an end. When he pulled away, Ben stopped within centimeters of Kathy. She stared at him in astounded silence. Ben didn't figure he looked any less shocked.

Now what? The unspoken question hung between them, demanding an answer—an answer Ben did not have. Kathy didn't, either, if her stunned expression was anything to go by.

Ben had never planned this. At least not today. Not now. He'd purposed to take everything slowly. He detested his own weakness.

"I—I'm sorry." He edged away.

Kathy blinked. "It's okay," she whispered. A shy smile revealed her endearing dimples and made Ben want to kiss her all over again. "I . . ." she swallowed, "enjoyed it."

No joke, Ben thought. "Me too," he said, sounding every bit as enthused as Kathy looked. *I might as well buy an engagement ring now,* he scoffed. The very thought of marriage sent Ben to his feet. A wave of heat instigated his clutching the front of his polo shirt and fanning himself with the shirt.

When an unyielding voice urged him to grab Kathy and kiss her again, Ben stumbled backward. Kathy's expression guaranteed she'd heard the same voice. *What have I done?* he thought. *If Dad doesn't like her . . .*

Maybe I could keep the relationship a secret like Alaina, he reasoned. Thoughts of sneaking around behind his father's back brought to mind Alaina's fall. The *last* thing Ben needed was that level of temptation. His whole ministry loomed before him. Ben rubbed his tender forehead, his eyes, his face.

"Ben?" Kathy's uncertainty twisted his gut. He never wanted to hurt or confuse her. From their first meeting, he'd celebrated her whimsical nature. Kathy Moore was like a spring breeze: cool, fresh, pure.

She's also eight years younger than I am, and I should have been mature enough to exercise constraint. As things stood, Ben figured there was plenty of opportunity for her to believe an older man had taken advantage of her youthful innocence—especially if tonight didn't go well. *She'll be calling me the biggest cad of the century by sunup tomorrow.*

"I've got to go," he mumbled out and didn't bother to explain.

Kathy's lips drooped. Her brow wrinkled. She toyed with the French fry box.

"I'll see you tonight, I guess," he continued and softened his words with a mild smile.

"Okay," she agreed, a veil of confusion clouding her eyes.

"Well, okay, then," Ben echoed and didn't move.

"Don't forget the coffee." She extended the foil bag.

As Ben took the coffee, the doorbell's chime spurred him to action. Head ducked, Ben dashed for the store door. While he received the vague impression of a familiar person entering the store, Ben was so agitated he didn't register the significance of the man's presence.

Eighteen

Reeling from the kiss, Kathy watched Ben leave and didn't bother to acknowledge the customer. She looked down and realized she'd tortured a French fry into tiny bits. In a breath, Kathy recalled the unexpected kiss—a kiss that obliterated the memory of every passing crush she'd ever experienced for any other guy. This attraction to Ben Tilman was far more than infatuation.

Am I falling in love with him? Dazed, she stared out the window until she captured the last glimpse of Ben hurrying from the store. Briefly she went through a mental list, checking off the qualities of the man she would like to marry.

A man of strong faith and high moral character. Check.
Someone who's dedicated to the church. Check.
A person I can respect. Check.
A hard worker. Check.
A guy who's balanced and mature. Check.
Someone who knows who he is. Check.
He has to be willing to accept and respect me the way I am. Check.

Ben Tilman fit everything Kathy wanted in a husband. Everything and more. Kathy nibbled one of the salty fries as a disturbing realization trotted through her mind. *I'm expecting more spirituality from my future husband than I'm living.* While Kathy lived high morals, she wasn't so certain if the faith she knew was her own or her parents'. *And I don't even want to think about my dedication to church these days.*

Deciding the vein of her thoughts was too disturbing, Kathy went back to Ben. *On top of everything else, he's also attractive, a good dresser, and charming*, she thought. *With blue eyes that make me melt . . . and a kiss that rocks.* Kathy touched her lips.

But he can be really weird and unpredictable. She frowned. Kathy could no longer doubt that Ben was drawn to her, but something about the attraction disturbed him. What, Kathy couldn't determine.

Maybe I'll figure it out tonight, she thought, *or maybe Alaina will give me a clue.*

"You don't listen very well, do ya?" a gravelly voice challenged.

Kathy jumped and looked toward the person.

Thurston Manley placed both hands on the service bar and leaned toward her. Riveted by his gnarled features, Kathy stepped back until she bumped into the counter. Tempted to scream for help, she reminded herself there was no one to hear. Simultaneously, Kathy was astounded the man had slipped in without her noticing who he was.

"I know where yer goin' tonight." The smell of tobacco wove through Thurston's claim.

"Y-you do?" Kathy stuttered and noticed a pack of thin cigars sagging from his shirt pocket.

"You bet I do," Thurston drawled. "You're goin' to that darned chalet I tol' you to stay away from." His evil eye gave her the willies. While Kathy wanted to look away, she could not find the strength.

"H-how do you know that?"

"I've lived in this town my whole life. Nothin's a secret 'round here! Get used to it. If ya sneeze, the whole town'll know it by sundown."

Kathy remained silent. Her heart pounding in her throat, she debated which was more formidable—the chalet owner or Thurston Manley.

"I also know about you and Ben Tilman."

She gulped. "What about us?"

"You're sweet on each other, that's what! And you and Alaina are thick, too. She was at yer place 'til after 'leven the other night."

Gaping, Kathy wondered if he'd made spying on her his primary goal.

Thurston reached into his Western shirt's pocket, pulled out a pencil-thin cigar, and clamped it between his teeth.

Goose bumps crept along Kathy's back. "Why are you watching me?" she blurted. "You—you have no right."

He frowned, released an oath, and shifted the cigar. "I already tol' you!" he yelled through clamped teeth. "You look like her!" His eyes took on a crazed glare; his voice resonated with amazement. "Sometimes I even wonder if you *are* her—come back from the dead." Thurston's mouth twitched. The cigar jiggled.

Kathy gripped her throat and imagined her photo sprawled across the *Northpointe Gazette*'s front page with the headline reading, "New Northpointe businesswoman murdered in her own store." An unexpected whimper leaked from Kathy's lips.

"What's the matter with you?" Thurston bellowed and yanked the cigar from his mouth. "You don't need to be scared o' *me*!" He jabbed his finger against his stained shirt. "It's that no-'count murderer up the hill you need to worry about!" He pounded his fist on the bar, making Ben's root beer bottle dance.

Kathy started and yelped. She glanced toward the cordless phone near the end of the bar. Kathy calculated she could be at the phone in five giant steps. The police station was only two blocks away. She jerked her attention back to Thurston.

"When Zachariah Tilman gets you in his claws, ya can't say I didn't warn you!" Thurston's prediction hissed out like a crocodile smelling meat.

He lunged at the service bar as if he were going to crawl across it. The cigar was crushed beneath his work-worn fingers—fingers that took on the crook of river reptile talons. Kathy pressed herself against the back counter until it ate into her flesh.

"Yore crazy to be messin' around with those Tilman kids. Crazy!" With another pound on the service bar, Thurston glared at her for a final challenge. "All I'm tryin' to do is stop you from gettin' killed like she did!" he screeched.

Too scared to reply, Kathy compulsively swallowed and begged God to make the maniac go away.

"Fine, then!" Thurston backed down from the bar and lifted his hands in disgust. "Have it yer way. Don't listen to me! When they lay ya in yer coffin, you'll regret it!"

But I'd be dead, Kathy pondered. *How could I regret it if I'm dead?* The thought penetrated her fear and offered an avenue of release—in a wacky, tangled sort of way. An unexpected giggle, rooted in delirium, trickled through her shaking lips.

Thurston's dreadful scowl suggested she should stop.

The very idea that she *should* stop increased Kathy's need to laugh. Her initial giggle grew into a chortle. The chortle merged into a hysterical cackle. "I won't regret it when I'm in my coffin," she wheezed out, voicing her sarcastic thoughts. "How can I regret it? I'll be dead!"

Thurston's leathery face flashed red. He shook both fists at Kathy and released a primitive growl.

Every scrap of laughter vanished. She covered her mouth with her hand and held her breath.

The old man whipped around and stomped toward the door, his worn boots pounding out a dreadful rhythm. He flung open the door, trudged outside, and slammed the door.

Kathy released her breath. "Oh, God, help me," she whispered and slumped against the counter.

In the excitement of being with Ben at the dinner party to-night, the chalet and all its secrets had seemed a secondary concern. Now the whole mystery mingled with the excitement of Ben's ardent kiss. She imagined herself trapped in the chalet's dark corridors with the blood-thirsty Zachariah Tilman chasing her. She had no one to turn to . . . no one to help her . . . until Ben appeared, scooped her in his arms, and carried her through a hidden doorway to the safety of sunshine.

A foreboding shiver wracked her body. Kathy had moved to Northpointe to find adventure . . . intrigue . . . romance. It looked like *they'd* found *her*.

That evening Kathy drove her Impala along the winding stretch of road up Northpointe Mountain. Even though the blazing sun inched toward the horizon, there might as well have been a treacherous storm underway. A cloak of doom, as dense as a bank of storm clouds, settled on Kathy's soul. The closer she drew to the chalet, the more she felt like an island maiden being tugged to the precipice of a volcano where she would be hurled into its mouth as a human sacrifice to appease the gods.

Not only did her arrival at Northpointe Chalet terrify, it also mesmerized. While Zachariah Tilman had taken on demon-sized proportions, Kathy could hardly wait to see Ben again. With every passing hour, the memory of their kiss had grown more poignant and pleasing. Kathy could only hope Ben would be inclined to repeat the gesture . . . if he could overcome whatever it was that continued to trouble him in regard to her.

Kathy rounded the route's final bend and spotted the driveway to the chalet beside a large brick mailbox, just like Alaina had described. She hung a right and steered her trusty vehicle across the graveled driveway lined with oaks and aspens. The drive ended in a circular parking area where several vehicles already resided. Kathy recognized Alaina's Volkswagen and Ben's cream-colored Toyota Corolla. A black Hummer and a taupe Chevy truck also claimed spots in the graveled circle. Kathy didn't know who the truck belonged to, but she figured the Hummer's owner must be Zachariah Tilman. The vehicle's square structure reminded Kathy of an army tank and was perfect for someone who'd once been a military officer.

Dots of perspiration attacked Kathy's upper lip despite the air conditioner's cool blast. An invisible tremor danced along her nerves, and Kathy forced herself to put her Impala into park, turn off the engine, and get out. She clutched her duffel purse to her midsection, shut her door, and began the trek to the home's long, railed porch. The smell of grilled beef mingled with the cool mountain air and suggested the evening was nothing more than a gathering of new friends. Kathy knew differently. While friendship definitely played into the scheme of things, the presence of Zachariah Tilman sealed the evening with the kiss of mystery. Thurston Manley's repeated warnings knotted her stomach, and Kathy began to pray as she'd never prayed in her life.

Her high-heeled boots crunched across the gravel as she sized up the chalet she'd lived in dread and awe of ever since the day she arrived in Northpointe Village. Her neck muscles stiff, Kathy absorbed the vast cedar exterior, numerous windows, and Swiss-style roof that draped across the third story. Never had she imagined the place could be any bigger than what she'd conjured in her mind. But as she stepped onto the long porch, the home loomed larger than life.

Despite her attempts to be silent, her boots tapped along the porch with a telltale staccato that Kathy was certain they must have heard in downtown Northpointe. A surprised "Woof!" echoed from the end of the porch, and Kathy realized her mistake too late. A giant black beast arose from his snooze and bounded forward, his meaty tongue rolling from his jowls like the hound of the Baskervilles. Kathy's scrambling retreat was no match for the canine's pace. Before she realized his intent, the panting dog bounded forward and jumped at her.

By divine miracle, Kathy managed to sidestep the attack. Too scared to even scream, she maneuvered a swift pivot, only to dangerously wobble on her heels. While the dog's playful prance and joyous yelp indicated he meant no harm, his friendly bump knocked Kathy off balance and sent her into a forward topple. By the time her knees crashed into the porch's cedar floor, the black canine was whining and attempting to lick her face with a tongue the size of a dinner plate. His breath couldn't have smelled worse—dog spit and beef chews.

When his tongue connected with her ear, Kathy raised her arm and tried to push against the calf-sized animal. "Stop! No!" she wailed and imagined all the hard work on her appearance being gobbled up in an ocean of canine slobber.

"Duncan!" an abrupt voice commanded. "Back, boy! Back!"

With a pathetic whine, the oversized puppy inched away from Kathy, lay down, and rested his head on his paws. Her knees burning, Kathy lowered her arm.

A man's steady gait boomed across the porch. Kathy looked up into a pair of blue eyes every bit as kind as Ben's, except this man's eyes were lined in deep crow's-feet that spoke of years of wisdom . . . and maybe sorrow. His silver-streaked dark hair winged away from his broad forehead in an attractive wave. His square jaw and prominent nose bespoke a man of strength and character.

"You're Kathy Moore, I presume?" The man squatted beside her. He wore a chef's apron over stiff jeans and a Western shirt, and he smelled of grilled beef.

"Y-yes," she stammered.

"I'm Zachariah Tilman," he said with a roguish, white-toothed smile.

Kathy gasped and inched away from him. Everything Thurston Manley said crashed to the front of her mind. But in the middle of all the warnings and predictions came a thought that would not be ignored: *He doesn't* look *like a murderer!*

"No need to be scared," Zachariah said and laid his assuring hand on her shoulder. "I'm not like Duncan," he gruffly teased. "I don't try to lick our guests' faces."

With a timid smile, Kathy accepted Zachariah's callused hand and allowed him to help her to her feet.

"I don't know why all you gals these days think you have to wear shoes with mile-high heels," he groused. "Alaina's got some that raise her altitude so high, I'm sure she'll have a nosebleed."

Adept at saying what she was thinking, Kathy quipped, "Well, not if she doesn't stick the heels up her nose."

Zachariah tilted his head back and laughed. His rich tenor bounced along the porch in a celebration of mirth.

Kathy emitted a weak chuckle while brushing the smudges of porch dust from her trousers. *Wonderful,* she thought, *the man has what every successful murderer needs—a sense of humor.*

"Oh my goodness." Zachariah placed his hand on his forehead in a gesture similar to Ben's. "I haven't laughed that hard in ages. Ben's right," he said with an accepting light in his eyes. "You're a keeper!"

"He is? I am?" Kathy blurted and forgot about her stinging knees. "Ben—he—he said that?"

The front door opened. Still dressed in the shorts and polo shirt, Ben rushed onto the porch. "Kathy!" he called and strode forward as the screen door whacked behind him. "I was watching for you. How'd I miss you?"

"I don't know," Kathy said and tried to straighten her disheveled jacket. She touched something damp along the neck of her cinnamon-colored top and figured it was dog drool. *Oh, great!* she thought. *How attractive is that?*

Ben stopped a few feet away, dubiously examined his father, then hesitantly smiled. "Great to see you again." Even though his eyes were full of caution, they stirred with a warmth that suggested he hadn't forgotten their kiss—not by a long shot. "You look great!"

"Thanks." Kathy touched her hair and wondered how well the spritzer held this time. "Duncan thought so, too."

At the mention of his name, the dog released a worried whine and thumped his tail against the porch. A breeze swished through the trees, offering nature's music in perfect rhythm with Duncan's tempo.

"When I came around the house, he was on top of her trying to lick her face off," Zachariah rumbled.

"We have a rule around here," Ben said through a chuckle. "If you survive our welcoming committee, you're worthy of dinner. If not, we make you go back home."

"Well, I should get a whole side of beef," Kathy chirped.

Ben's dad didn't hold back another guffaw.

"Didn't Alaina and I tell you she's a hoot!" Ben exclaimed.

"I was just saying I think she's a keeper, just like you said," Zachariah enthused and slapped his son on the back.

Zachariah slipped his hand above Kathy's elbow and propelled her toward the door, leaving Ben behind. "I'll get you inside," he said, "and show you where the restroom is. If you're anything like Alaina, I have a feeling you'll want to freshen up after that roll on the porch."

Kathy looked over her shoulder at Ben, who was gawking at his father. She cut a swift glance toward Zachariah's face, lined, tanned, and handsome. All these weeks Kathy had imagined him shriveled and warted and bent like an evil being from a horror tale. In reality, Zachariah looked like a cowboy model she'd seen in a magazine ad for Bush's Baked Beans. The last thing she'd ever expected her murderer to do was protect her, laugh at her, and immediately like her. Not knowing what else to do, Kathy allowed Zachariah to urge her toward the chalet's doorway.

But as he opened the screen door, Kathy remembered a very important element from every mystery novel she'd ever read. The murderer always turned out to be the least suspicious character. She clutched her purse and made a mental note not to allow Zachariah to charmingly dupe her into believing he could never be guilty. Too many amateur detectives in too many novels made that mistake—a mistake that could be fatal.

Stupefied, Ben stared at his father and Kathy as they entered the chalet. Zachariah Tilman almost never immediately accepted a newcomer. Ben had anticipated spending the evening searching for any clue about his dad's opinion of Kathy. Then, in about a week, he expected Zachariah to make some cryptic statement in favor of or against Kathy.

The only other time Zachariah had behaved so nicely was when their new next-door neighbors brought over a pecan pie as a get-acquainted offering a few months ago. Zachariah and the couple had sat in the porch's wooden rocking chairs and chatted until sundown. The thing Zachariah liked about them was what he'd referenced with Kathy. They made him laugh.

Maybe he's going soft in his old age, Ben thought and reminded himself that mid-sixties wasn't really all that old. He fingered the scar at his hairline as the implications of his father's actions settled into his mind. Ben's reason for not pursuing Kathy had just been swept aside in a matter of seconds.

Ever since his dad invited Kathy over, Ben had been trying to prepare his father for meeting her. He'd methodically dropped hints about her spontaneity and quick wit. Earlier this evening, when they were starting up the grill, Ben even dared to mention that he thought Kathy was a "keeper." His father had looked up from the grill and stared at Ben with a keen-eyed sharpness that implied Zachariah Tilman knew something was up. At that point, Ben had begun to worry that maybe he'd said too much.

But maybe he hadn't said enough . . . at least not to Kathy. And maybe he could remedy that tonight.

The screen door's clap jolted Ben back to the moment. The door opened again, and Zachariah peered out at his son. "Benjamin, are you going to just stand there like a zombie all night or what?" he barked.

"No." Ben hurried toward the doorway.

From inside, his elder brother Phil's voice boomed as forceful as his father's. "So this is the famous Kathy Moore? Glad to meet you. You're as gorgeous as your reputation."

An unexpected flame of jealousy burned Ben's stomach. Philip would be home for the next couple months. He was single, five years older than Ben, and ten times better looking—at least in Ben's eyes. Phil's popularity with the ladies had never bothered Ben . . . until now. The last thing he wanted was for his elder brother to so impress Kathy that she forgot him and that dynamite kiss they'd shared—a kiss Ben ached to repeat before the night was over.

Nineteen

Alaina opened the oven door and examined the twin apple pies. The crust was browning; the mixture beneath, bubbling. A few bits of apples protruded through the lattice-work crust. She closed the oven door, turned back to the counter beside the sink, and continued tearing the mixed greens.

She and her father and Ben had struck a deal on tonight's meal. Alaina was in charge of buying and baking the frozen pies and making the salad. Zachariah had volunteered to grill pork chops, chicken breasts, and ribs. Ben brought the rolls and drinks. When Phil got an unexpected leave from duty and showed up last night, he'd insisted on buying a boatload of potato salad at the deli.

Once her dad fired up the grill, the mixed smells of apple pies and succulent meats filled the kitchen. Normally, such scents would make Alaina's stomach rumble, but not tonight. Alaina had barely been able to eat since her father got home yesterday morning. With the glass bowl full of salad greens, Alaina wiped her fingers on the butcher's apron that covered her linen pants and sleeveless blouse. She reached for a plump tomato and relived her father's arrival yesterday morning.

After their usual hug, he'd scrutinized Alaina and said, "There's something different about you. Did you get a haircut or something?"

"No," Alaina had hedged and touched the ringlets Caleb so loved. "I changed makeup colors," she'd mumbled and begged

God that if He was still listening to her, He would make her father move to another subject. The makeup excuse was true. Alaina had visited the Clinique cosmetic counter the day before she and Caleb got married. In a fit of dizzy excitement, she'd bought all new products and a collection of vibrant colors they called "Summer Sunshine."

"Maybe that's it," Zachariah had rumbled before hauling his leather suitcases to his small second-floor bedroom. He'd moved from the third floor suite the day Alaina's mother died. The room remained as it had been during Laura Tilman's life. Nobody in the family was allowed to even mention going up there now. But that didn't stop Alaina from frequenting her mother's room while everyone else was sleeping.

She'd never missed her mom more than now. Laura Tilman would have known exactly how to break the news of Alaina's marriage. Alaina was at a complete loss. What seemed a grand idea in her father's absence now appeared an insurmountable obstacle.

She diced the tomato, dumped it into the glass bowl atop the greens, and stared out the opened kitchen window, framed in knotty pine. A refreshing breeze tumbled up the mountain and invaded the kitchen. It rustled the lace curtains and whisked in the scent of pine and earth. The smells reminded her of the day she and Caleb walked hand in hand along a secluded mountain stream. That memory ushered in another and another. Alaina closed her eyes and daydreamed about the last time she and Caleb were together. They'd danced around the Denver hotel room until they fell onto the bed in a tangle of laughter and love.

The next time they planned to meet was tomorrow afternoon—Saturday. He had the day off. Alaina was going to Denver for a "shopping trip." Of course, she *would* be making a trip to the mall . . . after she met Caleb at the hotel.

Alaina's hands quivered. She opened her eyes and noticed a

movement at the kitchen's edge. Alaina jerked toward the movement. Ben strode closer, his thick-soled sandals scuffing across the ceramic tile.

Her knees weakened, and she looked past her brother rather than into his eyes. Alaina hoped she could maintain the charade yet another day. This was the first time the two of them had been alone since Alaina's marriage nearly three weeks ago. If Ben suspected something was different about her, he might not be put off by her "new makeup" excuse. Even though she'd come within a breath of spilling her news to Kathy, Alaina was now glad she'd chosen not to tell. She didn't need to start her marriage breaking her word.

"Dad asked me to see how things are coming," Ben said. "He and Kathy and Phil are heading out to the grill to take the rest of the meat off."

"Kathy's here?" Alaina asked.

"Yes. I would have thought you'd heard her come in. She's been here about fifteen minutes."

"Oh." Alaina pulled out a nearby drawer and grabbed two wooden spoons. "I guess I'm in another world tonight. I didn't hear her." She attacked the salad and began ferociously tossing it.

Ben's silence increased Alaina's salad fervor. A sizable section erupted and plopped into the spotless sink. "Here, I've got that," Ben said.

"Thanks," Alaina said. "Wash your hands first."

"I just did in the bathroom, Miss Clean Freak," he teased while dumping the salad back into the bowl.

"Thanks," Alaina said and dared a glance up at her brother. At first glance, Ben's expression appeared as pleasant and supportive as ever. But the longer she looked at him, the more she absorbed the questions, the disillusionment, the tinge of pain that marred his gaze.

A burst of nausea spun through Alaina. Ben had never looked

at her like this before. She concentrated on the salad; it blurred through unshed tears.

"Believe it or not, I think Kathy's made an instant conquest of Dad," Ben drawled. "It took her three whole minutes."

"That's really good for you, isn't it?"

"Why would you think that?" Ben asked.

Alaina blinked away the tears and forced a laugh. "You two have it bad, that's all. Anybody can see it from a mile away. If Dad likes her, then the marriage is on."

"Marriage?" Ben blurted. "I'm just getting to know her."

Alaina watched from the corner of her eye as Ben leaned toward the window and strained to peer to the right, to where the grill was positioned.

A chorus of laughter floated in on the breeze. Alaina couldn't remember the last time she'd heard her father laugh so. *Not since before Mom died*, she thought.

"Problem is, I think Phil's as enamored as Dad," Ben complained.

"Hark, do I hear jealousy?" Alaina teased, and the nausea began subsiding. Apparently the questions and pain in Ben's eyes had nothing to do with her and everything to do with Kathy.

"Hark yourself," Ben mumbled.

"I don't think you have anything to worry about," Alaina said. "You know how Phil is. He's a hopeless flirt. He doesn't mean a thing by it."

"I know that, and you know that, but will Kathy?" He leaned away from the window and relaxed against the counter. "She's so young." He crossed his arms and stared toward the oven. "And Phil's *way* better looking than I'll *ever* be."

"Give her some credit, will you? And give yourself some credit." Alaina handed Ben the salad bowl. "She's had a thing for you nearly since the first time she laid eyes on you."

"She told you that?"

"She didn't *have* to tell me that," Alaina said and patted the front of Ben's polo shirt like she'd grown in the habit of doing with Caleb. Deciding eye contact with Ben was totally safe, she looked him full in the eyes and emphatically added, "It's all over her."

Ben looked at Alaina's hand for several silent seconds. When he raised his gaze back to her, a veil of disenchantment cloaked his features. Alaina snatched her hand back and rapidly blinked. "Wh-what's the matter with you, Ben?" she stammered. "You're treating me like . . ."

He studied the salad and remained silent. Duncan's rambunctious "woof" mingled with Zachariah's voice. "That's it! Looks like it's done. Phil, if you'll get that platter, I'll get this one. I don't know what happened to Ben. I guess we'll have to come back out for the ribs."

"I'll get them," Kathy volunteered. "That dog can eat them in one gulp. I speak from experience."

"Ben?" Alaina prompted.

"I saw you and Caleb," Ben choked out. "Two days ago. At the hotel in Denver."

"What?" Alaina hissed. She plucked at the pocket of her butcher's apron and could only imagine what Ben must be thinking.

He raised his gaze to hers as a sea of pain heaved through his soul. "Alaina, I never imagined you'd—"

"Just stop right there." Alaina held up her hand and couldn't believe the firmness of her own voice.

He jerked his head back and stared at Alaina like she was growing tusks.

"Caleb and I are *married*," she emphatically whispered.

"What?!" Ben whispered back.

The sound of voices floated from the home's back entry. The French doors clattered shut. And Zachariah's voice blasted through the kitchen's swinging doors. "Time to eat!"

"We got married the day after Dad left," Alaina mumbled and shot a nervous glance toward the kitchen doors. "Please don't say anything," she pleaded and gripped Ben's arm.

"I won't."

"I promise, I'll tell you everything later."

Ben had barely nodded when Zachariah invaded the kitchen. His cowboy boots thudded across the tile, and he eyed his daughter. "Salad done?" he asked.

"Yes." Alaina lowered her head. "I just have to get the dressing out of the refrigerator. Ben, if you'll put ice in the glasses, we can be ready in a minute."

"Good," Zachariah said. "I put the meat on the table. Kathy wants to see my aquarium. Call us when it's ready." He pivoted back toward the swinging doors, shoved them open, and was gone.

Alaina released her pent-up breath, and the implications of Ben's assumptions fueled an onslaught of ire. She glared at her brother. "How could you think that about me?" Alaina whispered, her eyes stinging.

"Well," Ben spread his hands, "what was I supposed to think?" he whispered. "I never imagined you'd haul off and get married without telling me. You've always told me everything—except when it comes to Caleb. You didn't even tell me you were seeing him in the first place. What was I supposed to think?" he repeated.

"You were supposed to have enough faith in me to give me the benefit of the doubt!" Alaina stomped to the stainless-steel refrigerator, yanked open the door, and reached inside. She pulled out three different bottles of salad dressing, rammed the door shut, and turned to face her brother again. A new wave of anger surged to the top of her head. She leveled a glare at Ben and watched him shrivel on the spot. Alaina searched for something clever and original to say but couldn't come up with anything except a scandalized, "How dare you!" Then she flounced from the kitchen.

By the time Kathy swallowed her last bite of apple pie, she didn't doubt who ruled the chalet and the whole Tilman family. Zachariah Tilman put capital letters in PATRIARCH. While Kathy's mother could be somewhat controlling, Kathy believed even her mom would classify Zachariah as a control freak.

During the meal, he'd had Alaina hopping back and forth to the kitchen for this, that, and the other like some slave. He'd corrected Ben both times he'd said something, and interrupted Phil half a dozen times. Just about the time Kathy was sure she'd had enough, Zachariah would smile at her and ask if everything was fine or strike up a new vein of conversation about her store or compliment her in some other little way.

At the meal's end, Kathy labeled him a *charming* control freak. *The perfect personality for a murderer,* she thought. The memory of Thurston Manley's convinced warnings insisted she alter her diagnosis. *He's a charming-control-freak-murderer,* she decided.

"Did you enjoy your pie?" Zachariah asked through one of those magazine-model grins.

"Yes, it was great," Kathy replied and smiled in his direction without making eye contact. "Alaina's a great baker." She darted a glance toward her friend, who was just finishing her chicken.

"Oh, I didn't bake it," Alaina said.

"Sara Lee did," Ben teased.

Alaina ignored him and went back to her dinner.

Ben cleared his throat and leveled a searching stare at his sister. She ignored that, too.

The level of tension at the table went through the ceiling. Kathy exchanged a concerned glance with Phil. He shrugged and winked.

While Phil looked more like Zachariah than did Ben, he was far from the mirror image of his father. His sandy blond hair, close to the color of his sister's, was cropped short in a military cut that complemented his chiseled features. While Ben's eyes were deep blue, Phil's were that rare shade of light blue that nearly shocks at first glance.

His sandals, loose jeans, and button-down shirt reminded Kathy of Ron Thaine's style of dress. So did the cocky tilt of his head. While many women might think Phil was better looking than his younger brother, Kathy had never been attracted to tall, blond, and arrogant.

When she realized Phil noticed her staring, Kathy shifted her attention back to Alaina and Ben. Alaina's back was stiff. She'd been silent most of the meal. And she focused on her chicken with a vengeance that spoke volumes. Kathy nervously glanced at Ben, who fleetingly grimaced before sipping his coffee. She eyed her own steaming mug and lost her desire for another swallow of the fragrant brew.

Kathy had been so busy sizing up Zachariah Tilman and being amazed at Phil's flirting, she decided she must have missed the undercurrents between Alaina and Ben. She studied the tatted placemat peeking from beneath her empty pie plate and remembered Ben speaking only twice during the whole meal.

Neither Zachariah nor Phil had attempted to hide their instant appreciation for Kathy and had manned most of the conversation. By the time they sat down to dinner, Zachariah had insisted Kathy call him Zach, and Phil was mentioning coming by her store.

"Is there something you two would like to share with the rest of us?" Zach eyed his younger son and daughter.

Kathy's shoulders stiffened, and she dubiously watched Ben and Alaina.

Ben held his father's gaze for several seconds and then looked away.

"I've . . . I'm having a bad day," Alaina said, her voice unsteady.

Sensing a potential family crisis, Kathy decided a journey to the bathroom was in order. "If you'll excuse me," she said, her words strained. "I'm going to make a trip to the restroom."

"Here, I'll show you where it is," Ben offered and stood with Kathy.

"Oh, that's okay," she said through a smile. "I've already been once. It's just right down the hall beside your dad's study."

"No, I was going to show you one on the second floor," Ben said, his gaze pointed and full of a silent message. "It's next door to my old bedroom. My train collection's still there if you'd like to see it."

"Hint, hint, hint," Phil teased. "Watch out, Kathy. Don't let Ben fool you with the reverend business. He's full of moves."

"I'd say if he is, he learned from a pro," Kathy shot back before thinking.

Phil jerked his head back. Alaina giggled. Kathy slapped her hand over her mouth.

Zach laughed as loud as he did earlier on the porch. "You had that one coming," he said and whacked Phil on the back.

"Go on up and see your trains, Ben," Zach said and dismissed them with a wave of his hand.

"I can't believe it," Phil taunted. "I've been beat out by my own brother."

"No, I think Ben won a long time ago," Zach deduced.

Twenty

Ben guided Kathy from the dining room into the great room, replete with pine walls, a vaulted ceiling, and a massive rock fireplace. The suede couches and sparse decor spoke high taste yet simplicity for a less-is-more effect. As she walked across the Southwest-style area rug, Kathy once again pondered if the deceased Laura Tilman had decorated the home. If so, she had unbelievable talent. While Kathy had a sixth sense in regard to arranging her store, the best she could achieve in her home was the feel of a cluttered hodgepodge.

"Do you like the chalet?" Ben paused beside the stairway, constructed in the same rich pine as the rest of the room.

Smiling, Kathy shifted her focus to him. "No, not at all," she teased and was amazed that a home that appeared so sinister from the valley could be so beautiful inside. "Why do you think I'd like it? What's *wrong* with you?" She lightly tapped Ben's arm, and the contact sparked the memory of their kiss . . . and the desire for a repeat.

He snickered. "I decorated it," he said with a hint of satisfaction.

"No way!" Kathy gaped at him.

"Don't look so shocked," he chided. "You're going to hurt my feelings." He laid his hand on his chest. "Some of us guys have talents, too, you know."

"Oh, poor baby," she crooned.

Ben's mouth barely quirked.

"Does *your* house look like this?" she asked.

"Well, it's not near this big," Ben admitted, "but yes . . . I guess you could say I've pulled off a similar look."

"What motivates you?" Kathy blurted and lifted her hand. "I mean, I couldn't do this if I tried for a year."

Ben shrugged. "Beats me," he said. "I just get this vision in my head, and I do it. When I get through," he nodded, "everybody's pleased. Actually, my mom was a lot like that. I guess I got the gene from her. But our styles were totally different. She's the reason Dad wanted me to redecorate. You know, after her death . . ." He trailed off and gazed toward the window, spanning from floor to ceiling.

"I understand," Kathy mumbled.

Ben slipped his hand into the crook of Kathy's arm and nudged her toward the stairs. "Let's go check out the trains, okay?"

"Sure," Kathy replied.

The thud of their shoes on the wooden steps was all that broke their silence. When they got to the second floor, the scent of food and coffee faded, and the odor of spicy potpourri reigned. Ben moved forward, but Kathy looked up and back toward the stairs leading to the third floor.

"Those go to my mom and dad's old suite," Ben explained. "Dad has pretty much told us it's off-limits."

"Oh, really?" Kathy inquired, her mind conjuring all sorts of reasons why Zach Tilman would ban the family from the room. *Maybe there's a murder clue up there*, she mused and recalled one of the *True Crime* stories she'd recently read. The thing that incriminated the murderer was one tiny drop of the victim's blood on his bedroom carpet.

"My old room's this way," Ben explained.

Kathy followed Ben up a wide hallway and made a mental note

to explore the suite. How and when, she didn't know, but Kathy would not rest until she examined every inch and determined if a murder took place there. *Of course, a lack of evidence doesn't mean he didn't murder her,* she argued with herself.

Ben paused near a bedroom's doorway and motioned Kathy in before him. "Ladies first," he encouraged and flipped a light switch.

While his attention was diverted, Kathy took the opportunity to scrutinize Ben. So far this evening, he manifested no trace of the restraint that was proving her nemesis. She hoped he was getting over whatever his problem was.

Kathy stepped into a room that reflected the same flair for decor as the great room but still looked like it belonged to a high-school guy. A multitiered train track ran around the walls about two feet from the ceiling. Near the French doors, an enormous knickknack shelf housed a plethora of train cars.

"Mom didn't want to change the room after I left home for college," Ben explained and pointed to a banner hanging on the north wall. It read, "Go Bearcats." Beside it hung a cork bulletin board with thumbtacks holding up old photos and memorabilia.

Hungry for every detail about Ben, Kathy wandered toward the bulletin board and examined the photos of a young, lean guy, sometimes dressed in basketball gear, sometimes pictured on family outings.

"Oh, I forgot!" Ben said from behind. "I was supposed to show you to the bathroom."

"That's okay," Kathy said with a mischievous grin. "I was just looking for a way to give you guys some space. I thought you might need to have a family powwow."

"Whew!" Ben rolled his eyes. "Alaina is *not* happy with me right now."

"Really, I couldn't tell," Kathy said.

"Yeah, right," Ben admitted with a smirk. "I bet Duncan would have picked up on her vibes. She's mad because—" Ben stopped, clamped his mouth shut, and looked away. "I can't tell you," he admitted. "Or anybody, for that matter."

"She has some sort of a secret, doesn't she?" Kathy guessed.

"Can't say." Ben looked down, shook his head, and rubbed his upper lip.

Kathy's curiosity bounded in all directions as Ben's body language screamed, *I wish I could tell you!*

"I bet it involves a man," Kathy deduced.

Ben snapped up his head. "Why would you say that?"

"Oh," Kathy toyed with the fringe of her hair, "I read a lot of novels, and beautiful young women always have secrets that involve a man. They just do!"

Ben crossed his arms and leaned away from her. "What all do you read, anyway—I mean, besides those books about crazy criminals?"

"I read some self-help books along the way, but my first love is modern mysteries or romantic suspense, and sometimes paranormal stuff like *Dr. Jekyll and Mr. Hyde.*"

"Does any of that ever scare you?"

Kathy slipped her hands into her pants pockets and feigned a shiver. "Sure," she said with a delighted smile.

"And you enjoy this?" Ben raised his brows and looked at her like she was an adorable kitten he wanted to take home.

Feeling encouraged, Kathy decided to turn the wacky charm up a notch. "One time," she whispered in a conspiratorial tone, "I even dreamed Frankenstein was growing mushrooms in the bottom of my dishwasher."

Ben placed his hand on his forehead and laughed out loud.

"Of course, that was *after* I'd indulged in caffeine and went to sleep reading *Frankenstein.* That stuff makes me hyper and makes me have wild dreams once I do get to sleep."

"You slay me!"

"Oh, and I read *A Christmas Carol* every Christmas," she added as an afterthought.

Ben mimicked a ghastly face. "I am the Ghost of Christmas Past," he said in a haunted voice. "No wonder you liked my line."

"What possessed you?" Kathy asked.

Ben chuckled through his response. "I have no earthly idea. I asked myself the same thing almost as soon as I said it. That was some night, wasn't it? I think I'd have drowned if I hadn't spotted you."

His appraisal took on a spellbound quality that left Kathy speechless. The longer she searched for something to say, the more vacant her mind became. Her thoughts wandered back to that magical kiss, and she could feel her face growing warm.

Out of desperation, Kathy peered at the bulletin board again and latched on to the first photo she spotted—a snapshot of Ben and Alaina as teenagers, hanging on to the side of an old stagecoach.

"Alaina has hardly changed," Kathy exclaimed and wondered if Ben noticed her voice wasn't steady.

"In appearance, I guess," Ben mused.

Kathy cut him a sideways glance and wished more than ever he'd tell her why Alaina was mad at him. *That's going to drive me nuts!* she thought and went back to her scrutiny of the photos.

One particular picture snared her attention as no other. Ben stood beside a lovely young woman as blond as Alaina and as attractive as Liza Thaine. Ben, who looked to be in his early twenties, was dressed in a tuxedo. The young woman wore a tea-length dress that demurely draped off the shoulders like melting cream. A rose corsage decorated her wrist. Ben's lapel sported a boutonniere. The writing superimposed across the bottom of the photo read, "Athletic Banquet, Sweetheart and Beau."

Kathy frowned. Even though she'd known a thirty-year-old attractive male would have naturally been involved with a girlfriend or two, seeing the reality didn't sit well. Her active mind wondered if the two had gone steady in college. *They might have even been engaged,* she stewed. Kathy didn't realize she was balling her fist until her fingernails pressed into her palm.

"You're jealous," Ben declared.

Kathy turned toward Ben, mere inches away. "Why . . . why would you say that?"

Ben's ecstatic smile brightened his eyes and deepened the crow's-feet around them. "I love it," he taunted, and Kathy caught the hint of a male ego in full function.

She narrowed her eyes. "I'm glad you're so impressed," she snapped.

"If it's any consolation, that girl and I weren't even a couple. We just happened to be the ones chosen that year."

"Oh," Kathy said. She lowered her head and picked at a piece of Lucy's cat hair stuck to her pants leg.

"I guess I did my share of taking women here and there in college," he explained, "but I never met one I thought I should get serious about until . . ."

Kathy peered into his face and awaited some true confession about the one woman he was never able to get over. Part of Kathy was stuck to the spot, craving the information. Another part of her insisted she cover her ears and run.

"Uh," Ben looked past Kathy, "would you like to see the balcony?" he asked, his voice strained.

"Sure," Kathy agreed and imagined all sorts of scenarios. *Maybe he's been married,* she worried, *and has four-year-old triplets.* She stifled a groan and imagined what three kids that age could do to her neat bookshelves. *What have I gotten myself into?*

"Come on." Ben pointed toward the French doors.

Kathy peered past a heavy wooden bed and through the doors to an expansive balcony decked out with wicker furniture. She walked forward. Ben stepped beside her, placing his hand on her lower back.

When they arrived at the doors, he paused and glanced toward the shelves full of trains. "You don't care about my train collection, do you?"

"Well . . ." Kathy eyed the train cars and pieces of tiny villages. While she longed for any link to Ben's interests, she wouldn't lie awake at night wondering about his trains.

"Once you've seen one train collection, you've seen 'em all," he claimed with a sly smile. "I didn't ask you up here to see the trains anyway."

"You didn't?" Kathy bleated.

"You're *so* naïve," he teased.

"So Phil was right? You were just putting some moves on me?"

"What if I was?" Ben's attention trailed to her lips. "Would you still have come up?"

"What do you think?" Kathy quipped and turned the knob to the French doors. She pulled open one door and stepped into the invigorating mountain air that smelled of earth and rocks and pines.

Ben's laugh resonated with Zachariah Tilman's tone.

Kathy suppressed her smile. She stepped to the rail, gripped it, and absorbed the miles and miles of breathtaking Rockies bathed in the light of a sun hiding behind cotton-candy clouds. At this vantage, Northpointe Village appeared to be snuggling down for a nap at the base of the jagged mountains that were topped in what looked like white frosting.

With a flippant decision as whimsical as the breeze stirring the nearby wind chimes, Kathy dismissed the ex-wife and triplets as a figment of her imagination. *Besides,* she thought and crossed her arms, *if Ben had been married before, Alaina would have told me. Either her or that creepy Thurston Manley*, she thought with a grimace. *He seems to know everything.*

"Why the frown?" Ben asked from her left.

Kathy slid a saucy glance his way. "I just decided you don't have an ex-wife and triplets."

"And that's something to frown about?" Ben parried. He faced Kathy, propped his elbow on the elevated balcony rail, and leaned into it.

"No. I just—"

"Actually, I have *quadruplets*," he said.

Kathy's mouth fell open.

"Out of wedlock," he continued.

She narrowed her eyes.

"That's by one woman. Then, by another, there are twins."

"You're lying like a dog," she accused.

"I guess that's better than lying like a cat," he retorted.

"You also tell very, very goofy jokes." Kathy rolled her eyes and loved every minute of his flirting.

"Actually, I've never been," he rubbed his fingertips along the rail and glanced down, "you know, active in that way."

"Me either," Kathy replied, her respect for Ben sailing to the sky.

His affirmative nod reflected no surprise. "I knew that."

"You did? How?" She cut him a sideways stare.

"Sometimes you just know these things." He touched the tip of her nose with his index finger and allowed it to trail to her jaw.

An enchanting flurry of tingles cavorted down her neck.

"You're really a sweetheart," Ben mumbled. "You've got my dad eating out of your hand. I don't know if I've ever seen him so easily won over."

"I have a hunch he could be hardheaded if he wanted."

"Very," Ben admitted. "That's part of the reason I . . ." He faltered, looked down, and stroked the railing again. "We need to talk."

"Really? Why would you say that?" Kathy asked.

Ben shot her a sour glance and continued. "When I first met you, Kathy, I tried to tell myself you were too young."

"I know."

"You do. How?"

Kathy wagged her head like a sage. "Some things you just know," she said in a low masculine voice that mimicked his.

Ben snickered. "Anyway," he continued, "once I got over *that*, I had another problem."

"Let me guess," Kathy babbled. "You really don't like brunettes because your first-grade teacher was also brunette and was meaner than a junkyard dog."

His grin took on an adoring glow. "I wish it had been that simple," he admitted. "Actually, it involved my dad. His parents—especially his mom—couldn't stand my mom," he explained. "They fought the whole time I was growing up. I guess if you want the truth, I've got some really bad memories and the scars to go with them. I made a vow a long time ago never to get very involved with a woman unless my parents liked her."

"So that explains why you were so—"

"Yes. That explains it. I just don't have the heart to put someone through all that grief. The morning my mom died, she'd been on the phone with my grandmother. They'd had an awful argument."

"That's terrible," Kathy breathed and shook her head.

"And Grandmother is as strong-willed as my dad any day of the week. She never once even hinted that she thought she contributed to my mom's death. My mom had a heart defect from childhood," he explained. "So it's really easy for Grandma to blame the defect and take no responsibility." Ben shook his head.

"My dad has *not* done well. He even yelled at his mom at the funeral home the night before the funeral. He dragged up all sorts of stuff my grandmother has done—including the time she slapped my mom over my sister's Easter dress. I can't imagine what he'd have done to her if he knew everything. I won't get into all of it right now, but that night at the funeral home was a nightmare. All his brothers and sisters were there. One of his sisters—who believes my grandmother is a saint—is still mad at him even now."

Kathy remained respectfully silent but wondered if maybe Zachariah was using his mother as a cover for the murder. *That sort of stuff does happen in real life*, she thought and averted her gaze toward an eagle soaring near a distant mountain. The last thing she wanted was for Ben to detect her suspicions.

"Well," Ben drawled, "enough of the sad, sorry saga of the dysfunctional Tilman clan."

Kathy leaned into the railing. "My family has some problems, but I'll admit yours are more . . . interesting."

"Interesting." He shook his head. "That's a good way to put it. Anyway," Ben rubbed his hands together, "I think we can safely say my dad likes you. I think he'd probably ask you out himself if he wasn't old enough to be your father." Ben shifted his weight and laid his hand on hers. "As things stand, since you've passed the test, I might as well tell you I *really like* you a lot, Kathy. And I'd like to get to know you better." Finally his earnest eyes were clear of any trace of restraint.

The balcony seemed to tilt, and Kathy gripped the handrail.

"I also owe you an apology," he continued. "I shouldn't have kissed you this afternoon when I didn't know how things were going to go tonight."

"You don't owe me an apology at all," Kathy insisted. "It wasn't like I was trying to beat you off or anything." Bucketfuls of mirth filled her words.

"I know," Ben said, his lips twitching. "But it wasn't fair. I mean, if my dad *didn't* like you, I would have just got some distance and prayed I could forget . . ." He looked down, straightened, and gently kicked the balcony rail with the tip of his thick-soled sandal. "I'm not really sure how well I'd have done, for that matter," he said, gazing toward the horizon. "But I wasn't planning on us being . . . you know, together, if things had gone too badly with my dad."

All the attraction Kathy had bottled for weeks spilled forth with renewed potency. She longed to move closer to Ben . . . to touch his hair . . . to feel his lips on hers. The evening sun peeked from behind the fluffy clouds and showered Ben in a fleeting dash of sunlight as he said, "Anyway, I was wondering if maybe we *could* start to date."

A compulsive voice insisted she take advantage of the moment. Before Kathy anticipated her own actions, she flung her arms around Ben's neck and pressed her lips on his.

His surprised grunt coincided with his arms wrapping around Kathy.

She closed her eyes and drowned in Ben Tilman. The kiss was every bit as electrifying as the one this afternoon, and then some—even without the boa-infested jungle, the gorillas, or even the crocs. As she tangled her fingers in the back of his hair, the wind chime took on the resonance of wedding bells. And Kathy could have vowed she felt rice pelting her lacy veil.

Once the kiss reached its end, Ben lifted his head and said, "Wow! I guess that's a yes!"

"Yes, yes, yes!" Laying her head against his chest, Kathy wasn't surprised that his heart's rapid rate matched her own. "I knew there was something wrong," she babbled and relished the faint whiff of his masculine cologne. "I just didn't know what. I could see you liked me, but you kept me at arm's length. I couldn't figure it out. Now it all makes sense. And I don't blame you for not wanting to be with someone your family disapproves of. I understand completely. My grandmother made my father *miserable*. In-laws can be so *awful* to each other. And I respect you for not wanting to marry someone who . . ." Realizing her thoughtless words had led her into the most awkward situation of her life, Kathy closed her eyes and ground her teeth together.

The vibration of Ben's rich chuckle tickled her cheek. "I guess since you brought up the subject, I might as well tell all," he said. "A few minutes ago, when I said I'd never met a woman I thought I should get serious about, what I didn't say was 'until now.'"

He placed his hands on her shoulders and nudged her away until Kathy met his gaze.

"Kathy, we've only known each other since early June, but I have to tell you, I already know there's something special between us." He paused as a ribbon of uncertainty fluttered through his eyes. "At least, *I* feel that way."

"I do, too. I do, too," she hurried as her embarrassment slipped away. "You *know* I do. I think you're *wonderful*," Kathy said. "I'd just about stopped thinking there even *were* any guys like you left."

Ben beamed. "I'm a long way from perfect."

"You're perfect to me." Kathy placed her hands on either side of his face, then touched the scar on his forehead.

"I saw your picture in the paper," she confessed. "I think you've got to be the bravest man on earth."

"Not by a long shot," Ben said, although his eyes shimmered with pleasure.

"Was the car on fire when you pulled that boy out?" Kathy rested her hands on his shoulders.

"No." Ben shook his head. "I drove up right after the accident. The mother was hysterical. I smelled gas, and something . . . someone . . . told me to crawl into the car and get the kid out. I guess it was God." He shrugged. "The next thing I knew, the car was exploding and I was running with the boy. My head was bleeding like crazy." Ben shuddered. "Yesterday somebody told me my name was up for Citizen of the Year. But really, I think anybody would have done the same thing."

"I disagree," Kathy whispered as she snuggled her head against his chest once more. "I think you're one in a million."

Twenty-One

Two weeks later, Kathy stood in her store's mini kitchen, trying to get a new can of whipped cream to dispense. Ben and his family were due in her shop in thiry minutes, and Kathy had put together a large strawberry shortcake. The thing looked like a work of art, but it had taken her only fifteen minutes to create. She'd popped the angel food cake out of the wrapper, swathed whipped cream all over it, and plopped the fresh strawberries on top. She stepped back to admire her creation.

"Walmart rules," she said and dipped her index finger into a frothy dollop of topping. When she licked off the treat, her taste buds begged for more. Three hours ago, Kathy had dashed to the Walmart Supercenter and gathered the ingredients for the dessert. Even though she'd known all week Ben and his family would be here for a special dessert party, she'd put off the purchases until the last minute.

She ignored the can's nozzle, stared at her cappuccino machine, and revisited the odd encounter she'd had with Alaina in Walmart. When Kathy spotted Alaina coming into the back of the store through a doorway, she hadn't noticed the door was marked "Employees Only" until she waved at Alaina. While Ben's sister had waved back and even spoke, she'd acted sheepish. Kathy, focused on tonight's party, had called, "See ya later!" and moved along in her shopping. Before Kathy got to the dairy section, she'd wondered why Alaina had been behind a door marked "Employees Only," and why she looked different.

Kathy strained for what was missing and finally realized that Alaina hadn't been wearing any lipstick. Considering Alaina's vibrant makeup was always perfect, the absence of her brick-red lipstick struck Kathy as odd. The only other time Kathy recalled seeing Alaina without lipstick was the night they watched movies together in her apartment. *Also that first time she came to see me,* she thought, *the day she'd been crying.*

Kathy focused on the empty strawberry carton and tapped her toe while something elusive tugged at the back of her mind. *Ben hinted that Alaina has a secret,* Kathy deduced. *I figured it must involve a man. If it does . . .* Her eyebrows flexed as she recalled that hunk of a manager who had the audacity to barge out of the "Employees Only" door when Kathy decided to get nosy and investigate.

"Do you need help finding something?" he'd asked from his hulking height.

"Uh . . ." Kathy had hedged long enough to note his name tag read "Caleb Manley, Manager." Then she lamely asked where the canned whipped topping was.

With suspicious grace, Mr. Manley had pointed her in the right direction.

Kathy examined the can of topping and decided to get on with her creation. She'd worry about Alaina later tonight. *I might even get the chance to find out what she was doing,* she thought.

"Now, if I could just get this stupid whipped topping to come out of the can." Gritting her teeth, Kathy placed the can on the counter, examined the nozzle, and pressed it harder than she had yet. The thing sputtered, hissed, and shot a stream of cold topping straight into her face.

She screamed and jumped. "Oh no!" Kathy wailed and blinked against the shower of dots clinging to her eyelashes. She'd spent an hour getting ready for tonight. Her hair . . . her makeup . . . everything had been perfect, right down to the new dress she'd bought at a boutique.

"I cannot believe this!" she wailed and groped for the dish towel lying on the counter. Kathy gingerly dabbed at her face and prayed she didn't look like she had leprosy. She licked at her glossy lips and was encouraged when she detected no sweetness.

Once Kathy rid her lashes of most of the topping, she hurried to the closet-sized bathroom at the back of the store and pulled the chain hanging from the ceiling. The bare bulb obliterated the darkness. Dreading the sight, she peered into the new, brass-trimmed mirror and groaned. Her makeup was splotchy. Her mascara was smudged. And the front of her hair looked like someone had sprayed it with Christmas snow.

In a fit of desperation, she scrutinized her linen blouse, void of white spots. "Whew!" she breathed.

Kathy checked her watch and decided to do the best she could with a twenty-five-minute repair job. The door's opening made her groan. "They're early!" she said and plopped the towel in the sink. *I'll never again buy spray whipped cream as long as I live!*

Like a brave soldier going to war, Kathy marched back into her shop, fully prepared to face Ben, his family, and their laughter. Instead, she spotted her brother, Liza, and Ron.

She hovered behind a bookcase and thought, *Not tonight!*

The last two weeks had been awkward, to say the least. While Jay and Liza were definitely in a world of their own, they assumed Kathy should tag along as Ron's date wherever they went. Since Ben and she both agreed that, considering his position, they should keep a low profile romantically, not even her brother knew they were officially dating. Not that Ben or Kathy minded his knowing. But Jay, unlike Gloria and Sigmund, was so distracted, he failed to notice the subtle clues.

Just to keep the peace, Kathy had gone on a few outings with the three during the past two weeks. Each time she'd purposefully removed Ron's hand from her leg. The guy seemed determined to move in, no matter what boulder-sized hints Kathy dropped on his head.

"Anybody here?" Jay hollered. "Kathy?"

"I'm here!" Kathy said and stepped from behind the bookcase.

Liza rushed forward in an ecstatic fit. "Oh my goodness," she babbled and waved her left hand. "I can't wait to tell you! We're going to be sisters-in-law!"

Kathy stopped herself from gawking at Liza, then asked herself why she was so surprised. Jay had as good as told Kathy he was going to propose before he went back to New Mexico next week. As calmly as possible, Kathy glanced toward her brother. Arms crossed, he was smiling and rocking back on his heels like he had achieved his greatest victory. Ron, not far behind Liza, arrived at Kathy's side at the same time Liza shoved a diamond cluster in her face.

"See!" Liza squealed. "It's official! We're engaged!"

Hiding her dismay, Kathy conjured the most genuine smile she could fake. "Congratulations!" she said and took Liza's fingers in hers. She tilted the dazzling ring and had to admit the thing must have cost a boatload of pennies. *What is my brother thinking?*

Jay arrived at Liza's side, pulled her close, and kissed her cheek. The bedazzled warmth in his eyes made Kathy realize Jay *wasn't* thinking.

"We're going to celebrate!" Ron declared and looped his arm along Kathy's waist. "Go get your purse. We're hitting the town!"

"No, wait!" Kathy held up her hand and noticed the three were dressed as nicely as she. Even Ron had retired the baggy jeans for a pair of twill slacks. "I've got—"

"Oooh, girlfriend," Liza said and pointed at Kathy's hair, "what's with the white stuff?"

"I sprayed myself with whipped cream," Kathy said, her voice flat.

Her admission gained Jay's attention. He looked at his sister and didn't hide his humor. "You've got it all in your hair!" he mocked.

"Yes, I know." Kathy stepped away from Ron. "I was just going upstairs to try to get it out. I've got—"

"Well, hurry up!" Ron urged. "The night is young, and we've got some *serious celebrating* to do!"

"But I've got company coming."

"Company?" Ron blurted and looked at Kathy like she'd announced the arrival of space aliens.

"Yes." She nodded. "They're due in . . ." Kathy checked her watch. "Yikes! In twenty minutes."

"Ah, Kathy," Jay argued while Liza wilted, "why don't you just call them and tell them something important has come up?"

"Jay, I can't do that."

"Who is it, anyway?" Ron huffed. "Should I be jealous?"

"Well, if you must know, it's Ben Tilman and his sister and brother and father. Oh, and Aunt Gloria and Uncle Ziggy."

"And you didn't invite us?" Liza pouted.

"Well!" Kathy raised her hands and shrugged. "You guys weren't around when I was making the plans."

"Should I be jealous of this Ben character?" Ron demanded.

Feeling like a cornered mouse, Kathy stared at Ron and debated how best to tell the guy he didn't have the *right* to be jealous.

"Just call 'em, Kathy!" Jay asserted. "This is more important than any ol' whipped-cream get-together." He jabbed his fingers against his chest. "Your brother's engaged!"

"I'll call them," Ron spouted. "I know!" He grabbed Kathy's shoulder and looked her full in the face. "I'll tell them you're sick . . . barfing your guts up . . . and you asked me to call and cancel for you."

"Perfect!" Jay squawked and clapped once. "Now, what's their number, Kath?"

Kathy didn't hide her grimace. "Jay Moore," she snapped, "I am *not* going to be a part of a lie like that! I might not be the Christian of the Year, but I *don't lie*. Even if I didn't want them over—and I do—I wouldn't cancel on them at the last minute. It's not fair to—"

"Kathy," Jay barked like he was about to start bullying her.

She stiffened and glared at him. "Listen, Jay, I don't know when you started lying, but—"

"Look," Liza lifted her hands, and her ring sparkled, "why don't we just hang out here? We can celebrate here as easily as we can at Impressions."

"That works!" Ron crowed and moved closer to Kathy.

She inched away and didn't doubt that Ron's motives involved sizing up Ben's intentions.

"What do you have to eat besides the cake?" Liza asked and pointed toward Kathy's creation.

"That's all," she admitted.

"That won't be enough," Liza decided.

"But—" Kathy said.

"It's not finished, either, is it?" Ron asked.

"No, I was just trying to finish it up when the whipped cream sprayed me."

"I'll take care of it while you go upstairs and clean up." Ron went to the service bar before Kathy could stop him.

"The Diner on the Corner has a deli," Jay said. "The last time I was in there they had these German chocolate cakes." He exaggerated the size with his hands. "I think I could eat a whole one myself."

"That sounds perfect," Liza exclaimed and adjusted her

glasses. "They also have party trays of all kinds—meat and cheese and veggie trays, too."

Feeling as if she was losing control of her own party, Kathy attempted to protest again, but to no avail.

"Here . . ." Licking his index finger, Ron turned from his project, pulled out his wallet, and removed a twenty. "Take this for my part." He dropped the bill on the bar and stuffed his wallet back into his hip pocket.

"We'll take care of it," Jay assured. After retrieving the money, he grabbed Liza's hand and pulled her toward the door. "Don't worry about a thing, Kathy. We've got it under control."

Kathy mutely watched as her brother and Liza sailed out the door. Her shoulders drooping, she tried to fathom how her carefully planned evening would go now. She'd so hoped to seal her place in Zachariah's good graces. If Ron continued in his territorial pursuits, no telling what Ben's father would think. If Ben's father ultimately disapproved of her . . .

She folded her arms and squeezed her forearms. The last two weeks cavorted through her mind like the plot of a fairy tale. At the first of their courtship, Ben explained that he wanted to keep their relationship low-profile because of his church position. The last thing he said he needed was the grapevine to get started. Kathy readily agreed and preferred to enjoy their romance without the arched eyebrows and probing questions of a whole congregation. Word would get out soon enough.

Still, Kathy had attended church with Alaina and her dad the last two Sundays. Her whole life she'd gone to church out of a sense of duty to her parents and the way they raised her. But listening to Ben's insightful messages had sparked something new in Kathy—something that transcended the fact that the man she adored was the deliverer. Kathy wasn't sure exactly what all that meant, but she did know she wanted to create a better church attendance habit. And this time it would be for her, not her parents.

Once Ben declared them a couple, he'd been nothing short of Prince Charming. He'd called every day, personally delivered flowers twice, and even arranged for Kathy to visit his home—with Alaina as chaperone, of course. The house had been everything Kathy thought it would be, right down to the collection of porcelain birds on the mantel and the masculine decor, as tasteful and balanced as the chalet's. The whole visit, Kathy had imagined what life would be as the lady of the house.

But that will only happen as long as Zachariah approves, she worried. Her attention slid to Ron, diligently bent over the cake. Kathy blinked against the unexpected sting of tears. *After tonight, no telling what the charming-control-freak-murderer will assume.*

An unforeseen surge of resentment plagued her soul. Even though she and Ben's father had gotten along famously the past two weeks, Kathy felt as if she were under his microscope. One mistake might reap his disapproval. *Then Ben would probably drop me,* Kathy thought and wondered if she could fall all the way in love with a man who allowed his father such power in his life. *But then, I haven't had to live with Zachariah all these years,* she thought. *And I don't have Ben's scars, either.*

Last week, Ben told her that the Easter slap wasn't the only one he'd seen his grandmother inflict on his mom. He remembered at least five other instances. According to Ben, she always made certain her son was well out of the way before her attacks. One time when Ben was eleven, he'd even blocked his grandmother's abuse and wound up with a black eye. Kathy decided Zachariah had probably been slapped around in his childhood, as well. That meant Laura Tilman understood all too well the nature of the Tilman clan's uncanny control and abuse. This realization brought even more credence to Thurston Manley's claim.

Kathy shivered and tried to convince herself that her worries were a figment of her imagination. She failed. And that third-floor suite beckoned as never before.

"All finished!" Ron declared.

Kathy jumped, turned to face Ron, and covered her chest. "Oh my word, you startled me."

"What? Did you already forget I was here?" Ron complained as he placed the cake on the service bar.

"No." Kathy shook her head and glanced at the cake. "I was just thinking." She raised her brows. "That cake is gorgeous!" she exclaimed and hurried forward.

"I thought you might like it," Ron admitted, his words dripping with satisfaction.

"This is a work of art!" she gasped and took in every curl and dip of the whipped topping. "It looks like . . . like a wedding cake almost. I can't believe you did this with a can!"

"My uncle—Mom's brother—is a caterer in San Francisco," Ron admitted. "I used to spend my summers with him. We did a lot of weddings."

"You guys just blow my mind. Jay can barely make coffee. And even though his apartment is always clean, he couldn't decorate it to save his life. Ben's as good at decorating a house as you are this cake."

"Ben Tilman?" Ron questioned.

Nodding, Kathy continued to admire the cake.

"As in, that Ben guy who's coming tonight?" Ron's voice held a possessive edge.

Kathy observed him. While his short, spiked hair, angled features, and keen brown eyes usually turned heads, they still did nothing for her. Even though Ben's external features weren't as classically handsome as Ron's, or even his brother Phil's, his character superseded both men's.

"Isn't he the guy you tried to do the Charleston with?"

She nodded.

"You never told me if I should be jealous of him."

"Ron, I . . ." Kathy grappled with how to tell Ron his interest was hopeless. The guy just wasn't getting it.

"I guess he probably has oodles of money," Ron griped. "What does he do, anyway?" He laid his hand on the service bar and leaned toward Kathy.

"He's a pastor," Kathy said and wondered if Ron was going to shine a bright light in her eyes to up the pressure of the interrogation.

"You're joking, right?" he chided.

"No, I'm serious. He's a pastor." Kathy never blinked.

Ron arched his back and laughed out loud. "And to think I was worried about competition," he scoffed.

Kathy frowned. "What's that supposed to mean?"

"You're too wild and crazy to ever interest a pastor!" Shaking his head, Ron snickered.

"I'm not wild and crazy!" Kathy placed her hands on her hips.

"You're right. Maybe that's not the best description, but you're just too young and pretty and full of life to ever be a preacher's wife," Ron declared, his features softening. "If you got tangled with a pastor, you'd have to dress like a nun and act like an old woman. Ha!" he added. "It would never work."

"Ben's not—"

"Forget Ben. Why don't we get engaged and celebrate with Liza and Jay?" Ron's playful tone and dancing eyes declared him so far from serious, Kathy didn't see the need for a decline.

"You'll never get married, Ron," she retorted and touched her sticky hair. "You're too big of a flirt!" She checked her watch. The Tilmans were due in ten minutes. She debated whether taking the chance to leave Ron to greet her company was worth having presentable hair and makeup, and decided she really didn't have a choice. Mirrors didn't lie. She looked a mess.

"Kathy . . ." Ron began

She started toward the doorway that led to her apartment. "I'm going upstairs to get this goo out of my hair," she said over her shoulder. "If they get here before I come back down, just send Alaina up for me, will you?" Kathy hoped Ron understood she did *not* want him coming up to her apartment.

"Alaina," Ron drawled. "My all-time favorite person."

Twenty-Two

Kathy took one look at herself in her tiny bathroom's cracked mirror and decided it would take a solid thirty minutes to re-create what the whipped topping had obliterated. The longer she thought about leaving Ron to greet the Tilmans, the more Kathy realized she didn't even need to use the full ten minutes she had.

With Lucy twining around her legs, Kathy reached for the portable showerhead that hung above her claw-footed bathtub. In five minutes she had washed her hair and face. Enveloped in the smell of peach shampoo, she towel-dried her hair, shrugged, and decided she looked about like she did the first time Ben saw her.

"Like I'm sixteen," she said and pragmatically accepted her fate. Leaving the damp towel and shampoo on the counter, Kathy bent to pick up her cat. "I love Lucy," she crooned. The purring cat propped her damp feet against Kathy's arm and stretched to sniff her hair.

"Hey, your paws are all wet," Kathy said and looked down. "Did I leak on the floor?" She examined the faded bathroom tile and noticed a puddle of water oozing from near the toilet. "Oh no, not again!" she groaned and placed Lucy in the doorway. The orange striped cat released an offended "meow" and trotted into the bedroom with her tail in the air.

Kathy squatted beside the toilet and examined the cut-off

valve near the wall. Just as she'd figured, the thing was leaking. The first bout of leaking had been a four-towel ordeal. But after Kathy removed the fourth wet towel, the drip had stopped and she forgot about calling a plumber—even though the plumbing still groaned like an aching hippo.

She grabbed the towel she'd used on her hair and began a quick cleanup. All the while, she prayed, "Please God, let it stop again, and I'll call a plumber first thing Monday morning." She repeated the prayer a dozen times while she retrieved a dry towel, slipped it under the leak, and hurried downstairs.

The second after she closed the doorway to the staircase, Ben led the way into the store, followed closely by Alaina, Zach, and Phil. Kathy sighed.

"Hello!" she called and hurried forward before Ron spoke. Kathy spotted him rising from a corner chair. He laid a magazine on a nearby table and glanced toward Kathy.

"Sorry about my wet hair," Kathy said as Phil closed the door. She stopped in front of the Tilmans and lifted a strand of hair. "I was making the strawberry shortcake and sprayed myself with whipped cream. I had to go upstairs and wash it out of my hair and off my face."

Zachariah's guffaw bounced around the store. "Nobody else but you, Kathy," he declared and rested his hand on her shoulder for a fatherly squeeze. "Better be careful, Ben. That whipped cream can sounds like bad news." Zachariah folded his fist and nudged his son's chin. "I guess we could say she's armed and dangerous."

Ron neared Kathy on one side while Ben stepped to her other side. "She looks like she did the night I first met her," Ben said.

Kathy couldn't deny the indulgent gleam in Ben's eyes. Once again, she felt as if she were an adorable kitten he wanted to take home. *If I'd known having wet hair and no makeup would have this effect, I'd have done this a long time ago,* she thought. Ben's expression gained more warmth, and Kathy was almost sure he'd read her mind.

Squinting, Phil leaned closer and tilted his head from side to side. "Do I know you?" he teased.

"Oh, leave her alone," Alaina said and gently slapped his arm. Tonight she was dressed in the denim jacket with the leopard collar and the matching skirt—the same thing she'd worn the day she'd been crying.

"I think Kathy looks just fine." Ben slipped his hand in hers and smiled into her face.

"Me too," Ron said.

"By the way, Ben," Kathy said, "this is my . . . friend, Ron Thaine. My brother and Ron's sister—her name's Liza—have gone to the deli. They'll be back soon. If you remember, they were here the night you and I nearly killed each other trying to do the Charleston."

"Good grief," Ben said and covered his eyes. "Did you have to bring that up?"

"I hope you don't mind us crashing your party," Ron said like he couldn't care less. "My sister and Kathy's brother just got engaged. We came to get Kathy to go out with us, and she invited us to stay."

I did? Kathy thought and fingered her damp hair.

"Well, the more the merrier." Phil slipped off his jacket and peered around the store. "Great place you've got here, Kathy," he said as Zachariah ambled toward a bookshelf.

The door opened and Jay and Liza bustled in. "We made it back!" Jay said while manning two oversized deli bags. Liza, right in front of Jay, carried two bags, as well.

Phil took one look at Liza's radiant face and said, "Looks like things are going to be *really* merry."

"They just got engaged. Behave!" Ben admonished.

Liza flushed and smiled at Phil, who stood about two inches

taller than Jay and was also a notch higher in external appeal. While Jay was loaded with boyish charm, he lacked the knock-'em-dead effect of Phil's shocking blue eyes and chiseled features.

"Hey, Ben," Zachariah called, picking up a fishing magazine, "why didn't you tell me she carried all these sportsmen magazines?"

Ben squeezed Kathy's hand and released it. "You just scored another point," he whispered before strolling toward his dad. Kathy didn't stop herself from admiring Ben's graceful gait or how nicely the navy sport coat accented his broad shoulders.

In Kathy's mind, there was no comparison between Ron Thaine and Ben Tilman. *Ron's crazy to even try*, she thought as Ron relieved Jay of one of his bags.

Liza bumped into Kathy. "Oh, sorry," she mumbled.

"Here. Let me have a bag," Kathy said. "We'll just put everything on the service bar."

"Be careful with that one," Liza explained. "It's a shrimp ring with a cup of sauce in the middle. I'm afraid it might spill."

"Got it covered," Kathy said.

In the following bustle, Liza sidled over next to Kathy and whispered, "Who is that guy?"

She followed Liza's speculative gaze. "Ben's older brother," Kathy explained. "Don't pay him any attention. He's a die-hard flirt."

"He's also a knockout," Liza replied.

"Yes, but you've got the better guy by far." Kathy pulled the shrimp ring from the bag. Even though she'd grabbed a sandwich at five, a mild whiff of the red sauce and chilled shrimp made her stomach beg for a sample.

"Oh, I'm fully aware of that, girlfriend," Liza assured. "But just because I'm engaged doesn't mean I'm blind, you know." Her hungry gaze slid from Kathy back to Phil.

Kathy stopped in the middle of trying to open the shrimp

ring long enough to glimpse Phil. Dressed in a pair of faded jeans and a T-shirt that clung to his defined muscles, he stood near his brother and father. While Zach and Ben were engrossed in the magazine, Phil's attention was all for Liza. He smiled and Kathy was almost certain he threw in a discreet wink. The gesture was so subtle, she debated if she'd imagined it . . . until she looked back at Liza.

Her cheeks flushing, Liza bent her head and focused on removing a large vegetable tray from her cellophane bag. Her strawberry-blond hair swung forward like a curtain of glistening silk and hid her features.

Forgetting the shrimp ring, Kathy searched for her brother. The poor guy was so tuned in to his prized cake, he missed the whole exchange. "Hey, Liza," he called from five feet down the bar, "get a load of this German chocolate baby. I think I could eat the whole thing!"

That seems to be a recurring theme, she thought and cut another glance to Phil. At least the guy had the decency to look interested in the magazine now.

"And did you see the size of these shrimp when we were in the diner?" Liza called toward Jay.

Kathy's mouth turned down at the corners.

Liza now acted as if she'd never even noticed Phil. She picked up the shrimp ring and hurried toward her fiancé with an adoring smile.

After admiring the shrimp, Jay removed the cake's plastic bubble, dipped his finger into the frosting, and offered the morsel to Liza. She nibbled at the end of his finger and closed her eyes. "That's delicious," she declared.

Squinting, Kathy observed Phil. He looked up from the magazine and took in every inch of Liza's snug-fitting pants and shirt. Nobody with half a brain had to look far to find out what Jay and Phil both saw in Liza. As far as her brother was concerned,

Kathy wasn't naïve enough to believe it had anything to do with what he *should* be looking for in a future wife.

She glanced at the clock hanging near the photo of her and her Impala. It was Saturday night, and by ten she'd be on the phone with her mom. In the past month, the mother-daughter calls had dwindled from daily to weekly. Kathy figured her mother received enough updates from the Averys and Jay to keep her happy.

Well, tonight she's going to get an update on Jay, Kathy thought. *Maybe Dad can talk some sense into him before it's too late!* She doubted that a newly engaged woman would be so easily affected by a man if she were truly in love with her fiancé.

Her finger's barely warmed that ring, and she's already making eyes at another guy! Kathy fumed. Despite her doubting Jay's wisdom in such a hasty engagement, her neck tightened, her legs stiffened, and she wadded the shrimp ring's bag into a tight ball.

I'm not blind, either, she thought and sized up Ron, who was stiffly standing near Alaina. *I know handsome when I see it.* Kathy's attention shifted to Ben, who pointed at the magazine page and said something to his father. *And if I were engaged to Ben, there's no handsome out there who could distract me from who I belonged to.*

Shaking her head, Kathy began removing the plastic top from the veggie tray and idly wondered if having Phil around was such a bad idea after all. If Liza was apt to wander, better to find out now than after the wedding.

Kathy barely detected the doorknob's rattle over the varied conversations. She turned toward the door in sequence with a light rapping noise. Gloria peered into the store while Sigmund gazed over her shoulder. When she spotted Kathy, she pointed to the doorknob.

"It's locked," she mouthed.

"Oh!" Kathy said and hurried forward. A swift examination of the deadbolt attested that it had somehow been bumped into the locked position. Kathy went through the usual deadbolt tango and finally flung open the door.

"Hey, you guys!" she greeted.

"Hey yourself!" Sigmund quipped and followed his wife inside. He stopped when he grew even with Kathy, pointed toward the ceiling, and swung his hips. "We're here to par-tay!" he sang, his baggy shorts flopping around his knees.

"You crazy man!" Gloria gently slapped his tummy. "Stop that now. Everybody's going to think you're batty. You need to act sixty instead of sixteen!"

Sigmund ignored her and continued his jig. "You're just mad because I can out-jitterbug you," he claimed.

Jitterbug? Kathy thought and slammed the door.

"Look, everybody!" Gloria beckoned. She dug through her orange tote bag, as festive as her capris and matching jacket, and pulled out a CD and a folded chart. "We went back to that party shop today and found out how to do the jitterbug. We brought the Charleston CD, too!" She pulled out a second case.

Kathy's gaze flew to Ben. He stared at Gloria, then looked at Kathy. His befuddled expression said, *I'll kill myself trying to do that!*

A gurgle bubbled from Kathy, despite the fact that Zachariah was observing Gloria and Sigmund like they were nuts. Images of Zach trying to do the jitterbug in his cowboy boots and jeans frolicked through her mind. Another giggle escaped Kathy.

So much for my quiet dessert party, she thought and touched her drying hair. *So much for my hair.* Kathy rubbed her eyes. *And my makeup.* She leaned against the door, shook her head, and decided laughing again was a much healthier alternative to sitting down and crying.

"Ah, man!" Jay said and pressed his fingertips against his temple. "I meant to buy a bottle of ranch dressing. They had some right beside the vegetable trays." He looked at Kathy. "Do you have any upstairs?" he called.

"Sure!" Kathy pushed away from the door and hurried past her godparents, who were wasting no time getting to know Zachariah. "I'll go get it," Kathy offered and figured the charming-control-freak-murderer wouldn't know which end was up in half an hour.

"I'm coming with you," Ben said and trailed her to the stairway door.

Thrilled to have him close, Kathy opened the door and smiled up at him. As she stepped into the narrow passage, she noticed Ron straining for a last glimpse of them. *Good grief,* Kathy thought as the door closed, *I hope he doesn't follow us.*

Twenty-Three

"Even with wet hair, you look cute, Kathy Moore," Ben said and once again relived that first night he'd met her. Kathy had been like a ball of unexpected energy erupting all over his predictable world.

"Thanks," Kathy said and beamed up at him.

The evening sun cascaded through the lone window high in the staircase and shimmered in her damp hair. For the first time, Ben noticed a faint chicken pox scar in the center of her forehead. The flaw was one more thing Ben added to his growing list of Kathy's endearing qualities.

Ben rested his fingertip along the bridge of her nose and stroked it to the end. "Your nose turns up at the end. Did you know?" he teased and lowered his hand.

"No, I've never noticed," Kathy rasped and looked up at him like he was a superhero.

"I love your wit," he continued.

Kathy swallowed hard.

"And your energy." He reached for her hand.

She held on tight.

"As a matter of fact . . ." Ben stroked the edge of her mouth with his thumb. "Would you think I was rushing too much if I admitted—"

"No—not at all!" she hurried and shook her head.

Ben chuckled and brushed his lips against hers. He draped

his arms around her waist, nuzzled her ear, and whispered, "I think I'm falling in love with you, Kathy. And it started when you pulled me into your store that rainy night. I couldn't stop thinking about you after that."

Kathy clung to Ben and made him feel even more like her hero. "I feel the same way," she gushed. "I really do!"

He smiled and said, "Your hair smells like peaches. I think that just became my favorite fruit!"

She pulled away from Ben, placed her hands on each side of his face, and smiled. "*Ben* is my favorite. I don't know how anyone could know a Ben and not adore him."

"Well, all Bens are not equal, I'm afraid," he replied.

Kathy giggled.

"There might be a few out there much better than me."

"Never!" Kathy gasped, resting her hands on his shoulders.

Ben tilted his head and decided to voice the worry that had nagged him the last couple of days. Despite his mind's logical assessment of what he saw Thursday night, his heart wouldn't rest until he heard the facts from Kathy.

"What's with this Ron person?" he cautiously questioned. "Should I be jealous?"

She sputtered out a laugh. "Not on your life!"

"Promise?" Ben prompted and despised his own weakness. "I mean . . . I saw you guys out together a few nights ago—with Jay and what's-her-name."

"Liza," Kathy supplied and backed away, but not out of the circle of his arms. "If it was Thursday night—"

"Yes. I came to town for some groceries, and well, to see you . . . and . . ." Ben gazed toward the pine wall. His arms tensed. "There you were, walking into the movies with him."

"They roped me into going," Kathy explained. "I've gone out with them off and on all summer." She stood on her tiptoes, grabbed him behind the neck, and kissed him full on the lips.

"Whoa!" Ben exclaimed.

"I wouldn't let Ron Thaine touch me with a ten-foot pole," she whispered and smacked a trio of repeat kisses on him. "He's nothing but a Ron Juan."

"I think that's supposed to be Don Juan," Ben corrected through a huge smile.

"Whatever. I can't wait until Tuesday," she said after her final peck.

"What's Tuesday?" Ben would have vowed the narrow passage was spinning.

"The day Ron leaves. He's driving me nuts! Have you been eating mints? You taste minty." Kathy indulged in another kiss. Ben held her tight while the kiss lengthened, and a primeval longing signaled his internal warning system.

He forced himself to break away and gasped, "Time out!" Ben placed his hands on her shoulders and got some space. Her wide, innocent eyes hinted at her disappointment. Kathy was so young and so guileless, he figured she had no idea of the power of her nearness.

"Are you on caffeine again or what?" Ben gasped.

"No caffeine," Kathy admitted and shook her head. "I just want to make sure you know I'm serious about you—and not about Ron. And," she moved in to steal another smooch, "I like kissing you."

"Yes, me too, but—"

"You like kissing you, too? How exactly do you do that?" she joked and gave him some breathing room.

"No, I mean—I like . . . I like . . ." His attraction growing more intense by the second, Ben focused on her lips. "I like kissing you," he admitted and stepped out of reach, "but we can't—I can't—we shouldn't. Enough is enough! Comprendé?" He crossed his arms and managed a smile.

"Is that German?" Kathy asked with a saucy grin. "Because

if it is I've never learned German, so I can't answer one way or the other." She lifted her hands and shrugged.

"You're an incurable tease," Ben growled.

"Tell me you don't love it!" Kathy shot back and twined her fingers. Her hazel eyes assured him she was falling as hard as he.

Ben stifled a groan. "You know that answer." He glanced toward the door, slipped his hand into his jacket pocket, and pulled out a roll of Mentos. "Want a mint?" He lifted the roll and it trembled with his hand.

"No, thanks." Kathy wrinkled her nose. "I've already had mine."

"Right," Ben drawled and helped himself to another. "I guess we better get the ranch dressing before somebody comes after us," he said and slipped the mints back into his pocket. "I'd really rather just hang out with you all evening."

"They'll never miss us."

"Maybe not us," Ben admitted, enjoying the fresh burst of mint, "but I have a feeling they *will* miss the ranch dressing."

"Right." Kathy turned for the steps, and Ben reminded himself to go easy on the kissing from now on. While Kathy had made her point about her feelings for him—not Ron—the last thing either of them needed was a trip to the brink of temptation.

"Not much comes between Jay and his ranch dressing," she chattered. "He even eats it on his French fries."

"I actually like vanilla ice cream with my fries," Ben admitted.

"Now that's just gross," Kathy accused and shot him a grimace. "Oh, yuck! I thought I'd heard of everything. That should be outlawed!"

Ben laughed. "I've been eating it since I was a kid. It tastes like sweet potatoes, actually."

Their light banter continued until they topped the staircase. When they paused at the top of the landing, a cat's panicked meows seeped through the doorway.

Kathy looked at Ben. "That's Lucy," she said. "I wonder what's got her so upset."

She opened her apartment door. Ben gazed past her to discover the plump, striped feline pacing across the back of the couch, howling. The second she spotted Kathy, the cat bounded from the couch and ran to her owner. She then raced into the bedroom and back to Kathy. When Kathy bent to pick her up, Ben scrutinized the passage into Kathy's bedroom, searching for an intruder or a fire . . . anything.

"Her paws are wet," Kathy gasped. "Oh no!" she shrieked and maneuvered past an overflowing laundry basket.

"What?" Ben hollered and followed close behind. "What is it?" he asked.

"The plumbing!" Kathy shrieked and ran toward her bedroom.

"Oh no," he moaned and hurried after Kathy. "Don't tell me you never got a plumber!" Ben bellowed.

"I never got a plumber!" Kathy hollered from the bathroom. "Help! Come here! Stop it! Help!"

He trotted the rest of the way to the bathroom's door, gripped the frame, and stopped. Kathy hovered beside the toilet, surrounded by water.

Ben examined the aging taupe carpet covering Kathy's bedroom. It was oozing water like a dirty wet poodle. About two inches of water had already pooled on her bathroom tile.

"Move!" Ben ordered and shoved past Kathy as she backed away. Fighting against the stream of cold water, he found the cut-off valve and twisted it until the water stopped.

The panicked silence lasted only a second.

"Kathy!" Jay's frantic voice erupted into the apartment. "You've got water dripping down the back wall. What's going on?"

His fingers dripping, Ben looked up over his shoulder. Kathy hovered near the sink, her arms crossed, her face void of color. "Why didn't you call someone?" Ben asked.

"I . . . I . . . I . . ." Kathy helplessly shrugged. "I forgot."

"Kathy?" Jay yelled.

"In the bathroom," Ben replied and stood. He twisted to face Kathy. "Do you have a Shop-Vac? Or can you get one—maybe a couple?"

"Wh-what's that?" she stuttered.

Ben grabbed the back of his neck and looked down. The water was oozing into the seams of his loafers and moistening his toes. He could only imagine the damage to Kathy's store if they didn't do something—and soon.

"At least the carpet's absorbing a lot of it," he mumbled and stepped from the bathroom, just in time to run headlong into Jay. The two men bounced off each other and scrambled for their footing. Ben waddled into the wall and regained his balance. Jay, not as fortunate, slammed into Kathy's bed and landed on the floor with a moderate splash and a disgruntled "Humph!"

"Yikes." Ben winced. "Sorry there."

"What happened?" Jay demanded. "This place is like a wet sponge!" He gazed at the carpet in dazed disbelief.

"Your sister's plumbing sprang a leak." Ben offered Jay his hand and helped him to his feet. "Ah, man," Jay exclaimed and wiped at the seat of his pants. "I'm soggy!"

Under any other circumstances Ben would have laughed, but he didn't have time. He wrestled with his cell phone lodged firmly in his pocket. After a brief battle, Ben dislodged the phone and dialed the one number he hoped would solve their problems. He turned toward Kathy to explain the call. She stood just inside the bathroom doorway, her hands fully covering her face. Assuming she was weeping, Ben stroked the back of her hands.

"Hey, honey, don't cry," he assured as the phone started ringing. "I'm calling my church treasurer now. She and her husband own a hardware store just inside town. They sell new and used

Shop-Vacs. They're like special vacuum cleaners that can suck up water."

Kathy lowered her fingers to just beneath her eyes. But the emotion spilling forth was far from sadness. Instead, unbridled hilarity spilled out. A laugh bounced past her hands, and Kathy pressed her fist against her lips.

"You've got a really sick sense of humor," Jay barked as he shifted from one foot to the other.

"I can't help it," Kathy squealed as Ben's friend answered the phone. "You two looked like Laurel and Hardy!"

Twenty-Four

By ten o'clock, Kathy's sense of humor had died. She stood in her kitchen and rubbed the back of her aching neck. Never again would she have to ask what a Shop-Vac was. She now knew how to manage and operate one of those water-sucking, vacuum-cleaner contraptions. Ben's church member had arrived in ten minutes with two of them. Kathy, Ben, Zach, Jay, Gloria, and Sigmund had either vacuumed water or moved furniture.

Ben's hardware buddy explained that the carpet in her bedroom was so wet and so old he recommended replacing it. He claimed the moisture could warp her wooden floors and make the whole apartment smell like a souring, wet mongrel for months. Once Kathy gave the nod, the man began pulling up the ruined carpet, cutting it into manageable squares, and stuffing it into garbage bags. Kathy told him he might as well go ahead and pull up the carpet in the living room, as well. Even though the pile hadn't gotten wet, it was the same age and the same ugly.

The carpet knife the guy used looked sharp enough to slit someone's throat. The second Kathy saw the blade, she decided to use the thing as a murder weapon in a future novel. The possibilities were gruesome.

She shivered and decided her future was more gruesome at the moment than any fictional murder. In the middle of all the upheaval, Ben had gone outside and found her apartment's water valve. He'd shut it off and told her not to turn the water back on until the plumber could fix everything—unless she wanted to risk another flood episode.

Now that all activity had ceased, Kathy dubiously eyed her living room. The wooden floors, battered by decades of use, lay barren. Her living room furniture was out of place, as was her bed and dresser.

Bewildered, Kathy leaned against the breakfast bar and considered where she would stay until her plumbing was fixed. The only logical option was the bed-and-breakfast across the street, where Gloria and Sigmund were spending the summer. They were scheduled to leave soon. Gloria had already insisted that Kathy should bunk in their suite and then rent the rooms when they moved out. Ben said a plumbing job of this magnitude might take a week or two to be completed—especially if the plumber wasn't immediately available and there was damage to her internal walls. Kathy tallied the cost of staying at the B and B on top of the great unknown plumbing bill and wilted. But she didn't see that she had another option.

"You okay?" Ben asked as he pushed a Shop-Vac from the bedroom. The hardware man had left it just in case.

"Yes, just tired." Kathy's smile felt as limp as her soggy carpet.

Like the other volunteers, Ben was damp around the edges, and dark circles marred his eyes. Everyone had left except Ben, Alaina, and Zachariah. Alaina and Zach went downstairs for a final inspection. Kathy prayed they came back with good news. The last downstairs report came from Phil an hour ago. According to him, everything was in good shape.

Twenty minutes ago, Phil announced that since he'd come in his own vehicle, he was going to rope in a late movie. The last Kathy heard, Jay, Ron, and Liza were going with him. She imagined Phil sitting beside Liza in the theater and playing footsies with her while Jay blissfully held her hand. Even in the midst of the flood chaos, Kathy envisioned Phil and Liza sitting on stools, sipping root beer, and flirting while Jay slaved away upstairs and Ron and Alaina mopped the downstairs leaks with towels.

Those two probably even ate all the shrimp ring, Kathy griped, and her stomach rumbled. That five o'clock sandwich wore thin hours ago.

Ben entered the kitchen and wrapped his arms around Kathy. "You look like you need a hug."

"I think what I really need is a new brain," Kathy mumbled against his shirt, which smelled of musty carpet.

"Don't beat yourself up too badly," Ben fussed and stroked her hair. "You didn't know."

"I should have. You told me. I can't believe how dimwitted I can sometimes be."

"Hey, don't talk about yourself like that," Ben admonished and nudged her away. "You're *my* dimwit now, remember?" He kissed the tip of her nose and smiled.

"Thanks for the support," Kathy drawled.

Ben pulled her close again, and Kathy rested in his embrace. The hardware guy sauntered back through her mind. "I guess I owe that hardware person big, don't I?" she asked. "What was his name, anyway?"

"Roger Rodriguez," Ben replied, his voice pleasantly vibrating her cheek.

"He and his wife are some of my best church members. Don't know what I'd do without them."

She couldn't help but wonder how special it would be to relax in Ben's arms for the rest of her life . . . to be a part of his ministry and his church. Even though Kathy wouldn't dare jump into a quick marriage like her "logical" brother was doing, her imagination wouldn't be stopped.

Ben's nearness, his warmth, his breath tickling her ear all worked together to make Kathy forget her worries about the

Zachariah factor. All that mattered was that Ben was falling in love with her, and she with him. Tilman Senior would have to accept the facts. And if he didn't, Kathy was willing to brave his disapproval. If Ben's love ran as deeply as hers, she knew he'd eventually feel the same.

He has to, she reasoned. A breathtaking new hope spread its wings in Kathy and swept her along the warm river of uncharted dreams. She held on tight. Ben was hers . . . all hers. Nothing could ever change that.

Someone entered the apartment door and discreetly cleared his throat. Kathy and Ben sprang apart. Kathy gripped the counter's edge and stared wide-eyed at the charming control-freak-murderer-turned-helpful-handyman. Zach's silver-streaked hair stood out in tufts here and there, and a smudge of dust marred his lined cheek. He looked from Ben to Kathy, back to Ben, then grinned.

Alaina stood beside her father and observed Kathy with a shy-yet-knowing smile.

Looking down, Kathy relaxed her grip on the counter and remembered she never got a chance to discover what Alaina was doing behind the "Employees Only" door at Walmart.

"Phil was right. Downstairs looks fine," Zach proclaimed. "It's going to need some paint to cover the water marks, but other than that you're in good shape."

"Good." Kathy laid her hand across her chest.

"You're going to need a place to stay for a while, aren't you?" Zachariah asked.

"Well, yes. I am," Kathy admitted. "But Aunt Gloria is expecting me in her suite tonight. I guess I'll just stay at the bed-and-breakfast until the plumbing is finished."

"Nonsense." With the wave of his hand, Zach dismissed the whole plan. "You're staying with us."

I am? Kathy thought.

"There." He nodded, his bottom lip protruding. "It's settled." He reminded Kathy of a hawk-nosed Indian, standing tall and proud on top of his own mountain.

"We've got an extra room that shares my bathroom," Alaina explained.

"What about my cat?" Kathy asked.

"Well . . ." Zach hedged.

"Lucy can stay with me," Ben announced.

He squeezed her hand, and Kathy figured that was her cue. "Okay," she heard herself say while her tired mind raced with the magnitude of the invitation. She'd just agreed to stay in a mysterious chalet that held who-knew-what secrets . . . with a man Thurston Manley swore was a murderer . . . and a third-floor suite that begged to be explored.

"Oh no!" Zachariah snapped his fingers. "I forgot. I won't be here part of next week."

"You won't?" Alaina queried and lifted a ringlet away from her eye.

"No. I'm leaving Wednesday morning for a fishing trip. I'll be gone until Saturday. I guess I never told you."

"You're right." A hint of glee stirred beneath Alaina's impassive expression, and Kathy wondered if her reaction had anything to do with what went on behind that store door this afternoon. "But we'll be okay. Don't you think, Kathy?" Alaina's grin seemed to go past Kathy and target someone unseen.

"Sure," she agreed.

"I'll be around, too," Ben said. "Maybe I could take you ladies out to dinner one of those nights."

"I'd love that," Kathy said and reveled in Ben's doting.

"Great, then. We're all set," Alaina said and touched her father's arm. "Don't worry about a thing, Dad."

Despite her exhaustion, Kathy's active mind hopped from one bit of information to another. *Zach's gonna be gone. Alaina's already making plans. Who knows what or who they involve? I want to explore the suite. I'll be staying at the chalet. There's no better time for Zach to be gone!*

The telephone's ringing pierced Kathy's brainstorming. "Oh my word," she said and looked at her wristwatch. "I think that's my mom. She was supposed to call at ten."

"Well, it's ten"—Ben said, checking his watch—"on the button."

"She's never been late for anything in her life," Kathy explained. She hurried from the kitchen, stepped around an askew end table, and dashed toward her bedroom. Kathy crawled across her unmade bed, now shoved against the wall, and nabbed her cell phone from the window ledge.

"Hi, Mom," she said into the receiver.

"Hello, honey," Michelle replied in her sweet Southern drawl. "How's everything goin'?"

"Everything's fine with me," Kathy said and looked at her bare floors. "Except my plumbing flooded me out tonight, and I'm going to stay with some friends for a while."

Kathy squirmed off the bed, stood, and slipped into her bathroom. She hooked her finger through the doorknob hole and discreetly closed the door. She hated airing her family upheavals in front of Ben's father.

"The important news is," Kathy continued in a low voice, "Jay has flipped his lid. He's gone and gotten engaged to a woman he met this summer."

Michelle's lengthy silence prompted Kathy's "Mom? Are you still there?" She rested her backside against her bathroom counter and crossed her ankles.

"Yes, I'm here," Michelle said. "I'm just trying to process what you said. Did you say your apartment flooded?"

"Right—but don't worry about that right now." She lifted her hand, palm outward. "It's under control. The deal here is Jay!

He's asked this woman to marry him. Bought her an engagement ring the size of Mars!"

"What about your inventory?" Michelle rushed. "Was that harmed at all?"

"No. My store's fine!" Kathy straightened, turned, and gripped the shampoo bottle, still out from when she'd washed her hair. "Listen." Kathy picked up the bottle and began tapping it against the counter in rhythm with her words. "Your son, Jay—the logical one—he's hauled off and gotten engaged!"

"Jay is thirty years old," Michelle said. "Your dad and I always said when he fell, he'd fall hard. It's not like they've eloped or anything, is it?"

"No, but—"

"Well, Jay's got a square head on his shoulders."

"It's not square anymore," Kathy said. "It's gone all gooey! Trust me—he's lost the whole square. And I don't think he's in love, either! You should see her. She's a knockout."

"He's probably planning for a long engagement," Michelle reasoned. "Jay can take care of himself. You're the one I'm worried about. Now tell me about this flood."

Kathy plopped the shampoo bottle against the counter. The bottle tilted sideways, toppled into the sink, and leaked a stream of golden liquid in its wake. "Mom, I can take care of myself, too," she snarled as her day crashed around her. "You really don't have to keep baby-sitting me." Kathy observed her reflection in the mirror and grimaced. She looked as haggard as she sounded.

"Kathy!" Michelle gasped. "You've never spoken to me that way before."

"Well, you treat me like you think I'm ten," Kathy said as the wad of frustration in her gut began to dissolve. She'd read and reread that book on boundaries but hadn't possessed the courage to start implementing the concepts—until now. "Jay's going off the deep end, and you aren't even concerned about him. It's like

you have this blind trust in him and nothing but *distrust* in me."
Kathy yanked up the shampoo bottle and slammed it against the
counter while the smell of peaches enveloped her. Being fully
honest had never felt so good.

"It's not that I don't trust you, Kathy. It's just . . . well . . . I
worry about you. You can be a little . . . just like that night you
let that man in to use your phone—"

"That man is now my boyfriend," Kathy injected, "as I'm
sure Aunt Gloria has already told you."

"No! Nobody's told me a thing! You mean you've started seeing that guy? Kathy, he just showed up at your door and now,
boom, you're dating him?"

"He's a pastor," Kathy explained and decided now was not the
time to admit that her apartment flooded because she forgot to
call a plumber. But it was the perfect opportunity to hold what
personal territory she was gaining. "And it wasn't a 'boom' deal.
We've gotten to know each other, and now we're just getting to
know each other better."

"Oh," Michelle said.

"I like him a lot," Kathy added, and couldn't imagine how
she sounded so practical about something she was so ecstatic
about.

"Well, maybe he's okay. I don't know why Gloria hasn't said
a thing."

"Maybe because she thought *I* should tell you," Kathy replied
like she was sealing a business deal.

"Are you okay?" Michelle asked. "Because you don't sound
anything like yourself."

"Mom," Kathy pleaded and bent forward, "would you please
believe me when I tell you Jay is making the biggest mistake of
his life? Liza—that's the woman's name—I saw her making eyes
at another guy tonight even."

"Oh my," Michelle worried, and Kathy at last found some

satisfaction. "What's gotten into him? What are we supposed to do?"

"I *don't know*," Kathy moaned and covered her face. "I guess get ready to pick up the pieces, and hope it happens before the marriage, not after."

A light tap on the door reminded her she had visitors. "Kathy?" Alaina called.

"Oh no. I forgot my company!" She flung open the door.

Alaina stood on the other side and smiled an apology.

"Mom, just a minute," Kathy said and lowered the phone.

"Sorry," Alaina said, "but Dad's ready to leave. He can get . . . impatient."

"No, *I'm* sorry. I can't believe I forgot you guys!" Kathy exclaimed and pressed the phone to her ear. "Mom, I have to go. I forgot my company."

"Okay, Kathy," Michelle said with an indulgent tone. "And did your apartment flood because you forgot to call the plumber?"

"Uh, I'll call you later. Love you," Kathy replied and disconnected the call.

Twenty-Five

That night, Kathy lay in one of the chalet's bedrooms with the covers pulled up to her chin. The digital clock on the nightstand proclaimed one o'clock was swiftly approaching. Kathy, shrouded in fatigue, was too uptight to even think about sleep. She'd lived and relived the events of the evening until her mind was numb.

Much of her thoughts were occupied with Ben, with his thoughtfulness. After she packed and put Lucy in her carrier, Ben followed Kathy to the chalet and carried her suitcases up to her room. He'd even made her a cup of herbal tea and helped her make a sandwich before leaving at eleven. Every day that passed, Kathy grew more and more convinced that Ben Tilman was a rare treasure she should make every effort to keep.

Too bad he has a charming-control-freak-murderer for a dad, she thought and trembled with the dread of falling asleep in the same house with a killer. Unlike Ben, Zach had ended his hospitable attitude when he entered his home. He'd declared he was going straight to his room and encouraged Ben and Alaina to see to Kathy's comfort.

At that point, Gloria's previous question, *"Are you sure that's what you want to do?"* had begun to haunt Kathy. Gloria and Sigmund had been all set for Kathy to crash in their suite until Kathy phoned with her change in plans. Now that the lights were out and the uncertainties were setting in, Kathy prayed Gloria's misgivings were unfounded. She also couldn't even imagine her mom's response to this decision—if she were told all the details.

Kathy gripped the fresh-smelling sheets in her clammy hands and imagined that horrid morning when Laura Tilman met her fate. Kathy stared at the ceiling that also served as the floor for Laura's old suite. Fifteen minutes ago, the swishing wind had begun harassing the trees, producing specter-like shadows that cavorted across the ceiling in a silent dance of doom. As a result, the yard light's eerie sheen resembled a flickering, ancient candle heavy with wax. Kathy's mind raced with the plots of hair-raising novels she'd read and reread . . . of dungeons and crooked-backed doorkeepers . . . of Edgar Allen Poe's ghastly stories . . . of the ghost of Ligeia.

Her whole body went rigid. *That man had a weird imagination,* Kathy told herself. *He did take opium, after all. There are no such things as ghosts, and no such thing as Ligeia. It was all made up.* Despite her logic, her body remained as stiff as a corpse.

A flicker of lightning illuminated the paneled room in a blinding white flash. A boom of thunder rattled the brass lamp. Kathy jumped and squeaked. She bit a wad of sheet as her heart's wild palpitating pounded her temples. *I was crazy to come here!*

The sheers cloaking the window shifted, and Kathy clamped down on the sheet. The faint scent of bleach filled her senses. A wave of sticky heat flashed over her body. And all she could think was, *Lucy isn't here to move the drapes this time. There's nobody in here but me!*

A noisy swoosh of wind slammed into the chalet, and the sheers pranced from the window. Kathy released a silent scream as a current of cool air drifted across her face, beaded in sweat. Then the sheers hugged the window and puffed out. Kathy relaxed her jaw and released the tormented sheet. *The window must be open,* she thought. Before she could measure her courage, Kathy cast off the covers, swung her feet out of bed, and hurried to the window. As suspected, it was open a couple of inches.

Oh, duh! she thought and pressed down on the metal frame. The window slid into place with a thud.

Headlights illuminated the yard in twin splashes of light as a truck glided into the driveway. Kathy stepped behind the column of heavy drapes hanging beside the window and peeked from behind them. When Kathy arrived, she hadn't expected Phil to be back at the chalet. The late show didn't start until nearly ten. But it should have been over around eleven thirty.

Why's he so late then? Kathy hoped the answer didn't involve Liza.

Something bumped against the ceiling, and Kathy snapped her head up. She stared at the shadowed ceiling and waited in agony. Nobody was supposed to be up there. Ben said his father declared the room off-limits.

What if it's off-limits because Zach keeps his wife locked up there? Kathy's frantic mind grappled for any thread of logic in the suspicion. *But how could she be alive if everyone saw her dead?* She clutched the sides of her cotton pajamas and strained for an answer. Finally it came. *What if it was a closed-casket funeral and Zach didn't let anyone see the body?* Kathy stared at the rocker in the corner and allowed the idea to grow. *That would fit his control-freak personality,* she thought, *and nobody would have the guts to question his decision.*

Another crack of lightning sent Kathy into a frenzied jump. She pressed the heels of her hands on both her temples and swallowed a scream. Scurrying for the bed, she glimpsed a movement across the room. Kathy stopped. Her bare toes dug against the area rug as she realized she was not alone. Another person stood on the other side of the room like a pale phantom, watching . . . watching.

It's her! Kathy thought and covered her mouth with her chilled hand. *Laura Tilman!*

She scrambled toward the doorway, the whole time looking over her shoulder. Interestingly enough, the phantom did the same. Kathy stopped, leaned forward, and scrutinized the invader, who looked more familiar all the time. Finally, she realized she'd been scared of her own reflection in the closet's mirrored doors.

Kathy went back to the bed, fell forward, and buried her face in the plump pillow. *I have never felt so dumb in my whole life*, she thought as her mother's words from childhood rang from the past. *One day your imagination is going to get you into more trouble than you can get out of!*

Another bump on the ceiling ended Kathy's embarrassment. She flopped onto her back and again stared at the ceiling. Once more she pondered the closed-casket funeral and the possibilities of Laura Tilman being held captive in her own home.

Thurston Manley said I resembled Laura, she worried. *What if Zachariah plans to lock me up there with her?*

Kathy sat straight up. She picked at her pajama top's buttons and debated her options. *Matlock would investigate*, she thought. *Mr. Chicken wouldn't.* For fifteen seconds Kathy was trapped in an identity crisis, trying to decide whether she was more like Matlock or Mr. Chicken. Finally, she knew she had no choice but to be Ms. Matlock.

Grabbing her lightweight robe off the end of the bed, Kathy hurried for the door. With a new rush of wind splattering raindrops against the window, Kathy turned the doorknob, peeked into the hallway, and discovered it vacant. A crystal lamp sitting on a decorative table illuminated the hall in a silvery aura. Zach's door, at the hall's end, was closed as tightly as Alaina's. Kathy slipped out of her room, eased her door shut, scampered up the hallway, and paused at the base of the stairs.

The passage loomed upward, a forbidden corridor leading to an unknown realm. Gulping, Kathy wished she'd packed her flashlight but was thankful for the meager light the lamp provided. She gripped the handrail and forced herself to take the steps. Her bare toes, as cold as tombstones, padded along the polished wood until she arrived on the carpeted landing. She paused and sized up her surroundings. A trace of light from downstairs provided enough illumination for Kathy to detect a closet between what appeared to be a large bathroom and a bedroom's closed door.

A faint musty odor—the fragrance of the unused—heightened her uneasiness. *What am I doing up here?* She relived the last five minutes to evaluate how she'd talked herself into entering the unknown. *I wasn't thinking,* she decided and pressed her fingers between her brows. *I've got to get logical here. That bumping was probably just a tree limb hitting the side of the house. There's nobody trapped up here in this room.*

Kathy further deduced that there was no way Zach would have forbidden his own children from seeing his wife's body. Ben was convinced his mother was dead; so was Alaina. Suddenly, Laura Tilman being locked up here was as ridiculous as Kathy thinking someone was in her room when it was her own reflection.

The ambulance had to have been called. The paramedics would have been witnesses to her being dead. Kathy placed her hand on top of her head and squeezed as she recalled Alaina saying she'd found her mother's body.

Okay, okay, okay, she reasoned. *So nobody's up here, but that still doesn't mean Laura Tilman wasn't murdered.* A few days ago she'd been flipping through one of the *True Crime* books in search of any murderer who might have induced a heart attack with chemicals. She discovered a story about a doctor who used a chemical injection to trigger a heart attack in his wife. Nobody questioned that she died of natural causes until a snoopy investigator found the syringe and needle in the doctor's briefcase.

Like a doll maneuvered by forces beyond her control, Kathy pivoted to face the suite's door. Even though her eyes were gritty,

Kathy's agitated mind refused to allow her to even think about sleep. She'd wanted to prowl through this suite ever since Ben told her it was off-limits.

Here I am, she thought, *and there it is. I might as well go for it while I have the opportunity.*

Another round of thunder grumbled from the distance. *It was a dark and stormy night*, she thought and swallowed a delirious giggle. Kathy rubbed her damp palms together and stepped toward the suite's door at the same time the knob rattled and turned. Her heart lurched and pounded against her ribs. As the door inched open, a sob, low and desperate, floated onto the landing.

All Kathy's logic vanished. *Laura Tilman really is up here!* she thought. Kathy sprang toward the closet and whipped open the door. When the hinges complained, she grimaced. Silently, she stepped inside, slowly pulled the door within centimeters of closing, and prayed the whole time the thing wouldn't make another peep. Goose bumps swept Kathy from head to toe. As she peeked through the door's tiny opening, smells of moth balls and yesterday's treasures closed in for a stifling hug.

A fair-haired woman dressed in pale, gauzy nightwear floated from the suite. She sniffled and rubbed at her face while holding a lighted object next to her ear.

Kathy pressed her fist against her mouth and shivered.

"Caleb, I have to go now," the woman whispered, and Kathy recognized the wobbly voice as Alaina's.

Relaxing her fist, Kathy closed her eyes, gulped at the air, and tried to recall how she knew the name Caleb. *I've seen it somewhere in the last few days*, she thought.

"I'll—I'll call you back once I get to my room and can stop crying," Alaina continued. She stepped toward the stairway. "Dad will kill me if he finds me up here." She paused for a series of sniffles.

"I know you didn't mean it that way," Alaina whimpered. "I love you, too." A swallowed sob, faint and full of feeling, punctuated her claim before she ended the phone call. Dropping the cell phone into her robe pocket, Alaina descended the stairs.

Kathy rubbed her face and realized a thin film of perspiration covered her forehead. Two new facts spun through her mind like informational nuggets to be savored and analyzed: Alaina was in love with somebody named Caleb, and she was convinced her father would kill her if he found her upstairs.

"If he'd kill his daughter, he'd kill his wife," Kathy mouthed and rested her forehead against the door. Closing her eyes, she allowed her system to slow in the aftermath of the adrenaline rush. After a moment of inactivity, Kathy indulged in a languid yawn. Her shoulders drooped. Her feet felt like boulders.

She pondered the suite, mere feet away, and debated whether now was the best time to investigate. *I need a flashlight*, she thought, and made a mental note to get one from home. Kathy determined she'd be crazy to go into that suite and just flip on the light. *And I won't find many clues in the dark*, she thought. *Zachariah will be gone Wednesday, Thursday, and Friday nights.*

With a nod, she made her final decision. "I should wait until later," she whispered, then welcomed another yawn.

Kathy inched open the closet door, silently closed it behind her, and quickly walked across the room and out of the suite. She glided down the steps and paused at the base to peer up the hallway. All was clear. Kathy scurried along the corridor, slipped into her room, closed the door, and locked it. She hurried to her rumpled bed and dove under the covers. After rolling onto her back and placing her hand under her head, Kathy planned to close her eyes but found herself staring at the ceiling again.

"Caleb . . . Caleb . . . Caleb," she whispered and was trying to make herself remember how she'd heard that name when a ray of light sliced across the floor. Kathy tilted her head toward the restroom she shared with Alaina. The door was closed but the light filtered beneath it. She propped herself up on her elbow and gazed toward the bathroom. The sound of running water mingled with the splash of rain on the window.

Wondering if Alaina would call that Caleb person again, Kathy hopped out of bed and tiptoed across the room. She plastered herself against the wall by the bathroom door and strained for any vein of a conversation. A cell phone's high-pitched tune wove a melody of satisfaction through Kathy before its immediate ending.

"Caleb, what are you thinking?" Alaina's hasty greeting, urgent and low, was now void of tears. "I'm supposed to call you. You're going to wake somebody up. Kathy's just in the next room."

Alaina's lengthy pause prompted Kathy's pressing her ear against the door.

"I'm tired of this, too, Caleb," Alaina said. "But how do you propose we tell him?" Her voice faded until Kathy couldn't decipher another word.

Tell who what? Kathy thought. She rested her head against the wall and pressed her fingers against her eyes. *Caleb . . . Caleb . . . Caleb*, she chanted to herself until the image of a Walmart name tag with *Caleb Manley* written on it floated across her vision.

"Bingo!" Kathy whispered and lightly snapped her fingers. She slowly slid down the wall as she pieced together the implications. Whatever was going on behind that employees-only door at Walmart, Alaina did *not* seem like the type. Kathy plopped to the floor. The jolt joggled her memory. Only hours ago, she and Ben had stolen a few kisses of their own. Kathy smiled as the recollection warmed her all over again. *Maybe that's all that's happening with Alaina and Caleb*, she reasoned and decided to give her new friend the benefit of the doubt.

Meanwhile, a new realization gnawed at Kathy. She doubled her fist against the carpet and fixed her gaze on the oak highboy dominating the room's corner. *Thurston's last name is Manley—just like Caleb's!* She scraped her memory for any familial resemblance between the two men. While Thurston looked like a sun-baked cowboy, Caleb was a tall, robust hunk-of-a-guy who bore zero resemblance to the aging codger.

Maybe their last names being the same is just a coincidence, Kathy thought. *For that matter, I'm not the only Moore in Northpointe.*

She pulled her knees closer to her chest and wrapped her arms around them.

"This family has a lot of issues," Kathy whispered and wondered how Ben had turned out so balanced, charming, and generally wonderful. She figured her answer lay in the woman who once occupied the third floor.

Twenty-Six

By Wednesday noon, Kathy was counting the hours until Ron left. *Only two more,* she thought and eyed him sitting at the end of the service bar. He'd come in an hour ago and alternated reading a magazine with trying to help.

Kathy resumed her task of unpacking an order of nonfiction books. *Setting Boundaries* had made such an impression on her that she decided to carry it and a few others by the same author. Since she'd conjured the courage to implement some of the concepts, things were gradually changing with her mother. Michelle had called yesterday and never once tried to tell Kathy what to do. Kathy backed away from the front-and-center display and then adjusted the books.

She couldn't stop another peek at Ron and wondered if she should have been more forceful in setting a few boundaries with him. For some unknown reason, Ron had altered his original plans to leave Tuesday when Jay did. Much to Kathy's surprise, he'd hung out at the store all day, despite the fact that she encouraged him to "move along" because she was so busy.

The guy had misconstrued her hints about his leaving for a request for help. He'd even gone to the hardware store, bought some paint, and painted the wall that was stained from the Saturday-night flooding. The smell of new paint now mingled with the morning's batch of cinnamon rolls. While Kathy was grateful for Ron's work, she wondered if he thought she was indebted to him.

She dug through a mound of packing paper and pulled the final book from the box. Glancing toward Ron again, Kathy found him looking back. His smile suggested her attention didn't surprise him. "Are you ready for lunch?" he asked.

"Uh . . ." Kathy hedged and wondered where this was leading. Somehow she didn't think he was about to offer to get everyone a burger.

"I was thinking maybe you and I could check out the new steak house." He pointed south.

"Go ahead, Kathy," Sigmund said from a few feet away. He and his wife were removing books from the shelves and meticulously dusting every inch of exposed wood. "It's not that busy today. Gloria and I will take care of the store for you. You might as well enjoy some freedom before we leave Saturday."

Kathy looked over her shoulder and wondered if Uncle Ziggy even had one memory about where her affections lay. She widened her eyes toward Gloria, who squeezed her husband's arm and discreetly shook her head.

Oh! Sigmund mouthed and nodded.

Gloria rolled her eyes.

"Let's go, then," Ron said and slid from his stool.

Shooting a silent plea for help toward Gloria, Kathy debated her options. The last thing Kathy needed was for Ben to see her out alone with Ron.

Just tell him! Gloria mouthed.

Kathy placed the final book on the display and decided she wasn't going to be able to get around the tasteless task of telling Ron Thaine to get lost *permanently*. She'd so hoped he would take her hints or that his leaving for the summer would mean he'd forget her. But yesterday after Jay left, Liza said that Ron was talking about coming back to Northpointe for Christmas. How the guy could think Kathy was interested in him was a mystery.

"Ron," she said, "let's step outside for a few minutes, okay?"

"Sure." He shrugged. "Whatever."

Kathy led the way out the door into the August warmth and was thankful this was an off day for the downtown merchants. Only a few cars claimed parking places along the street. A trio of elk stood on the edge of the parking lot, near Kathy's Impala. The rascals had roamed the streets most of the morning and even blocked traffic more than once. They observed her and Ron with bored stares. She recalled thinking how charming the elk were earlier in the summer. Now she was beginning to view them as pests—especially when they were impairing her navigation. She couldn't wait until hunting season started, when they would head to the mountains.

Ron closed the store door, and Kathy decided this was not the time to worry about elk. She had another problem to face. "Ron," she began and looked up at him.

"I'm all ears," he said.

Kathy crossed her arms, tilted her head, and wrestled with what to say. Finally, she blurted, "I'm seeing Ben Tilman."

Ron laughed and stroked the front of his snug knit shirt. "What gives, Kathy? Did you drag me out here for a comedy routine?"

"No. I'm serious." Kathy tapped her thick-soled sandal against the sidewalk. The smell of burgers drifted from The Diner on the Corner. One of the elks snorted. And the sunshine bore through Kathy's sleeveless blouse.

"*We're* serious," she added.

His eyes went from scornful to incredulous. "What? Are you crazy? That guy's as exciting as a two-by-four."

"I like him," she defended. "A lot."

Placing his hands on his hips, Ron shook his head and stared toward the mountains. "I cannot imagine what she sees in him," he mumbled as if Kathy weren't there.

While Ron pondered his dilemma, Kathy examined her polka-dotted toenails and smiled. She saw more in Ben Tilman than Ron could ever imagine. Yesterday evening, Ben had arrived at the chalet minutes before Kathy pulled up after work. He'd met her at the door and informed her that they were cooking supper for his father. According to Ben, Alaina was working late and Phil was "out." Kathy and Ben had laughed through placing a frozen casserole in the microwave and dumping a bag of salad in a bowl.

After dinner, they'd sat on the porch together while Zachariah retired to his room with a book. Before the night was over, Kathy convinced Ben he should paint her toenails with the new purple polish she'd bought at the drugstore. While he jovially complained through the whole task, he was the one who insisted on adding the white polka dots.

And he was the one who insisted that Kathy should attend his church's Wednesday night "Fruit of the Spirit" Bible study tonight. Kathy had never been so excited about being fruity. After the study, Ben had invited her and Alaina to come to his house for a visit with Lucy, who he was still boarding. Kathy could hardly wait.

The more she was with Ben, the more she liked him. The more she liked him, the more she wanted to know of him . . . and of the woman he called Mother. As planned, Zachariah had left town this morning for his fishing trip. Kathy had a midnight appointment with the third floor.

Tonight's the night, she thought and was so overtaken with anticipation she nearly forgot Ron's presence and her date with Ben.

"Maybe once you understand what my plans are, you'll change your mind," Ron said.

She lifted her gaze and tried to recall what Ron was referencing. "Your plans?"

Ron raised his chin to an assured angle and gazed back at Kathy. "Well, yes. I mean, maybe I haven't been clear here."

"About what?"

"About . . . I guess what I'm trying to say is, if you knew you could have me for keeps," he extended his arms and pointed to himself, "I can't see you wasting your time on Ben."

Kathy stopped a sputter.

"Looking back, I guess I haven't come across like I was serious. But I meant what I said Saturday night."

Eyes wide, Kathy tried to remember.

"You know," Ron prompted, "after I fixed your cake, I told you we ought to get engaged and celebrate with Jay and Liza."

"You were serious?"

He spread his arms. "Of course! I've never painted for any other woman. That ought to tell you something. Here I am, baby. I'm all yours. You can tell the Reverend Boring Ben he can find himself another chick."

A spontaneous giggle bubbled within Kathy. She pressed her fingertips against her lips and examined the sidewalk until she could control her mirth. Ron Thaine was an arrogant idiot if he thought he could compare to the likes of Ben Tilman. She imagined Ron zooming past that little boy trapped in the overturned car because he was too busy adjusting his rearview mirror to reflect his "perfect" face.

Ron sidled over close to Kathy, placed his arm along her shoulders, and said, "Look, babe, I know you're shocked speechless here. Why don't we just go on to lunch, and we can talk some more, okay?"

Kathy lowered her hand from her lips and looked up at Ron. "I hate to have to be so blunt, Ron," she said. "But I'm not your woman. You aren't—I'm not—We're just not."

"You mean you aren't—"

"No!" Kathy said. "Like I already said, it's Ben and me."

"But he's a preacher!" Ron jerked his arm from Kathy like she was spreading anthrax.

"So? My father's a preacher, too. He's not so bad!"

Ron gazed skyward and huffed. "You'll change your mind after I leave," he decided.

"No, I won't!"

"Yes, you will." He crossed his arms and rocked back on his heels. "I'm glad I waited to leave until today. It's good we've had this talk. I can see why you'd be confused about Ben. But I just can't see you serious about someone so . . . so, well, drab."

"Ben is up for Citizen of the Year," Kathy defended. "And there's a reason! He's not drab! He—"

"What I mean is," Ron droned, "you're just too full of life for the likes of him. I think once I'm gone, you'll figure it all out. Jay even thinks we should make a go of it."

"Jay? You talked to Jay about this?"

"Sure, he told me to go for it."

Kathy sighed and covered her eyes. "My brother doesn't know which end is up right now. He and I have barely talked all summer—not alone, anyway. I don't guess he even knows about me and Ben."

She uncovered her eyes, allowed her attention to trail up the street, and attempted to come up with a line that would facilitate Ron's swift departure.

"So are we still on for lunch?" Ron asked.

Squinting against the persistent sun, Kathy looked back at him. "No!" she said and shook her head. "No! I already told you—no!"

"Ah, come on, Kathy! Be a sport for ol' Ron, okay?" He flashed her the same smile he'd used on a few gals around town, and Kathy wondered if the guy had ever been turned down.

"No!" she repeated. Kathy stepped around him and marched toward her store. *If I have to, I'll lock myself in my apartment until he leaves*, she thought.

Kathy was determined not to stop until she entered her store. Then she spotted Phil Tilman's Chevy truck outside the colonial bed-and-breakfast across the street—where Liza and her mother were still staying. Kathy halted and stared at the vehicle until she convinced herself it couldn't be Phil's.

Ron's voice penetrated her concerns. "Oh, looks like Phil's here again."

"Again?" Kathy turned to face him.

"He came over last night. We all stayed up until midnight playing cards. Mom loves him. She asked him back over today."

"Oh," Kathy said and doubted Phil was there to develop a relationship with Dory Thaine. *When the cat's away, the mice will play,* she thought and wondered what her optimistic mother would think of this new development.

"Well, I guess this is it, then?" Ron asked. "You're serious about us not doing lunch?"

Thankful the guy was finally admitting defeat, Kathy nodded and decided gazing past him was the best option.

"Okay, then." He hooked his thumb through the belt loop of his jeans and shifted his weight. "I'll be in touch." Before Kathy realized his intent, Ron bent down, brushed his lips against hers, looked her in the eyes, and said, "There's something for you to think about while I'm gone."

Too stunned to answer, Kathy mutely stared at him. Before she could form a rebuttal, he sauntered past her and crossed the street. Once he strode onto the B and B's white porch, Ron gave Kathy a thumbs-up and blew her a kiss. The second he went inside and closed the door, she scrubbed at her lips and then laughed.

This is too ridiculous for words! She was still laughing when she went back into the store.

"Everything okay?" Dust cloth in hand, Sigmund stepped from behind a bookshelf. "Sorry I tried to send you off with him. I wasn't thinking."

"It's okay," Kathy said. "Everything worked out anyway." She chuckled under her breath and picked up the empty book box she'd left behind.

Gloria peeked out from the other side of the shelf. "What's so funny?" she asked, a sprig of dust clinging to her curls.

"Ron Thaine. He's so full of himself it's ridiculous."

"Glad you can laugh about it." Gloria frowned. "His mother was always that way when she was younger. Of course, *some* people were too blind to see it and actually went to homecoming with her."

"Now, now, dear," Sigmund chimed, "let's don't drag up old bones." He disappeared behind the bookshelf. Three seconds later, Gloria squealed and vanished. Sigmund's laughter mingled with hers. Then silence reigned.

Kathy shook her head and meandered to the back of the store. *Those two act like newlyweds, and they've been married almost forty years. I'm going to miss them when they're gone,* she thought and hoped they planned to visit next summer. As things had turned out, they'd been less focused on spying and more interested in support.

Since Sigmund and Gloria were leaving Saturday, they were dedicating this week to helping Kathy get everything in top shape. After scheming with Kathy's mom and dad, they'd even surprised her with the offer to pay for new carpet. Even though Kathy preferred to maintain her independence, she decided now was not the time to assert it. She accepted the gift. The carpet people were arriving tomorrow.

So was the plumber. Kathy dropped the box near the back door and estimated that she'd be in her apartment within a week. Zachariah's fishing trip couldn't have been better timed. She smiled and paused by a display of murder mysteries. The one she focused on featured a female private detective gazing around the corner of a brick building and holding a gun. Kathy stroked the cover and thought about what clues she might find in Laura's suite.

Then she confronted a dilemma she had yet to consider: *What should I do if I find out Zachariah Tilman really did kill his wife? Will Ben and Alaina believe me? If they don't believe me, will they get mad if I turn their father over to the police? Will Ben break up with me?* Her fingers stiffened against the novel's cover. Kathy debated whether she should leave well enough alone and be assured of her relationship with Ben or stay true to justice and snoop for details.

She looked at the dark-skinned private eye and whispered, "If I don't find any clues, then I still don't have anything to worry about." Kathy picked up the book. "If I don't look in that suite while I have the chance, I'll probably regret it for the rest of my life." She rested her nose against the pages and breathed deeply. *Nothing smells better than a new book*, she thought and made her decision.

Kathy Moore refused to neglect justice. If Thurston Manley was right, then Zachariah Tilman needed to be uncovered for what he was.

Ben cares for me, she thought. *He'll stand by me.* She placed the book back in the rack and pledged to stick to her original plan.

Twenty-Seven

At five thirty, Alaina stepped into Kathy's store and glanced around for signs of the owner. The smell of furniture polish and glass cleaner mingled with the odor of fresh paint. Every book was in place; every speck of dust gone. But, as with the street, the bookstore appeared to be deserted.

"Hello," Alaina softly called. Her wedge heels tapped along the floor as she meandered between a pair of bookshelves. "Kathy?"

A crash, tumble, and "oomph" erupted from the back of the store.

"Kathy?" Alaina repeated.

"Back here!" Kathy yelled.

Alaina followed her voice to the far corner and stopped on the edge of a literary disaster. Kathy sat in the middle of a mound of paperbacks that appeared to have collapsed with the wall shelf lying near her legs.

"The thing fell on me." Kathy rubbed her head, then examined a small tear in the leg of her cotton pants.

"Ouch!" Alaina grimaced. She secured her purse on her shoulder, lifted her long cotton skirt, and knelt beside her friend. "Are you okay?"

"Yes." Kathy's weary smile didn't match her claim.

"Here, let me help you up."

"Be careful," Kathy cautioned. "I don't want to bend the books any worse than they already are."

"Okay. I've got you." Alaina stood, scooted her foot beneath the edge of some of the books, and reached for her friend's hand.

With a heave-ho, Kathy pulled herself up, and Alaina offered the leverage to get her out of the books and steady on her feet. "Man!" Kathy huffed and placed her hands on her hips. "I can't believe this. I thought I had that shelf secure."

Alaina examined the bent nails marring what looked to be a fresh coat of beige paint. *This must be where the paint smell is coming from.* She examined the wall that had been marked by water spots the last time she saw it.

"I'm just impressed you got the wall painted so soon. You don't waste time, do you?"

"I didn't do it," Kathy admitted. "Ron Thaine did."

"Oh," Alaina said and looked at Kathy, who examined the metal rack like a scientist studying a new experiment. "He's big on helping, isn't he?"

"Who?" Kathy asked and glanced toward Alaina.

"Ron Thaine," Alaina supplied and didn't bother hiding the aversion in her voice.

"Oh, him." Kathy brushed a streak of dust off the front of her white sleeveless blouse and rubbed her palms together. "He's gone back to New Mexico. I'm glad. Good riddance."

"Really," Alaina agreed. "He acted like he owned you or something. Even Ben said—"

"What did Ben say?" Kathy prompted, her intense hazel eyes begging for more details.

"Now that I have your attention . . ." Alaina teased.

Kathy gripped Alaina's arm. "Seriously, did Ben say anything?"

"He just said . . . I think it was Friday . . . He said he hoped there was nothing between you guys. I think he was a little worried."

Kathy nodded. "He said something Saturday to me, as well. Ben saw me going to the movies with Ron and my brother and Liza. I told him Saturday night that I'm not even close to interested in him."

"You know, Kathy, Ben likes you a lot," Alaina said and tried to recall ever seeing her brother so distracted by a woman. "Up until now, I had about decided he was married to his ministry and that was the end of it."

Beaming, Kathy motioned toward the front of the store. "Come on. I'll make us some coffee or something, and you can tell all."

"Actually," Alaina hedged and followed Kathy toward the service bar, "I can't stay long. I just came to tell you . . ." She hesitated and paused near the cash register.

Stopping her journey toward the coffeemaker, Kathy pivoted to face Alaina. Her quizzical eyes and calculating appraisal hinted that Kathy Moore already knew Alaina was hiding something. A hard knot formed in Alaina's stomach, and she wondered if her father also suspected.

"I . . ." Alaina moved to the service bar, plopped down her leather purse, and perched on a stool. She'd debated a dozen different ways to tell Kathy about her absence tonight. She'd invented as many excuses. None of them were as appropriate as the truth. Caleb agreed.

"I'm not going to be home tonight," she explained.

"You're not?" Kathy asked and never changed her position or her expression.

"N-no." Alaina toyed with the strap of her purse.

"You're going to be gone all night?" A cloak of doubt marring her features, Kathy leaned against the counter and reached back to grip the edge as if she were trying to hold herself up.

"Before you jump to conclusions . . . there's something I need to tell you," Alaina hurried. "I'm married."

Kathy fixed her focus on Alaina and silently examined her like a private eye piecing together the final clues to a nearly finished case. "To Caleb Manley?"

Alaina held her breath and straightened her spine. "How did you know?" A panicked mantra pummeled her mind. *If Ben saw us, and Kathy figured it out, what about Dad?*

"I knew you were hiding something when you came to my apartment that first time. You'd been crying."

"I wasn't married then," Alaina explained. "I'd just told Caleb we'd get married when Dad was gone on the mission trip. I was scared stiff."

Kathy licked her lips and nodded. "Then Ben—"

"Did Ben tell you?" Alaina leaned forward.

"No." Kathy vehemently shook her head. "No," she repeated. "But he wouldn't tell me why you were mad at him that first night I had dinner at your house. I just figured it involved a man. It always does. Well, in the novels, anyway."

"You and your novels," Alaina said. "Ben says you're a mystery junkie."

"What would give him that idea?" Kathy rapidly blinked.

Alaina chuckled and shook her head. "Oh, I don't know. Maybe the fact that you've got a whole store full of them." Alaina pointed her thumb over her shoulder.

"Right," Kathy agreed and threw out another question. "So why were you mad at Ben?"

"He saw Caleb and me leaving a hotel in Denver." Alaina looked down. "He thought . . ." She stiffened and tapped her sculptured fingernail against the service bar. "I got really angry. It was like he believed the worst without even asking me."

"Brothers can really be a pain." Kathy moved forward and leaned into the service bar. "Mine drove me crazy when I was a kid. Once I left home, we got to be friends. But now he's—" She shook her head. "Let's talk about that later. We're not finished with you yet." Kathy's calculating smile mingled with Alaina's next words.

"So how did you figure out I was married to Caleb? Do you

know him?" Alaina asked, worried that whatever clues Kathy picked up might also be visible to her father.

"No, I don't know him," Kathy admitted. "But when I saw you coming out of that 'Employees Only' door at Walmart, I got curious. I went and investigated. Caleb came out at the same time I was going in. I saw his name tag. Your lipstick was gone, so—"

"Maybe all those mystery novels you've read have paid off. You don't miss a beat, do you?"

Kathy's grin couldn't have been prouder. "Anyway, I didn't know you were actually married to Caleb . . . until now," she admitted.

"That's a relief." Alaina propped her arm along the service bar. "I was worried that if you had figured it out, and Ben saw us, then maybe Dad suspected something, too. As far as I know, he doesn't know yet."

"Why don't you just tell him?" Kathy asked and tilted her head.

Alaina's hand shook, and she rubbed her fingers along the polished wood's grain. "I wish it were that easy." She lifted her gaze to Kathy's. Alaina certainly wasn't coming up with any answers. "Caleb's father and my dad—they can't stand each other. They've been enemies since before I was born."

Kathy's eyes sharpened.

"I'm afraid if my dad finds out he'll kill me."

"You're scared of your dad," Kathy stated.

"Well," Alaina's eyes stung, "when you put it like that, it sounds so . . ." She shrugged and dashed away a tear. "I've just never done anything to go against him. And now I feel so—so guilty."

"But you love Caleb."

"Of course."

"You loved him enough to marry him." Kathy crossed her arms.

"Yes—behind my dad's back." Alaina studied the knots in

the aged pine wall. Her life couldn't have gotten more tangled if she tried.

She thought about the conversation she and Caleb had yesterday. When Alaina explained that she was worried God was frowning on her for disobeying her father, he'd laughed. Once Caleb understood she was serious, he'd apologized and told her that her dad was the one who was in the wrong, not her. According to Caleb, Zachariah had taken his parental influence to a level God never intended. Their hour-long conversation had been therapeutic, but Alaina had yet to be free of worries regarding divine disapproval.

"Who are you going to spend the rest of your life with?" Kathy's soft voice floated from nearby.

Alaina glanced toward her friend, now standing across from her. "Caleb, of course."

"I think you need to just tell your dad."

"But you don't understand," Alaina said and balled her fists. "I've never done anything so—so disapproved of. Have you ever done anything huge that your parents disapproved of?"

"Huh, yes." Kathy waved her arm to encompass the store. "You're lookin' at it."

"They didn't want you to open the store?"

"Nope. When my grandmother died, she left Jay and me both nest eggs. Jay invested his for retirement. Mom and Dad wanted me to do the same, but I wanted to be my own boss somewhere besides my hometown. They nearly flipped when they realized I was serious. Up until the Averys got here, my mom was calling me every night to check on me—like I'm ten or something."

"She wouldn't worry so much if she didn't love you," Alaina said.

"I know." Kathy sighed. "But sometimes I feel stifled, I guess."

I wish my mom were still alive to call me, Alaina thought. *I sure could use her now.* Her lips quivered as the memories rolled in like a melancholic fog. Laura Tilman had pushed Alaina on her first bicycle. She'd cheered for her tennis games. She'd helped her learn to drive. *Of course, Dad did a lot, too,* Alaina thought and wondered if part of his possessiveness involved not wanting to be alone . . . not wanting to release the last person who was a link to his wife. If simply releasing Alaina was an insurmountable obstacle, she shuddered at the thought of having to tell him she'd married his enemy's son. Alaina imagined her dad's angry glare, and she wanted to crawl under the stool. *But I do love him a lot,* she thought and dreaded hurting him as much as angering him.

"I still say you should just tell him the truth," Kathy said and pointed toward the front of the store. "I've been reading a book that has helped me a lot. It's about setting boundaries, and that starts by just being honest."

"But he'll *kill* me!" Alaina said and wasn't so certain the news wouldn't kill *him.*

"That is a problem," Kathy replied. "A big problem." She lifted both hands. "Why don't you and Caleb just disappear and start somewhere new? You could even change your identities."

Shaking her head, Alaina sighed. Kathy's options seemed melodramatic, like something from one of her spy novels. She couldn't imagine that Kathy was serious. "Anyway," Alaina continued and didn't attempt to reply to Kathy's extreme solutions, "I'm not going to be home tonight, like I said. Caleb and I are meeting at a hotel in Denver. I just wanted to let you know you'll be on your own."

"What about Phil?" Kathy questioned, her words dripping with worry. "Will he be at the chalet tonight?"

"Oh, don't worry about that." Alaina shifted on the stool and crossed her legs. "Phil's going out of town for a day or two," she explained. "He said something about Colorado Springs this morning."

"Good." Kathy toyed with the base of her hair. "Not that I have anything against Phil, I just wouldn't be, well, comfortable."

"I understand. I wouldn't expect you to stay there alone with him. It just all worked out this time."

"Phil's kind of a force unto himself, isn't he?" Kathy picked up a dish containing creamer and sugar packets. Then she set it down, pulled out a packet of sugar, and rolled the edge.

"I guess." Alaina shrugged. "The deal with Phil is, he knows how to pull off *appearing* to do what Dad wants—at least to Dad. He's never been married, but he's lived with a few gals. And probably been with more than any of us knows."

"Does your dad know?"

"No way! Dad would blow a fuse."

"Phil seemed to really notice Liza the other night." Kathy tore the edge of the sugar packet and dropped it on the service bar.

"Really?" Alaina asked and wondered where this was leading. "I think he noticed you, too, for that matter. Phil seldom misses a pretty face," she said. "Ben was even a little worried at first, I think."

"Ben doesn't have a thing in the world to worry about," Kathy said with a clever smile. "I think he knows that for sure by now. I just hope . . ." She retrieved a creamer packet from the dish and looked out the front window. "Phil's been hanging out with the Thaines ever since my brother left."

"Oh, I see," Alaina said. "I really wouldn't worry about it. When it comes to engaged women, Phil's usually a harmless flirt at best. The last thing he wants to tangle with is a woman with marriage on the brain—even if it's not with him." Alaina chuckled at her own joke.

Kathy ripped the creamer packet. "What about Ben?"

Alaina toyed with a tendril near her eye. "Ben? He knows more about Phil than I do, but I'm sure he'd tell you the same thing."

"No. That's not what I meant." Kathy's laugh oozed uncertainties. "I guess I just sprang that one on you, didn't I? What I was thinking was, if Ben did decide I was 'the one,'" she drew imaginary quotes in the air, "and your dad decided he disapproved of me . . . well, do you think Ben would dump me?"

"I don't know," Alaina drawled. "He's pretty wild about you."

"You really mean that?"

Alaina slid off the stool. "I mean it," she said, her thick heels meeting the floor with a decisive click. "I've never known him to be so intense about a woman—not that there have been a long line of women by any means. But I think he's probably thinking you might be 'the one.'"

"Really?" Kathy said. "He said that?"

"You mean he hasn't hinted to you at all?"

"Of course," she admitted. "But it means a lot coming from you, that's all."

Alaina nodded. "I understand." She glanced at her watch and calculated the drive time. "If I don't hurry, Caleb's going to wonder what happened to me."

"Okay." Kathy nodded and dimpled. "I hope you enjoy your evening, Mrs. Manley."

"Oh, I will." Alaina's stomach fluttered. As her torso warmed, she eyed the gleaming wooden floor. "Don't tease me too much." She glimpsed Kathy out of the corner of her eye and tugged on the neck of her short-sleeved sweater. "Turnabout's fair play, and you might be a newlywed one day yourself."

"If that happens, you can tease me all you want. Believe me, I won't care!" Kathy snickered, and Alaina joined her.

Kathy tossed the tormented creamer package onto the service bar. Fine white powder dusted the wood. She picked at her thumbnail, then worriedly eyed Alaina. "I guess since I'm going to be at the chalet alone, maybe I should get a hotel room or stay with the Averys or something."

"No way!" Alaina laid her hand on the service bar and leaned toward Kathy. "It's empty and completely available tonight! Which reminds me," she opened her purse and pulled out the key she'd inserted into an inside pocket, "here's an extra house key." Alaina laid the key on the bar next to the sugar and creamer dish. "It fits the front and back doors."

"Okay." Kathy retrieved the key and tapped it against the bar. "What do you want me to tell your dad if he calls?"

"Just tell him I haven't gotten home yet and to call my cell if he wants to talk to me. I've had to work late a few nights lately. He'll think I'm at work."

"I can't tell him that though."

Alaina shook her head. "Of course not. I'm not asking you to lie for me. Just tell him to call my cell."

"And if he asks for Phil?"

"Tell him the truth—that Phil's gone to Colorado Springs. Dad doesn't worry about him like he does me. Phil left home a long time ago. Dad's used to him doing what he wants."

Twenty-Eight

Kathy stood on her tiptoes and watched as Alaina's Volkswagen eased down the street. The second the car was out of sight, she grabbed her purse, raced to the window, switched the sign to "Closed," and flew out the door. After manhandling the lock, she strode toward her Impala parked in the next-door lot.

The chalet's key warmed in her palm. She looked toward the chalet, shrouded in sunlight. As usual, the long windows peered on the valley like menacing eyes absorbing every move, missing no detail. But this evening the eyes evoked no fear, only anticipation.

With no one at the chalet, Kathy didn't have to wait until midnight to explore Laura Tilman's suite. She could go immediately to the room the second she entered the home. Her stomach rumbled, and Kathy lambasted her own appetite.

I don't have time to eat, she thought and decided to drive through a burger joint on her way home.

"Yoo-hoo! Kathy!" The sound of quick footsteps accompanied the familiar voice.

Oh no, Kathy thought, *Dory Thaine can talk for hours.* She turned to face Ron and Liza's mom and recalled something from a freshman public relations class about using body language to your advantage.

Kathy smiled toward Mrs. Thaine but allowed the buxom lady to approach her, rather than meeting her halfway. Dory's red cheeks and lips matched her scarlet pants with matching blouse, and made her look like a red-light special on wheels. Her tinted blond hair took on a pinkish cast in the evening sun and heightened the effect.

"Oh my goodness," Dory said and grabbed Kathy's arm. "I'm so glad I caught you. I've *got* to buy some books. I need you to open the store back up for me," she said with no hint of doubt that Kathy would comply.

"Okay," Kathy agreed and wanted to groan. The few times Mrs. Thaine had used the word "buy," she'd wound up shopping for hours and writing a sizable check when she was through. Normally the prospect was enough to make Kathy willing to stay open until late evening, but not tonight. Her shoulders sagging, she followed the chatty Dory toward the store door. With a longing glance toward the chalet, Kathy unlocked the store and allowed Dory access.

As soon as Kathy closed the door, Dory said, "I smell paint. Ron told me he painted the back wall for you. Isn't he the sweetest thing?" she said as if she possessed a well-hidden secret.

"He can be, I guess," Kathy absently admitted and hoped nothing she said would be twisted and then repeated to Ron.

Her diamond rings flashing, Dory scurried toward the new display of Christian fiction. "He and Phil and Liza have all gone to Colorado Springs for a few days," she said.

Kathy clutched her duffel-style purse against her stomach and nodded.

"They wanted me to go, too, but I just didn't feel like it. My arthritis is flaring up." Dory picked up the first book of a five-book series and quit chattering long enough to read the back cover.

Kathy focused on Dory's profile as a numb awareness spread through her mind. *Liza is flirting with temptation,* she thought. *No, Liza is flinging herself into the arms of temptation.*

Half an hour ago, Alaina admitted that Phil's morals were

low. Despite what Alaina said about his avoiding women with marriage on their minds, he'd driven off with one. Kathy wasn't naïve enough to think that Ron would serve as any kind of a stabilizing chaperone. If Phil had seduction on the brain, Liza could fall prey.

And where does that leave Jay? Kathy worried. *It leaves him with his eyes opened,* she answered herself. *But what if he doesn't find out before there's a wedding?*

"Oooh, this novel sounds *great!*" Dory exclaimed. "It's just what I need—mystery, romance, and four more books in the series." She grabbed up the other titles. "Liza will be back Monday. Ron's going on home then. It's going to be a long weekend," she added and nodded toward Kathy. "Plenty of time for reading. This ought to do me." She held up the books. "I won't keep you any longer. I know you were on your way out."

"Mrs. Thaine," Kathy began and inched toward the lady. Even though she was as eager as ever to get to the chalet, she was more interested in her brother's welfare. Kathy paused within feet of Dory and debated how best to pose her question. Finally she arrived at a safe approach. "Did Liza say anything about Jay meeting them in Colorado Springs?" she asked and decided she was at the height of clever.

"No." Dory shook her head. "I think Jay's team starts preseason practice tomorrow. Ron's doesn't start until Monday. I thought you knew that."

"Well, I . . ." Kathy placed the chalet key into her purse's side pocket and slipped the purse strap on her shoulder. "I did, of course. I just thought maybe they'd invited Jay for the weekend." She relieved Dory of her books and walked toward the cash register.

"For all I know, Liza might call him on the way," Dory explained as she followed Kathy. "This whole thing was Phil and Ron's idea. Liza just went along to keep from being bored."

Kathy halted behind the cash register and observed Mrs. Thaine, who was pausing near the magazine rack. *Do you really believe that?* The question bulged against Kathy's lips, but she stopped herself from blurting it.

While Mrs. Thaine picked up a magazine and thumbed through it, Kathy laid her purse aside, flipped on the store lights, mutely rang up the novels, and slipped them into a bag. All the while, she was reliving the plot of a movie she'd seen a couple of years ago. An engaged woman indulged in a brief flirtation before her wedding just to be sure marriage was the right choice. In this particular plot, the lady realized she shouldn't get married and canceled the wedding.

But what if Liza wants to marry Jay anyway? Kathy worried. *And what if this weekend in Colorado Springs turns into more than just a flirtation, but Liza never tells Jay?* She rubbed the plastic bag holding the books and blindly stared out the window. Alaina said Phil had probably been with more women than they ever knew about.

Liza might just be another weekend fling for him, she thought.

"Well, I guess this is all, my dear," Dory said.

Kathy focused on Liza's mother and studied her for a second. "All right," she said and accepted the three magazines Dory extended over the counter. Except for her concerns about being alone this weekend, the aging lady showed no signs of distress regarding Liza's trip. Kathy deduced that either Liza's going off with men was a regular event, or Dory was so gullible she'd believe anything.

She rang up the total and kept the conversation light and encouraging while finalizing the sale. By the time Dory called, "Bye, now!" and meandered out the door, Kathy decided to question the Averys. Since they were staying in the same bed-and-breakfast as the Thaines, maybe they'd witnessed signs of Liza's straying. The front door rattled to a close.

As smitten as Jay is, I doubt he'd believe me if I had a video of Liza kissing Phil, Kathy thought. She shouldered her purse and turned out the store lights. *If the Averys speak up, though, maybe he'll listen.*

The closer she drew to the store's door, the more the chalet whispered her name. By the time she placed her hand on the knob, Liza and Jay floated to the fringes of her mind while the chalet boldly claimed the center.

When she was halfway out the door, her demanding stomach growled with a fierce determination that insisted she could ignore it no longer. Kathy stroked her midsection and said, "Down, girl!" while recalling a Snickers bar lying near her refrigerator. The treat belonged to Uncle Ziggy, but Kathy decided a candy bar offered a quicker alternative to driving through a burger joint. She retraced her steps and grabbed the snack. Deciding a sugary cola would give her a sugar overdose, Kathy chose a caffeine-free diet soda from the fridge and hurried to her destiny while devouring the treats.

By the time she opened the chalet's front door, her heart was battering her ribs. Clutching her purse, Kathy pounded up the stairs and didn't even stop by her room. Instead, she stormed the steps to the third floor and barged into the suite like a missile from the present erupting into the past.

Panting, she stopped on the room's edge and absorbed the cool tranquility, so opposite her overwrought psyche. Kathy dropped her purse on a king-sized cherry bed draped in a gauzy comforter. The room's musty smell couldn't obliterate the faintest hint of lavender, and Kathy thought of soft summer evenings, full moons, and ballads longing to be sung.

She was a gentle spirit, Kathy thought, *like Alaina . . . and Ben.*

Slowly, Kathy turned and absorbed the chamber's ambiance. Gossamer curtains, as delicate as the comforter, covered the floor-to-ceiling windows that commanded the south wall. Spears of sunlight bathed the sitting area in a golden aura that made the love seat, recliner, and rolltop desk look like they belonged to graceful royalty. A cherry dresser, ornate and regal, claimed the wall opposite the windows. In the corner stood an armoire. A full-length mirror hung beside it. Near the mirror, a house robe drooped on a brass clothing hook mounted to the wall.

"Just like she left it," Kathy whispered. She walked to the velour robe, extended her fingers, hesitated, then stroked the fabric. The soft folds whispered against her skin. Kathy lifted the housecoat, pressed it against her nose, and breathed in a trace of the sweet lavender. She closed her eyes and tried to imagine what Laura Tilman must look like.

Thurston Manley said she looked like me, Kathy thought. When she opened her eyes and raised her head, Kathy caught sight of a framed photo on the dresser's corner. Still holding the robe, she hurried toward the dusty dresser and snatched up the photo. Kathy blew on the glass. The first layer of dust swished into the air and tickled her nose. She sneezed. Kathy grabbed the hem of the housecoat and started to wipe away the rest of the dust but stopped herself.

"Can't do that," she admonished. "Zach will know somebody's been up here." Kathy eyed the place where the frame had sat and said, "Whew!" Fortunately, when she'd picked up the picture, she hadn't dragged it across the dresser. The dust remained in place.

Focusing on the picture, Kathy strained through the film of yesteryear to detect a thin, blond woman with short hair. She stood in the circle of Zachariah Tilman's arm. He appeared to be about ten years younger. They were in front of the chalet. Both smiled. Both looked content.

Kathy searched for any resemblance between her and Laura and saw nothing, except perhaps their size-six bodies. She looked into the mirror, held the photo up to her face, and leaned forward. Finally Kathy shook her head and decided Thurston Manley had a bad memory if he thought she strongly resembled Laura

Tilman. The only people she'd seen who resembled Laura were her kids—especially Alaina.

Maybe Thurston's half crazy, she thought. With a shudder, Kathy recalled the wild look in his good eye, the smell of alcohol on his breath. *If he's so off about Laura and me looking alike, maybe he's hallucinating about Zach murdering Laura.* The very possibility so dashed Kathy's hopes of discovering clues, she immediately dismissed it and decided not to be thwarted by anything—not even logic.

When she replaced the picture, Kathy examined the taupe carpet. If there were signs of blood, this was a great color to show it. Kathy flopped the housecoat on the end of the bed and perused every inch of the exposed carpet. By the time she got to the recliner, the only stain she'd found was near the window—a water ring, possibly from a live plant.

Kathy collapsed onto the recliner, propped her elbows on her knees, and rested her chin in her hands. She stared at the stack of magazines spread across the glass-topped wicker table. The dated covers brought back memories of two years ago when Kathy was struggling to survive college. She sighed while the weight of her day hung on her shoulders.

As the minutes ticked by, the sun's intensity waned. The windowed room, once bright with summer light, languished in the coming shadows. Kathy yawned and touched the tear in her pants. She rubbed the sore spot on her head and pondered the pile of books she'd left on the floor in the back of the store.

She flopped back in the recliner and gazed around the room. The initial rush and thrill of being in the mysterious suite had vanished. In its place remained the anticlimactic wilt of disappointment. The room was nothing like she'd ever imagined or read about in her novels. There were no signs of struggle. No feelings that something horrid had transpired. No eerie furnishings or traces of the bizarre. Not even one drop of blood.

"Edgar Allen Poe would be *so* disappointed," Kathy said.

She stood, stretched, and gazed toward a set of folding doors on the other side of the bed. Kathy snapped her fingers. *Of course*, she thought, *the closet. I still haven't looked in there or in the armoire.* She scanned the room for any other spots that cried to be foraged and made a mental list of the nightstand, the dresser drawers, and a bookshelf.

A new surge of optimism propelled Kathy to action. Only the sight of the purple housecoat lying on the end of the bed could detour her mission. Kathy snatched up the robe and marched toward the brass hook.

I don't want to leave a thing out of place, she thought.

When she tried to hang up the robe, she realized she had it upside down. In the process of righting the housecoat, Kathy's fingers brushed something hard. Puzzled, she fumbled with the robe, searching for a pocket. Only when she opened the garment and looked inside did she spot a hidden pouch, weighted with a burden.

A thrill zinged through Kathy as she imagined any number of things the pocket might hold. At the top of the list was a digital recorder into which Laura Tilman whispered the name of her murderer before gasping her last breath. Her fingers unsteady, Kathy fumbled with the pouch until she extracted a petite leather book about the size of a small Bible.

On closer inspection, Kathy realized she was holding a pocket journal. She gasped, flung the robe onto the hook, and flipped open the journal. Sure enough, the pages were covered in feminine scrawl, and a faint whiff of lavender attested to the owner.

Kathy turned to the first page and noted a date from five years before. She scanned the words and picked up details about the fabric of Laura's life, including a wild deer named Bo who was starting to take food from her hand. While the brief story was charming and helped Kathy understand Ben's mother, it did nothing to satisfy her hunger for intrigue. By the time Kathy waded through one-fourth of the diary, she understood that Laura Tilman was exactly the kind of woman she expected her to be. Her quiet demeanor was her legacy to Alaina. Her big heart was all Ben's.

She was swiftly becoming as disenchanted with the diary as with the carpet inspection when she flipped the page and the words *Zachariah's temper* leaped out at her. Her interest soaring, Kathy walked toward the bed, settled onto the end, and drank in the words penned two years before Laura's death:

I don't know that I've ever seen Zachariah's temper so high! He came home in a bad mood in the first place. Then, when he realized I'd forgotten to buy the peanut butter, he threw the empty jar across the kitchen and turned on me like I was a criminal or something. His temper scares me to death! I never know when he's going to explode or what's going to make him go off. I just wish he wouldn't yell at me. Thank you, God, he's only hit me once. I guess even in the middle of tears, I have something to be thankful for. When he's like this, he's so much like his mother I don't even like him. I just wish he could be more like my dad. Oh, Daddy, I never even heard you raise your voice!

Kathy's heart thumped behind her eyes as she stroked the words, blotched by tears. "What if Zach lost his temper and hit her again?" she whispered. "Then Laura's temple slammed into the nightstand, and it killed her." Kathy nodded, but soon shook her head.

"Wouldn't work," she admitted. "The autopsy showed a heart attack."

She peered across the room at her own reflection in the dresser mirror. The young woman who stared back sat in a long shaft of remaining sunlight, her face pale, her eyes intense.

"What if Zach paid off the autopsy director?" she schemed.

Hunching over the journal, Kathy consumed the next fifty pages, only to discover more commentary on Laura's daily life. While enlightening and moving, especially when Laura talked about her walk with God, the writing did nothing to implicate Zach as a murderer. By the time Kathy had read a few more accounts of his moodiness and temper, she realized Laura wasn't saying anything that Alaina hadn't already told her or she hadn't already realized.

As much as Kathy wanted to believe Zachariah Tilman was a murderer, she was beginning to think there was no hard evidence—not in this room, anyway. The idea that Zach paid off the autopsy director now struck her as ridiculous as her assumption that he was holding Laura Tilman hostage in this suite.

The shadows deepened. The light faded. And in the sun's final glimmers, Kathy read the last page of Laura's diary:

I'm not sure why I feel the way I do today. It's like heaven is closer than it's ever been. I don't know if it's because of Mom's death a year ago or just because I've fallen so in love with the Lord these last few years. All I know is that I belong to Jesus, and He belongs to me. I'm ready for Him when He comes for me. I'm so proud of Alaina. I see the beginning of my walk in her. I only hope she's strong enough to stand on her own if my time is near. And Ben . . . my dear, sweet Ben who'd never hurt a soul. His commitment to God leaves me breathless. Oh, Father, give Ben a good wife who'll appreciate him and never leave him. Somehow I don't think I'll be here to meet her. Lord, are you trying to tell me I'm going home soon? Jesus, Son of God, be with Phil. If Zach suspected what I already know,

it would kill him. Father, be with Zach. You know I love
him. He loves you in his own way. Help him to be patient
with the kids. Help him to know when to let go. Help him
to stop hating Thurston.

Kathy sighed and blinked against her stinging eyes. Laura's
last entry indicated that she suspected her death was imminent.
Many times Kathy had heard or read of people who reported
that they knew they were close to eternity before they stepped
over the threshold. Laura's words read like a woman who was
intimate enough with her Creator to understand when He was
calling her name. She didn't sound like a battered woman who
was fearful for her life.

Maybe Thurston Manley is wrong, Kathy thought as Laura's
claims echoed through her soul: *"I've fallen so in love with the
Lord these last few years. All I know is that I belong to Jesus, and He
belongs to me."*

An unexpected longing stirred Kathy's spirit, a restlessness
that would not be denied. She had never experienced the level
of love for God that Laura's diary bespoke. Before she left home,
her devotion to God had been wrapped up in her devotion to her
parents and their expectations. Now that Kathy was on her own,
she hadn't spent a lot of time analyzing her relationship with God
or even altering her schedule that much to attend church . . .
until she met Ben. Then she'd attended church mainly because
she enjoyed seeing and pleasing Ben. But still, there had been
something in his messages that stirred Kathy as did the thread
of holy devotion in Laura's diary.

A yawn wouldn't be denied, and Kathy checked her watch.
In the last vestiges of evening light, she determined it was 8:45.
Her stomach rumbled, and Kathy realized she was slumping into
the blood sugar drop that usually occurred after she indulged
in too much sugar. She looked around the room and decided

to continue her snooping after she ate some protein. When she stood, her head felt light, her legs weak.

Deciding to reread the diary over a sandwich, she picked up her purse, shoved the dairy inside, and turned toward the door, only to realize the stairs leading to the suite were releasing faint, irregular creaks. Convinced she must be hearing things, Kathy gripped her throat, held her breath, and listened. A few seconds revealed her first impression was correct. Someone was ascending the stairs, not with the regular rhythm of sure footsteps, but with the near-silent creeping of a predator.

Conjuring a dozen different scenarios involving burglars and villains, Kathy frantically scoured the room for the best place to hide. The closet was the only answer. Before she could take two steps toward it, the door sighed open, and Zachariah Tilman's towering frame filled the entry.

Twenty-Nine

"Kathy!" Zach exclaimed.

"Mr—Mr. Tilman," she stammered. "I thought you were fishing."

"This is my wife's—*our*—old suite." He glowered. "I guess you didn't know it was off-limits." His lips stiff, Zach stood aside and motioned for Kathy to exit.

She lowered her head and scurried toward the door. "I—I'm sorry. I was just . . . I was curious, I guess." She ducked past Zachariah and stood near the stairs, ready to dash down them should he start yelling at her.

Tilman flipped on the room's light and leaned into the suite as if he were inspecting it for signs of violation.

Kathy swallowed and thanked God she hadn't been in the middle of scrounging through the closet.

Finally Zach turned off the light and closed the door. As he turned to face Kathy, she hovered against the wall and convinced herself not to burst into tears before he gave her reason. Still frowning, Zachariah scrutinized Kathy for a second before his features softened.

"I'm not going to eat you alive," he said. "It's just that—" Zach glanced toward the door. His shoulders drooped. "You wouldn't understand." He shook his head. "No harm done. I'm glad you're okay. When I saw the door cracked and couldn't find you, I wondered if you'd stumbled into the room by accident.

Then I was afraid something had happened. Maybe an intruder. Where's Alaina, anyway?"

Kathy inched away from the wall, fumbled with her purse, and groped for something to say. "Did your fishing trip—did something happen? I thought you weren't due back until Saturday morning."

"Oh, that." Zach smiled and extended his hand toward the staircase.

She gripped the handrail and coaxed her trembling legs to carry her down the steps.

"There were three of us—me, Harold Ivory, and his son, Devon. We were renting a cabin on the side of a mountain. Harold fell off the back porch midafternoon. It was a pretty good drop. By the time he stopped rolling, he'd broken his arm in a couple of places." Zachariah touched his forearm.

"Yeow," Kathy said as they paused at the bottom of the steps.

"We took him to the emergency room." Zachariah shrugged. "Just one of those things. He won't be able to fish for a while, that's for sure."

"I'm sure the fish will miss him," Kathy quipped and was astounded she could conjure even the subtlest humor after her scare.

Zach's chuckle rumbled from his chest. "I'm sure."

She turned toward the hallway and said, "Well, I'm going to my room for a few minutes. After that, I'll be down. I still haven't had dinner. I was thinking I'd just fix a sandwich."

"Okay, you mustn't have been here long. Had to work late, did you?"

She curled her toes. "Well, I . . ."

"Hey, did you say where Alaina was?"

Kathy tightened her stomach and tried to remember what Alaina told her to tell her father. Just as she recalled something about Zach calling Alaina's cell phone, Kathy's cell began playing the theme song from *The Twilight Zone*.

Zach jerked his head back and looked toward her bag. "That's interesting," he said through a fond grin.

Wondering if her smile appeared as nervous as it felt, Kathy lifted her bag, groped past Laura's diary, and retrieved her cell phone from beneath last week's grocery receipt. One look at the screen showed it was Ben.

"It's Ben," she said. "I wonder what he wants?" As soon as Kathy swiped to answer, she remembered exactly what he wanted. "Oh my word," she blurted and placed the receiver to her ear. "I totally forgot tonight! Oh no, Ben! I am *so sorry!* I stood you up, didn't I?" Kathy questioned while Zach motioned that he was going downstairs.

Kathy nodded and waved him on. Her relief at not having to talk about Alaina mixed with her growing anxiety over what Ben must think. "We were supposed to study fruit and visit Lucy!"

His soft laugh eased her worry. "It's okay. I debated whether or not you just forgot or you were having second thoughts about . . ." The uncertainty in his voice made Kathy want to kick herself. "I guess there are no second thoughts, then?"

"No! Absolutely not! Only first thoughts. And they're the same as always!" She walked into her room, decorated in oak furniture and frilly eyelet, and dropped her purse on the dresser. "Ben, I'm *so sorry!* I'm just so brain dead, that's it! It has nothing to do with you or me or—or us." The handbag flopped sideways and coughed up Laura's diary. Frowning, Kathy glanced over her shoulder toward the open door and shoved the diary to the bottom of her purse.

"So it'd be okay if I were driving to the chalet now to see you?"

"Absolutely!" Kathy breathed and laid her hand over her heart.

"Good," Ben replied, "because I'm pulling into the driveway now."

"Now!" Kathy exclaimed.

"Yes, now. Meet me at the door. Okay?"

"Okay," she agreed and disconnected the call. Kathy looked at herself in the mirror. She hadn't bothered with makeup this morning, and her hair had flopped many hours ago. The dark circles under her eyes spoke of the state of her blood sugar, now plummeting.

I've got to get some protein down me! she thought.

Kathy tossed the phone into the top of her purse. She scurried up the hallway, down the steps, and whizzed through the living room.

"Yikes!" Zach fumbled with his newspaper and scooted to the edge of his recliner near the fireplace.

Pausing at the front door, Kathy focused on Ben's dad. His reading glasses crooked, he looked at Kathy as if she'd dropped out of the ceiling.

"Whoops!" Kathy paused at the front door. "Did I scare you?"

"A little," he complained and settled back into the recliner. "I guess I just wasn't expecting you like that."

"Ben's driving up now," she explained. "I'm going to meet him."

"By all means then, go meet him." Zachariah's gaze took on a quizzical intensity that made Kathy squirm. If she weren't hurrying out the door, she wondered if Zach would have interrogated her again.

Not wanting to give him time to begin, she bumped out the door and into the cool mountain air. Trotting along the railed porch, she dubiously searched for "the Hound of the Baskervilles" and didn't spot him. Duncan hadn't attempted to knock her down and lick her again, partly because Kathy had learned to sidestep him.

When she got to the end of the porch, Ben's Corolla was rolling up beside her Impala. Deciding now was not the time to hold back her emotions, Kathy trotted along the drive to his vehicle. The smell of evergreens and earth bathed her senses as she jittered in place while Ben turned off the engine and got out.

The second he slammed his car door, Kathy bolted forward and grabbed him.

"Hel-*lo!*" Ben burst out.

"I'm so sorry!" Kathy hugged him tight and laid her head against his chest.

Ben wrapped his arms around Kathy and swayed from side to side. "If this is the treatment I get when I'm stood up, here's hoping you stand me up for every date!"

Kathy backed away, looked up at him, and absorbed the angles of his face, accentuated by moonlight and shadows. She didn't attempt to hide her unbridled admiration, her respect, and her overwhelming sorrow for having forgotten their date.

"I just can't believe I forgot like that," she hurried. "Earlier today all I could think about was you—and Alaina and me going to the Bible study. I've never been so excited about fruit!" she babbled. "Then Alaina came by right before closing and told me she wouldn't be home tonight. I got so distracted over her and—and—"

She backed away and sobered. "She told me she and Caleb got married," Kathy whispered and glanced over her shoulder. "She's with Caleb now."

"Ohhhh," Ben said and looked around the dark parking area. "I guess her car *is* missing."

"Yes. They're in Denver," she hissed.

"Wait a minute." He pointed toward his father's Hummer. "Dad's home. I thought he was fishing."

"He just got home. One of the men he was with broke his arm. I think his name was Harold."

"Harold Ivory?"

"Yes. That's it."

"So Dad's home and Alaina's out," Ben stated. "Does Alaina know Dad's home?"

"No. I guess I should call her."

"Maybe," Ben said and thoughtfully observed Kathy. "Maybe not. Let me handle it. Okay?"

"Well, all right," Kathy agreed and wiggled through a shiver.

"Cold?" Ben asked.

"A little I guess." She crossed her arms and rubbed. "This sleeveless blouse was fine this afternoon, but now it's a little light."

"Here." Ben slipped out of his jacket.

"But then you'll be cold," she protested.

"Not me." He winked. "I'm a big tough man. Besides, I'm wearing a sweater vest and a long-sleeve shirt."

"Well, okay," Kathy agreed and gladly allowed him to help her into the jacket. "If you're going to twist my arm, I guess I'll go along." She grinned up at him and reveled in the jacket's mild masculine scent mixed with a hint of taco sauce.

"There," Ben said and tugged the front together.

"Have you been eating tacos?" Kathy asked and sniffed at the jacket. As hungry as she was, she considered taking a bite.

"Oooh, I've been caught," he teased. "I went through Taco Bell on the way here." Ben rested his hands on her shoulders, then touched her cheek. "I can't get anything past you, can I?"

Kathy shook her head. "Don't even try," she said as a thrill zipped through her. "Hey, how's Lucy?" she asked. "I was supposed to be visiting her by now."

An impulse to kiss Ben's whole face sprang out of nowhere, and Kathy wondered what his reaction would be. Then she recalled what Ben said Saturday night when she kept kissing him. *"I like kissing you . . . but we can't—I can't—we shouldn't. Enough is enough. Comprendé?"*

His attention settling on her lips, Ben stroked Kathy's chin with his thumb. "Who's Lucy?" he rasped before he kissed the corner of her mouth. Kathy pressed her lips against his and welcomed his cinnamon taste.

Sighing, she held Ben tight and drank in his closeness, holding back none of the youthful eagerness brimming from her tender heart. Soon Northpointe Mountain was quaking, and Kathy was certain it was on the verge of spewing lava. When Ben started pulling away, Kathy longed to test the lava, but she also sensed the time had come to draw the line.

By the time Ben lifted his face and traced her lips with his index finger, his hand was trembling as violently as her legs. Images of Liza leading Jay and Phil to the brink of who-knew-what gave Kathy the strength to ease back. The last thing she ever wanted to be was somebody's temptation.

"Wow!" Ben breathed and got some space. He pulled Kathy's hands between both of his and held them tight.

Kathy dimpled, twined her fingers through his, and lifted his hand to her lips. She generously kissed every knuckle and said, "Please don't ever let me stand you up like that again. Next time, call me sooner. Okay?"

"It's a deal," Ben said and slipped his arm around her waist. "I was really worried that you'd decided maybe . . ."

"No way!" Kathy exclaimed as the two headed toward the chalet. "I love you to death, Ben!"

He stopped and swiveled to face her. "Do you really mean it?"

"All the way," Kathy oozed and was sure the Colorado stars gleaming like crushed diamonds against the infant night glimmered brighter.

"You know I feel the same way, Kathy," he admitted. "I never dreamed I'd fall like this. It's just so . . . it's everything all the songs say and even more. Honey, *please* don't go breakin' my heart," he begged, his shadowed eyes saying even more than his words.

"I won't, Ben," she whispered, the crickets echoing her pledge. "I promise with all my heart."

"Come on." He tugged her toward the porch. "Let's go to better lighting. I've got something for you."

Kathy didn't resist. "Okay, but I need to tell you that my blood sugar's dropping. I'm starting to shake pretty badly. I need to get something to eat." She took the steps as eagerly as she'd embraced Ben and couldn't imagine what he had for her.

"All right," Ben said. "Tell you what, let's go in and get you a bite, and I'll wait until you're through eating to give you the gift."

"No," Kathy protested. "I won't be able to stand it! I've waited this long. I can wait another minute or two."

"Great, because I can't wait to give it to you!" He squeezed her hand.

They paused near the chalet's door, and Kathy bounced on her toes like a little girl about to ride her first pony. Ben reached into his pants pocket. He was pulling out an oblong box when the chalet's door banged open.

Both Kathy and Ben looked toward the doorway. Zachariah stepped onto the porch and slammed the door behind him. His blue gaze, all for Kathy, bore an icy chill through her spine. Slowly he lifted his hand, and Kathy recognized the small leather book his white-tinged fingers pressed into.

Her face flashed hot, then slowly cooled.

"You little snooping two-faced witch!" Zach spewed and strode straight for Kathy.

Recalling Laura's claims about her husband's horrid temper and Ben's stories about his grandmother's physical abuse, Kathy yelped and stumbled backward until she rammed into the porch rail. Her retreat meant nothing to Zachariah. He met her step for step and lowered his menacing face to inches from hers.

"How dare you!" he snarled, his breath laden with coffee. "I haven't even removed her diary from her robe, let alone read it!"

"Dad, don't," Ben said and stepped to Kathy's side.

Zach turned to his son and bellowed, "Didn't you say you told her the suite was off-limits?"

"Well, yes," Ben admitted. His eye twitched. He licked his lips. He observed Kathy, then his father.

Whirling back to Kathy, Zach lifted the diary between them. "I saw the edge of it sticking out of your purse when you dug out your cell phone," he explained in a voice as calm as death, as hard as hate. "At first I didn't realize what it was. Then the more I thought about it, the clearer it became."

"You went through my purse?" Kathy gasped.

"Now you know how *I* feel!" Tilman growled. "You went through my suite. You went through Laura's diary. You stole it! You had no right!"

Her face heating, Kathy lowered her gaze to the top button of his plaid shirt. "I wasn't stealing it," she mumbled. "I was just borrowing it."

"Now that's an original excuse," Tilman scoffed and looked toward Ben.

Helplessly, Kathy gazed at Ben, whose lax features and open mouth suggested he believed his father.

Zach looked at Kathy, and her gaze riveted on his menacing eyes. "By the time I found the diary, I remembered Ben telling me he'd explained about the suite being off-limits. You see," he snarled, his white teeth flashing in the porch's lighting, "I specifically asked Ben if he told you to stay away from the suite because I wanted to make sure you understood the house rules before you got here! And to think I was dumb enough to trust your conniving ways." He lifted his fist.

"Ben?" Kathy whimpered, her blood sugar dizziness increasing past discomfort.

"Dad, no!" he yelled and pushed his father.

Shoving Ben, Tilman grabbed Kathy's upper arm and squeezed until his fingers ate through the jacket. As Ben crashed into a wooden rocker, Zach shook Kathy. "You had no right to go into that room!"

"Please, Mr. Tilman," Kathy begged. Her knees buckled, and she clung to the porch's post to keep from collapsing.

"Don't you even have enough character to respect a grieving man's wishes?" his voice boomed around the yard.

Duncan's startled barking erupted from the other side of the house.

"Dad, stop!" Ben barged between them and rammed into his father. Zach's staggering footsteps rumbled along the porch before he slammed into the side of the house.

Tears seeped from the corners of Kathy's eyes as she imagined Ben doing the same for his mother as an eleven-year-old boy.

"What possessed you, Kathy?" Zachariah roared while Ben rammed him against the chalet again. The two men grunted, and Kathy didn't know how long Ben would be able to thwart his father.

She also figured if she didn't tell the absolute truth, Zachariah Tilman would reach into her soul and rip it out of her. "Thurston Manley told me you m-murdered her," Kathy choked out.

"Thurston Manley?" Zach bellowed. His face contorting into a mask of hate, he forced Ben aside and rushed at Kathy. "He's crazy!" Tilman screamed in her face. She slumped against the railing. "And you're an idiot if you believe a word of what he said."

He turned to Ben, who was preparing for another war tactic. "Would you stop it!" Zach smacked his flattened hand against Ben's chest. "You're as big of an idiot as she is!"

"You better not hit her!" His face flushed, Ben knocked his father's hand away and didn't flinch from the stare-down.

Zack stepped back and clenched his fist at his side.

"Apparently your stupid girlfriend went into that suite to see if she could prove I murdered your mother!" he said. "I think I deserve some answers."

"Not like this!" Ben barked.

Glaring at each other, the men labored to breathe. So did Kathy. Finally Zach stomped toward the doorway and snarled, "Fine! Have it your way, then!"

But before entering, he pointed at Ben and said, "All this time she's been pretending she likes me. She's a two-faced liar! If she'd do that to me, she'll do the same thing to you. Go upstairs, get her stuff, get her out of my sight. And I don't ever—*ever*—want to see her again! If you have any sense, you'll tell her to get out of your life."

He glowered toward Kathy, and she considered slithering under the house. "You get *off* of my porch and don't ever come back!"

She crossed her arms, hunched forward, and hugged herself.

"*Now!*" Tilman screamed.

"Dad, that's enough!" Ben hollered.

Nevertheless, Kathy jumped and scurried to the end of the porch, her legs as unsteady as licorice sticks.

"Kathy!" Ben called as the chalet's door slammed. He trotted after her until she collapsed against her car door, opened it, scrambled inside, and propped her forehead on the steering wheel.

While Ben hovered in the open door and stroked her heaving back, he felt like he was eleven all over again. But this time he was defending Kathy, not his mother.

"Kathy, I'm so sorry. He had no right!" Ben said and rubbed at the stinging streak along his chest. When he knocked away his father's hand, Ben reaped a scratch.

A broken sob ripped through the night. "He sc-scared me to—to death!" Kathy wailed. Covering her face with her hands, she turned toward Ben and then clutched at his torso.

Awkwardly, Ben attempted to keep his balance, and finally managed to lower himself to the seat. Kathy scooted over. He placed his arm around her. As she rested her head on his shoulder, the chilly leather cooled his thigh and the back of his arm.

"I've got to have some protein," she said through her sniffles. "I'm as limp as a dish rag. I might—might faint." She hiccoughed. "Orange juice. Do you have some orange juice?"

"Uh . . . I don't. Dad might!" Ben clambered out of the car and reconsidered the offer. His father probably wouldn't give Kathy a crumb right now.

"Wait!" he said. "I've got a leftover taco in my car and half a large Pepsi. It's probably a little soggy by now, but—"

"Anything!" Kathy begged.

Ben scratched through his pocket for his car keys, dragged them out, dropped them, and finally managed to pick them up and press the button that unlocked his Corolla. He whipped open the passenger door, scrounged through the fast-food bag for the taco, and retrieved the cup of Pepsi from its holder near the gear shift.

The second he extended the gifts, Kathy grabbed the taco, and Ben didn't think Duncan could have swallowed a pork chop any faster. After inhaling the taco, she sucked on the straw until it gurgled and coughed. Then she scrubbed at her cheek like a toddler and looked at Ben.

"Gone, gone," she said with a weepy grin.

His heart aching, Ben took the cup and set it on the concrete. He settled behind the steering wheel into the scent of tacos mixed with something feminine and sweet.

"Kathy, I'm sorry about my father," he breathed and shook his head. Still trying to process the magnitude of what happened, he voiced the next thing that trotted through his mind. "But at the same time, I really can't believe you went into the suite like that."

She looked down and fumbled with nothing. The antique car's dome light cast a ghostly glow on her paled features.

"And you stole my mom's diary?" He propped his hand on the base of the steering wheel.

"I didn't steal it!" Kathy looked up. Fresh tears trickled down the sides of her nose. The crickets' shrieking increased to a deafening shrill, and the cool night air grew tombstone cold.

"I really didn't." She clung to his arm. "I just found it and was reading it. My blood sugar was dropping. I was going to take it down to the kitchen and read it while I was eating, so I put it in my purse. Then I heard your father coming up the steps, and there he was." Her earnest eyes, shadowed and damp, begged Ben to trust her word.

"I believe you," he admitted and didn't know if he had what it took not to believe Kathy Moore. "But why did you go up there in the first place, Kathy? You knew it was off-limits. *I* haven't even gone up there."

"Alaina has," Kathy monotoned.

"Well, Dad doesn't know about it," Ben assured. "If he did . . ." He shook his head. "Alaina's getting headstrong in her old age."

"Maybe she's just tired of being under your dad's thumb." Kathy shivered. "I don't like him. He's a *tyrant.*"

Ben's back stiffened, and he didn't bother to analyze the desire to defend his dad from Kathy's barbs only minutes after defending Kathy from his father. "He's a grieving husband," he said, "and that should be respected by Alaina *and* you."

"But Thurston Manley told me—"

"Thurston Manley is a lying alcoholic," Ben said, his voice as rigid as his spine.

Her forehead wrinkled, Kathy stared at Ben. "But I didn't know that."

He held her gaze and finally shook his head. "How could you *not* know? He reeks of alcohol most of the time. Anybody who's with him five minutes can see he's nuts!"

"You're taking your dad's side," she whispered.

"I'm not taking anybody's side, Kathy." Ben rubbed at his chest again. His day had started at six this morning when one of his church members had a miscarriage. Then Ben's checker-playing buddy at the nursing home passed away at one. Now he'd just tried to beat up his own father after an eloquent Bible study titled "The Fruit of the Spirit: Longsuffering." Ben didn't know an optimist alive who wouldn't call this a bad day.

"What were you trying to do, anyway?" Ben asked. "Be like one of those detectives you read about?"

Kathy peered at him like an overwhelmed puppy.

"Hmmm." Ben looked across the yard to Duncan, trotting up the porch steps. He envisioned Kathy's wild imagination spinning her into a frenzied search for clues against his father. Ben chortled and rubbed his eyes.

"Oh, Kathy," he groaned, "what have you gotten yourself into?"

"Now you're laughing at me," she huffed.

"No, it's just that—" An outright guffaw sprang from Ben.

Kathy scooted away and crossed her arms. "Would you please get my stuff?" she demanded. "I'm ready to leave now."

"Where are you going to stay?" Ben asked. "Your place doesn't have any water."

"My shop does," Kathy said, her face turned toward the window. "I can sleep in my bed and use the bathroom downstairs."

Thirty

Kathy didn't open her shop the next day until ten, and only because Gloria had the audacity to call her cell and awaken her at 9:50. Since the Averys were leaving Saturday, she'd already given Kathy her key to the shop. In a panicked stupor, Kathy told her godmother she'd meet her at the door in ten minutes. Still groggy, she now unlocked the store door and allowed Gloria to enter.

"You look awful!" Gloria exclaimed the second she stepped into the store. "When we woke up at seven thirty, we saw your car in the parking lot. Did you spend the night here?" she questioned, eying Kathy's rumpled clothing.

"I guess you could say that," Kathy replied and rubbed her puffy eyes. "If lying awake most of the night is considered sleep. I drank half a Pepsi last night after nine. The caffeine kept me awake."

"Looks like the crying kept you awake," Gloria observed, her brows arching.

Looking down, Kathy rubbed her hands along the front of the white sleeveless blouse she'd worn yesterday. Other than shedding Ben's jacket, Kathy hadn't even bothered to change last night when she flopped onto her bed. The apartment had been so empty without Lucy. Her heart had been just as empty without Ben's approval.

He hadn't said much when he placed her suitcases in the back of her car and handed Kathy her purse. The dark circles under his eyes and the uncertain angle of his mouth said enough. All Kathy's worries from yesterday now crashed around her.

Whether or not Ben would allow his father's disapproval to end their romance was still unanswered. Her heart cold, Kathy blinked against fresh tears and staggered behind the service bar. As she groped for the coffee carafe, she reminded herself that Ben hadn't officially started their romance until he thought she could coexist with his dad.

Sniffling, she shoved the carafe under the waterspout, turned on the water, and reminded herself that Ben hadn't hesitated to defend her. Maybe that was a sign he'd also go against his father and continue their relationship.

"Did you and Ben have a fight?" Gloria's question came from inches away.

Kathy glanced up at her godmother. As usual, every silver hair was in place. Her makeup was meticulous, right down to the fuchsia lipstick that perfectly matched her cotton blouse. And she smelled as sweetly as Laura Tilman's lavender.

Not wanting to admit what she'd done, Kathy concentrated on watching the water fill the carafe. Finally she said, "Yes. Sort of. I guess."

"Oh," Gloria responded. "Look," she covered Kathy's hand with hers, "why don't you go upstairs and get your things. Go on over to our suite and take a shower. And you might want to put on some makeup," she hinted.

Allowing Gloria to take the coffeepot, Kathy touched her swollen eyelids. The brief glimpse in the mirror this morning told her she looked like a space alien with bubble eyes.

"The warm water will help some," Gloria advised, her voice tender and void of judgment.

"Okay," Kathy meekly agreed.

"I'll take care of the store. The plumber is coming at one. Remember?"

"No. I forgot," Kathy mumbled and yawned. The pasty taste in her mouth reminded her she still hadn't brushed her teeth.

"Go on up now!" Gloria shooed her from behind the service bar. "By the time you get your things together, I'll have a hot cup of coffee for you and a cinnamon roll you can eat on the way over."

"Make the coffee with caffeine," Kathy said, "and cut the cinnamon roll. I've eaten too much sugar lately. I've got some already-cooked sausage in the freezer. I'll zap it in my microwave up there."

"Okay," Gloria agreed. "But honey, as tired as you look, I don't even know if caffeine will affect you."

Within an hour, Kathy maneuvered past a pair of elk claiming the street corner and bounced back toward her store. Her short cotton skirt swayed above her knees as her flip-flops cheerfully slapped the sidewalk. Her hair smelled like peaches. Her skin prickled in celebration of clean. And she snapped a wad of cinnamon gum she'd found in her purse. Somewhere about the middle of her shower, the caffeine had indeed kicked in, and Kathy wondered how she could have been so out of it when she awoke. By the time Revlon had camouflaged the signs of her tears, even last night's episode took on a more positive light.

I can face anything, she thought. *It's all going to be okay! I just know it is. If Ben would nearly beat up his dad for me, he'll keep our relationship going. That's a no-brainer!*

With the opening of her shop door, Kathy was on such an optimistic tear she convinced herself that Zach would calm down and not hold her curiosity against her. After that, Ben would call and tell her all was well.

We'll be planning our wedding in a year, she thought.

Managing her canvas tote in one hand, she closed the door with the other. The gum's invigorating flavor reminded her of Ben's kisses. Kathy would never think of cinnamon the same again.

A movement in the far corner snared her attention. Ben stood from one of the cushioned chairs and laid a magazine on a nearby table.

"There you are!" Gloria neared from the back of the store. "Someone's here to see you." Still out of Ben's sight, Gloria pointed toward him and wiggled her brows.

"Hey, Ben," Kathy softly called and walked toward him.

"Hi," Ben replied and awkwardly waved. As usual, he wore a pair of nice pants and a long-sleeve dress shirt. As usual, his hair was neatly groomed and his smile was intact. But his eyes lacked the adoring sparkle, and his lips were stiff.

Kathy stopped. Her caffeine-induced buoyancy deflated with her spirit. She gripped the tote's handle and talked herself out of spitting the gum onto the floor, bursting into tears, and racing up the stairs.

"I was thinking the two of you might enjoy talking upstairs." Gloria neared Ben and directed a sly wink toward Kathy. "I'll take care of the shop, Kathy."

"That would be best, I think," Ben said with a calm nod.

"Sure," Kathy agreed and realized her fingers were performing their post-caffeine jitters. "I slept here last night," she nervously chattered while Ben followed her toward the stairs. "It was okay, really," she added and wondered how to stop herself from talking. "I missed Lucy. How is she?" Kathy tackled the stairs with Ben at her side.

"She's fine," Ben replied.

"I guess it would probably be okay for you to bring her back home. I've decided to just stay in my apartment and do the best I can. I can get my showers in Aunt Gloria and Uncle Ziggy's room at the inn until they leave Saturday. After that, maybe the owners will let me borrow a shower for a few days. We can make it work. The plumber is coming this afternoon."

They paused outside Kathy's door while she opened it. "The

apartment smells way more musty. I guess the wood's not quite dried out yet. But I think it'll all be okay once the plumbing gets fixed." Kathy stepped through the entrance, allowed Ben to enter, and closed the door. Hurrying forward, she dropped her tote on the sofa and turned toward Ben. Afraid to make eye contact, she looked past his ear and then glanced away. "I think I've got some bottled water in the fridge. Want one?"

"Yes," he agreed. "That would be nice."

"I'll have some, too," Kathy said and opened the refrigerator. "Maybe it'll water down the caffeinated coffee I had this morning. Am I talking too much?" She grabbed two bottles of icy water from the cluttered shelf and rapidly blinked at him.

Ben's tired smile met his eyes this time. "No, you're just fine," he said with a hint of the old endearment.

The refrigerator's cold air blasting her bare legs, Kathy closed the door and handed him the water.

Ben twisted off the lid and laid it on the breakfast bar. He settled onto the lone barstool and sipped the liquid.

Gripping her bottle, Kathy stood on the other side of the counter and stole a long look at Ben. The dark circles under his eyes were as prominent as hers had been this morning.

"Kathy," he began and set down the bottle, "I . . . This isn't easy." He pinched the side of the bottle cap and never looked up.

She stared at the top of Ben's wavy hair, still damp around the edges, and remembered that first night she'd met him. His hair had been even more wet. Her frenzied mind toiled to comprehend the impact of Ben's presence in her life.

I'll never forget that night, she thought and adoringly eyed the diminishing scar near his hairline. *I'll never forget him!*

Her soul ached with the implications of her own thoughts. Ben wasn't here to make up or to proclaim his dad had reconsidered a thing. Kathy unscrewed the water lid and guzzled the liquid. Somehow in the mix, her cinnamon gum washed to the back of her throat, and she hacked against the wad lodged at her tonsils.

Ben looked up.

"I just swallowed my gum." She wheezed, leaned forward, and coughed again. A pink mass propelled from her mouth and squished onto the bar. "Well, howdy-do to you, too," Kathy rasped.

Fresh laughter erupted from Ben.

Kathy survived another hack and downed a new swallow of water.

"I'll never forget you, Kathy Moore," Ben said.

She pulled a tissue from the box on the breakfast bar, covered the gum, and wadded the tissue around it. "I was just thinking the same thing about you," she whispered and dared to peer into Ben's soul.

Her miserable night was reflected in his eyes. So was her agony.

"Why, Ben?" she asked and shook her head.

"My dad, he was serious last night."

"But you're thirty years old," Kathy stressed. "Are you going to let your dad control you your whole life? Even Alaina's got more guts than this."

He narrowed his eyes. "What are you saying?"

"I'm saying Alaina's got more guts than this!" Kathy plopped her water bottle on the counter. A dollop splashed out and splattered the bar. She smashed the tissue against the droplets.

"I've got plenty of guts," Ben claimed and crossed his arms. "I defended you last night, didn't I?" he challenged.

"Sure, but—"

"And just so you know, Dad and I had a knock-down drag-out last night after you left."

"He hit you?"

"No!" Ben held up his hands, palms outward. "I didn't mean that *literally*," he explained. "I just mean we had an awful argument. I told him some things I've needed to tell him for a long time, including that it's time for him to bury the hatchet with Thurston Manley."

"Oh," Kathy said and dug her toes into the flip-flops' spongy soles. "Sorry."

"I didn't sleep at all last night," Ben continued, his voice tight, "especially not after Dad called Alaina, and she told him."

Her mouth fell open. "About her marriage?"

"Yep."

"Whoa!" Kathy shifted backward. "I guess she took my advice after all. Yesterday, I told her to just tell him."

"Well, she did. And," he sighed, "I heard him crying in the night. I decided to stay this morning until Alaina and Caleb arrived to get her stuff."

"And?"

"The minute they drove up, Dad shut himself up on the third floor. As far as I know, he's still in there. I don't know that I've ever seen him so miserable—except at Mom's funeral."

"But Alaina said she thought he'd *kill* her." Kathy shook her head from side to side.

Ben squinted. "Did you take her literally, too?"

"Uh . . ."

"Kathy," Ben said. He looked down and worked his mouth.

"Well, Thurston Manley kept telling me he was a murderer. What was I supposed to think?" She yanked on the hem of her T-shirt.

"Oh, Kathy." Chuckling, Ben placed his elbow on the breakfast bar and rested his forehead against his hand.

She stiffened and crossed her arms. "Why do you always have to laugh at me?"

Ben raised his head, observed her, and stroked his bottom

lip. "Sorry," he said. The corners of his mouth quivered, and he ducked his head.

"So get on with it. Break up with me and get it over with," she said, her voice thick. "I don't like all this beating around the bush."

"What bush?" His gaze intensifying, Ben scrutinized her. "There is no bush. I wanted to tell you everything I've told you."

Kathy tapped her foot.

Ben pressed both palms against the bar and leaned toward her. "I don't like this any more than you do, Kathy!"

"Then why go through with it?" she demanded and lifted both hands like a lawyer in her final argument.

"Because my father no longer likes you!" he explained, his voice even and hard. "I already told you, I watched my mom and grandmother fight my whole life. I don't want that kind of a life. I'd rather just end us now while we have half our hearts left."

"If you *really* cared for me, Ben, you'd tell your dad to take a hike!" She doubled her fists at her sides.

"Maybe breaking up with you is a greater act of love than staying with you," Ben defended. "Do you really want to spend the rest of your life dealing with him?"

"No, I don't!" Kathy said. "But I wouldn't have to, would I? Why couldn't you just tell him to stay out of our lives? Break up with *him* instead of me!"

"Do you want to break up with *your* parents?"

Ben's staccato words rendered Kathy speechless.

"Put yourself in my position, why don't you?" He stood and scooted the stool aside. It growled against the exposed wood and teetered to a stop. "My dad's still grieving for my mom. My sister's dropped a bomb on him. I'm not saying she shouldn't have done what she did. I'm just saying it's like a bomb! My brother is lying to my dad and doing who-knows-what in his spare time. That leaves me!" Ben pressed his fingers against his chest. "My father's not always right. He's done some things really wrong. But I will tell you that he's worked like a dog for our family. He was there for me when I was a kid. I can't just ditch him in his retirement years. I at least owe him some loyalty, don't I?"

"Are you breaking up with me for good?" Kathy's words wobbled as badly as her legs.

Ben pressed his index finger into the bottle cap and fixed his attention on it. His affirmative nod was barely perceptible.

"I'll stay single my whole life before I'll relive what I had to put up with as a kid," he said. "I'm pretty sure I'm still not over it. I don't think Dad knows how bad it really was. I don't even like my grandmother."

Her head spinning, Kathy crossed her arms and rubbed. Her breaking heart suggested she should get down on her hands and knees and beg. She imagined wrapping herself around Ben's leg and his dragging her down the stairs in an attempt to escape. The very absurdity of the image gave her the strength to remain standing.

"You know what I just figured out, Ben Tilman?" she said through a curtain of hot tears.

"What?" He put the cap back on his bottled water.

"You're not perfect."

Ben jerked his gaze to Kathy. His eye twitched. "You couldn't have really believed I was."

"Y-yes. I did!" She stomped her foot and detested herself for crying. The more she detested, the harder she cried. "But you're not!" She hurled the wad of tissue at him. It bounced off his shirt and dropped to the floor. "If you were, you'd tell me your father's disapproval doesn't matter because you love me, and we'd make it work!"

"That sounds like something from a romance novel." He rubbed the corner of his mouth.

"Maybe it is!" Kathy bellowed.

"Well, I'm sorry, Kathy!" Ben hollered. "I'm not some perfect hero! I've got flaws. A lot of them! And even if I didn't, life is tough. It's not some black-and-white, easy-choices kind of plot that places everything in neat little boxes with happy endings."

His face gradually reddened as his voice's volume increased, and Kathy saw more of Zachariah in him than she had yet. "I can't help the way this has turned out. It's just the way it is. In the real world, bad stuff happens, and we have to do the best we can to make the most sane choices." Ben rapped his knuckles against the bar. "Shoot me at sunrise. Hang me at sundown."

"Both of those options sound pretty good right now," Kathy growled and strode around him, toward her bedroom.

"I'm just trying to do what's best for both of us!" he claimed. "You're young. You'll find somebody else! I'll find someone my dad can get along with."

"Your dad couldn't get along with Mother Teresa!" Kathy stomped into her bedroom, slammed the door, collapsed against it, and stared straight ahead. Her gaze encompassed her cluttered dresser. The book on boundaries still lay among a pile of clothes. On an impulse, Kathy marched across the room, grabbed the book, and charged back the way she came. Not bothering to check the increasing flow of tears, she whipped open the door, only to discover Ben walking toward the apartment's door.

He swiveled to face her with a questioning lift of his brows.

Not knowing what to say, Kathy hurled the book in his direction. It sailed over the sofa and landed with a page-ruffling thump four feet from Ben.

"What's that for?" he demanded.

"Since you're so smart, *you* figure it out!" she bellowed and slammed the door again. Kathy threw herself on the unmade bed, buried her head in the covers, and shook with the force of her emotions.

After a season of hard sobs, Kathy lifted her face and grabbed the covers to blot away the tears. Before the fabric touched her skin, she realized she'd been crying on Ben's jacket, dribbled in stale-smelling taco sauce.

"Oh, phooey!" Kathy exclaimed and thrust the jacket to the edge of the bed. She gripped the rumpled sheet and scrubbed her face until it stung.

Kathy stood on quivering legs and mumbled, "What I said *is* from a novel, you . . . you . . . It's from *my* novel!"

She stumbled toward her open suitcase, strewn with askew clothing. Beside it sat a laptop case. Kathy picked up the case and plopped it onto her bed. Within a few minutes she had booted up the computer and was scrolling through a list of her documents. When she highlighted the file titled *The Chalet*, she hit the Delete button and removed all traces of the gorillas, the crocodiles, and the boa-infested jungle. As Kathy fully absorbed the demise of her precious boas, the mourning began anew.

She collapsed onto the bed, stared at the ceiling, and allowed the tears to drain down her temples, into her hair. "Oh, Jesus," she whispered, "how did all this get to be such a mess?"

Kathy rolled to her stomach, hiccoughed, and swiped at her tears. She recalled Laura Tilman's claims of spiritual assurance, depth, and peace. And she wondered, as she'd wondered through the night, exactly how to have peace in the midst of such awful pain.

By midafternoon, Kathy opened the door of Lighthouse Community Church and stepped inside. The stained-glass windows filtered pristine sunlight across white pews. Clasping her car keys behind her, Kathy hovered at the chapel's entrance, absorbing the smells of hymnals, the cool shadows, the spirit of faithful worship. Her gaze trailed to the oak cross attached to the wall behind the pulpit. Kathy's eyes stung anew.

This time she wasn't in church out of habit or duty or for

her parents. She was here for herself and for God. After she had exterminated the boas and cried awhile longer, the tiny frame church two streets from her store began to beckon. She'd gone downstairs and found Gloria laboring in the customer-free store. Gloria hadn't asked a thing when Kathy told her she was going out. The compassion spilling from her eyes said it all.

Now the altar waiting in front of the pulpit whispered Kathy's name. She lingered no longer. New tears splashing her cheeks, she stumbled across the short-piled carpet and collapsed to her knees.

"Oh, Jesus," she cried, draping her body over the altar, "I'm hurting. Bad. I'm confused. I don't know what to do or think or feel. I've made a mess of the whole thing. I should have never listened to Thurston Manley, or gone into the suite, or . . . or read Laura Tilman's diary."

Kathy blindly groped for the box of tissue under the altar, pulled out a fistful, and swabbed her face. When the tissue was thoroughly damp, she grabbed more and started the process all over again. The whole time, the passage from Laura's diary echoed through her mind: *"I've fallen so in love with the Lord these last few years. All I know is that I belong to Jesus, and He belongs to me."*

She rested her head on the altar, took in the smell of furniture polish, and watched as the tears dripped from her lashes and sank into her skirt. Kathy contemplated her whole life of religious activity. Even though she had long ago accepted Christ as her Savior, she couldn't say that she'd ever been involved in a deep love affair with Him. She wasn't sure she even knew how to get there.

"Oh, Jesus, show me," she breathed. "And forgive me for all these wrong choices with Ben. Please, somehow, work a miracle and bring him back. But whatever happens, please show me how to get where Laura was."

A holy peace Kathy had never known swooped from the corridors of heaven and invaded her soul. She held her breath, hung
on to the altar, and waited before her Lord. A deep and lasting
Presence assured her He'd heard her prayers, that her request
had begun a process that would take a lifetime to complete.

Thirty-One

Two weeks later, Kathy hustled into her apartment's diminutive utility room. She twisted the blind rod to the open position and peered out the petite window. The colonial bed-and-breakfast across the street was the backdrop for Kathy's latest attempt at spying on Liza. She placed the grocery bag full of canned cat food on the floor near her feet. Even though Lucy was howling for her meal and pawing at the bag, Kathy concentrated on the street below.

Minutes ago, as she was entering her store, Kathy noticed Phil's truck pulling up next door. She had barely seen Liza the last couple of weeks. When Phil's truck wasn't at the B and B, Kathy assumed Liza was out with him.

Twice Kathy had hinted to Jay about what was going on. Once by phone, once by text. Both times Jay swept aside Kathy's concerns and continued chatting about Liza's great qualities. Meanwhile, Kathy's mom also had tried to encourage Jay back to planet Earth. Even in the face of her common sense, Jay was doing a free-float in outer space.

"The poor guy has lost all sense of logic," Kathy whispered while straining for any signs of Liza's disloyalty.

The scene below, like several before, offered nothing but the image of a helpful young man taking a mother and daughter on a Saturday-afternoon outing. Liza and Dory exited the bed-and-breakfast with Phil close behind. He pressed a button on his key chain and the ladies opened the passenger door. Liza climbed in first with Dory close behind.

After Phil took his place behind the wheel, Liza leaned over and kissed him near the ear.

"Gotcha!" Kathy whispered. She doubled her fist and thrust it toward her torso as if she'd just scored a home run. For the last two weeks, Kathy hadn't spotted Phil and Liza alone, although she knew in her heart they must be seeing each other. Even Gloria and Sigmund, before they left town, testified to having never seen Liza alone with Phil.

But now Liza had reduced herself to showing open affection in broad daylight. Kathy dashed into her kitchen, thrust her hands in the air, swung her hips, and chanted, "Oh yeah . . . oh yeah . . . oh yeah!"

Lucy pranced into the kitchen and peered up at her owner. Her tail straight, she meowed, ran toward the breakfast bar, and hopped onto it. She trotted toward another grocery bag sprawled atop Ben's jacket.

Kathy scooped up the feline and said, "Lucy, you aren't supposed to be up there. You crazy thang!" She stroked the purring cat's body. "Listen, I've got great news! Liza Thaine is history! I'm gonna call Jay and tell him what I saw. If he doesn't believe me, I'll get a picture of the two of them and send it to Jay. All my spying these last two weeks has finally paid off."

"Meow!" Lucy responded and sniffed at Kathy's burrito-splattered T-shirt.

"You're hungry, aren't you?" Kathy crooned. She retrieved the bag of canned cat food by the back door and dropped it beside the other bag on the breakfast bar. It, too, landed on Ben's jacket.

Kathy scrounged through the bag, pulled out a can of tuna delight, and tugged on the tab that opened the can. When the lid clicked off, the can tilted sideways and dribbled a stream of fishy juice on Ben's jacket.

"Oh no," Kathy groaned while Lucy propped her paws on the side of the cabinet and began a series of impatient yowls. "Okay, okay, cat," Kathy said and dumped the strong-smelling feast into Lucy's bowl. The cat hunched down and began smacking with delight.

Kathy tossed the can into the trash basket under her kitchen sink and turned back to the new problem: Ben's jacket.

I guess I get to wash it again, she thought. Kathy had already laundered the jacket once to wash off the taco sauce and the evidence of her blubbering all over it. She'd planned to return the jacket when Ben brought Lucy home. But he hadn't brought her. Instead, Ben asked his new secretary to take care of the deed. Kathy had been so flabbergasted when the tall brunette walked into the store with the cat carrier that she hadn't even thought about Ben's jacket. All she focused on was whether or not the attractive lady wore a wedding band. Once she spotted the diamond solitaire and wide gold band, Kathy had been so relieved, there was no room for remembering the jacket.

All week she deliberated about how to return the coat. Careful not to get the cat food juice on her jeans or T-shirt, Kathy picked up the jacket. As of yesterday, she'd decided to buy a large manila envelope and mail the jacket to Ben. That seemed to be the most logical answer.

Of course, that will be after I wash it again, she thought. With a resigned sigh, Kathy stepped into her utility room, tossed the jacket into the washing machine, and threw in a few other dark-colored items lying in a basket near the dryer. Despite her determination not to think about Ben, Kathy's vision began to blur. By the time the water was running and she was dumping in the powder detergent, her hands were unsteady. So were her knees.

"Oh, Ben," she whispered. "Dear God, help me get over him." Even though Kathy had begun a new chapter in her walk with the Lord, her heart still ached for Ben. She recalled the many times she'd heard her father say, *"Being a Christian doesn't mean you won't have pain or that you won't take time to heal. It does mean you've got Jesus to walk through the pain with you."* For the first time in her life, Kathy fully understood what her father meant.

The muffled notes from *The Twilight Zone* penetrated her thoughts; the sound of her cell phone reminded her she needed to call Jay. With a thud and a metallic *boing*, Kathy dropped the washer's lid into place.

"I can't believe I still haven't called him," she mumbled as she scurried into her living room.

Kathy stopped near the sofa, where she'd dropped her purse on the way in. She scrounged to the bottom and found her cell beneath a pair of pantyhose she'd shed in the church parking lot Wednesday night. She'd discovered a hole in the knee one block from Lighthouse Community Church. After parking the car, Kathy had squirmed out of the nylons and stuffed them into her purse, all the while wondering why she ever put them on in the first place. Today was their debut appearance from what her father dubbed "the black hole." When she pulled out her cell phone, the top of it lodged in the large hole and she dragged out the hose with her. After fighting with the nylons during several measures of *The Twilight Zone* theme song, Kathy finally just answered the phone through the pantyhose.

"Kathy?" Jay questioned. "You sound muffled."

"Jay!" she said. "I was about to call you! Just a minute. My cell phone is tangled in my pantyhose."

"Are you *wearing* the pantyhose?" Jay asked.

"No, you goofball," Kathy retorted. "They were in my purse." She pulled the phone away from her ear and managed to dislodge the cell from the hose. They drifted to the floor and settled against her red carpet. Relishing the smell of new carpet, Kathy returned the phone to her ear, then scooped up the hose.

"There," she said and traipsed into her kitchen. "I'm pantyhose free." She opened the cabinet door beneath the sink, tossed the hose into the trash receptacle, and clicked the door shut.

"And I'm not *even* going to ask why you had pantyhose in your purse." Jay's listless voice held no traces of humor. "You can really get yourself into some fixes, that's all I know."

So can you, Kathy thought and debated how to best tell Jay that his fiancée was unfaithful.

"Have you seen Liza lately?" Jay questioned.

Grappling with what to say, Kathy moved back into the living room and collapsed onto the dormitory-green love seat. She hadn't visualized just how badly her furniture would clash with the cheerful carpet until *after* it was laid.

Dismissing the decor dilemma, she leaned forward and decided to just be honest. "Yes, I've seen her."

"And . . . ?"

"And?"

"What'd she say? Did she tell you?"

"I haven't talked to her much since you left," Kathy explained. "I've *seen* her, like I said. But I haven't talked to her."

"Well, she called last night and dumped me," Jay explained, his voice flat.

Kathy covered her eyes. "I am *so sorry,*" she breathed and decided not to mention the kiss. That would be like pouring acid into Jay's wound.

"You were right," Jay said. "She's got a thing going with Phil."

"But I hate that I was right, Jay," Kathy said, her heart swelling with the pain in her brother's voice. "I wish she'd been more like—more like—"

"Like Ben?" Jay queried.

Kathy winced. "I didn't realize you knew about us," she said, straining to keep her voice steady.

"Ron told me."

"Well, while I can say I don't believe Ben would ever two-time me, we aren't together anymore."

"Oh," Jay said while Kathy's mind raced ahead.

"But don't tell Ron, okay? I mean, even though Ben and I broke up, that doesn't mean I'm interested in Ron."

"Humph. I don't think you have a choice. Ron is talking about nothing else but you. The second he hears about you and Ben being off, he'll probably be on your trail. Even if I don't tell him, I imagine Liza or her mother will the second they find out. Chances are high they will, since Liza is seeing Phil."

"Please, Jay," Kathy plead, "*please* tell him it's useless."

"I'll try," Jay agreed. "But he's pretty hardheaded."

"I know. I know." Kathy slipped off her sandals and relished the feel of carpet fibers against her feet. "How well I know."

"I just wish I'd had enough sense to steer clear of Liza like you have Ron. I have been a fool, Kathy."

"Don't be so hard on yourself."

"Why not? It's the truth. I let a pretty face and a great figure get to me."

"Well, it happens to the best of us." Kathy stood and strode toward the framed poster of Lucille Ball, which had somehow gotten crooked.

"It's just that here I am, twenty-eight and still not married. I guess I just—I'm starting to really want a wife. She seemed perfect."

"Of course," Kathy soothed and adjusted the poster. "But you just can't rush into such a huge decision."

"I can't believe we're having this conversation," Jay mused, his voice filled with weary mirth.

"Just remember, you can call your sister, Kathy, any ol' time you need advice," she drawled and stepped away from Lucille to eye her angle. *Perfect*, she thought.

"Okay, this has gone far enough," Jay threatened.

"Seriously," Kathy encouraged, "I'm sure you'll find somebody else." The second the words left her mouth she cringed. Those were some of the last words Ben said to her. They'd done nothing to comfort. Even now, the idea of getting involved with another man brought only dismay.

I don't want another man, Kathy thought. *I want Ben!*

"Actually, there's a new tennis coach here at school," Jay admitted.

"Oh, really?" Kathy questioned.

"Yep. She's nothing like Liza. Very athletic and practical. But, well, I'd already had some thoughts—especially when she showed up at my church. I think I might ask her out."

"I wish you would," Kathy enthused and eyed Andy Griffith. "As in tonight!"

"Tonight!" Jay blurted.

"Yes. Why wait?" She nudged at the poster until it was centered.

"Didn't you just tell me not to jump into anything?"

"I'm not suggesting you should get married!" Kathy placed her hand on her hip. "But I don't think it would hurt for you guys to go get a burger and be friends. The sooner you start getting Liza out of your system, the better. She's not even close to what you need, Jay. I knew that early on."

A tired huff was his only answer. In the lull, Kathy adjusted Dick Van Dyke and decided the rest of the gang was in place.

Finally Jay said, "I guess I'll go, oh great, wise Kathy." A grin colored his words. "I think tennis practice might be on this afternoon."

Kathy laughed out loud. "I'm really glad to hear the old Jay is back," she teased.

"Yes, and do you think he'd be back so soon if he was really in love with Liza?"

"Probably not," Kathy agreed. "Sometimes it's easy to get attraction mixed up with love."

"Here's hoping I don't make this mistake ever again."

"Really," Kathy affirmed. "You could go broke buying engagement rings."

"Ow," Jay complained. "Did you have to mention that?"

One week later, Kathy scrunched lower in her bed and gripped the sides of the novel *Castles*. She'd chosen the book because the title was nearly identical to the first title of her novel. Now her damp palms oozed perspiration on the pages. This new thriller featured a twenty-first-century woman trapped in underground passages between two medieval castles. She'd started out a tourist and wound up witnessing a murder. Now the killers were after her.

Kathy, absorbed in the plot, smelled the cramped underground corridors. She lived the heroine's terror. She imagined the horrors awaiting her at every turn.

Lucy, purring profusely, snuggled close to Kathy's arm and rubbed her head against her owner's hand. "Hang on, girlfriend," Kathy mumbled. "We're in a tight place." She once again immersed herself into the heroine's psyche and fell with her through a trapdoor into a den of cobras.

"Oh my word," she whispered and imagined staring eye-to-eye with one of those hooded serpents. *This is better than boa constrictors any day*, she thought. Her skin delightfully creeping, Kathy braced herself against a hard cringe just as her phone rang.

"Aaaahhhh!" she shrieked, lunged, and dropped the novel. Lucy jumped from her repose and darted off the bed. With the phone's peals continuing, Kathy placed her hand over her heart and flopped back onto the stack of pillows. As the ringtone began to replay, Kathy laughed.

That was a good one, she thought and stretched toward her cell phone. She answered it just before it would have gone to voicemail.

"Kathy?" a teary-voiced female questioned.

"Yes. It's me." Kathy sat up in bed and tried to decipher the voice.

A chorus of sniffles preceded the next words. "This is Liza."

"Liza?" Kathy asked, her forehead wrinkling.

"Yes. Oh, Kathy, would you please open your store and let me in? We've always been such good friends."

We have? Kathy thought.

"I'm out here w-waiting on you! I need to t-t-talk to you." Liza's weepy declaration preceded the call's immediate ending.

Kathy pulled the phone away from her ear. "Well!" she said. "Thanks for giving me a choice." She picked up the novel, longingly stroked it, and placed it on her nightstand. Kathy had spent the last week reading more than ever in an attempt to obliterate Ben from her mind. The last thing she needed was to be Liza's psychiatrist. Kathy threw the phone onto her bed. After what Liza had done to Jay, Kathy struggled with even seeing her. She stood and paced toward the kitchen. During the brief journey, she put together the pieces of Liza's crisis. Alaina had admitted that her brother was a flirt who wasn't the least bit interested in marriage.

I bet he broke it off with her, Kathy thought.

Pausing in front of the refrigerator, Kathy gripped the handle, placed her forehead on the cool surface, and bumped her head against the refrigerator several times. *No duh!* she thought. *Everybody and their brother can see Phil Tilman is a womanizer.*

Kathy opened the fridge, retrieved a bottled water, and slammed the door. The cool air enveloped her shorts-clad legs and she shivered. She found her flip-flops by the barstool and slipped them on. Before taking another step, Kathy unscrewed the bottle lid and downed a generous swallow of water. The icy liquid created a pleasingly cool path to her stomach. Running through those stuffy underground passages from castle to castle had left her panting for liquid.

In less than a minute, Kathy set her water bottle on the service bar and unlocked the store door. Liza rushed inside. Her brown mascara smeared from lash to lips, Liza grabbed Kathy before she could even shut the door.

"Oh, Kathy, I've made a dreadful mistake!" she wailed and crushed Kathy in a hug.

Kathy, gripping the knob, stopped herself from falling against the door as it whacked shut. Not knowing what to do with her arms, she gently patted Liza's back while being engulfed in a cloud of designer fragrance that was as powerful as the wearer's ability to perform.

"Have you heard? I broke up with Jay." Liza lurched backward and rubbed at her tears.

Kathy nodded. "He told me last week," she admitted and tried to conjure at least a scrap of compassion for Liza. She failed. "I figured you and Phil were—"

"We were! And that was the mistake!" Liza wailed. "We aren't now! He left for the military base y-yesterday and—and before he left he *d-dumped* me!" She covered her face with her hands. "Do you think there's any way Jay would ever take me back?" Liza cried against her palms.

Uh, no, Kathy thought. She crossed her arms and backed away. *Not if he has any sense.*

"I've still got his ring and everything! I've been *sooooo stupid!*" Liza lowered her hands and gripped Kathy's upper arms. "We've been great friends from the first time we met!"

We have? Kathy asked herself again. She stepped away from

Liza's grasp, moved toward the service bar, and retrieved her water bottle.

"I need your help!" Liza wailed.

Kathy guzzled the water.

"Would you *please, please* talk to Jay for me? I'm sure he'd listen to you, and then I could call him, and we could get back together."

"Liza . . ." Kathy swallowed more water, plopped onto a stool, and debated how best to say no. She couldn't even find a scrap of pity for Liza, let alone help her reconcile with Jay.

"Kathy, you're such a wonderful friend," Liza oozed through a deluge of fresh tears. She hurried forward and claimed the stool next to Kathy. Her short denim skirt rose halfway up her slender thighs, which were tan and bare.

Kathy squeezed the near-empty water bottle until the sides met.

"I just know this hurts you as bad as it does me, and you'll be so glad to see me and Jay back together. When you call him, please let me know what he says. Then I can call him. He *loved* me *sooooo* much! I don't know why I let Phil come between us!"

"Probably because Phil's better looking than Jay," Kathy stated and couldn't seem to stop herself from sounding aggravated. Her fingers digging into the plastic bottle, Kathy stood and marched toward the trash can near the cash register. She drained the last swallow of water from the crumpled bottle and dropped it into the receptacle.

Liza's crying gradually ceased. "What are you saying?" she whimpered.

"I'm saying you dumped Jay because Phil's better looking." Kathy crossed her arms and leaned against the retail counter.

"Don't say that," Liza complained and toyed with the hem of her short T-shirt. "You know me better than that. That sounds so . . . so . . ."

"Shallow?" Kathy questioned and realized she'd never sounded so much like her mother.

"Uh!" Liza said and hopped from the stool. Her sandals slapped the wooden floor with as much vehemence as Kathy's reddening face indicated.

"Liza," Kathy continued and purposefully softened her voice. "I'm sorry, but I cannot call Jay for you." Silently she prayed for God's wisdom . . . and His forgiveness. Never had Kathy so struggled with wanting to hold a grudge.

"Well, you don't have to sound so spiteful about it!" Liza snapped, all tears amazingly gone.

"I'm not trying to be spiteful," Kathy said. Her spine stiff, she gazed past Liza toward the display of antique books near the front window.

"Would you care to tell me why you won't call him?"

"How would you feel if you were me?" Kathy asked. "I really love my brother. You hurt him. I just happen to think it's best for both of you to find someone else," Kathy said and hoped Liza stopped pushing there.

"And?" she prompted. "You're not through. I can see it all over your face. Go ahead and *say* it!"

Okay, since you put it like that, I will, Kathy thought. "I don't think it's a good idea for you and Jay to get back together because . . . because I'm not so sure you won't do the same thing to him again."

"Well, a fine sister-in-law you're going to be!" Liza railed and stomped her foot. "I don't even know what Ron sees in you."

"Sister-in-law?" Kathy croaked.

"When you and Ron get married!" Liza explained, her voice rising with every syllable.

"I'm not marrying Ron!" Kathy squared her feet and placed her hands on her hips.

"That's news to me *and* him," Liza snorted. "He told me since you and Ben broke up—"

"I am *not* marrying Ron!" Kathy repeated.

"Isn't this like the pot calling the kettle black?" Liza advanced on a napkin holder like a general gaining new territory. She stopped only three feet from Kathy and pulled out a wad of napkins.

Tempted to back up, Kathy held her ground and didn't flinch. "I have no earthly idea what you mean."

"I mean, oh dense one," Liza pontificated, "that you're acting so high and mighty over me and Jay when you've treated my brother just as badly." She wagged her head from side to side.

"I have not!" Kathy locked her knees. "I never wanted anything but friendship, and I made that clear!"

"Not to him!" Liza growled and pointed her finger at Kathy's nose. "And you looked pretty cozy to me, too!"

"How?"

"You just did!" Liza subjected her face to a final rubdown, then whirled around like a tyrannical queen and stomped toward the front door. Halfway out of the store, she pivoted and delivered a final glare. "I'm *glad* you aren't interested in Ron!" she snarled. "I'd *hate* having you as a sister-in-law!" She slammed the door with such force that the front glass rattled and the bell clanked to the floor.

"Well, later-gator to you, too," Kathy retorted and recalled a handwritten note in the Bible she'd inherited from her grandmother . . . something about forgiveness taking time. Kathy rubbed her tense face and had never been so thankful for God's grace. She certainly needed it every time she thought of Liza Thaine.

With the store floor pleasantly creaking beneath her feet, Kathy walked toward the bell. She picked it up and examined the red ribbon, which was worn in two. Kathy examined the knob and decided the satin ribbon was being nipped every time she turned the knob. She was so engrossed in her problem that she didn't realize someone was standing on the other side of the door until she absently glanced up. Not expecting another human being so close, Kathy jumped. Then she realized she was staring into Ben Tilman's beseeching blue eyes.

Thirty-Two

Ben rested his hand on the window and gazed at Kathy, who stared back at him as if he really were the Ghost of Christmas Past. The seconds stretched, and Ben wondered if she'd welcome him or call the police.

He offered a weak smile and mouthed, "May I come in?" while pointing at his chest, then inside Kathy's store.

She vigorously nodded and whipped open the door. "Hi, Ben!" The hero worship awe that haunted Ben's every dream oozed from Kathy and assured him he was more than welcome. A warm glow started in his gut and spread to his soul.

A fresh breeze, whispering about courage and love, swirled from Northpointe Mountain and urged Ben to recite the speech he'd rehearsed while cruising past Kathy's store all last week.

"I was wondering, um, if you'd mind if I came in for—"

"Yes!" she declared. "Oh, I mean no! No, I don't mind. I mean, I'd be thrilled," she babbled yet never opened the door farther or moved aside. Instead, she continued to stare up at him like she was eight and he was the biggest ice-cream cone she'd ever seen.

"Okay," Ben said, his voice cracking like an adolescent's. He cleared his throat. "Well, uh . . ." He stepped forward and hoped she took the hint.

"Oh!" she exclaimed and swept open the door. "I guess I was in the way, wasn't I?"

Ben walked into the shop and felt as if he'd come home. Until now, he hadn't realized how much he'd missed the store's yesteryear ambiance, the smell of books, and the odor of gourmet coffee. He faced Kathy, inserted his hands into the pockets of his golf shorts, and debated where to begin.

"Do you want to sit down or something?" she asked and shut the door. "I make a mean lemonade."

"So I've heard," Ben drawled. "Actually, I was wondering if maybe you'd let me borrow your phone. My car broke down, and I don't have my cell and it's raining."

"Of course!" Kathy agreed, then looked toward the street, ablaze with late-afternoon sunshine.

Ben followed her gaze. His Corolla was parked at the curb.

"It's not raining," Kathy chided with a crooked smile. "And you're not serious." She fidgeted with a bell attached to a red ribbon.

"Well, that's the way we met, isn't it?" Ben questioned.

Kathy nodded and tilted her head.

"So if that line started something once, I was thinking it might . . . maybe it would help us start over."

"Me and you?" Kathy pointed to Ben when she said "me," to herself when she said "you."

Chuckling, Ben nodded. "Yes, me," he pointed at her, "and you," he pointed to himself.

"Oh, Ben!" Kathy gushed and flung herself into his arms. She dropped the bell behind him and it jingled to the floor. "I've been hoping and praying, but I never dreamed you'd come back!"

Ben laughed out loud for the first time since he'd walked away from Kathy. He wrapped his arms around her, held on tight, and swayed from side to side.

"These last few weeks have been the most miserable of my life," he said near her ear and relished the faint scent of peaches as her hair tickled his nose. "I thought I could be strong and move on without you, but I found out it was impossible. I felt like I was only half living."

"I felt the same way," Kathy said, her voice thick. She sniffled and pulled away while wiping at her eyes.

"Hey, I didn't come here to make you cry," Ben coaxed.

"I'm not crying." Kathy smiled up at him, her eyes brimming with tears. "I'm raining joy."

Ben's throat tightened. His eyes burned. "So am I, sweetheart," he said and stole a brief kiss that sealed their new romance.

Kathy wrapped her arms around him again and rested her head against his chest. "Your dad—did he change his mind?"

"No." Ben shook his head and stroked Kathy's hair.

"He didn't?" Kathy lifted her head and gaped at Ben. "Then why are you here?"

"After about two weeks I realized I'd never be happy with another woman," he explained, "and that I didn't want to break up with you any more than I did with him. So I spent another week reading that book you threw at me, trying to figure out how to make this whole thing with my dad work."

"Does he totally hate me now?" Kathy sheepishly asked.

"I wouldn't say *hate*." Ben rubbed his forehead, searched for the best explanation, and decided to just be honest. "I think he's still pretty hot about everything that happened. But he's not as mad as he was when he first found out."

"I'm so sorry I did what I did." Kathy backed away from Ben. Her lip trembled as she hugged herself.

"I know," Ben said and stroked her cheek. "You're just too curious for your own good."

"That and Thurston Manley—"

"Since you brought him up," Ben interrupted, "Dad went to see him last week."

"No way!"

"Yes." Ben nodded. "Once he read Mom's diary, he decided

he needed to try to make peace with Thurston. And even though he's still upset with Alaina, he's at least trying to like Caleb. He's also had a few really honest conversations with Phil about what he's up to."

"Wow!" Kathy enthused. "This is a miracle, isn't it?"

Ben nodded.

"Does he think I'm the weirdest woman on the planet or what?"

"Not quite," Ben said through a chuckle. "I think it's just going to take some time for him to get to know you. I just wish Mom was still around to meet you." Ben put his hand into his pocket and jiggled the simple cross keychain that had been his mother's.

"She was really a special person. I could tell by her diary. It had some pretty powerful stuff in it," Kathy said, her eyes wide. "It helped me make some changes, too."

"My mother really knew the Lord."

"I don't know if I'll ever be able to fill her shoes." Kathy gazed across the room.

"I don't expect you to replace my mother," Ben explained and rested his hand on her shoulder. "I want you to just be you."

"Boa constrictors and all?" Kathy asked with a mysterious grin.

"You have boa constrictors?" Ben imagined a fifty-gallon fish tank full of serpents.

"Not in real life," she admitted. Kathy pulled his hand from her shoulder and clasped it between hers. "But I was writing a novel that had them—oh well," she waved her hand as if sweeping aside an unseen object, "it doesn't matter anyway. I deleted it off my laptop."

"You deleted something you were writing?" Ben asked and squeezed her hand.

"Yep." Kathy shook her head. "Sure did. I got so mad about . . . about . . . well, I just got mad and decided to delete it."

"I would have liked to have read it."

"Really? You don't think me trying to write is goofy or anything?"

"Not in the least. I think it's kind of cool. My girlfriend's an author," Ben said and purposely infused his voice with loads of pride.

"Now you make me wish I hadn't deleted it," she admitted with a worried wilt to her features.

"Wait a minute," Ben said. "Have you emptied your laptop's recycle bin?"

"No," Kathy said, her face gradually glowing. "It's in there, isn't it?"

"Of course!"

Without another word, she ran for the stairs. Only when she'd opened the door did she look over her shoulder and say, "Are you coming?"

"Sure," Ben replied and hesitated. He had two gifts in his car. He hadn't brought in either because he didn't know what kind of reception he'd receive. "But I have something I wanted to give you first."

"You do?" Kathy released the doorknob and stepped toward him.

"Well, yes." Ben jutted his thumb over his shoulder. "It's still in the car. I didn't bring it in because I didn't want to assume . . ."

"Is it that thing you were going to give me before your dad got mad at me?"

"Actually, yes." He couldn't stop the spontaneous smile. "And a little something else." Ben hadn't dared hope he could present her both gifts now. But just in case, he'd gone ahead and put them in the glove compartment.

"Wait here," he said and hurried out the door. "I'll be right back."

"I can't *wait*! I'm coming with you!" Kathy chased after him, her face shining.

"Well, okay," Ben agreed and grabbed her hand. "Come on." They approached his car and Ben opened the passenger-side door. He helped Kathy into the seat, then flipped open the glove box and retrieved two jewelry cases. The first one was the oblong box he'd planned to give her three weeks ago. The other one was much smaller.

After eying both boxes, Kathy turned her adoring gaze on him, and Ben detected more signs of a joy shower. He lowered himself to one knee and didn't worry about the road's bumpy texture eating into his knee.

Who can think of knees at a time like this, anyway? he thought.

"The first gift," he said and opened the lid, "is a sterling silver bracelet. I found it in Denver." Ben lifted the piece from the box and extended it to Kathy. "Look," he pointed to the middle of the flat, shiny silver, "I had our names engraved on it."

She took the bracelet, moved it closer, and read, "'Kathy and Ben.'" Smiling into his eyes, she said, "I love it!" and slipped the bracelet over her arm. "I really love it! I'll always wear it," she rushed as her gaze slid to the tiny velvet box Ben still held.

Ben chuckled. "Kathy, your subtlety is your best trait."

"Really?" she asked and tilted her head. "You think so?"

He laughed outright. "No, there's really nothing subtle about you. I'm just teasing you because you can't keep your eyes off of this." He lifted the ring box.

"Well, what do you expect?"

"Nothing else. At least not from you," he admitted. "So I guess this is the moment we've all been waiting for." Ben glanced up and down the street. A mixed potpourri of food smells wafted from The Diner on the Corner. The collection of cars parked near the restaurant testified to their quality food. Other than those patrons, the street was empty. Ben looked back at Kathy and told her he loved her without ever saying a word.

"I didn't exactly expect to do this here and now, but I can't wait." He opened the box. A half-carat diamond solitaire winked in the evening sunshine. "Kathy, will you marry me?"

"Yes!" she squealed. "Yes! Yes! *Yes!*" Kathy grabbed at him and pulled so hard Ben struggled to keep his balance. Before she was through, she kissed his whole face, messed up his hair, and thoroughly boggled his brain with a lip-lock that shook the mountains.

As Ben was slipping the white-gold ring onto her finger, she said, "But what about your father? What are we going to do? He's not going to be happy about this, is he?"

"Here's what I've decided," Ben explained. "I've been doing a lot of thinking and praying and reading this last week. I've decided to do what my father never did with his mother. I'm going to put some boundaries on our relationship with my dad." Ben snapped the ring box closed. "Kathy," he continued, "you were right about something."

"I was?" she asked and laid her hands on her chest. Ben's diamond winked at him, and he was tempted to wink back.

"Yes, you were. You said my dad couldn't get along with Mother Teresa. That's pretty close to the truth, although I do think he's starting to at least try to do better. Even so, he can be a real pain when he wants to be, but he's still my dad and I still love him."

"Of course." She twined her fingers around his.

"Anyway," Ben said, "I've realized that Alaina and I both have put my dad in the place of God. It looks like Alaina is breaking free. And, well, so am I. All that to say, I'm willing for us to put up whatever boundaries we need to—even if you prefer not seeing him."

"I don't mind seeing him, Ben," Kathy said. "As a matter of fact, I think he can be really charming when he wants to be."

"Yes, when he wants to be," Ben echoed. "And if he doesn't want to be . . ." He shook his head, looked down, and decided his knee had taken all the road it could stand. He stood and rubbed at his knee cap.

"Oooh, your knee looks like the road," Kathy observed.

"What knee?" Ben asked and offered his hand to assist her in stepping from the vehicle. "I don't even remember if I have any knees."

"Mine are all wobbly," Kathy said through a giggle before grabbing Ben for another bear hug.

Ben enveloped her in his embrace and relished her closeness. He hesitated to introduce his next thought but decided to plunge forward because he wanted to make certain they both shared the same expectations.

"I was thinking we'd take this engagement business slow," he said. "Maybe start making wedding plans in a year or so?"

"Perfect," Kathy agreed and nodded against his chest. "Even though I know beyond a doubt you're my man, we still have so much to learn about each other."

"Yes," Ben agreed and rested his cheek against her silky hair, "and a lifetime to study." He lifted his head and edged back. "By the way," Ben added with a tilt of his head, "I need a date for tonight. Are you available?"

Kathy inched away and beamed up at him. "Absolutely!" she exclaimed. "Where are we going?"

"To the City Council's annual banquet. I got a call a few days ago." He couldn't stop his enormous grin. "I won Citizen of the Year! They're giving me the award tonight."

Kathy squealed and gently drummed her fists against Ben's chest. "I knew it! I knew it!" she cheered. "I knew they'd know a good thing when they saw it!"

"Well, they're not the only ones," Ben claimed, his heart warming with her praise. "I know a good thing when I see it, too." He placed his hands on each side of her face. "And Kathy Moore, *you* are the best thing that's ever happened to me!"

Debra White Smith continues to impact and entertain readers with her life-changing fiction and nonfiction books, including the JANE AUSTEN SERIES and the LONE STAR INTRIGUE series, *Romancing Your Husband*, and *The Divine Romance: Experiencing Intimacy with God*. She has been an award-winning author for years with such honors as Top-10 Reader Favorite, Gold Medallion Finalist (*Romancing Your Husband*), and Retailer's Choice Award Finalist (*First Impressions* and *Reason and Romance*). Debra has 60 titles to her credit and over a million books in print.

Debra and her husband of 35 years co-pastor a small church in East Texas, and she speaks at ministry events across the nation. She has been featured on a variety of media spots, including *The 700 Club, At Home Live, Getting Together, Moody Broadcasting Network, Fox News, Viewpoint*, and *America's Family Coaches*. She holds two graduate degrees—an MA in English and an EdS in Education—and is a PhD candidate at Northwest Nazarene University.

To write Debra or contact her for speaking engagements, check out her website at www.debrawhitesmith.com.

More Jane Austen Fun from Debra White Smith!

Visit debrawhitesmith.com for a full list of her books.

In this entertaining, contemporary retelling of Jane Austen's most famous work, lawyer Eddi Boswick tries out for a production of *Pride and Prejudice* in her small Texas town. When she's cast as the lead, Elizabeth Bennet, her romantic co-star is none other than the town's most eligible—and arrogant—bachelor . . .

First Impressions by Debra White Smith, THE JANE AUSTEN SERIES

In this witty, contemporary retelling of *Emma*, Amanda, a bit of a busybody, always has her friends' best interests at heart. She prides herself on her matchmaking skills . . . but when nothing seems to be going according to plan on the beautiful island of Tasmania, can she learn to listen to her own heart?

Amanda by Debra White Smith, THE JANE AUSTEN SERIES

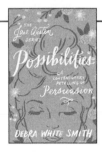

In this charming, contemporary retelling of *Persuasion*, Allie falls in love with a young man her family thinks is unworthy of her wealthy Southern upbringing. Yielding to the pressure, she ends the relationship. But when they find themselves in the same city years later, can she face her regrets before he falls for someone else?

Possibilities by Debra White Smith, THE JANE AUSTEN SERIES

⬥ BETHANYHOUSE

Stay up to date on your favorite books and authors with our free e-newsletters. Sign up today at bethanyhouse.com.

Find us on Facebook. facebook.com/bethanyhousepublishers

Free exclusive resources for your book group! bethanyhouse.com/anopenbook

anopenbook

You May Also Like...

The lifeblood of the village of Ivy Hill is its coaching inn, The Bell. When the innkeeper dies suddenly, his genteel wife, Jane, becomes the reluctant owner. With a large loan due, can Jane and her resentful mother-in-law, Thora, find a way to save the inn—and discover fresh hope for the future?

The Innkeeper of Ivy Hill by Julie Klassen
TALES FROM IVY HILL #1
julieklassen.com

Forced to run for her life, Kit FitzGilbert finds herself in the very place she swore never to return to—a London ballroom. There she encounters Lord Graham Wharton, who believes Kit holds the key to a mystery he's trying to solve. As much as she wishes that she could tell him everything, she can't reveal the truth without endangering those she loves.

A Defense of Honor by Kristi Ann Hunter
HAVEN MANOR #1
kristiannhunter.com

In the aftermath of tragedy, Grace hopes to reclaim her nephew from the relatives who rejected her sister because of her class. Under an alias, she becomes her nephew's nanny to observe the formidable family up close. Unexpectedly, she begins to fall for the boy's guardian, who is promised to another. Can Grace protect her nephew . . . and her heart?

The Best of Intentions by Susan Anne Mason
CANADIAN CROSSINGS #1
susanannemason.com

◊BETHANYHOUSE